Canadian **Dani Collins** knew in high school that she wanted to write romance for a living. Twenty-five years later, after marrying her high school sweetheart, having two kids with him, working at several generic office jobs and submitting countless manuscripts, she got The Call. Her first Mills & Boon novel won the Reviewers' Choice Award for Best First in Series from *RT Book Reviews*. She now works in her own office, writing romance.

Maisey Yates is a *New York Times* bestselling author of over one hundred romance novels. Whether she's writing stories about strong, hard-working cowboys, dissolute princes or multigenerational families, she loves getting lost in fictional worlds. An avid knitter, with a dangerous yarn addiction and an aversion to housework, Maisey lives with her husband and three kids in rural Oregon. Check out her website: maiseyyates.com.

THE BABY
HIS SECRETARY
CARRIES

DANI COLLINS

THE ITALIAN'S
PREGNANT ENEMY

MAISEY YATES

MILLS & BOON

First published in Great Britain 2024
by Mills & Boon, an imprint of HarperCollins*Publishers* Ltd,
1 London Bridge Street, London, SE1 9GF

www.harpercollins.co.uk

HarperCollins*Publishers*, Macken House, 39/40 Mayor Street Upper, Dublin 1, D01 C9W8, Ireland

The Baby His Secretary Carries © 2024 Dani Collins

The Italian's Pregnant Enemy © 2024 Maisey Yates

ISBN: 978-0-263-31990-3

01/24

MIX
Paper | Supporting
responsible forestry
FSC™ C007454

This book is produced from independently certified FSC™ paper to ensure responsible forest management.
For more information visit: www.harpercollins.co.uk/green.

Printed and Bound in the UK using 100% Renewable Electricity at CPI Group (UK) Ltd, Croydon, CR0 4YY

THE BABY
HIS SECRETARY
CARRIES

DANI COLLINS

MILLS & BOON

For you, Dear Reader,
for your endless love of dramatic,
glamorous, passionate romance.
I hope you find all of those things in this one.

PROLOGUE

MOLLY BROOKS WAS already hyperaware of her sale-rack blouse, cotton culottes and discount sandals when she stepped off the elevator onto an upper deck of the *Alexandra*. She hadn't had time to shop and had had to make do with what was in her closet, not that she owned clothing that belonged in this setting, anyway.

The superyacht was gliding past Cyprus as though barely touching the water, but she was thrown off balance when someone in a crisp white uniform asked sharply, "Are you supposed to be here?"

No. Definitely not.

Her immediate supervisor, Valentina, had twisted her knee while skiing yesterday. Molly had been on a plane within the hour and was strictly here as a gofer so Valentina could stay in her stateroom and keep her leg elevated.

"I'm bringing this to my employer, Georgio Casella." She nodded at the leather portfolio she held with the freshly printed document inside it. "For his review and signature."

"Why isn't he doing it electronically?" the man asked with a scowl.

Because it was a court document detailing the theft of proprietary information, not that it was any of his business.

"I'm not privy to his reasons." Molly channeled Valentina's polite smile and cool tone. "Perhaps you'd like to ask him when you show me where to find him?"

With a grumble, he led her through an opulent lounge, where emerald cushions accented ivory sofas placed to view the wall of windows overlooking the sea. A crystal chandelier sparkled and the fresh flowers on an end table perfumed the air as they passed.

They moved into a darker room with tinted windows and a curved cherrywood bar. Colorful bottles were arranged behind it and glasses dangled above. The stools were low-backed and upholstered in black leather. Highboy chairs and drink tables were arranged near the windows and the doors opened onto—

He was in the freaking *pool*.

Please don't keelhaul me, she pleaded silently as she looked into the mirrored finish of Gio's unforgiving sunglasses.

If she hadn't felt his attention zone in on her like a raptor swooping for a bunny, she would have thought he was asleep. He didn't even lift his head. He sat low with his arms splayed along the edge of the free-form pool. The water cut across his tanned, muscled chest, right in the middle of his brown nipples.

Don't look!

Molly jerked her gaze back to his sunglasses, hoping he hadn't seen her ogle him. She didn't mean to, but the man absolutely fascinated her, leaving her mouth dry every time she had to talk to him. Thankfully, that wasn't often. Valentina was his executive assistant and Molly was Valentina's support. Until this trip, she had never seen him outside the London office and he was only there on and off, as he traveled constantly, usually with Valentina by his side.

Today, he had a topless woman next to him. She lowered her sunglasses to give Molly a look that asked, *What on earth has the cat dragged in?*

Oh, God.

Gio was a guest aboard this yacht. He wouldn't like her embarrassing him or jeopardizing the deal he was working out with the yacht's owner, Rafael Zamos.

She sent a wavering, apologetic smile to the handful of people here with him: the other couple in the pool, also mostly naked, the two men at the bar, one with his shirt hanging open over his barely there swimsuit, and the two women lying topless on nearby loungers.

"I—" Her throat closed and her heart stalled as she recognized... Sasha?

She looked so different! Her burnt caramel hair was tinted a bright blond. Her face and figure were elegant and lean, not rounded by youth and pregnancy. She wore pink gloss on her lips, eyelash extensions and diamonds in her ears.

She also wore a look of horror as she yanked her filmy cover-up across her naked breasts.

"What are you doing here?" Sasha—or Mrs. Alexandra Zamos, Molly was realizing through the rushing sound filling her ears—sounded livid.

All the blood in Molly's body drained into her sandals. A plummeting sensation assaulted her gut. She genuinely thought she might faint.

"What's wrong, Alexandra? Is the help supposed to stay belowstairs?" Gio's topless paramour was laughing at Molly, though, not her friend. "You're such a snob."

"Molly is my assistant's assistant," Gio said crisply. Now his head came up. "What do you need, Molly?"

"Valentina, um..." Molly cleared her throat, trying to recover from seeing her adopted sister's mother for the first time in eleven years.

She should have done her homework! Her coworkers had been green with envy that she was leaving the blustery November streets of London to spend a week aboard the Zamos yacht, but Molly hadn't bothered looking up photos or gossip about the owners. She had used her time on the flight to Athens to study the deal the men were negotiating. It had been made clear to her that she was expected to stay on the crew level. If anyone would rub elbows with Gio's vaunted peers, it would be Valentina, exactly as it always was.

And how could Molly ever imagine she would bump into Sasha like this? She had known Sasha's family was wealthy, but not *this* wealthy.

"Valentina finished the, um…" She waved the portfolio, mind splintered, voice still jammed. "She said you wanted to sign it as soon as it was ready."

She hoped Gio attributed her raging blush to the mortification of finding them all like this, rather than the anguish that she was dragging Alexandra's painful past into what seemed to be the happily-ever-after she very much deserved. Would she tell Gio to fire her? No. She wouldn't do that to her. Would she?

"Your executive assistant has an assistant?" the man behind the bar drawled as he poured from a silver shaker into martini glasses. "No wonder it was so difficult to get hold of you to extend this invitation."

He must be Rafael Zamos, the yacht's owner and Sasha's husband. Molly couldn't make that detail work in her head, but she pushed aside her utter astonishment, even though she was highly curious about him. He was very easy on the eyes, with dark hair and a tanned, powerful chest, but she made herself look away.

She glanced once at the ashen face that Alexandra was

smothering with big sunglasses and a floppy hat, and pulled herself together. Betray *nothing*.

"I'm very sorry I've interrupted your…" Orgy? "Shall I leave this?"

She forced herself to meet the glint in Gio's sunglasses again when she actually wanted to sprint to the bowels of the ship.

"No. Valentina is right. I want to keep that moving." He turned and set his hands on the ledge, propelling himself upward, seemingly without effort. One foot touched the ledge and he was standing before the water had fully sluiced off him.

How dare he? Now he was nothing but swarthy skin, sculpted muscle and neatly trimmed body hair. He had the lean physique of a swimmer with broad shoulders and long limbs. His narrow hips wore a slash of black that barely contained whatever cockatiel he was smuggling. Not that she was looking!

"Sir." The purser hurried forward with a towel.

Gio—he was always Gio in her head, even though she'd never called him anything but Mr. Casella—took the towel in a laconic reach of his arm and wrapped it around his hips. He rolled his wrist to invite Molly closer.

With her heart pounding, she picked her way past Sasha's painted toenails and opened the leather portfolio.

She felt everyone's gaze pinned on them as he read the top page, then swiped his fingertips on the towel before he lifted the second page.

Rafael began dishing out martinis, briefly distracting everyone's attention.

"Thank you, my love," Sasha said, then took a hefty gulp of hers. Her hand seemed unsteady. Did Rafael's gaze linger on his wife an extra second, noticing that?

The yearning to talk to her old friend was so strong, it was like a scream trapped in Molly's throat. Her hands felt sweaty and all her muscles were threatening to twitch violently, purely to discharge the tension trapped within her.

"Pen?"

Gio had finished reading. She stared at her own reflection in his sunglasses, wishing she could see his eyes, but also glad that she couldn't. His mother's Icelandic blood was crystal-clear in his blue eyes and they often felt as though they pierced into her soul. His eyes always mesmerized her, being such a contrast to the rest of him, which was a reflection of his father's Italian heritage.

She shakily fished into the pocket of her culottes.

"Calm down," Gio said in an undertone that only she could hear. "I'm not angry that you're here."

He had noticed how rattled she was. As much as she loved her job, however, getting fired right now was the least of her worries. She was terrified of exposing Sasha when she had promised so sincerely and solemnly that she would never, ever reveal her secret.

Gio took the pen she offered and grasped the edge of the portfolio. His cool fingertips grazed the overheated skin of her own hand.

What fresh hell was this?

She stayed very still while he applied the weight of his signature, holding her breath until she could bolt.

"You can get this to the mainland for me?" he asked Rafael as he returned the pen to her. "I'd like it in London by morning."

"Of course." Rafael nodded at the man in the white uniform, who continued to stand by, waiting to escort the riffraff back where she belonged.

"Again, I'm very sorry," Molly said to the gathering, closing the folder and doing her best to hide behind it. "I'll stay below from now on."

"I was just surprised," Sasha said in a defensive tone. She adjusted the fall of her bathing suit cover so it was level across the top of her thigh. "I like to know who is on board, including any staff our guests bring along."

"You thought we had a stowaway?" Rafael was sipping his martini, once again watching his wife with a narrow-eyed, inscrutable expression.

"What exactly do you do for Gio?" Sasha asked without answering her husband.

"As Mr. Casella said, I report to his executive assistant, Valentina. I help her with emails and correspondence, assist with reporting and presentations. I also run personal errands to free her time, so she can be more accessible to Mr. Casella. She suffered an injury so I came along at the last minute to be her legs. That's probably why you didn't see my name on the passenger list."

"I didn't see 'Legs,' either," Sasha said, prompting a few dry chuckles. She turned a pout upward to her husband. "Much as it pains me to admit it, I think you may be right, darling. I need my own assistant. Either that or you should hire an assistant for Tino, so little things like sending me an updated passenger list doesn't fall through the cracks."

"Happy wife, happy life. I'll have Tino call an agency today."

"I'll reach out to him myself once I know exactly what I want. Tell me a little more… Molly, is it?" Sasha didn't give her a chance to reply. "Never mind." She flicked her hand. "We don't need to discuss that here. Come by my stateroom tomorrow. Have breakfast with me," she offered with a pleasant smile. "You can tell me about your duties so I can hire exactly the right person. Would you mind, Gio?"

"If you're planning to poach her, then yes. I mind very much." He threw off his towel and levered himself back into the pool. "I'm sure Valentina would, too." He took little notice of the woman who drifted closer, bare breasts practically grazing his rib cage as he stretched out his arms again. "Molly may make her own choice, of course."

Was that a threat? She shot a look of alarm toward the water, but he didn't sound worried.

"Come by at ten," Sasha said. "The men will be in their meetings. Everyone else will still be sleeping. Won't you, dolls?"

"Oh, I expect to be up all night and needing my beauty sleep, yes," the woman in the pool purred as she slithered even closer to Gio.

Ugh. Molly did her best not to think about that and smiled weakly at Sasha. She didn't know if she should be relieved that she would be able to speak privately with her, or filled with dread. Should she call her mother? Pack her bag and prepare to find her way back to New York?

"I'll see you tomorrow," she said and quickly made her escape.

CHAPTER ONE

Eight months later...

"MOLLY. MY OFFICE."

Molly jolted as she came back from the powder room to find Gio standing in the doorway between her office and Valentina's.

How did the man get more compelling each time she saw him? He wore one of his tailored suits. This one was a dark gray pinstripe, but he'd removed the jacket.

She was a sucker for any man wearing a vest and tie over a crisp white shirt, but when he wore it, she was dazzled. Maybe it was the way his icy blue eyes glittered and the way his jaw gleamed from a fresh shave. Maybe it was the fact he wore his hair in a more rakish style these days, still short at the sides, but a little longer on top, giving him a lean, hawkish look that was intolerably sexy.

Not that she wanted to notice, but she was a woman with a pulse, wasn't she?

"Let me get my tablet." She rubbed her clammy palms against her hips, nervous because today was the day she was asking Valentina for a medical leave. They had a meeting with Gio in the diary. Afterward, she planned on talking to Valentina privately.

"You don't need it." He waved for her to move through

Valentina's sumptuous office ahead of him. Valentina's office was empty, the lights not turned on yet.

Strange.

Gio's office was a massive, airy space in relaxing earth tones. There was a comfortable lounge area where an ox-blood sofa and matching chairs faced a view of London's skyline. A discreet nook held a bar and a kitchenette to service the small table for dining or hosting a one-on-one meeting. Nothing so crass as a whiteboard existed in here. That was saved for the boardroom down the hall, beyond the carved, double doors.

She reflexively moved to stand in front of the chair she used when she and Valentina met with him in here.

"I understood you were coming in at ten for our meeting. Is Valentina on her way?"

"Valentina isn't coming." After shutting the door to Valentina's office, he moved to close the double doors as well. The click seemed overly loud and ominous.

"No?" Molly's stomach gave a dip and roll that warned her she might not be fully past the morning sickness after all. Her lungs compressed as she waited for him to circle his marble-topped mahogany desk and take his seat.

This was already a very nerve-racking day. Now she was also hyperaware that she was alone with him.

Despite a crush on her boss that she was certain she had not hidden well, Gio had never once acknowledged it or acted with any hint of impropriety. Nevertheless, his masculine energy radiated toward her like a heat wave. She couldn't seem to ignore it. She needed Valentina's buffering presence—especially when she caught his gaze flickering over her light gray pants and pale pink blouse when he nodded at her to sit.

She had made great strides with her wardrobe and hair,

given her generous salary and Valentina's sophisticated example, but she still felt like a bumpkin from New Jersey, always obvious in her awe. She didn't feel she had anything close to equal footing with this man, which was glaringly obvious to her so it must have been to him.

"I hope Valentina's all right?" The last time her boss had failed to come into the office had been while she was still recovering from her knee injury.

"She's perfectly fine." He leaned back in his chair. "She wanted to be here for this, but I sent her to New York last night. She's taking over as executive director of R and D."

"What?" There she went, sounding like an uncouth hayseed. "I mean, that's fantastic for her. Wow. I had no idea she was even interested in taking a position like that."

Molly was genuinely pleased for her mentor while also experiencing immediate panic. Had Valentina not wanted to bring Molly along?

What does this mean for me?

Her brain took another sharp swerve. What did it mean for the *baby*?

Her hand started to reflexively cover her unsettled stomach, but she caught it with her other hand, resisting the urge while her mind continued to stumble and race.

"This promotion has been in the works for some time, but we kept it between us. She needs to clean house on arrival. Aggressively." His eyebrows went up with the significance of that.

Heads will roll.

She blinked. She was often privy to confidential information, but never like this, where he was not only sharing the actions that would be taken, but also his view of it. She felt as though she was being invited into the inner circle. It was flattering, if disconcerting.

"You'll draft the announcement, with her input," he continued. "Once I approve it, you can send it out. There will be several releases as we restructure. Brace yourself for some busy days."

"Of course, but…" She barely stopped herself from stumbling into an *um*… "Sensitive press releases usually happen at Valentina's level. They should include the name of her replacement as a contact. Has that been decided?"

"You tell me, Molly." He tapped the keyboard beneath the monitor on his desk. The screen flickered to life. "Valentina assured me you are the best person to take her place. I agree. All of your reviews are excellent." He angled the screen so she could see the column of nines and tens in the matrix she and Valentina had filled out two months ago.

"Wait." Molly almost fell out of her chair. She genuinely wanted to lean forward and dangle her head between her knees, but clung to the arms instead.

"I encourage promotion from within. You know that."

"Yes, but…" That's how Molly had come to London, by applying for an internal posting while she'd been assisting in the marketing department in the New York office. She had a business degree with a focus on marketing and analytics, but she had never expected her PR position to lead to a top-floor job here, let alone *this*.

"I'm not ready to work for the president and CEO." The *owner*.

Even as she blurted out her protest, she could hear Valentina chiding her in that very same review.

"Confidence inspires confidence," Valentina had insisted. "Believe in yourself, Molly.

"Valentina deliberately increased your responsibilities after this review, ensuring you could seamlessly take over for her."

"Because there was a mandate for every department to have a succession plan. For emergencies," she blurted. A lovely young woman named Yu had job-shadowed Molly for a week, to ensure she could cover Molly's desk in a pinch.

That pinch was supposed to happen three weeks from now, when Molly went on medical leave.

"R and D is leaking like the *Titanic*," Gio said starkly. "Not just money, but information. I consider that an emergency. Valentina has been dispatched to right that ship. I need a qualified assistant. You are qualified." He waved at the screen. "Welcome to your new title of executive assistant."

"But—" She once again stopped herself from covering her belly. Her stomach was churning with a load of gravel. "I was…" She crushed her own fingers as she clenched her hands in her lap. She couldn't announce her pregnancy. She'd signed a nondisclosure agreement committing to hiding it.

Hiding it was becoming an issue, however. Two days ago, a coworker had had the temerity to ask if the salad she was eating was an attempt to drop the weight she was gaining.

"I have a thyroid condition," Molly had lied coldly.

She had hoped to speak to Valentina after the twelve-week scan and be on leave by now, but Valentina had been traveling with Gio. Molly had just rounded fourteen weeks and even though her bump wasn't pronounced, everything about her was becoming rounder, from face to breasts to tummy to backside.

Offering three weeks' notice as they entered July seemed more than fair. Things usually slowed down in summer. She could finish training Yu and not be missed too badly.

She had thought.

Gio was watching her with raised eyebrows, awaiting whatever words she was trying to find.

She couldn't take this job without disclosing that she didn't intend to be here.

"May I have a few days to think about this?" She needed to ask Sasha— Well, she couldn't explain her predicament to her, could she? Everything that happened in this office was strictly confidential. What the heck was she going to do?

"I know you've been taking meetings with headhunters, Molly," Gio said with a jaded blink.

"What?" It truly felt as though the room was spinning, she was so disoriented by this conversation. "What makes you think that?"

"Valentina said you've booked personal time during work hours lately. Afternoons here and there. I respect that." He shrugged it off. "Everyone should test the waters now and again to find out what they're worth. Now you're better prepared for this meeting."

She really wasn't. A bubble of hysterical laughter was trapped in her throat because those meetings had been about engaging her for something far more personal than "assistant."

"Of course, now I'm also prepared," he said dryly as he tapped a few more keys. "If I must compete for your loyalty, I'll bring more to the table. This is the salary I'd like to offer with a signing bonus if you commit to at least two years. You'll hire your own assistant, of course. Valentina said you seemed to like Yu, but she pulled a handful of other résumés she thought might be a good addition to this floor. You'll have an allowance for wardrobe, since you'll accompany me constantly. Also, a company expense account and use of a car service. I think you'll find I've been very generous, but by all means, let's negotiate. No one is irreplaceable, but I'd rather not replace you. Not when we're so comfortable with each other."

Comfortable? That was the last thing she felt around him!

Dear Lord, those numbers on the screen were positively blinding.

Why did he have to offer her dream job *now*? She had not only agreed to be a surrogate for Sasha, but she was also three months pregnant with the couple's baby!

She couldn't take this job. Not only was it demanding as hell, but she also couldn't become visibly pregnant, take a few weeks off, then come back without a baby. There would be a *lot* of questions.

The thought of refusing made her want to cry, though.

"This is a lot to take in," she managed to say in a cracked voice. "I won't leave you in the lurch now that Valentina is gone, I swear. But I'd like a few days to give more thought to all of this."

He sat back, tongue sliding across his teeth behind his closed lips as he used his laser vision to x-ray her insides. Could he see the baby?

For some reason she blushed and dropped her gaze, feeling transparent in other ways. Could he see how deep her crush went?

"Are you romantically involved with someone?" If there was gruff dismay in his tone, it was work-related, she knew that, but his question made her nerves go taut.

"No." Her throat was hot. She watched her own fingers torture themselves. Dating was a nonstarter. She compared everyone to him, but she couldn't help pointing out, "Not that you're allowed to ask that."

"I was asking as a friend." His tone was heavy with irony. "I understand why you want time, Molly. That's another reason I know you're right for this job. You're not impulsive. You manage a crisis with a cool head and not a lot of hand-wringing. Typically." His gaze penetrated the marble desktop as though he knew she was knitting an invisible scarf in her lap.

She could have laughed uproariously at his judgment of her. He should have been in that stateroom with Sasha eight months ago, when a mere hour after reuniting with her friend, she had declared, "I'll do it. I'll be your surrogate."

She had no regrets. None. But she hadn't thought she would inconvenience Valentina with her absence. An assistant to an assistant was an easy job to cover. Executive assistant to a man like Gio required near twenty-four-seven accessibility. Travel at a moment's notice. He needed to be comfortable granting access to his most personal details—which woman required flowers after staying over, for instance.

A potent silence grew between them as she searched for some way to explain her reluctance. Dare she explain that her recent meetings were medical in nature? That's what she had been planning to tell Valentina. She had a note from a doctor and everything.

The burble of an incoming call had him glancing at the screen and hitting a button.

"Valentina," he said crisply. "Molly is here with me and she's being modest, trying to persuade me that she's not qualified."

"Gio, I'm so sorry." Valentina's cultured, boarding-school accent had never sounded so pained. "Ilario called me. He didn't know that I've been sent to— It's your grandfather. He's very ill and refuses to see a doctor. Would you like me to meet you in Genoa or…?"

As Molly watched the color drain from Gio's swarthy complexion, her heart was nearly pulled from her chest. It was well known that he was estranged from his parents. His grandfather had raised him and the pair were very close.

She snapped into the reliable assistant she had trained so scrupulously to become.

"I'm here, Valentina. I'll arrange everything and go with him. It sounds like you have your hands full, but please keep your line open. I'd like to know I can call with any questions that might arise."

"Absolutely. Thank you, Molly. Keep me posted."

"I will." Molly stood and reached across to hit the button that ended the call. "I'll have the jet readied."

"Signor." Ilario was the *maggiordomo* here in Gio's grandfather's Portofino villa. He had worked for the family since Ottorino's marriage sixty years ago.

"He's in his room?" Gio asked.

"Sì."

"Have the doctor come. I'll go up and persuade him to let him in."

"Grazie." Ilario flicked his gaze to Molly.

Gio had hold of her arm again. He kept doing it and didn't mean to. She wasn't his date. She wasn't wearing five-inch heels and an evening gown. She didn't need a supportive hand as she climbed in and out of his jet or his car.

Nevertheless, he had offered assistance every single time.

She was so damn warm, though. He felt encased in ice. His frozen fingers kept seeking out the warmth that seeped through the sleeve of her silk blouse, trying to thaw blood that had slowed and thickened with dread.

He *hated* this sensation, so he was seeking the most immediate and efficient means of melting it away: touching her.

"I'm Molly." She offered Ilario the sunny smile that Gio had felt like a strike of lightning through his center the first time he'd met her. That extreme reaction was the reason he had kept her firmly in the role of employee, enjoying the heat of being near her, but staunchly avoiding stepping into the fire.

"Valentina is tied up," she continued, notably *not* introducing herself as Valentina's successor, which annoyed him. "She told me you usually have a room set aside for her. Perhaps you could direct me to it and I'll keep myself out of the way?"

"No." Gio firmed his hold on her arm. "Let me see him so I know what I'm dealing with. Then you and I have things to discuss."

He might have dropped everything to come straight here, but he had also dropped a proverbial bomb on the New York office by sending Valentina there. He'd descended into a bleak place on receiving this difficult news about his grandfather. His mind had become fully occupied by the ways he'd have to reassemble his life if it shattered.

The demands of his position waited for no one, though. Molly had been fielding calls the whole flight, rising to the challenge, he had dimly noted with satisfaction. She maintained an air of smooth aplomb, calming the most hysterical voices while keeping a force field of untouchability around him, providing him the space and privacy to process whatever was about to happen with his grandfather.

She was also being ridiculously accommodating, murmuring things like "If that's what you prefer." She slid her hand into his, as though he was a damn child needing a sense of security.

He knew better. There was no such thing as "security," but he accepted the interlacing of her fingers. There was a sick knot in his gut that grew bigger and thornier as he drew her up the wide staircase and along the black-and-white checkerboard tiles of the upper hall.

"Gio?" Her voice was small, but it was the first time she'd ever called him by his first name. That startled him enough to halt him in his tracks.

He tried not to notice his female employees in any way beyond the skills they brought to their positions, but he had always been aware of Molly. She was a natural beauty with a pale peach skin tone and big brown eyes. In the year she'd been working under Valentina—who was an example of the Swiss boarding school she'd attended, full of heiresses and aristocracy—Molly had begun making the most of her own attributes. Her rich brunette hair was in a smooth twist, her makeup had been freshened on the plane and her slacks had a chic flare over her wedged heels.

Lately, she had put on a few pounds. They added a voluptuous softness to her already very feminine figure, making it harder than ever for him to keep his eyes off her.

"You're hurting my hand." She wiggled her grip in his.

He swore and released her, then pinched the bridge of his nose, realizing that a terrific pounding sensation had lodged behind his eyes.

"It's okay. I understand," she murmured. Now she was petting his sleeve. "This is a difficult thing to face. If you want me to come in with you—"

"I do." He would swear that he wasn't a dependent person. He didn't allow himself to be. He removed people from his sphere before they had the chance to cut him out. It was a lesson he had learned very early. Too early.

Perhaps that was what was at play here. He was irritated that she hadn't leaped to swear allegiance to him this morning. He was keeping her where he could see her until he understood exactly which way she would jump.

Why? When Valentina had asked to be promoted and leave his day-to-day world, he had made it happen without a single qualm. "Everyone is replaceable," he had told Molly this morning, and he'd meant it.

This isn't about Molly, he chided himself. This was about the inevitable loss of his grandfather. Death could be delayed, but not escaped. No one lived forever.

He took a deep breath and looked to the door into his grandfather's private suite, dreading what awaited him.

Molly's warm hand tucked itself into his again. She covered the backs of his knuckles and gave him a patient look. How had he never noticed those gold flecks in her dark brown eyes? Her skin looked so downy, he wanted to cup her cheek and run his thumb along her wide bottom lip. Maybe his tongue.

Her lashes flared wider, as though she sensed his carnal thoughts.

He yanked his attention back to the door, away from a weak attempt at self-distraction.

Taking greater care this time, he clasped her hand then quietly opened the door, drawing her through the sitting room to the bedroom, where his grandfather was lying in his wide bed.

Gio had occasionally come in here as a child, but couldn't remember being here as an adult. It looked the same, though. Ottorino's bride had redecorated the entire villa when they'd married and Nonno hadn't changed a thing in the decades since. He'd never remarried and never had more children beyond the son his true love had given him.

The sheers were drawn so the view of the sea was blurred. Muted light fell on his grandfather's pale, aged face.

"Nonno," Gio said gently as he stood beside the bed.

Ottorino was eighty and wore his pajamas, but his iron-gray hair was neatly combed, his jaw shaved. He blinked his eyes open. His dark brown irises were immediately alert.

"You're here," he said in raspy Italian. "That's good. Who's this? Not a nurse."

"No, this is Molly. My…" He still had her hand in his. She hadn't yet agreed to the job so it seemed a misnomer to say "My assistant," but that's what he called her.

"Oh?" His grandfather seemed to perk up, drawing some significance from Gio's brief hesitation. His gaze slid to their linked hands.

Gio released her.

"What does the doctor say?" Gio asked.

"It doesn't matter what he says. If it's my time, it's my time." Nonno's fingers lifted off his chest. "I only wish you were married with a son, Gio. Then I could die in peace." His eyebrows inched into a wrinkled line. "A daughter even. *Someone* to carry on this legacy we've built. Why did we bother, if not for your children?"

"I know, Nonno." Guilt stabbed at Gio, along with old anger. He had tried to fulfill his grandfather's wish three years ago, but after spending a fortune on a lavish wedding, his fiancée had chosen to run off at the last minute with her childhood sweetheart, leaving Gio with the bill and the humiliation of being left at the altar.

He hadn't bothered with a serious relationship since.

There was a quiet knock on the sitting-room door.

"Not the doctor." Nonno rallied into sounding cross.

"Your legacy includes creating a stubborn man in your own image. What did you think I would do?" Gio asked. "Let's see what he says. Won't you feel foolish if I've come all this way and you only need more fiber in your diet?"

"You're not funny." Nonno had a stare like a basilisk, but his mouth twitched. "Let's see if I have time to plan my own funeral, then."

"I'll step out," Molly said quietly. "It was very nice to

meet you Signor Casella," she added in decent Italian. "I hope you feel better soon."

"Otto," his grandfather corrected. "Don't go far. You brighten up the place."

"I'll be here as long as Gio needs me," she said with a re-assuring smile. She walked away through the sitting room.

"Assistente?" Nonno pried gruffly.

Gio ignored that and turned to greet the doctor Molly let in on her way out.

CHAPTER TWO

NAUSEA STRUCK HARD. Molly had no choice but to seek out the nearest powder room.

She would love to believe this was food poisoning. She doubted it was even morning sickness. It was stress, pure and simple.

What a day! And it was only midafternoon.

As Gio had predicted, her phone had exploded once Valentina began composting the bad apples in New York. Panic had spread like a plague from the lowest receptionist to the board of directors. Everyone wanted to speak to Gio, to know if they, too, were going to lose their jobs. Molly had drafted the announcement, but Gio had been so withdrawn, she hadn't asked him to approve it.

All she had managed to do was put lids on fires with cryptic phrases like "An announcement is forthcoming" and "Leave that with me."

She usually thrived on days like this. She loved the challenge in this job, which made the new role, and her inability to embrace it, all the more frustrating.

That conflict had her moaning in suffering as much as this awful dry retching.

"Molly?" Gio knocked sharply on the door. "Are you sick, too?"

"What? Oh, God." She flushed the toilet and lurched

to her feet, then splashed water on her face and rinsed her mouth. Her mascara was smudged from her watering eyes and her cheeks were splotchy.

Wonderful. Not that she expected him to see her as desirable, but she didn't want him to be outright repulsed.

She dabbed herself back to presentable and yanked open the door, practically walking straight into Gio. He stood in the doorway, frowning with concern.

"Should I get the doctor?" was his baffled question.

"No. I'm fine," she insisted. "What did the doctor say about your grandfather?"

"Could be a virus that's got into his heart. Nonno has accepted IV fluids, but still refuses to go to hospital. He doesn't want major interventions." He raked his hand through his hair. "He lost my grandmother after fifteen years of marriage and says it's been too long without her."

"Oh." She covered her chest where her heart turned over in sympathy.

"I can't force him to accept treatment, but…" He wanted to. That's what she took from the tortured way he looked toward his grandfather's suite.

"I'm so sorry, Gio." Empathy overwhelmed her. These last hours had been so difficult to watch and now he was facing possibly his grandfather's last hours. It was unbearable.

She reacted on instinct, the way she would to anyone in such blatant pain. She closed her arms around his waist, trying to offer what little consolation she could.

He turned to iron, making her realize she was grossly overstepping their boundaries, but as she started to pull back in embarrassment, his arms clamped around her, squashing her to his front with a hard hug.

This was supposed to be comfort, but she found herself closing her eyes, absorbing the feel of him. This was what it

would be like to be with him in a different role. To be someone he cared about who touched him all the time. To know
intimately the beat of his heart against her cheek and the
precise degree of heat that radiated through his crisp shirt,
warming her torso. To draw in the fragrance of cedar and
spice, and recognize it as his and hers and home.

She had an urge to run her hands all over his back and tilt
up her mouth to his, one that was almost impossible to resist.

He released her abruptly, then muttered, "That wasn't
appropriate."

"I know, I'm sorr—"

He flicked his hand, dismissing the hug as inconsequential. Which made her heart pang.

He seemed to have pulled a cloak over himself, one that
made him impossible to read. He nodded jerkily toward the
powder room. "What was that, if not illness?"

"Nerves," she insisted and pushed her hands into her
pockets to keep from stacking them protectively over her
belly.

"Why? Not this job? You've stepped up exactly as I expected you would. It's done," he said with finality. His expression was hard, his vivid blue eyes piercing into her. "If
you want more money, say so, but quit being coy and let's
move on to addressing the day's business."

The air in her lungs turned to fire and evaporated, making her voice a thin squeak as she said, "I can't take it."

She hated to refuse when she knew he needed her right
now. She paced down the checkered tiles of the hall. How
apropos. She felt as though she was in a real-life chess
match, watching all the careful, strategic moves she had
planned being thwarted. She'd been racking her brain all
morning, trying to figure out new options.

"What is the issue?" He folded his arms, very much the

imposing boss who intimidated the hell out of her. "Spell it out for me."

Working for him was the chance of a lifetime, but it was also too much. *He* was too much. Even without this other secret she was carrying, she would struggle to hide her attraction. It was bound to become as obvious as her pregnancy if she worked closely with him, the way Valentina always had.

On the other hand, if she left, she would regret it forever. Professionally, it amounted to walking away from her career. Yes, in roughly six months she'd be able to return to it, but she wouldn't have *this* job, not if she turned him down now. On a personal level, she would lose the chance to know this extraordinary man a little better.

A maid bustled past with a tray, heading toward his grandfather's room.

Gio tossed an impatient look at the interruption, then clasped Molly's elbow the way he had been doing since leaving the London office. He steered her into a bedroom of masculine colors with a sitting area, a desk beneath a tall window and doors that opened onto a balcony overlooking the sea.

At any other time in her life, she would be charmed beyond measure by a room like this, but— She flung around in time to see him closing the door.

"This is my room. No one will bother us." He crossed his arms again. "Now speak freely," he demanded.

I'm not at liberty to!

She had to tell him something, though. She licked her lips and said haltingly, "The appointments that Valentina saw in my calendar were medical. I don't want to discuss it, but I anticipate needing time off—"

He swore sharply. "You're *pregnant*?"

* * *

"Wh-why would you say something like that?" Molly asked. Her hand grappled the air before clasping onto the back of the chair by the desk.

"It's the only conclusion that makes sense." His ears rang as though he'd taken an uppercut to the jaw. But, yes, this explained both her reluctance to accept a job that most people would kill for and the retching he'd just overheard. "Don't deny it. Guilt just landed on your face like a cream pie."

Her hand tightened on the chair and her color seemed to drain away. For one second, he thought she might faint, but she looked toward the window and her spine straightened.

He might pass out—his shock was that profound. Why? People were entitled to a private life. Even his employees, he thought ironically, but how? *Who?*

"You said you aren't seeing anyone."

"I'm not." Her voice was firmer than he'd ever heard it. "I don't want to talk about this. My personal health is not my employer's concern."

She shifted to face the door to the balcony, leaving it closed, but staring out. Her silhouette was the figure he had involuntarily memorized—average in height, narrow shoulders, a deliciously round ass. She was definitely plumper than a few months ago, though.

He ran his hand down his face, trying to assimilate this development with the rest of what had happened today.

"Valentina doesn't know." Would she have told him if she had? She was very loyal, but also very ethical. She wouldn't betray anyone's medical status without their permission.

"No one knows." Molly twisted around, voice taking on a note of warning. "It's common for people to keep things under wraps for the first trimester, in case it doesn't work out as planned."

If she was concerned about miscarriage, she obviously wanted this pregnancy. His mind filled with wild thoughts he wasn't entitled to have, but who the *hell* was this man who'd made love to her, but wasn't involved with her?

"Does the *father* know?"

Her mouth tightened. "None of this is information I am required to share with you."

"I'm not threatening your employment, Molly. I'm trying to preserve it." Wasn't that obvious? "If you need a mat leave, fine. Tell me what we're working with. We'll find a way around it. I don't see how this prevents you from becoming my assistant."

Assistente? His grandfather's skepticism rang in his ears, then his plea. *I only wish you were married with a son, Gio. Then I could die in peace.*

"This is a very private matter that is not up for discussion." She stubbornly folded her arms. "I was about to ask Valentina for a six-month leave, starting three weeks from now. Provided I have no health complications, I can offer that to you. I'll support whoever you pick to take over for Valentina—"

"*Three weeks?* How far along are you?"

"*Three,*" she said firmly, ignoring his question. She pointed at her middle. "Everything about this topic is firmly off-limits. It's as classified as any company information that you have ever sent across my desk. I mean that, Gio. Tell *no one.*"

He'd never seen her like this, with her chin up and her eyes sparkling with battle. It was hot. She was.

Shut up, libido.

Don't go far... Nonno's voice echoed in his head. *You brighten up the place.*

Could she brighten up an old man's final days?

"Three weeks," he repeated, swiveling the puzzle pieces in his head, trying to make them fit. "I'm not prying—" he was definitely prying "—but I need to know whether the baby's father will be annoyed at your devoting every minute of the next three weeks to me."

She clung to her elbows, shoulders hunched. After pursing her lips and seeming to debate her words, she finally gave a small, pained frown of concession.

"The father and I are not involved. Not in the way you're suggesting."

Good.

"I was intending to work until the twenty-first," she continued, looking to her toes. "I can give you that without any reaction from him."

"Does he plan to support you and the baby? Is that why you're refusing my offer?"

"Three weeks and this topic is off-limits." She drew a circle above her navel. "Those are my terms."

"Three weeks in which I will continue to sweeten *my* terms in order to persuade you to stay. You'll immediately take everything I offered you this morning." He kept speaking even though she opened her mouth to interrupt him. "You'll take the full signing bonus. I'll double it each time you double the timeline of your commitment."

"You don't mean—"

"I'll double it if you agree to stay another three weeks, double it again if you stay for twelve."

"That won't happen," she cried. "I'm not playing hardball, Gio. This is the reality of my situation."

"We see it differently." He shrugged. "You'll need more than one assistant because I am now your sole priority." Why did he like that thought so much? "We'll stay here and work out of the Genoa office. I understand you may have physical limitations, but outside of that, you're mine in whatever role I need."

Her eyes widened. A soft blush came into her cheeks.

He usually did his best to ignore that, too. A lot of women betrayed an awareness of him. He was rich, well-dressed, intelligent and kept himself fit. He never let female attention go to his head, though. With Molly, however, he always felt when she was watching him and he damn well liked it.

Being her employer, he'd always been careful to keep his low-key arousal to himself. There were enough mermaids in the sea that he didn't have to fish where he worked. In fact, his latent interest in her had been his only reservation in bringing her on as his executive assistant. He'd been confident he could keep his hands to himself, and still was, but everything about their relationship was changing, becoming far more personal than he had expected.

Which didn't matter. He could handle that, too.

He believed, until she bit the edge of her lip in a way that tightened his gut.

"If I agree to those terms, will I have your solemn promise that you will never, ever tell anyone about…?" She dropped her gaze to her thickening waistline.

"I can promise that." He didn't like it, but he could and would. He held out his hand.

She swallowed and searched his expression.

Was she waiting for him to clarify that he wouldn't cross any lines? Because he was about to wipe his feet on those lines and blur them into oblivion.

"Do we have an agreement?" he prodded. "Are you thinking about extorting more for the signing bonus first?"

"Don't be ridiculous." Predictably, she hurried forward to shake his hand, horrified by the implication she might be greedy. "You're already being very generous. Thank you."

He snorted. "I'm not generous, Molly. I'm merely willing to pay the price required to get what I want."

"What do you mean?" She tried to withdraw her hand, but he held on to it.

"I mean we're going to tell my grandfather that you're my fiancée."

CHAPTER THREE

MOLLY WAS STUNNED SPEECHLESS.

Gio's eyebrows went up, daring her to protest when her handshake of agreement was still withering in his hand.

The profound silence made the growl of her stomach all the louder and more cringeworthy.

"Let's have lunch." Gio dropped her hand and went to the door. "Then we'll give Nonno our happy news."

"Mr. Casella—"

"Oh, no, Molly." He did his thing where he used one glance to impale her like a barbed hook. "No take-backs. I accepted your terms. You accepted mine."

He opened the door, letting all the pent-up energy in this room flow out into the hall.

"You tricked me. You know you did." She walked through the door to escape the intimacy of his bedroom.

"Consider it a lesson in reading the fine print. Lunch on the terrace, please," he said in Italian to the first maid he saw.

Numbly, Molly accompanied him, too hungry to stage a mutinous walkout. All she could think was *I need to tell Sasha that he knows about the baby.*

"Where did my bag go?" she asked the young woman who poured them a cool glass of something that smelled of orange peel and nutmeg.

"We have a lot to cover, don't we? Let's get Valentina's announcement out of the way. What other business can't wait?"

Her laptop bag arrived and they worked while putting away a refreshing green-bean salad followed by a pasta course of pesto over gnocchi brightened with cherry tomatoes and yellow zucchini. A light cake with ricotta icing was their dessert.

By then, Molly was fully intoxicated by good food and the thrill of working directly with Gio, responding to his dynamic decision-making in real time. It was like dancing, but a really sexy tango, where she had to match every beat, count and step.

When Gio rose to speak to the doctor, who was on his way out, Molly finally caught a breath. She drew out her personal phone and sent Sasha a text, asking to set up a call.

It was tagged "read" immediately and three dots appeared.

"You have two phones?" Gio asked.

Molly jolted and almost dropped it.

"I didn't hear you come back," she said with a shaky smile. She clicked off the screen and set it face down on the table so only the bright floral phone case was showing. "It's for my sister, mostly. She knows I'm busy and in a different time zone, but she sends me things constantly. I love it, but I can't have that on my work phone. I would spend all day clearing notifications from her so I could see what's actually on my plate."

"I don't know much about your family. Do you have other siblings?" He retook his chair and nodded for coffee. "Where does everyone live?"

He wasn't really interested. He thought he should know these things because he wanted her to pretend to be his fiancée.

Molly had pushed that ruse to the back of her mind while they ate because it created such a disconcerting shiver in her chest.

"What did the doctor say about your grandfather?" she asked as a dodge against replying.

"Nothing good." His tone was very somber.

"I'm so sorry." She looked to her hands in her lap, thinking about how much his grandfather seemed to mean to him and how defeated the old man had sounded at not knowing who would steward the family empire after Gio.

"I want his last days to be happy ones, Molly," Gio said quietly.

"I know." It sounded as though Ottorino only *had* a few days. Where was the harm in a white lie? In a bit of hand-holding to comfort both of them?

The harm would be in the way it would feed into Molly's already thick catalog of fantasies, but she could bear it. It wasn't as though Gio was leading her on. She knew exactly what he expected of her and it was purely a pantomime for his ailing grandfather.

"It would only be him, right? That we would pretend for?" She lifted her lashes. "We would keep it inside that room?"

Would they kiss? She veered her gaze from his stern mouth. Surely, that wouldn't happen.

"*Sì.*"

"The promise you made me." She looked down again, so he understood she meant her pregnancy. "It includes him."

"I know." He nodded.

Her phone pinged, making her jolt at the possibility it was from Sasha, but even as she turned it over, it pinged three more times in rapid succession.

"See?" she said wryly. "Cat video, dance video. 'Can you

do my homework for me?'" She showed him the gif with a man on his knees, hands clenched in a plea, with the word *Pleeeze* pulsing over it.

"How old is she?" His eyebrows drew together with curiosity.

"Eleven. And this is such a dilemma." Molly pondered her response. "If I text back, I run the risk of her teacher realizing she's texting in class. She'll lose her phone for the day, which is a suitable consequence. On the other hand, I like her to know I'm here for her as much as possible." She spoke aloud as she replied, "'I'm in a meeting. Say you forgot it in the library, then do it while you're there.'"

"Not bad."

She shrugged and set aside the phone again.

"That's quite an age difference. You're twenty-five?"

"Six." She debated briefly, then told him what she told anyone if the topic of her much younger sister came up. "My mother wasn't planning to have more children. She and my father divorced when I was six, mostly because Mom's career as a midwife was so demanding. After that, I gave up on getting the little sister I wanted, but a situation came up where a young mother was looking to place her child in a private adoption. Libby joined Mom and me and she's been an absolute joy and blessing in every way."

So much so that Molly had wanted to help Sasha in the most reciprocal way she could.

Her melancholy must have reflected on her face because Gio said, "It must be hard to be so far away from her."

"It is. The age gap puts us in different life stages, too. I homeschooled for the rest of high school, then went to a local college, so I could live at home as long as possible. But when I finished my degree, I was ready to start my life. I wanted to live on my own and build a career. Mom was always adamant that she didn't adopt Libby so I could raise her. She's been nothing but supportive of my ambitions and encouraged me to put in for the transfer to London when I mentioned it. I honestly didn't think I'd get it, let alone wind up here."

In his family home in Genoa, about to pretend she was his fiancée.

"Ah. Now I understand." He nodded. "You want to go back to New York so you're with your family when—"

"Gio." She gave him her sternest look.

"Off-limits." He lifted his hands. "But we can look at working out of New York."

"You're relentless, aren't you?"

"I consider it one of my strengths, yes."

Her phone pinged again. She glanced and saw Sasha had responded.

Can't talk right now. Getting ready for a thing.

Molly didn't take offense at what seemed like a dismissal. For many reasons, Sasha and Rafael were being very secretive about having a baby by surrogate. If there were stylists and others milling about, Sasha wouldn't be able to talk freely.

"Everything all right?" Gio asked.

"Mmm-hmm." *Note to self: keep your thoughts off your face around him.* She clicked off her phone and dropped it into her bag.

"Good." He rose. "Let's go tell my grandfather."

Otto's color was still poor and he had an IV taped to the hand that rested on his chest.

"She's back." He weakly lifted his other hand.

Molly hurried forward to cradle his cool, stiff fingers in both of her own.

"Ah, *sei caldo*," he said of her warm hands. "Why have I never met you before?"

"I work in the London office." She glanced at Gio for guidance.

"But you're American?" He switched to English.

"Molly started in our New York office a few years ago." Gio's heavy hands arrived on her shoulders, provoking an acute, prickling awareness from the fine hairs on the back of her neck, down her spine.

Every cell in her body switched its polarity to align toward him. Her stomach muscles tensed and her breasts tingled. Her cheeks stung with a blush she fought to reveal, but she was certain Otto read her reaction to Gio like a neon sign.

"For the last year, she's been working under Valentina. I dispatched Valentina to New York, to deal with that issue we've been chasing there," he said in an aside.

"Bene, bene," Otto said distractedly, his sharp gaze moving from Molly's pink cheeks to the way Gio's hands lightly massaged her upper arms.

"I wasn't entirely honest with you earlier, Nonno," Gio continued.

"I can see that. *Assistente?*" he scoffed.

Molly was reacting so helplessly to Gio's caresses on her arms, she used her free hand to cover his, stilling his touch.

He immediately brought her into the cage of his body, folding one arm over hers while sliding the other around her stomach. He pulled her into the wall of his chest and settled her backside against his pelvis.

Heat flooded through her, melting her bones like wax. She found herself leaning into him, blushing hard while helplessly trying to hide her profound reaction and certain she was failing. She stared at the hand she still held so Ottorino wouldn't see directly into her soul.

"This is happening faster than we expected." The rumble of Gio's voice vibrated from his chest into her back. "But I've asked Molly to marry me and she has agreed. I wanted you to know, to put your mind at ease."

"This is good news." The old man gave a long, shaky sigh. Tears came into his eyes. The cool hand in Molly's shifted to turn hers over. "But no ring? Fetch Nonna's from the safe, Gio."

Gio's whole body jolted and she heard his breath catch.

His reaction was so visceral, her heart lurched and her veins stung with alarm.

"Oh, I—" *Couldn't.* Molly's instinctive protest was cut off by Gio's light squeeze of warning before he gently released her.

"I would be honored, Nonno. Thank you."

Gio walked away, leaving Molly feeling chilled despite the fact the room was being kept as toasty as a sauna for Otto.

Gio moved to a large black-and-white photo of a couple in wedding regalia from the 1800s. He swung it back on its hidden hinge, revealing a wall safe.

"The ring belonged to my grandmother," Otto told her. "Then my mother wore it, then my Theresa." His shaking fingers were moving restlessly on hers. "It will be good to see it on you."

What about Gio's mother? she wondered, but Gio was bringing a velvet box toward her. His gaze locked to hers, some hidden meaning sparking behind his eyes as he approached. It was a message that urged her to keep looking at him. *Stay with me.*

He went down on one knee!

"Oh!" she blurted, slapping both her hands over her mouth.

"Molly Brooks, will you marry me?" He offered the ring, which she could barely see because her eyes welled with tears. Her throat closed and her mouth couldn't form any words. Why? This wasn't even real!

Otto chuckled. "Give him your hand, *carina*."

She offered her right hand. *No, silly.* Her left. It was visibly shaking, which made her feel so horribly obvious.

This isn't real. It isn't real.

Gio slid the ring onto her finger—it fit beautifully, as though it was meant for her. He kissed her knuckles.

She had the wildest thought that she wanted to tell her mother she was engaged. She wanted to tell Libby. *Sasha.*

She really was going to cry. Why were all her dreams coming true at the worst possible time?

Gio rose, bringing her hand upward so he held it between them. His expression was impossible to read because her eyes were too full of mist. She looked at their joined hands, dying of embarrassment.

"I feel so foolish." What must he think of her acting this way?

"You're perfect." He sounded tender as he gently cradled her face, tilting up her mouth before setting the lightest of kisses on her lips.

Perhaps he only meant it to be that chaste performance for his grandfather, but as he drew back a hairbreadth, her lips clung to his. It was the hug all over again. She was instigating something she shouldn't have, but feelings were brimming out of her. Everything in her wanted to hold on to this moment. To make it real.

Her vision hazed over even more. Her bloodstream was

hot and fizzing. Her weight tipped forward ever so slightly while she lifted against him, inviting a firmer kiss.

His nostrils flared. There was a flash behind his eyes like sheet lightning, then his mouth sealed to hers. He angled his head, parting her lips without effort, then plundered in a way that sent a shock wave into her belly.

She had never been kissed like this. Not just the rough-gentle expertise that threw her so off balance she had to cling to his shoulders. No, the greater difference was the way her whole body reacted, as though she'd plunged into a fire that burned away the rest of the world, promising to leave her forged into something new.

But even as her cells and synapses were calibrating to his, he was pulling back. She heard Otto give another dry chuckle.

It had only been a few seconds, but she'd been bronzed and changed, and no longer made of one element, but two. She held particles of Gio within herself and they made her feel radiant.

"*Now* you have given me something to live for," Otto said in his paper-thin voice. "Call the ambulance, Gio. The hospital can keep me alive long enough to see you married."

Hours later, Gio exhaled a mountain of tension as they entered his apartment in Genoa. It was located closer to both the office and the hospital, so it made sense to sleep here instead of the villa.

The transfer to the hospital had been taxing on Nonno, but he was accepting oxygen and some antiviral medication. He had even sipped a little soup.

While ensuring his grandfather was settled, Gio had overheard Molly speaking to a boutique. She had arrived without luggage and was making the whole thing sound a lot more complicated than it needed to be. He'd asked her to let him speak to them.

"You have her sizes? *Bene.*" He'd mentioned a generous budget. "She needs everything, top to toe, every type of occasion, for several weeks. If you don't have it, call around to one of your competitors. Whatever she doesn't use will be returned within the month." His name had been enough to guarantee their fullest cooperation. He'd given them the delivery address and had handed her back the phone. "Learn to delegate."

They'd taken him at his word and, judging by the parcels and bags lined up along the wall, had spent every last euro of the amount he'd mentioned.

The rest of their afternoon and evening had been spent working late at the Genoa office.

"Do you want something?" He went to the bar.

"You have no idea." She sounded exhausted and was staring at the parcels as though they were a fresh mountain to climb.

Pregnant, he recalled. He kept forgetting that incredibly significant detail, probably because he didn't want to believe it. It was not only inconvenient on a professional front, but it also bothered him at a deeper level. Who was this man she had slept with? Why wasn't he fighting for the right to be in her life and his child's life? *I would.*

Gio knocked back the Scotch he'd poured, trying to erase that errant thought. Trying not to remember a kiss that had shaken his foundation.

Emotions had been running high. That's all it had been.

The whole episode had been surreal, from the way his hands had found their way around Molly's delicious figure to the way she had melted into him.

Through a haze of unexpectedly sharp arousal, he'd heard

Nonno offer the ring he had refused to give to Gio's father, for Gio's mother, and had neglected to offer to Gio for his own engagement four years ago.

It had made his willingness for Molly to wear it seem doubly impactful. It meant Nonno truly expected to die.

That, too, Gio was refusing to believe. The hospital had assured him a mere thirty minutes ago that his grandfather was sleeping, his fever under control and his color good. They would call him immediately if there was any change.

Molly had removed the ring so she wouldn't start rumors at work. He touched his shirt pocket to ensure the ring was still there, immediately feeling the weight of responsibility it entailed. He had always known he had a duty to marry and make children, but he was ambivalent about it. What if he turned out to be as feckless as his own parents? What if he broke his child? What if he failed his grandfather as gravely as his own father had failed both of them?

Molly seemed more than ready to become a parent. She was fiercely protective of her pregnancy, was off coffee and alcohol and had taken a few minutes in the afternoon to insist they pause for a healthy snack.

Had he pushed her too hard? It had already been a demanding situation before his grandfather's illness and he had asked a lot of her today.

"Which room is mine?" She gathered a number of bags by their handles and glanced down the hall.

"What are you doing? Put those down."

"They're not heavy."

"Your new assistant will put those away. Why is Nelo not here?" After weeding the applicants down to three, each with specific strengths, Molly had suggested utilizing all of them as a cohesive support team. They each happened to live in the cities where Casella Corporation had offices so they would have feet on the ground in New York, London and Genoa, which appealed to Gio.

"I sent him home."

"Why?"

"Because you said we were finished working for the night."

"*We* are. How many times did you pick up the phone at four a.m. to order breakfast for me and Valentina while we were traveling?"

"I don't know." She shrugged. "Dozens?"

"*Every* time. Otherwise, you wouldn't have kept that job. You wouldn't have this one. Call Nelo and tell him to make us a dinner reservation, then get his tail over here to put this away. If he gives you any excuse, he's not the right man for the job."

Molly glared a belligerent look at him, then let the bags fall to the floor.

"Do we have to go out?" she asked crossly. "If I'm off the clock, I'd rather have a bath and go to bed."

Pregnant, damn it.

He rubbed the stubble that was coming in on his jaw.

Now he was picturing her naked, skin shiny and coated with trailing bubbles. She wasn't even in the tub yet and he knew the image would persist for weeks.

"Fine. But don't you dare call in that dinner order yourself."

To her credit, she didn't roll her eyes, though he had a feeling she wanted to.

She didn't apologize when she reached Nelo, either. She politely said that she had thought they were done for the night, but explained, "This is a very demanding role and things will continue to surface unexpectedly. I hope you're prepared for that?… Oh?… I'm pleased to hear it. Dedication is rewarded over time, so do keep that attitude. We need a meal delivered. Something light for me with lots of vegetables, please. You might as well organize breakfast while you're at it and plan to be here bright and early to put some things away for me."

"Better," Gio said when she hung up.

Her eyebrows went up in a small commentary at his arrogant remark, but she only asked, "Which room does Valentina use?"

"She doesn't. We usually stay at the villa. I only keep this as convenience for late evenings or if I have a—" Date.

In those cases, if a woman stayed over, she didn't use the spare room. Gio didn't even know if his guest room had a bed in it, let alone whether it was made up.

Molly chewed the corner of her mouth, not meeting his gaze.

He led her down the hall. This was in a heritage building on the waterfront, but the interior had been completely redesigned and modernized into a his-and-hers pair of bedrooms joined by a shared bath.

Molly barely glanced at the rose-and-ivory decor in the second bedroom, seeming both uncertain and done in.

It was hitting him that she had been more than his professional support today. She'd been an emotional one and had even gone the extra mile, allowing him to hug her for comfort and kiss her for his grandfather's sake.

A fresh burst of carnal hunger struck his belly and rang behind his fly. In the same way that he had walked in here craving a strong drink, he longed to lose himself in sex.

Judging by the way they reacted to each other, sex with Molly would be all-consuming and deeply gratifying, but it couldn't happen. She was his employee, blurry as that distinction had become, and she was pregnant with another man's child.

A hard fist clenched inside him, a resistance. No. There were too many complicating factors to consider an affair with her, but he couldn't help envying the father of her baby, for knowing how it felt to make love to her.

Why wasn't that man in her life, though? Gio was grateful he was out of the way, but he had no respect for him. As someone who'd suffered parental neglect, he instinctually loathed a man who would leave a woman and their child to fend for themselves.

His thoughts were so frustrating and contradictory, he escaped them by moving into the bathroom to start the tub. He closed the door into his own bedroom, then decisively locked it, as though the action would lock her out of his mind.

He hesitated, though. What if something happened?

Nonsense. She was a grown adult. She wasn't going to drown in a thirty-minute bath.

And she was only his assistant. Why the hell was he in so many knots over her?

Concern. It was simple, human concern. Physically, she was in a vulnerable state and, much as he was not behaving like the best employer in the world, he valued the health of his employees.

"Listen," he said as he came back into her bedroom. "You know that my personality is to push until my strength gives out. I expect you to recognize your own limitations and tell me when you're reaching capacity."

"You mean that?"

"I said it."

"Okay." She nodded. "Then let me be very clear. I can't marry you. I won't. That's a hard limit." She had brought a few bags into the bedroom and dumped one onto the bed, spilling a powder-blue nightgown onto the bedspread.

Ignore it, he demanded of his inner barbarian, but he instantly had a vivid fantasy of her nipples lifting that fine silk while the gathers cupped her full breasts and scalloped lace fell around her thighs.

"I want your grandfather to recover, and if he does... This can't go any further, Gio. It shouldn't have gone this far." She shook moisturizer from another bag.

She might be right, but... "He's in the hospital accepting treatment. I won't apologize for my tactics in getting him there."

Including the kiss? She shot him a mutinous look, making him certain that's what she was wondering.

Despite his resolve to keep her from penetrating any deeper under his skin, he wound up holding her gaze, refusing to express regret over their moment of passion. It had been mutual. Her hand had been in his hair, urging him to kiss her harder.

Heat pooled in his groin at the memory.

She blushed and looked away, rolling her lips inward. Her very soft, luscious lips.

Once again, he was accosted by the most lascivious of fantasies, one where he kissed more than her mouth. He pushed silk upward to expose her curves and secrets, and tasted all of her, from that thumping artery in her throat to the humid heat between her thighs.

Both yearning and persecution flashed across her expression before she looked away. Her shoulders were heavy and her mouth tilted down at the edges, warning him that this day had taken more out of her than was comfortable on his conscience.

"I appreciate everything you did today, Molly." He was trying to drag this back to a professional relationship, but the way her bottomless brown eyes swept back to his, wary and soft, had him biting back a groan of hunger. "I asked a lot of you. You rose to the challenge, which is why I want to keep you on."

Was that disappointment that glinted in her eyes? A sting of rebuff that scorched her cheeks? If it was, she hid it very quickly behind a bland smile.

"This is you pushing for me to agree to a longer tenure?" She moved to the door to the hall, signaling that she expected him to leave.

"No." He came to stand in the doorway. "I'm reminding you that the company rewards dedication over time, so—"

"Oh, shut up." She sputtered into laughter, which was his goal in throwing her own words at her. "Three weeks, Gio. Minus today. Hard limit."

It *was* hard. And sharp. He wasn't used to being denied anything he wanted. Who knew it was such a diamond-tipped arrow? It penetrated his breastbone, vibrating there as he walked out and she closed the door behind him.

Molly dozed in the tub, then ate what had been delivered while she was catching up on her personal banking. After that, she slept like a log, waking feeling infinitely better.

The only awkward moment was when she almost walked in on Gio in the shower, hearing the water at the last second.

She bit back a groan as she pictured him running a cloth over his swarthy skin.

Okay, she *had* to shake this off. Yesterday had been an aberration of a day. She might have to pretend to be his betrothed when they were with his grandfather, but she was his executive assistant and she took her position seriously.

Thankfully, she had washed her hair after her bath last night, so she didn't need a shower now. She used the powder room off the kitchen to wash her face, then did her makeup and put her hair up in its simple twist before she dressed in one of her new outfits.

Gio had been ridiculously generous, forcing more than a handful of work outfits on her. There were cocktail dresses and casual wear, swimsuits and lingerie. It was pure bribery and an effective tactic for making her feel beholden to him.

There were a few skirts in the deliveries that she immediately set aside to return. She disliked wearing skirts to work. Valentina had once advised her to dress well, but comfortably. "You're not effective in your job if you're worrying about a wardrobe malfunction," she'd said.

That tacit permission to wear trousers had changed her life. She kept the style feminine, but her work clothes ran the gamut, from three-piece suits that were nipped and tucked to accentuate her figure, to crepe Bermuda shorts with a matching wine-colored jacket.

Today, she chose a pair of houndstooth capris and paired them with a flouncy green silk top that bloused over a stretchy band that hugged her hips, neatly disguising the thickening of her waist.

When Nelo arrived with breakfast, Molly showed him what needed to be done, then sat down to eat with Gio. He looked and smelled fantastic, freshly shaved and wearing his suit, seemingly engrossed in whatever was happening on his tablet.

"Valentina is asking for a conference call today," she said, determined to remind both of them this was a working relationship. "I told her we're visiting the hospital on our way to the office."

"They said he's showing some improvement. It should be a short visit to cheer him up." He offered the ring. "Before we head into the office."

"Oh, um." She glanced down the hall to ensure Nelo

didn't see, then put it on her finger, aware that Gio watched it go on. "That's good to hear, that he's improving."

"It is." He returned his attention to his tablet.

Molly checked her personal phone, but didn't have anything from Sasha yet. She sent a few silly memes to Libby. Then rose with the phone, taking it to the window.

"Do you mind if I send a photo of the view to my mother? I'd like her to know I'm working in Italy for the next while. She knows I can't say much about what I do, but I'd like her to know where I am."

"Fine," he said absently.

She took the photo, sending it with a text.

My view for the next while. I'll call later today to explain.

She would love to bring her mother and sister here to see it for themselves. She could easily afford it with her new salary, but Libby didn't know she was pregnant and likely never would. Her mother did. Sasha had fond memories of Patricia and had agreed that her discretion, advice and support would be invaluable to Molly as her pregnancy progressed.

With a wistful sigh, she walked back to the table.

"That's disturbing," Gio murmured.

"What is?" She curled one leg beneath her as she retook her seat.

She expected him to mention a conflict or disaster somewhere. Perhaps an unexpected plunge in market numbers.

"Do you remember the Zamos couple? You were with us on their yacht last year, when we began putting together a partnership agreement with their container division in Athens. We were actually due to finalize that next week."

Molly knew that, but *were*?

"I—I remember them," she said hesitantly, weirdly feeling as though the walls were both closing in and disappearing. Her ears were filling with water. "Why?"

"They've been in a terrible car crash."

"What?"

Gio thought Molly was leaning down for the phone she dropped and only realized at the last second that she was fainting. He barely reacted in time to catch her, saving her slumping body from crashing onto the floor. Her chair fell over with a clatter and he must have shouted something because Nelo came running.

"Signore?"

"Call the doorman. There's a doctor in this building. See if he can come. If not, an ambulance." Gio's knees were throbbing from the way he had plunged to the floor to catch her. Molly was a rag doll in his arms, but even as Nelo was snapping out instructions and Gio was still gathering her to pick her up, her eyelids began to flutter.

He got her onto the sofa, only then realizing how hard his heart was pounding. What the *hell*?

"The doctor is coming. I have first aid," Nelo said. "Please, let me do an assessment?"

Gio left Nelo taking her pulse while he opened the door to the doctor. As he showed him into the lounge, Molly was brushing Nelo away, trying to sit up.

"I'm fine. I was light-headed from moving too fast." She was still white as a ghost. The way she covered her mouth suggested she was fighting not to throw up.

"If you're finished here, Nelo, head into the office. I don't need to tell you this doesn't leave this room."

"Understood." Nelo nodded. He sent one worried glance backward and left.

Molly was hollow-eyed as she had her blood pressure

taken, but didn't seem inclined to share her condition with the doctor even when the man asked point-blank, "Is there a possibility of pregnancy?"

"I'll follow up with my own physician on that," she said firmly and shot Gio a glance that warned any word out of him would be grounds for her to walk.

The father must not know of her pregnancy. It was the only explanation for her secrecy. Who was he? Someone abusive? *Married?*

That started to make sense.

"I'm very sorry to have inconvenienced you," she said. Her voice was still shaky, but she was giving the doctor a firm brush-off. "Could we offer you coffee or croissants for your trouble?"

"No, thank you." The doctor sent a puzzled look to Gio, then cautioned her to have her iron levels checked. He accepted promised tickets to the opera as compensation for his house call.

Gio showed him out, then came back to find Molly had walked herself to the table and was texting someone.

"What are you doing? Sit down," he ordered. "And why the *hell* didn't you tell him you're pregnant?"

"I'm texting my physician right now, giving her my vitals. She'll tell me if she thinks it's serious."

"It *is* serious," he insisted. She was still pale. He came across to right her chair and pointed at it. "Sit."

"I don't want to talk about this right now." She set aside her phone, hand shaking, but did lower into the chair. She glanced at her half-eaten breakfast as though it was a bowl of worms. "Your grandfather is expecting us. We have a full day at the office."

"Molly, you have to tell me what is going on. Is he married?" That didn't fit with the type of person he thought her to be, but perhaps she hadn't known. Lots of people lied about that sort of thing.

Her mouth quivered. Tears came into her eyes. For one moment, she looked at him in a way that sent surprisingly deep claws into his heart.

"Are you afraid of him?" He braced himself for that answer because he didn't expect to react well if she was.

"What? No. I told you that topic is off-limits." She leaped to her feet, almost sending the chair flying again.

He caught at her, holding her still.

"Don't move so fast. Do you want to faint again?"

She seemed made of twisted iron, there was so much tension in her. She kept her head down, refusing to look at him, but her hand curled into his sleeve, almost as though she was hanging on for dear life.

"You *are* frightened." He sensed it in a primal way, at a level that made all his body hair stand on end in reaction.

"Not of him. Of—" She cut off her choked words. Suddenly she was made of something delicate. Strands of brittle frost. She was quivering like a leaf encased in ice. Anything could break her.

"What, then?" he demanded, trying to gentle his gruff voice.

She gave one sniff and crumpled into him. Clung.

He had woken this morning uneasy with how much of his inner life he'd allowed her to see yesterday. He hadn't just introduced her to his grandfather, he'd *kissed* her in front of the old man. They were pretending an engagement and she was sleeping in his home. More than that, she was in his thoughts, provoking sexual infatuation and very deep *concern*.

Now he had his hands on her again, reflexively trying to soothe away her trembles. Trying to absorb the emotions that had her in their grip while ignoring his own. He was furious, though. Furious with the man who had left her fainting and shaking, worrying for a baby on her own.

"If he's married or a criminal… I won't judge. I swear. But I can't help you unless you tell me."

She drew in a jagged breath and stepped away from him.

"I promised myself I'd be more professional today."

He barked out a laugh since "professional" had been thrown out of the car miles ago.

"You're the one who muddied the waters." She flinched and hugged herself, shoulders tense and defensive. "I know this is an illusion." She gestured at the ring she wore. "But…" Her brow pleated and she turned her gaze to the windows.

"What?" he prompted, experiencing a strange teetering sensation in his chest.

When she didn't say anything, he gently touched her chin, wanting to see what was going on behind her troubled expression.

She pulled away and blinked her red eyes, increasing the smudges around them.

"Come on, Gio." She swiped impatiently under her eyes. "You have to know every single, heterosexual woman in the company has a crush on you. Plus half the married ones and probably all the gay men."

"Do *you*?" He was a bastard for making her say it. He knew she was attracted to him. He'd always known. It was one of those things he actively ignored, but he wanted to hear it.

"Yes," she choked out. Her eyes brightened with tears of mortification. "Now we're hugging and kissing every five minutes…" She flung out a hand in an expression of how wretched she felt. "I want to help you with your grandfather,

I do. But I'm also a person and I'm not a sophisticated one. I don't date a lot or have casual relationships."

He lifted his eyebrows, dying to ask how she'd wound up alone and pregnant.

"Don't lead me on." Everything from her voice to her body language reflected how excruciating she found this, revealing her attraction and begging him not to exploit it.

He wanted to exploit it. This attraction was mutual. Close to irresistible, which was difficult enough to acknowledge privately, so he veered from admitting it aloud. He would be a cad for doing so when she had explicitly asked him not to lead her on. She wasn't a woman he could date casually to see where it led. He had to be explicit about his intentions.

"I don't accost my employees with unwanted attention. Or wanted," he said with an ironic curl of his lip. "Workplace romances makes for messy headlines."

Her gaze flashed up to his. Her lashes quivered unsteadily as she searched his eyes. Humiliation stained her cheekbones.

He looked away, not wanting her to read how his fantasies were flaring to life at the knowledge she reciprocated his interest. She would see how he wanted her. And *where*. The bath. The sofa. His desk. A flood of heat accompanied the reel of places and ways in which he wanted to make love to her.

In the charged silence, he heard her swallow.

Then there was a buzz from the table. Her personal phone.

She hurried across and picked it up, shoulders falling in what seemed to be disappointment. Expecting someone else? A sensation like breaking glass struck inside his ears.

"My physician wants me to get some blood work," she said stiffly. "I'll ask at the hospital where it would be best to have that done. Let me fix my makeup and we can go."

CHAPTER FOUR

SASHA AND RAFAEL had been side-struck while driving home from a gala, Molly learned as she surreptitiously scrolled the news on their way to see Otto. Rafael had broken bones and was in surgery. Sasha was still unconscious. Their driver was also listed as critical. They were in a hospital in Rome and all were expected to recover.

She grasped onto that. *Expected to recover.*

She wished she could go to Rome. So near and yet so far.

Gio's driver parked, so she put away her phone and dragged on an outward cloak of composure, but she felt as though she was walking through gelatin.

It was absolutely no shock to her that she'd fainted. She had made a life-altering decision when she had offered to become Sasha's surrogate, but her life kept turning and shaking out into new patterns faster than she could adjust to them.

Valentina was no longer her boss. That job was now Molly's, but she couldn't keep it. She was in Italy. Gio's grandfather thought they were engaged. The parents of the baby she was carrying were gravely injured.

She had accidentally thrown herself into her boss's arms, twice, and he had basically told her to put it away.

Which was exactly what he ought to say, but she was horribly disappointed and feeling rebuffed.

It ought to be the last thing she was turning over in her mind, but it colored all the rest in bleak shadows. It made her inevitable departure from her job and *him* all the more urgent.

Why had she opened herself up that way, revealing her attraction? She could have just shut up and moved on, but no, she'd had to spell out for him that she was having trouble remembering this engagement wasn't real.

In some ways it felt very real, though. She had come dangerously close to blurting out everything to Gio when he had offered to help her. He had seemed genuinely concerned, but he was only being decent. Indulgent, perhaps, since he wanted her to stick out this job and keep pretending they were engaged.

For a few seconds, however, she had been tempted to spill her guts and lean on the man who was posing as her partner in life. Her person.

That's not what he was, though. And there was nothing Gio could do to help her. Nothing she could do. There were contingencies in place. The surrogacy agreement had covered many scenarios, including the loss of both parents before the baby's birth. In that case, Molly had agreed to raise the baby herself, so it could inherit the fortune to which it was entitled.

Such an easy thing to say at the time, believing it would never happen, yet here she was, fearful it might.

No. Sasha and Rafael would recover. They had to. While they did, the very best thing she could do for them was keep their baby healthy.

She wanted to cry, though. She wanted to go to them. To Sasha. She wanted her mother to be here and tell her everything would be fine—even though her mother was a realist who would definitely never make that sort of false promise.

Molly was so wrapped up in her own thoughts, she was barely aware that they were walking into Otto's suite. It was tastefully decorated, looking more like a hotel than a hospital room. Only his IV and the oxygen tube under his nose indicated he was receiving care.

Gio swore and came up short as another couple straightened from hovering over the bed.

"What are you doing here?" She'd never heard his voice so ugly and cold. His hand on her elbow tightened.

"My father is dying. Where else would I be?" the middle-aged man said.

"You wish that was true, but it's not." Gio sounded so hostile, Molly instinctually grasped at his sleeve, subconsciously holding him back from attacking them. "There's nothing for you to gain here. *Leave.*"

Were they really his parents? The only thing Molly knew of them was that they were occasionally linked to scandals, like a politician turning up in the wrong bed or a party being busted for rampant drug use. Each time something like that had happened, Valentina would slip away with Gio for a few days. Sometimes there was an announcement that would distance Gio and the Casella Corporation. More often, their chaos was simply swept from the headlines and forgotten.

Curious, she studied the pair, thinking they looked much older than their years. They were dressed well, or rather their clothes were expensive, but worn sloppily. Neither was paunchy, but they both had faces that were well-lined. Not merely sun-weathered or full of laugh lines, but showing miles and miles of a dissolute life. His father's eyes were sunken, his skin sallow. His mother was probably a natural blonde, given her Icelandic heritage, but her blue eyes were glassy and her hair looked overprocessed and brittle.

When she came forward to try to embrace and kiss her son, Gio recoiled, not allowing her to touch him.

She gave an amused sniff and turned a smile on Molly that was both patronizing and ingratiating.

"Hello. I'm Fridrika, Gio's mother." She held out her hand. "This is my husband, Ambrose. And you are?"

"Molly," Gio answered for her, voice blunt as a hammer. He stopped Molly from lifting her hand to shake, bringing both her hands to his lips while holding his mother's gaze. "My fiancée."

Fridrika's wild-eyed gaze pinned itself to the ring. She raked in a breath.

"You gave her the ring?" She shot a look to Otto, who was watching from the bed, looking weary.

"No!" Ambrose came across and made to grab at Molly's hand himself, but Gio angled his body between them and brushed away his father's reaching hand.

"If I had thought you would have the gall to show your faces here, I would have told the hospital staff to refuse your entry," Gio said grimly. "Leave or I'll have Security escort you out."

"He's my *father*," Ambrose insisted. He was shaking, gaze pinned on Molly as though she was some multiheaded monster that had arrived to nip at him.

"When it's convenient," Gio shot back.

"It's convenient for you that I'm *your* father, isn't it? You think you can take all of this without a fight from me?" Ambrose waved his arm. "Think again."

"How much do you want? Hmm? Leave without a fuss and I'm more likely to be generous. Molly, go see that Nonno isn't upset by this while I walk them out." He gave her a small nudge in the middle of her back then jerked his head at the door.

The older couple wore disgruntled expressions, but shuffled out, glancing back once. Gio pulled the door firmly closed behind him.

Molly swayed under this fresh shock. It must be equally upsetting for Otto.

"Do you know that I've actually led a very quiet and boring life until the last few days?" She picked up his hand to warm it between her own. "At one point, I thought I might become a librarian because I was so content seeing the world through books, rather than with my own eyes."

He smiled faintly. "Tell me more."

"To help you sleep?" she teased. She told him about her first jobs babysitting, then her work in a bistro, where she had exploded the shop's popularity with social media. "Everyone said I had a flare for marketing so I started my degree in that field. Then I discovered *statistics*."

"Now I will sleep." He closed his eyes.

She chuckled and told him about her entry position in the Casella Corporation and the small successes that had allowed her to advance to London and work for Valentina.

"That was hard, leaving my mother and sister."

"No father?"

"He moved to California after their divorce. I still see him sometimes, but I'm much closer to my mother and sister. They're still in New Jersey. Not the exciting part of the state, either," she confided with mock glumness. "It's a rural town in the hills. Very beautiful, though, especially in the fall. I like to take my sister walking..."

She had first discovered those trails with Sasha. Her friend's dire condition rushed back with such force Molly began to choke up.

"I'm so sorry." She released Otto's hand and gathered a couple of tissues, trying to stem her tears before she smudged her makeup *again*. "I had some upsetting news about a childhood friend today. It keeps hitting me."

"Oh?" he prompted with concern.

"I…" She shouldn't talk about Sasha, she knew that, but her anguish was so great, she had to spill out something of what was going on inside her. "She was the closest friend I've ever had. Even though I was so envious of her when I met her that I was downright rude."

She still chuckled at the memory of Sasha, when she'd asked, "What is wrong with you? Your life is perfect. Gawd!"

"Her life looked very glamorous from the outside, but she had a lot of heartache." Molly blinked back tears, remembering quiet walks in the woods and playing board games. "I was at that age when you're in a hurry to grow up. She made me realize how lucky I was to have my simple life and the last pieces of childhood."

Sasha had been the sister she always wanted, then her baby had become that cherished sister.

"She sounds wise."

"And generous. She gave me more than I could possibly tell you." She swallowed. "We were so close for a short time, then I didn't see her for years. I thought she'd forgotten me." Sasha had probably tried. It had been a very dark period in her life. "I understood. Her world is very different from mine, but when I did see her, it was as though we picked up where we left off."

She couldn't help smiling as she remembered the huge hug she had received the moment she had stepped into Sasha's stateroom on the *Alexandra*. The mood between them had turned melancholy when Sasha burst into tears, then refused to hear about Libby. That had hurt, a lot, but Molly had seen the agony in her friend's eyes. It was too painful for Sasha to go back to that time. Molly had to respect that, especially when she learned that Sasha's life had become a fresh level of torture, trying to conceive and having that dream not work out.

"What can I do to help?" Otto asked.

"Nothing. There's nothing I can do, either." Sasha's parents were there. They didn't know about Libby or that Molly was carrying Sasha's second baby. Molly couldn't be seen at her side and risk revealing that. "But it helped me to talk about her. Thank you for that. I was feeling as though I was being held under water. Now I've finally caught a breath. Please don't tell Gio about this. He already has a lot to worry about—"

Gio strode back in looking like a pressure cooker emanating steam from its seams. His dial was definitely hovering at the red line.

"I have arrangements to make," he said flatly. "How are you, Nonno?"

"Better than you, I suspect." His voice was weak, but his gaze was sharp as he took in his grandson's simmering mood. His expression softened when he asked Molly, "When can you come back so we can talk more?"

"Why don't we bring dinner?" she suggested.

"I'd like that. Maybe a little wine, too." He winked. "Can I have a moment with Gio?"

"Of course." She faltered briefly, worried Otto would reveal something of what she'd just told him, but he gave her a reassuring smile so she went to inquire about the blood work.

"Keep this one," Nonno said after Gio had caught him up on how he planned to deal with his father.

"Molly?" Gio's fuse was already short, so Nonno's remark burned right against his skin. "I would have kept the last one. She chose to leave."

"You chose a woman you didn't love and expected her to be satisfied with wearing your name and spending your money. I could see it would never work. That's why I didn't give her Nonna's ring. Molly is different. She has a big heart. You can trust her with your own. Get her pregnant. Do whatever you have to do, but *keep her.*"

Good news, Nonno. She's already pregnant.

Gio pinched the bridge of his nose.

"Se insisti," he vowed, because what else could he say when his grandfather's eyelids were drooping so heavily. He was exhausted after being attacked by his own son, demanding he change his will. "Rest up. We'll be back soon."

The hospital staff had instructions to call Gio with any changes—or the names of any visitors—so he left Nonno drifting to sleep, found Molly and took her to the office.

"Here," Molly said in the car, surreptitiously offering him the ring she had removed and glancing at the driver, who had earbuds inserted to give them privacy.

"Wear it."

"Gio—"

"My parents will have the news of our engagement across the Italian Riviera by lunch. Draft a formal announcement as soon as we're in the office. I need this leverage against them. They see an opportunity because Nonno is ill, but anyone who is anyone understands the significance of you wearing the family ring. *I* am Ottorino's heir. Not my father."

"This wasn't our deal," she hissed, but pushed the ring back onto her finger. She faced forward, mouth tight, eyes shining with distress.

You can trust her with your heart.

Not if she had one foot out the door. On the other hand, Gio was not looking forward to another well-publicized breakup.

Keep this one.

He had promised his grandfather he would, but there was a knot of resistance within him. He knew he needed to marry, that he needed an heir. Otherwise, if something happened to him, his parents really would have a chance to swoop in and destroy everything he and his grandfather had built. But what was he supposed to do? Marry his secretary and claim her baby as his? It was ludicrous. Hell, until yesterday, they hadn't spoken two words about anything that wasn't work-related.

But that kiss...

Stop it.

"We have a lot to cover this morning," he said with more snap than he intended, making her stiffen. "I want to revisit the closing dates on the Athens deal. I'm not signing anything until I know that Zamos is in the clear." He began rattling off the rest of his priorities, pleased when she efficiently began delegating to Nelo, directing him to push tasks onto his counterparts in London and New York.

By the time they were striding into his office, the aroma of fresh coffee was in the air, a tray of biscotti was being delivered and Gio's desk phone was ringing.

"Signor Donatelli," Nelo said of the call, hovering with his tablet.

"Bene." Gio picked up the receiver and said, "Vittorio." Gio waved for Molly to shoo everyone from the room. "No, you stay in here, Molly."

"Buongiorno," Vittorio Donatelli said in Gio's ear. "I saw the report that your grandfather is in hospital. I'm so sorry, Gio. I hope he recovers quickly."

"So do I. And I'm pressed for time so I'll get to the point. I need an arrangement like the last for my parents. Double the amount, but in order to access it, they must relinquish all claim to the Casella estate and corporation. Is that something you can arrange or shall I get my own lawyers onto it?"

"I'll have a draft by end of day that your lawyers can look over."

"*Perfetto*. And thank you for excusing my brevity. It's been a difficult two days."

"I understand. Will we see you Saturday at our anniversary party?"

"I expected I would be in New York so I sent regrets." He shot a look at Molly. She had seated herself on the sofa and was concentrating on her tablet. Milan was less than an hour away by helicopter. "But if Nonno is well enough, yes. I'll bring my fiancée."

Molly lifted her head, eyes flaring with outrage.

"My grapevine is failing me," Vittorio said. "By 'grapevine,' I mean my wife. I had no idea you were engaged. Congratulations."

"For once you have a jump on Gwyn. It will be announced later today."

"Ah. I'm flattered to be one of the first to know and I shall be smug as hell when I pass your happy news along to her. I won't keep you. We'll speak later today on the other matter."

"*Grazie.*" Gio hung up and asked, "How is the announcement coming along?"

"Of our engagement? I put Nelo on it, didn't I?"

She sounded very facetious, so he asked, "Did you?"

"No! He would have spat his coffee across the office. Gio, think about this." She set aside her tablet and folded her hands in her lap. "You are my boss. A surprise notice that you are engaged to a midlevel employee—"

"You weren't my direct report until yesterday."

"It still looks terrible."

"Am I the first man to find his wife at the office? This isn't an affair. I'm marrying you. It's *romantic*," he said through his teeth.

She made a choked noise and reached for her tablet again, then stated firmly, "We are not marrying."

"But you're writing the announcement?" Rather than ask her to forward it to him so he could read it on his own screen, he walked over to settle next to her. She stiffened again, perhaps out of umbrage, but there was also a delicious crackle in the air between them.

I'm asking you not to lead me on.

He wasn't trying to, but this attraction was positively magnetic.

He heard his grandfather again. *Keep this one.* He had to stop himself from leaning closer to her, touching her.

He made himself focus on what she was writing. She kept it brief, calling it a "surprise engagement" to forestall anyone making a mountain of that. She stated that his new fiancée was not his direct report and "recently gave notice of her decision to leave Casella."

That part rankled.

"What about a photo?" she asked.

"We don't have time for a formal sitting." He picked up her phone with the floral case, since it was right there, and touched the camera icon. "Look happy, would you? You're going to break the screen."

"Gio." She made him lower the phone and angled to face him. "I know that you got as far as a church once before."

"This is nothing like that," he said flatly.

"It's exactly like that. I'm not going to marry you. And

I don't want to be the person who causes you another embarrassment."

Then don't be. The words were right there on his tongue, but it was only his sense of obligation to his grandfather prodding him to say that.

"Look." He set aside the phone and rose to pace off his restlessness. "I've always known I had a duty to marry and produce the next generation. I put my engagement together like any other merger and acquisition. She was beautiful and charming, well-connected and her family needed the money." He had thought that would buy her steadfastness. That's all he had really cared about. "When it fell apart, I was annoyed that I had put time into something that didn't work out, but I was not humiliated. My parents do things that are ten times worse. I've learned not to care how other people's actions reflect on me."

"I'm so sorry you had to see them today, Gio. Do you want to tell me—"

"No," he said flatly. "I never want to talk about them so don't bother asking."

She pursed her mouth into a circumspect pout. "So you weren't in love with your fiancée? Your heart wasn't broken when the wedding was called off?"

"No," he said with a choke of jaded laughter.

"Then why haven't you found someone else since?" Her lashes came up and it felt very much like she picked up a curtain and peered inside him.

"Fine," he muttered. "I was stung by it."

Rejection was something that landed in a very deep place when he experienced it. That's why he took steps to avoid caring too deeply about anyone. That's why he hadn't pursued someone new.

There was also that other piece. The part where he hadn't

been interested in anyone except a woman who was off-limits. There had been a certain comfort in that situation, where he saw Molly intermittently. He could hear her laughter down the hall or watch her ass leave a room, but he couldn't pursue her and therefore didn't risk a rebuff.

"I don't *care* if this ends in three weeks." That was a lie. It would grate like sandpaper. "But this engagement has become about more than easing my grandfather's mind. It signals that I am securing the Casella legacy. Our engagement solves a lot of problems for me."

"How nice for you. It creates an infinite number for me," she said tartly.

"But you'll go along with it," he pressed.

Her gaze cast about the room as though looking for some other solution. When it landed on her personal phone, her brow pleated.

"For nineteen days," she conceded.

A thousand questions leaped to his lips, the top one being "Who is he?" But he quelled them, coming back to sit next to her and picking up her phone again.

"Put your hand on my face. I want the ring to be visible. No, come closer or it will look ridiculous." He scooped his arm around her and pulled her snug against his side. "Better." Much better. She was a lovely armful of soft curves that melted into him.

"Don't take so many! I don't have time to delete a thousand useless photos."

"Kiss my cheek." He kept clicking as he extended his arm higher, trying different angles.

"No more kissing." Her fingertips were against his jaw, but one extended to cover his lips.

Her touch was lovely. The startling caress amplified his

craving for her. He turned his head to look at her and found her expression admonishing, yet filled with yearning.

Don't lead me on.

"For the camera," he said in a voice that emanated from the bottom of his chest. He dipped his head closer, allowing his lips to hover near hers, and clicked blindly.

She closed her eyes and said his name in such a helpless tone that he lowered his arm, dropping the phone between them.

He should have moved away, but he stayed right there, waiting for her lashes to flutter and lift. Her eyes were filled with more than longing. He read *hunger* and it made his whole body brick up.

Her gaze softened and her head tilted. Her hand on his cheek flexed, urging him closer.

A primitive noise left him, one that was possessive and carnal. He wrapped both his arms around her, taking the kiss she offered. Claiming it. It was the kiss he'd wanted for a year or more. Ever since Valentina had introduced her new assistant and Molly had nervously licked her lips while her cheeks turned pink.

She tasted of anise and tea and capitulation. Her hand slid around his neck and her mouth opened to his, drawing him into a long, dark tunnel of sensuality. He filled his hands with her curves, greedy for the flare of her hips and the small of her back and the swell of her breast.

A sobbing noise resounded in her throat, but she wasn't pulling away. She was pressing closer. Her knee bumped his.

He hooked his hand behind her leg and pulled her astride his thighs as he sat back on the sofa, dragging her to straddle his lap.

She gasped in surprise, drawing back to blink in startlement, but when he cupped her beautiful ass and slouched so she was pressed more intimately against his unmistakable arousal, her eyes hazed with lust. She dove her fingers into his hair and bent her head to kiss him with aggressive abandon.

He drank her unbridled desire straight, wanting the blindness it offered. Wanting to roll her beneath him and discover the full depth of her passion while proving to both of them that he was the only man who mattered to her.

That wasn't true, though. Maybe she didn't want to reveal the father of her baby, but that unnamed man was still a part of her life. A big part, if she was willing to draw such firm boundaries around that incredibly intimate connection.

What the hell were they even doing?

Gio dropped his head back, breaking their kiss.

They were both breathing heavily. She licked her lips and looked at him with such dazed longing he wanted to bottle it. Her hands were still cradling his jaw, but she self-consciously dropped them to her thighs. Remorse crept in around her mouth and eyes.

He fished for the phone, where it had fallen to the cushions.

"Don't you dare!" She stole the phone and clambered off him. "You're kind of a monster, do you know that?"

"I just wanted to see if we got anything we can use." He didn't usually ignore elephants or unwise kisses, but he was trying to break the mood so he wouldn't touch her again. His palms were burning with the imprint of her curves.

He watched as she swiped through the photos he'd taken before they kissed.

"That one," he said.

It was candid and tender. The ring was visible and they were looking into each other's eyes. The naked hunger she had revealed was already coloring her expression.

"That's too… This one," she insisted. Her eyes were closed and it was poorly framed.

As she flicked between the two, her phone pinged with a text.

Mom: I have some difficult news. Call me as soon as you can.

That was a douse of cold water. Gio swore with concern.

"That's—" She lurched to her feet.

"Stop getting up so fast," he ordered, still not over the way she'd crumpled to the floor this morning.

"I think I know what this is about, but I need to call her."

"She's a midwife, isn't she? Tell her you fainted. I want her number in case anything else happens to you."

Molly sighed with tested patience.

"I'm sending the announcement and the photo you like to Nelo, asking him to release it. All right?" She tapped and he heard the whoosh. "You and I are officially engaged. Happy? Now keep your nose out of my personal life."

She walked into the adjacent office that had been Valentina's and shut the door.

CHAPTER FIVE

HER MOTHER WAS as upset about Sasha's crash as Molly was.

Along with her busy midwife practice, Patricia Brooks had always done volunteer hours in a teen clinic. That's where she had met a troubled, pregnant sixteen-year-old. Sasha wanted to have the baby and place it for adoption, but she was hiding her pregnancy from her parents and the much older, married father. She needed somewhere safe to stay.

Patricia had a duty to report abuse, but Sasha had threatened to run away if Patricia involved the authorities. Talking to the teen, all Patricia could see was her own daughter, about to turn that age. She couldn't ignore Sasha's plight so she had brought her home. She gave her the care she needed through her pregnancy, hired lawyers and a counsellor who specialized in adoption, and personally caught Libby the day she was born.

Sasha stayed to nurse her daughter for almost two weeks, but as much as she seemed bonded to her baby, she insisted she had to leave without her.

By then, none of them could imagine Libby going to strangers. Patricia had adopted her. She made it clear to Sasha that she considered it an open adoption. Sasha could come at any time to see her daughter and be part of her life, but Sasha was adamant they never reveal she was Libby's mother. *This never happened.*

Given their close ties to Sasha, Patricia had understood Molly's willingness to surrogate for her. She was being as supportive as possible, but she worried, especially now that Sasha had been hurt.

"What does this mean for you?" she asked.

"I'm not sure," Molly replied. "The news reports say her parents are with her so I can't go see for myself. It sounds like she has a concussion, but they expect her and Rafael to make a full recovery. I'm sure Sasha will reach out to me as soon as she's able. In the meantime, I've been promoted and I'm in Italy right now."

"That's closer to Sasha, at least."

"Yes, but there's one more thing I have to tell you." Ironically, this was the hardest to say. "I'm engaged."

"To *who*?"

Ten minutes later, Molly walked back into Gio's office, probably looking as though she'd been run over by a truck because that's how she felt.

"Is your sister all right?" Gio frowned with concern.

"Yes. That was about a friend. I, um, warned Mom about the engagement. I told her it's not real."

His eyebrows shot up.

"I will lie to the entire world for you, Gio, even to my baby sister, but I will not lie to my mother." She and her mother had agreed it was best to let Libby believe it since she tended to overshare, especially when she was excited.

"Did you tell her you fainted this morning?" He narrowed his eyes.

"Yes. And while I was talking to her, my physician texted. She sent a requisition for blood work to a lab here in Genoa. I told Mom I'd make sure the results are shared with her."

"Get that taken care of, then." He jerked his chin toward the door.

"We have that conference call with Valentina," Molly reminded him. "Oh, I know," she said with mock discovery. "I'll send Nelo."

Gio didn't offer so much as a twitch of amusement. "That joke is wearing thin. Take Nelo, so I know someone is with you if you faint in the street. I'll handle Valentina."

Molly gathered her bag and hurried out because she needed a break from his nonstop lightning storm of commands.

She used the time in the car to personally send her "engagement" photo to her sister. Libby lost her pre-adolescent mind and rang through while she and Nelo were having a quick bite at a bistro after the lab, something Nelo said Gio had insisted they do before returning to the office.

Libby demanded to see the ring and meet her fiancé.

"He's not here, but we'll call you later." That would be just punishment for Gio for getting her into this mess. Libby would ask him all sorts of probing and awkward questions. "Right now, I have to go back to the office and you have to get ready for school, but I love you. Mwah, mwah, mwah." She blew her kisses through the screen.

If she had thought Libby's reaction was over-the-top, it was nothing compared to the way all the employees stood and clapped when she and Nelo entered the reception foyer.

"Oh, God." She covered her mouth. "The announcement has hit the internal channels, I presume?" She waved and smiled and blushed so hard, she thought she might actually die.

"Yes, and I'll apologize now," Nelo said once they were inside the elevator. "You were on the phone when I asked Signor Casella whether it would be appropriate to, um…" He swallowed loudly. "It's a very special occasion for the president to become engaged," he said, as though that was some kind of apology or excuse.

"No-o-o!" she moaned in premonition, even as the elevator doors opened to reveal balloons, streamers and a crowd of employees waiting to greet her. They applauded and someone began to play a romantic tune on an accordion.

"Are you kidding me?" she cried, which was the appropriate level of shock because everyone laughed with enjoyment.

"You told me last night to be prepared for anything," Nelo said, expression somewhere between a cringe and a grin of pride.

"Well done, getting her out of the office, Nelo." Gio beckoned her to join him at a table where a cake of ivory buttercream sat. It was in the shape of two interlocking hearts and read *Congratulazioni Gio e Molly.* Delicate cherry blossoms in pale pink icing were nestled between white roses and lavender sprigs that spilled off the side.

"This is a really beautiful surprise, Gio," she said sincerely. "It's such a pity I'm going to have to kill you for it later."

That provoked another roar of laughter from the crowd, who demanded a kiss.

Please, no. But also, *yes, please.*

She wasn't finished processing that other kiss, the one that she would have allowed to turn to lovemaking if he hadn't dropped his head back against the sofa to stare at her with those arresting blue eyes of his. His hands had mapped all of her and she'd loved it.

Gio drew her into his arms and she set nervous hands on his shoulders, fearful she'd make a fool of herself. She searched his eyes. She had warned him not to lead her on, but he was making this engagement seem so perfect. So real.

It would be over in three weeks, though. Less.

Even as she reminded herself of that, she wished the end would never arrive. Her arms slid themselves behind his neck and she lifted her mouth for the touch of his. He kept it chaste, but her lips clung to his, encouraging him to linger, her body not listening to her mind.

Her chest ached with loss when they drew apart.

The swoony "O-o-oh…" from their audience brought a blush to her cheeks, but now they were back to the business of selling this engagement. A series of photos followed, first as they cut into the cake, then as they shared the first piece.

A solid hour passed as they handed out cake, accepting congratulations. Everyone was so nice and genuinely happy for them that Molly began to feel ill with guilt.

When they finally got back into Gio's office, she collapsed onto the sofa.

"I cannot believe you did that to me," she groused.

"Neither can Valentina. She wants to hear from you before she decides whether to report me to HR. She wasn't joking," he added when Molly chuckled. "She said she'd risk her job if necessary. I assured her she is not at risk for doing her job, but I did tell her this is a pretense for Nonno and my father."

"Thank you for that," she said sincerely. It had been bothering her, wondering what Valentina would think of all of this.

The rest of the day was business as usual and very busy, but she was finding her feet with Nelo and the other assistants, which helped a lot.

They had an early dinner with Otto on their way home. He was sitting up and ate a few bites of the cake Molly brought him. His spirits were high because his doctor had told him he could go home in a day or two, to finish recuperating there.

Molly was equally pleased, especially because she could see that Gio was relieved, but the talons of guilt at their subterfuge were digging ever deeper under her skin.

"I hate lying to everyone, especially your grandfather," she told Gio when they returned to his apartment that evening.

Gio yanked at his tie, then poured himself a drink and a glass of sparkling water with lime for her.

"My grandfather would rather it wasn't a lie," he stated as he brought her the glass.

"Yes, I'm aware." She had already kicked off her pumps, so she curled her legs under her as she settled into the corner of the sofa and accepted her drink. "But as fond as I'm becoming of him, that's not the sort of love I intend to marry for."

"You're a romantic?" His eyebrows went up as he settled into the chair that faced her. "I've always thought of you as pragmatic, but you do let people prey upon your emotions, don't you?"

"You, for instance?" she asked with a facetious smile.

He sipped his drink, saying nothing.

She curled herself tighter into the corner of the sofa.

"I like to help people when I can." Who didn't? "But my desire to marry for love is actually a practical choice." Why did saying that make her feel so exposed? Maybe because it sounded as though she was refusing an offer he hadn't actually made?

"How do you mean?" he asked with curiosity.

"My parents married because they accidentally got pregnant with me," she explained with a pang of her old feelings of inadequacy. "In fact, my mother went into reproductive care because she felt so betrayed by how poorly she had been educated as a teenager about her own body, then neglected as she went through a difficult pregnancy. They both loved me, but they felt trapped in their marriage. I don't blame them for divorcing, but it was hard for me. When you're the reason your parents married, you also feel like a failure when they don't stay married."

"You knew all of that when you were *six*?"

"No. At six, I only knew that Dad moved out. Then he moved far away and started a new family. I visited a few times a year, but I didn't feel like I had a place there. Eventually, it came out that they had never been in love. They had tried to make the best of an unplanned pregnancy, but were better apart. They were trying to help me understand, but I still felt like the glue that wasn't strong enough. I don't ever want to put my own child through a divorce, but more than that, I don't want my child to suffer the pressure of holding a couple together."

Only two end table lamps were burning, so it wasn't easy to read his eyes, but she was certain his gaze slid down to her middle. She sealed her lips, reminding him they weren't talking about *this* baby or the fact she wasn't with its father.

"What happens in three weeks?" he asked after a long pause. "You go home?"

"No." Her thoughts flashed to the plans she'd made with Sasha to stay out of sight for the remainder of her pregnancy. Would the island villa still happen? Why weren't Rafael or Sasha texting her back?

Her uncertainty must have shown on her face.

"So stay. Continue to work until you take your mat leave."

"And let everyone, including your grandfather, believe this baby is yours? No. This lie has already gone too far. I don't even know how anyone is buying this engagement. It's obvious I'm a Podunk girl who doesn't belong in your world. I'm not even someone you'd have an affair with."

"Why do you say that?"

"Would you?" Her stomach swooped. Was he joking?

His expression was inscrutable as he sipped his drink, gaze seeming to pick her apart. "Would *you*?"

She had kind of implied that she would when she'd told him not to lead her on, hadn't she?

"That's neither here nor there," she quickly said. "I'm pregnant, so it's moot."

"Is it not safe?" He cocked his head with intrigue. "I was under the impression most women could have sex while pregnant."

She was struck dumb by that, then managed to answer him. "You're not wrong, but how on earth would you know that?"

"This is Italy." He shrugged. "Most men are trying to get their wife pregnant before she's delivered the one she's carrying."

"Oh, for heaven's sake," she sputtered, but she couldn't help a moment of speculation about whether he would find her growing curves sexy.

Don't, she cautioned herself. She couldn't let herself start thinking anything was possible between them other than this fake engagement.

"Have you received your results from today's tests?" he asked, technically pushing up against the boundaries of their deal, but she could tell he was asking out of concern.

"My doctor said she would call me once she reviews them."

"Hmm." It was another thoughtful rumble. "We'll table a discussion about an affair until after you've consulted with her, then."

"Oh, is that what we'll do?" Her voice went up an octave and so did her internal temperature. "Will I have any say in that discussion?" She was trying to sound sarcastic, but it was tough to pull off, especially when he rightly pointed out—

"You brought it up. I'm the one who's being sensible and saying we should check with your doctor first. I'll have a physical, too. Better safe than sorry."

"You're unbelievable." But it had been her Freudian slip. Was she out of her tree? She absolutely could *not* sleep with her boss while pregnant with the secret baby of her dearest friend...who was married to his business associate!

"I'm going to have a bath." She couldn't handle the way he fried her brain circuits.

"Let me know if you want me to wash your hair," he called to her back, taunting, but her skin tightened with anticipation at the thought of it.

She wanted him to touch her and see her naked and do all the rest. That was the stark, shameful truth.

She flipped him the bird. What was he going to do? Fire her?

The remainder of the week was a blur of work and training her team and getting Nonno settled back in his own bed. Molly also moved back to the villa with Gio, but Gio shrugged off her bringing more than a handful of essentials.

"Ilario has prepared the room next to mine with everything you'll need."

Indeed, the closet was completely stocked with yet another wardrobe from the same boutiques that had been raided when they had arrived. Evening wear had been added, and so many designer shoes that her mind boggled.

Molly had greater concerns than how Gio chose to spend his money, though. She found a report that Sasha had regained consciousness, but it didn't say anything else. Rafael was out of surgery and seemed to be recovering, but hundreds of other news stories had taken over, so she wasn't able to learn more than that. Her handful of texts to both of them remained unanswered.

Molly's physician, Dr. Kala Narula, reviewed Molly's blood work and saw nothing serious. She concluded what Molly suspected—she had fainted from shock.

Kala had been Sasha's fertility specialist and was equally concerned by the news about the pair. She had reached out to the hospital in Rome, but they refused to share anything more than what was released to the press. She agreed with Molly that the best thing they could do for Sasha and Rafael was continue to keep Molly's pregnancy as healthy as possible. She urged Molly to rest and eat smaller meals more often.

"And what about…" Molly almost swallowed her own tongue. "Sex?"

There was a beat of surprise, then Kala replied, "You're far enough beyond implantation and your pregnancy is not high-risk. Physically, there's no issue, but I wouldn't advise this become an experimental phase in your life."

"No." Molly's dry laugh held little humor. "That's not what I'm considering. It's someone I've known a long time and…" And she kind of wished the doctor had told her she was forbidden to have sex. Now the decision was all on her.

"I can't tell you what to do, Molly, but I would remind you that this is a distressing time. It's natural that you might be drawn to a relationship as comfort. Be aware that may be coloring your desire."

"Thanks," she murmured, even as she acknowledged that comfort was not what she was wanted from Gio.

She wanted what their kisses had promised. *Fire*.

She couldn't, though. Shouldn't. Beyond the immediate problem of her pregnancy, they really were from two different worlds. She was a smart, dedicated employee, so she didn't have imposter syndrome about her ability to do her job, but she felt the side-eye at work now that everyone knew they were engaged. They were all wondering how a midlevel employee had risen to the top and caught the boss's personal attention. None of the explanations were flattering.

On the other hand, her lack of a real future with Gio made a brief affair now, while she had the chance, seem justified. If her choice was no cake or a crumb, she wanted the crumb.

"We should leave soon," Gio said as he drained his coffee.

"Hmm? I didn't think we were going into the office today." It was Saturday and she was still in her yoga shorts and a loose T-shirt over her sports bra, having done her stretches before joining him in the garden for breakfast.

"We have the party in Milan tonight. You need to be fitted for a gown."

"I have gowns." She'd been planning to try them on after her shower.

"Those are samples that designers send in hopes of gaining your attention," he disclosed. "This is a very high-profile party and your first event as my fiancée. You'll want something you've chosen yourself."

That *she* chose? Or he did? This was exactly what she had meant when she called herself Podunk. She didn't know how to choose an evening gown for a high-profile event. Nor did she want to be molded by him into someone he thought was good enough to be seen beside him.

"I'll check in with Nonno, to be sure he's comfortable with our being away for the night." Gio rose.

"The night?" she repeated, halting him.

"We'll stay in Milan unless he wants us to come home. Can you be ready in thirty minutes?"

She was ready in ten, seeing as the maid had already packed for her. She had a quick shower and snuck her prenatal vitamins into her bag, then went to Otto's room to say *arrivederci*.

"What color is your gown tonight?" Otto asked her.

"I don't know yet. Apparently, I'm choosing something when we get to Milan."

"The white serpent, then," Otto said to Gio and pointed to the safe.

"Otto," Molly protested.

"Call me Nonno. Yes, that's the one." He nodded at Gio to open the velvet case.

It was a snake of diamonds—literally a serpent-shaped head biting its own dangling tail. Each reticulated scale held nine diamante diamonds and the head was an eye-catching sparkle of tapered baguets. Matching earrings were fashioned to appear as though the serpent had pierced through the wearer's earlobes.

"I had that made for our fifth anniversary. Theresa loved it. She didn't enjoy big parties, but these always sparked compliments and conversation, which put her at ease."

Molly was genuinely falling in love with this caring, old-world gentleman.

"I would be honored to wear it, Nonno. What else can I tell people about it?"

He told her about the designer and why he'd chosen it and where he'd presented it to his wife and how she had reacted. His eyes were damp by the time he'd finished.

"That's enough from me," he said, patting her hand. "You go enjoy yourselves."

"This is killing me," Molly said when they were aboard Gio's helicopter.

She ought to be getting used to the luxury that his level

of wealth afforded, but she was still agog at the private cabin with four armchairs arranged around a round table with drink holders set into it. The decor was slate-gray and silver, the windows huge and tinted, offering a view from ground to clouds as they lifted out of the city and traveled over green pastures and rolling hills.

"What is?" Gio prompted.

Molly was trying to be careful about not twisting the antique ring on her finger, but she constantly checked to be sure it was still there, terrified she would lose it.

"You have to tell your grandfather the truth, Gio. I like him too much to lie to him."

"Once he's fully out of the woods, I'll consider that, but not yet," he countered. "I have a clean bill of health, by the way."

"Wh-what?" She sat back into her armchair and stared across at him.

"It's information I want you to have." He was watching her through the screen of his spiky lashes. "What did *your* doctor say?"

"That my blood work was fine. I told you that," she mumbled and looked to the ground again. Was that a castle?

"You didn't ask whether—"

"Oh, my God, Gio!" A raging blush consumed her, licking her with flames of guilt and yearning and enticement.

"So you did ask." His mouth quirked with amusement. "And given that reaction, I hope to hear those words again soon."

Oh, my God, Gio? "You're not funny."

"I wasn't joking."

She ignored him for the rest of the flight. Or rather, tried to, which was impossible. Thankfully, the flight wasn't long. Very soon, they were touching down in Milan.

A drive through congested traffic ensued, then they arrived at the hotel, where they were shown into a beautiful suite with a sitting room, a terrace and two bedrooms. One bedroom was already occupied by a team of busy bees who looked up with smiles of greeting.

"Molly, this is Ursula." Gio came up behind her as Molly stood in the bedroom doorway, too intimidated to enter. "She and her team will look after you today."

A gorgeous woman with a wide smile and shimmering gold shadow on her eyelids stopped fussing with the gowns on the rack and came toward her to shake her hand.

"It's a pleasure to meet you."

"It's nice to meet you, too." Molly was agog at the gowns, the likes of which she'd only ever seen on coverage of the red carpet at award shows.

"I need to meet with Vittorio, to finalize the arrangements for my parents." Gio squeezed her shoulders. "Once you've chosen something, Ursula will take care of alterations while you relax in the spa. Have a massage, eat, nap if you can. She'll make sure you're back here in time to have your hair and makeup done."

"You're not…going to tell me what to wear?" She turned to face him, perversely disappointed and already bereft that he was leaving her.

"You'll look beautiful in whatever you choose." It felt very natural that he dropped a light kiss on her lips. It was the sort of kiss any engaged couple might exchange when one was heading out the door, but she wound up pressing closer and settling her hands on his waist, unconsciously urging him to linger.

He drew in a small, sharp breath, then swept his mouth across hers a few more times, more deeply, sending delicious tingles through her.

When he drew back, his blue eyes were the hot center of a flame. He trailed a caress in the curve of her throat, one that felt like a promise. Like anticipation.

"Until later." His voice had become a rasp in his throat that made her skin feel tight in the most pleasurable way.

He left and she turned into the bedroom in time to see everyone exchanging looks of raised eyebrows that said, *Ooh-la-la*.

CHAPTER SIX

THE CASELLA FORTUNE had its roots in the shipping trade and the earliest forms of cargo insurance, which had essentially been a series of gambling ventures on shipments making it to harbor. Most had, which had provided capital to a long-ago Casella son to build ships of his own. His son then married the daughter of a steel-mill owner. Together, they produced a dozen ships and almost as many children, one of whom had a passion for trains.

The locomotive enthusiast expanded the corporation into the manufacture of engines and rail cars. His brother, Otto's uncle, founded the Casella brokerage firm. Another uncle became an active buyer and distributor for the import-export arm of the company.

By the time Ottorino took over as president, the Casella Corporation was manufacturing airplane parts and owned enough farmland that they supplied and packaged their own brands of olive oil, pasta and pesto, among other goods.

Otto married the heiress to an automobile manufacturer, a move that was decried by the press as mercenary, but Otto had genuinely loved his bride. Sadly, they only birthed one son before she passed away from an undiagnosed heart condition when Ambrose was fourteen.

Otto became a withdrawn man and his son became a troubled teen. Ambrose was expelled from his boarding school twice for drug use.

As an adult, Gio was capable of some compassion for his father's desire to self-medicate his adolescent grief. If that had been the extent of Ambrose's failings, and he had subsequently sought help along the way, they might still have a relationship.

Ambrose had only paid lip service to rehab, however, using it as a means to get on Otto's good side when it suited him. Sobriety was not something he wanted. He liked to party and travel and spend money that was handed to him. At his core, he was an entitled, narcissistic parasite of a man.

When Ambrose found a woman as superficial, debauched and manipulative as he was, he married her and they produced a son in a calculated effort to oust his own father from his position as president of Casella Corporation. While Gio had still been an infant in the arms of a series of ill-treated nannies, a small war had raged around him, one that splintered the extended family and nearly sank the company altogether.

By the time Gio was leaving for boarding school, he had seen his grandfather only twice. Otto upended the challenges from his son by paying for Gio's schooling, taking guardianship of Gio in the process.

That had worked for a time, but Ambrose regularly reared his head, throwing out custody threats and other strong-arm tactics to squeeze more money from his father. If he had ever applied himself so diligently to actual work, he might have been an asset to the company, but all his efforts went toward ensuring he continued to enjoy a free ride.

Gio's mother was even worse. At least Ambrose was open about his financial motives. Fridrika liked to bait emotional hooks to drag people in and keep them serving her. Gio's earliest memories were thankfully blank, but later, he had fallen for her claims that she wished to know her son. He'd always been stung. Badly.

If his grandfather had not been alive to see it, Gio would have cut them off long ago, but Nonno still saw glimpses of his beloved Theresa in Ambrose. He also needed to know that her grandson, Gio, had inherited her sense of decency, even if her son had not.

Nevertheless, this latest exercise in buying them off reminded Gio that if something did happen to him, Ambrose would make every attempt to take control of the Casella Corporation. There were a handful of cousins who were excellent in their executive roles, but none as hardened by experience to deal with Ambrose as cold-bloodedly as Gio could.

Gio had always known he needed to produce an heir, but he had foolishly believed there was no urgency. With Otto's recent illness, however, Gio had to accept that even if Otto recovered, he would not live forever.

Gio had to ensure there would be strong, ethical leadership on the horizon. He needed a wife who would not only embrace motherhood, but would also understand the role her children were being raised to take on.

Molly and her protectiveness of her unborn child leaped to mind, mostly because they were already "engaged." With his grandfather improving, Gio would have to come clean about their ruse sooner than later. He hated to disappoint the old man, especially when Otto seemed so attached to Molly.

Was it really so far-fetched that he would want to marry her? She had wondered how anyone believed they were engaged and yes, they were from very different backgrounds, but he had learned from his first experience that knowing the same people and attending the same charity events didn't guarantee a happy union.

He and Molly had a far better rapport than he'd had with his fiancée. Her baby was not as big an issue as she might think. He understood firsthand that not every parent was meant to become one. Sometimes a man other than the baby's father had to step in for the good of the child, as Nonno had done for him.

Of course, he and Otto had a blood connection, but those kinship ties had been soured on both sides by the time the sullen and mistrustful Gio had been left with yet another stranger, this time a cynical and remote old man.

It had taken a long time for them to warm into the close relationship they enjoyed today, which only told Gio how important it was to bond with a baby from the beginning.

The more he thought about it, the further he went down the road of seeing marriage as a viable path for both of them. Rather than become a single mother, Molly would have a husband who could provide an excellent life for her and her child. There was a time when he had feared what type of father he might make, but he had Nonno's steady example to follow. Molly's innate warmth would counter any reticence he still possessed.

If he married Molly, he would gain a life partner whose company he enjoyed. His grandfather already adored her. That was incredibly important to him, given that Nonno had seen straight through Fridrika's external beauty to the ugliness inside her.

Then there was the animal attraction. Gio kept trying to put that aside so he could think clearly, but he kept hearing her say *You wouldn't have an affair with me. Would you?*

Hell, yes, he would. He was mindful that he was still her employer, though.

As he wrapped up the unpleasant business of forcing his father to disinherit himself, he allowed himself to replay their kiss the other day and her adorable blush today, when he'd asked what the doctor had said.

He couldn't press her into an affair if she didn't want one, but he didn't understand why she was hesitating. When they kissed, she encouraged him. She obviously wanted him as badly as he wanted her and he wanted her so badly, his blood was on fire.

By the time he had visited the barber and dressed in his tuxedo, he was downright impatient to see her again.

She was worth the wait, he decided, when she finally appeared. The sight of her knocked the breath out of him.

The top of the sleeveless gown was reminiscent of a breastplate in pale, metallic green. The skirt was a filmy waterfall that parted over her left thigh, revealing the three silver bands that formed her five-inch heels. His gaze ate up the glimpse of her leg, the roundness of her hips and the swells of her breasts plumped beneath the serpentine necklace.

She was a goddess, one who controlled all the fey creatures of the forest.

For once, she wore her hair down. The rich brunette waves framed an expression that awaited judgment, but how could she doubt she was anything but entrancing? Her makeup was heavier than he'd ever seen her wear it, but it was playfully dramatic with greens and golds accentuating her eyes. Her bold lip made him want that particular shade of crimson smeared all over his naked body.

"You look very nice," she murmured, looking down as she adjusted Nonna's ring on her finger.

"I would have said it first, but I'm speechless."

She lifted her long, thick lashes. "Don't mock me."

"Mock?" She might as well have hit him with a sledge-hammer, he was so at a loss as to what that was supposed to mean.

"I feel like a fraud, Gio."

"In what way?"

"In every way. I don't…" She looked over her shoulder toward the bedroom, where faint voices were still conversing in Italian, then came closer to him. "I don't belong here," she whispered. "I'm not one of you."

"I hesitate to say this, *cara*, because I've promised myself I won't come on too strong tonight. But if you belong to me, then you belong."

Her lips parted and her breasts rose in a shaken breath. "But I don't."

"But you will." The embers of want in his belly flared even hotter.

He wanted her to belong to him, physically, but in other ways, too. That desire was growing into such an intense imperative, he pushed it aside for examination later.

He brought her hand to his mouth and kissed her painted nails. "Shall we go?"

Molly didn't need a wrap. The party was in the hotel ballroom on a lower floor.

As they stepped into the elevator, she crushed a tiny, emerald-green clutch in her fist, as though it contained an elixir that would save her life.

Nothing could save her from the way Gio was looking at her, though. From the moment she had walked out of the bedroom, she'd been a bundle of nerves that she would disappoint him. Ironically, it was harder to take the burn of approval that ignited his gaze. It warmed her from the inside out, scorched away her insecurities and seared away any resistance she had left.

How could she not respond to being admired by a man like him? What had begun as a crush was now a full-blown infatuation with a man who seemed to reciprocate her attraction, but hadn't outright said so. She kept trying to convince herself there was nothing between them, then he would look at her or touch her or kiss the daylights out of her and make her think *if...*

If you belong to me...

"We don't need to stay long if you'd rather not."

She had slept a full hour in the spa's serenity room. That was after she had been soaked and massaged, mani-ed and pedi-ed, fed light snacks and hydrated with citrus-infused mineral water.

He wasn't suggesting they go upstairs to rest, though. When she met his glittering gaze, she saw lust. The bottom fell out of her heart.

The doors opened and she was so disconcerted, she was glad that he took her hand to lead her into the room full of pearlescent balloons and fairy lights, with tuxedos and gowns in every color.

He was right. She was glad that she wore something that could compete with the rest of the haute couture around her. It was a full-on runway, with enough sparkling diamonds to inspire a hundred jewel-thief movies.

A beautiful couple was greeting every guest personally.

"Gio! You made it," the tall, dark and handsome man said.

"Molly, these are our hosts, Vittorio and Gwyn Donatelli."

"Oh, my God, I love your necklace. We're so delighted to meet you, Molly." Gwyn was blonde, sounded American and was also very attractive.

"Thank you for inviting me," Molly murmured as she learned the art of cheek kisses, exchanging them with Gwyn, then her husband.

"Call me Vito, *per favore*," he murmured.

"Gio, you scoundrel," Gwyn greeted. "That was a very generous donation you made to my foundation, thank you."

Molly had asked if they were supposed to bring a gift, but the party was an annual fundraiser for an organization that promoted online privacy and helped victims of revenge porn. Apparently, Gwyn had met her husband after nude photos of her had been leaked without her knowledge or consent.

"You're American, too," Gwyn said to Molly. "I still stumble over cultural differences so please call me if anything comes up or you need help finding anything. Gio has my number."

"Thank you, that's very kind." Molly hadn't expected to be greeted with such warmth, especially after her experience on Sasha's yacht.

"Let's plan to connect, anyway," Gwyn urged. "I'd love to get to know you better."

"I'd like that," she said, even as she recalled that she wasn't really marrying Gio. In another twelve days or so, she would melt into the woodwork, never to see any of these people again. Not even Gio.

A chill wind whistled through the cavern of her chest.

"We'll let you greet the rest of your guests," Gio said, branding the small of Molly's back with his hand.

"*Grazie*. But find Paolo. He wants to say hello and Lauren is eager to meet you," Vittorio said with a wink at Molly.

"I seated you with my brother and his wife, Imogen," Gwyn added. "She's also American and very funny. I think you'll like her."

Molly was touched they'd gone to such trouble to ensure she was comfortable and entertained. Gwyn was right, too. Imogen was very witty. She lived with her husband, Travis, in New York. They had two children, six-year-old Julian, who was precocious, and three-year-old Lilith, who was a dreamer, often getting lost in her own imagination.

"I'm quite sure that Julian is setting us up for a water-damage bill as we speak, but Paolo insisted we leave our children with their four and Gwyn's two. That's ten children in an ancestral mansion full of priceless art. Paolo organized a clown and an extra nanny, as if that'll be any help. Lion tamers, Paolo! *That's* who you call. Am I right?"

Despite her jokes, Imogen was visibly pregnant and ecstatic with it.

"I notice you're not drinking, either," Imogen said, leaning close with a cheeky side-eye.

"I don't actually drink much. Alcohol gives me a headache," Molly lied. She was dying to compare pregnancy notes. It was one of the few things she was truly missing in this process.

"So much for Gwyn's theory for your sudden engagement. Tell me more about Genoa. We visit Italy at least once a year, but we always stay with Gwyn and Vito, either here or at the lake. We really should see more of the country. I say that, but I'll have a newborn in five months so when would that even happen?" Imogen rolled her eyes at herself.

"How long are you here this trip?" Gio asked, proving that he'd been dividing his attention between their conversation and the one he was having with Travis. "We're at the villa in Portofino with my grandfather. My apartment in the city is empty."

"That's kind of you to offer, but you don't want a pair of children tearing up the place," Imogen said with a wave of her hand.

"Immy." Travis waited for her to turn her head, then looked at her with heated adoration. "I love our children with all my heart, but *I* don't want our children tearing up his place. Not if I could have you to myself for a couple of nights. Gwyn will keep the kids, I'm sure."

"That's quite the anniversary present for her, isn't it?" Imogen joked, but Travis was already walking away.

Moments later, it was settled. The pair would fly to Genoa with them in the morning and stay for two nights.

"That was nice of you to offer your apartment to Travis and Imogen," Molly said to Gio, when dinner was over and they were dancing.

"Her husband is a useful connection." He shrugged it off. "And you seem to enjoy her company. See? My world isn't so different from yours."

She stifled a wild "Ha!" since there was a small orchestra providing the music and she was waltzing for the first time since being forced to take stilted, uncomfortable lessons in middle-school PE classes. If he hadn't been so skilled at leading, she would be stumbling onto his toes.

She was fighting the urge to crane her neck at all the starlets and royalty circulating the room, but others weren't being so polite. Despite the warm welcome Gio received when he introduced her, nearly everyone here viewed her as a curiosity. She could tell.

All of that faded away, however, when the music switched to an instrumental of a modern tune, one that was sensual and had Gio drawing her closer.

As his hand rested at the small of her back and his thumb shifted in a lazy caress against the sensitized nerves there, she felt herself melting into him. Her head grew heavy and sought the firm plane at the front of his shoulder. Lingering traces of his aftershave against his throat made her feel drugged.

"Are you trying to seduce me?" She picked up her head when the song wound down and he kept his arms around her, not moving them off the dance floor.

"I hope I'm succeeding." His fingertips skimmed up her

arm and across her bare shoulder, lifting a shivering wake of goose bumps. "*Mio Dio*, I want to kiss you." His gaze was so intent on her lips, they stung with anticipation.

She wanted that, too. But not here, like this. She wanted to be alone with him, where their kisses could progress to...

She dipped her head, fingers playing with the ruffle beneath his bow tie. She was very aware how short her window of time with him was. When Ursula had been fitting her, she had given Molly's midsection a curious moment of study, but the pins between her lips had kept her from asking questions with anything but her eyes.

Time was sifting like sand through her fingers. Molly had to wring out every minute that she could with him.

"It would only be for now." She peeked up at him and a small rasp entered her throat as she added, "You know that, right?"

"Let's take it one day at a time." He drew a tantalizing pattern in the hollow beneath her ear, but there was a faint curl of smugness to his lips.

Her heart pounded as they slipped out of the party without saying goodbye. In the elevator, he pressed her to the wall, caging her with his arms. She lifted her mouth in offering. His head dipped past her lips as he ducked to set a hot kiss against her neck.

A ragged groan left her, one of denial and enjoyment and agony at the delicate way he opened his mouth and sucked a damp spot against her skin. A flush of heat poured into her chest, making her breasts feel swollen. Her nipples stung.

She felt his smile against her tender skin. His teeth moved in the barest scrape of a wolf reminding his mate that he was dangerous, but would never hurt her. When his nuzzling gaze worked up to her chin, he leaned his hips into her abdomen, letting her feel that he was already hard.

"I'll be careful with you, I promise, but you'll tell me if I need to stop."

"You won't need to stop." She was pretty sure she would die if he stopped.

The doors opened and he whirled her out, then swept her down the hall, barely allowing her feet to touch the floor.

Inside the suite, all the lingering staff were gone. It was tidy and quiet, and dimly lit by a single lamp throwing golden light against the shadows.

Nerves struck and Molly brought her hands to her ear, as she started to remove her earring.

"You should take this necklace. I don't want anything to happen to these."

He shrugged off his tuxedo jacket and threw it over the back of the couch, then tugged his bow tie loose as he walked to the door into the bedroom.

As he stood there, opening his cuffs and setting fire to her with his gaze, he said, "I would love to strip you naked where you stand and have you on the floor, *bella*, but I just promised to take care with you. Come into the bedroom. I want you in my bed."

Her knees almost gave out.

Shakily, she crossed toward him, offering the one earring she had managed to remove.

He took it, then kept her hand as he drew her into the room and lazily closed the door behind her.

"I want to ask you what you like, but I don't want to hear about other lovers right now." He touched her shoulders to turn her, then his fingers searched under her hair for the clasp of the necklace. "Lift your hair."

She did, thinking she should warn him that her other lovers were as scarce as her sexual experience. It was another reason she was stealing this chance with him. No one had ever aroused her beyond idle curiosity. No one made her burn with the simple act of unclasping a necklace or lowering the zip of her dress.

"Stay just like that," he said of the way she held her hair gathered against her crown. "You're very beautiful." His voice seemed to resonate from the depths of his chest. His hot breath stirred the fine hairs at the back of her neck and the cool links of the necklace tickled her skin as he kept hold of it while shifting his fist to her shoulder. His other hand traced down her spine, sending more of those sharp tingles into her breasts and lower. A throbbing ache settled between her thighs.

Hot, hot kisses touched every single vertebra until he was on his knees behind her, dragging the gown down into a puddle on the floor. She was braless and, a few kisses later, divested of the lace that had graced her hips.

"I have a small obsession with your ass," he informed her in that gritty, erotic voice. He set a damp kiss on one cheek. As he rose, his hand trailed its way up her inner thigh, dipping ever so briefly toward the heat at her center before lingering to fondle each of her cheeks.

Then he was turning her into his arms. His shirt and trousers abraded her skin as he pulled her close.

"You're still fully dressed and I'm…" Wearing only shoes and a hard blush. Her hand reflexively shielded her mound.

"Oh, I am very aware," he said with molten satisfaction. He brought her hands to the buttons on his shirt while his own shaped her hips and waist, and spread over the subtle curve of her belly.

She faltered in trying to release his shirt buttons, shooting a look upward, worried how he was reacting to that evidence of her pregnancy, but his gaze was eating up her naked form. He was hungrily taking her in all the way to her toes, then coming back to her anxious eyes with a dazzled gleam in his own.

"You're so beautiful," he growled before he dove his fingers into her hair and sealed his mouth to hers.

A thousand sensations accosted her—the light pull on her hair that held her captive to his ravenous kiss. The rough-sweet way he devoured her lips and tagged her tongue with his own. The sense of being overwhelmed by him, by his wide shoulders and height. The crispness of his shirt against her hand, then the hot satin and fine hairs and underlying strength when she bared his chest. His torso scorched her own as they pressed closer. His possessive arm banded her against him and waves of pleasure emanated from the way his palm drew slow circles on her backside.

She could hardly bear how good it all felt and threaded her arms beneath his shirt, clinging around his waist as she strained to deepen their kiss, rubbing her breasts against his chest as she did.

When her knee instinctively came up, he took full advantage. He trapped it against his waist with his elbow. His palm slid to the underside of her butt cheek and his long fingers began to play in the eager slickness that had welled against her folds.

"Gio," she gasped.

"I have you. I won't let you fall." He tilted her and dipped his head, capturing her nipple to lick and lave and suck until she was groaning. All the while, his touch explored and discovered the spot that made her breath catch.

She clung across his shoulders, head falling back, never imagining she could be this helpless and uninhibited.

She wasn't. Not really.

"Gio, please," she sobbed.

"You're so close, *bella*," he said, offering one more lingering stroke of his fingertip across her swollen clit before he eased her upright. "I would never drop you, I swear."

She wanted to believe that, but she knew that one day, she would walk away, and she had a very strong feeling that despite all her warnings, he would not take it well. He wasn't used to being rejected.

Rejecting him was furthest thing from her mind in this moment, though. She opened his shirt wider and dragged the tails from his waistband. Then she tried to open his belt, but her hands were shaking too badly.

"That is possibly the most erotic thing I've ever seen," he told her, but took over, yanking his pants open. "Walk to the bed for me. Let me watch."

Wanton excitement gripped her. She started toward the bed, then glanced over her shoulder as she decided to take the long route around the foot of it. She deliberately set one five-inch heel in front of the other and let her hips ticktock in a shameless way.

When she looked back at him again, he was fully naked, fully aroused. He held himself in a light grasp of two fingers and a thumb, as though any more would finish him off.

It was flagrant and so sexy, she kind of lost the plot.

"Sit down," he said as he circled around to her. "As much as I want those shoes on my shoulders, I'd rather help you take them off."

Her legs were so weak, she sank down, then swallowed as she stared at his erection.

"Do you want me to—"

"I want *everything*, Molly." He cupped her face and tilted her gaze up to his. "The catalog of things I want to do with you will take years to accomplish. But we have time." He ran his thumb along her bottom lip. "Tonight, I just want to be inside you. Would you like me to wear a condom?" He went to his knees to remove her shoes.

"You s-said that your doctor said there were no concerns."

"I would still wear one if you want me to. I've never not worn one." His gaze flicked up to hers, steady, but there was a feral flash behind it that caused her stomach to swoop. "I want you very, very badly. I don't know how long I'll last."

"I think…without?" Was that too intimate? Too *naked*?

Her second shoe dropped away and he pressed her to the mattress as he rose, sliding her to the middle of the big bed, then covering her with every inch of his powerful body.

When she delicately took hold of his erection, he muttered a string of Italian that she didn't catch. He drew her hands above her head, stretching her out beneath him as he spread her legs wide with his iron-hard thighs and rocked to settle himself against her tender folds.

The intensity of his expression was almost too much to take. She wanted to shut her eyes, but she couldn't seem to look away. His gaze searched over her features as though memorizing them. He kept her hands pinned with his one hand while his other made a delicate dance along her temple and cheek, then traced her bottom lip.

Incredible yearning struck. She was getting everything she wanted, and loved the way he was drawing this out, but she wanted more. She wanted *forever*. She wanted that so badly, a scorching heat accosted the backs of her eyes.

She made the most of now by opening her mouth and turning her head just a little, keeping her gaze locked to his while she sucked his finger into her mouth and blatantly caressed it with her tongue.

His inhale was a torn sound, then he released another guttural few words in Italian. After a moment, he withdrew his finger and replaced it with his mouth. It was the most carnal kiss of her life, hard and hungry and infinitely possessive. At the same time, he shifted and his touch was there, where her folds were as wet as his finger. He pressed it inside her and they both groaned.

He held her like that for long minutes, trapped in his kiss, splayed for his pleasure as he slowly, slowly brought her to the brink.

When she was arching and writhing and moaning unabashedly, he replaced his touch with the damp crest of his erection and let his full length sink into her.

That was it. She had gotten her wish. She was his. Forever. Her heart quivered inside her chest as she acknowledged that.

He released her arms then, so he could brace on his elbow and tuck her more completely beneath him. He began slow, powerful thrusts.

"Don't close your eyes," he commanded in a rasp that made her blink her eyes open. "It's good? Does it hurt?"

"It feels so good, Gio, I can't—" She couldn't touch enough of him, couldn't take him deeply enough, couldn't sustain this height of arousal.

She couldn't bear to look him in the eye and let him see all this tortured ecstasy he was stirring within her, but she couldn't shut him out, either.

He was determined to wring every note of pleasure from the experience, thrusting in that steady, delicious way that strummed all her nerve endings and made her moan with abandon. Perspiration coated his back and his thigh was hot and tense where her foot stroked him. She was so lost to this experience that she trembled and grew feverish.

She had fooled herself into believing she could steal this time with him as though it was as inconsequential as a candy bar. This was the opposite of stealing. It was relinquishment.

Even as he gave her more pleasure than she could withstand, he stole her ability to ever settle for anything less than this with anyone else. She would never be the same after this. She would be his in ways that could never be undone.

Maybe she clutched on to him tighter in those seconds because she was trying to take back the pieces of her soul that were flowing into him. She was catching and clasping before it was too late, but then it *was* too late.

With a ragged noise, he began to thrust harder. Faster. Deeper.

"Don't hold back. Let go," he commanded, and she did.

She arched in ecstasy as her orgasm swept over her in a tsunami of breathless, wild joy. He rode with her through it, continuing to thrust, unevenly now. She was dimly aware of his muscles bunching, his body jerking, then his animalistic cries joined hers.

They clung and tumbled and withstood the powerful waves for a thousand years, bodies fused. It was the most perfect moment of accord she had ever experienced with another human being.

I want this, she thought. *I want him in my life. For the rest of my life.*

But as her postclimactic euphoria receded and the final flutters left her nerve endings, a harrowing sense of darkness took its place.

CHAPTER SEVEN

SHE WAS EVERYTHING he had imagined and more. *They* were.

He had woken to her ass spooned into his lap and they'd made love that way, with her breast in his palm and her delicate shivers of release milking his. It had been exquisite.

Now she was being adorably shy, blushing bright red when he said, "Let the maid pack for you. Surely you're as hungry for breakfast as I am?"

She gave up on her attempt to arrange her new cosmetics in the too-small case she'd brought. "Do you have the necklace?"

"Yes. It's safe. I reserved a table on the rooftop terrace, since we don't have time to see the city this trip."

"That was thoughtful. Thank you." She dropped her two phones into her bag, along with a lipstick and the pill dispenser he'd noticed she used for her prenatal vitamins.

"How do you feel?" he asked when they were alone in the elevator.

She gave him another admonishing look. "Yes, Mr. Smug. I've worked up an appetite."

"I meant… No adverse effects from our activities?"

"You make it sound like we went rock climbing or some other high-risk hobby."

"I've never had time for hobbies, but I see the appeal now. I'll start *making* time."

She giggled and flashed him a knowing look that was loaded with enough sinful speculation to have him wondering if they would have time to use the bed once more before they left the hotel.

"You didn't answer my question," he pointed out as the elevator let them out.

"I'm fine. Thank you," she said pertly.

Good. Because one night would not be enough. That certainty was crystalizing inside him. He wanted more from her. More time, more commitment. More of *her*.

Did he want her as his wife, though?

He considered that question while they enjoyed a pleasant, leisurely breakfast, intermittently speaking with a few guests from last night who were also staying in the hotel.

Molly was wrong to think she didn't fit in his world. People were curious about her, but much of it was around him and his history of being jilted. They wanted to gauge whether she was in it for the long haul. She didn't talk much about herself, though. She was naturally empathetic and curious and listened intently, which built trust and charmed everyone very quickly.

As they were finishing up, Travis texted to say they were on the way to meet them so they could drive to the helipad together.

"He sent me Imogen's contact details. Do you want that to go to your work phone or personal?"

"Personal." She had glanced over her work emails while they'd eaten, but now brought out the other phone.

It pinged with the text he sent her and she opened it to check it, then gave a few swipes as though checking for other messages. Her expression shadowed with dismay.

"What's wrong?"

"Nothing." She gave him an overbright smile. "I want to take a couple of photos for Mom."

She rose and moved to the rail while he signed their meal to the room, but he couldn't help wondering if she'd been hoping for communication from the baby's father.

The secrecy around that part of her life was really starting to irritate him. They would definitely have to dig into that before he brought up marriage.

He was pondering how he would open that topic as they walked out of the restaurant and were accosted by a woman waiting for her table.

"Gio! I heard you were here for the Donatelli anniversary party last night." She swept her talonlike nail through the fall of her raven-black hair. "I was supposed to be there, but I only arrived this morning."

He flickered through his mental contact list, coming up with… "Jacinda. It's nice to see you again." It wasn't. She reminded him of his mother. He would bet the Casella fortune that Jacinda had not received an invitation to last night's party and had arrived here this morning with the intention of running into him or some other poor sod she'd chosen to target.

"The rumors are true?" She took off her sunglasses and bit the tip of one arm as she studied Molly. "You're marrying your assistant's assistant?"

"I don't think anyone is so crude as to say that," he said with a note of warning.

"Oh." Molly jolted slightly. "We've met. I didn't recognize you with your, um, hair down."

"We weren't properly introduced last year." Jacinda swept a catty glance down Molly's flowing pants and the lace top that hugged her breasts and arms. "You've had quite the transformation yourself, haven't you?"

"We're meeting someone," Gio said flatly and set his hand against Molly's back to signal they were cutting this short.

Molly stubbornly dug in her heels, staying where she was. "I heard that Mr. and Mrs. Zamos were in a terrible car accident. I'm so sorry. I hope they're recovering?"

"Alexandra?" Jacinda dragged her attention from Gio's half embrace of Molly to Molly's penetrating gaze. "Pfft. I'd never worry about her. That woman has nine lives. They're already back in Athens."

Molly was visibly taken aback by the callousness of that response, as any decent human being would have been. Gio was.

"Excuse us," he said firmly, and escorted Molly to the elevator. He waited until they were alone inside it, then said, "You didn't have to try to be nice to her. She's not someone I cross paths with often." He couldn't think of any other reason she had made such an effort at conversation.

She didn't say anything and kept her nose forward. Was she pale?

"Molly?"

"Hmm?"

"You're upset." Of course, she was. Jacinda had been outright rude toward her.

For the barest moment, Molly's mouth quivered, then she firmed it, blinked rapidly and asked with a hint of belligerence, "Because I came face-to-face with one of your past lovers? That's none of my business."

"Is this you being possessive, Molly?" He didn't hate it. In fact, he found it heartening that she was invested enough in their relationship to be annoyed.

"No." She scowled and stubbornly kept her face forward. "I know where you slept last night. As long as we're monogamous while we're together, that's all that matters to me."

While we're together. That raised his own hackles of possessiveness.

"We all have a past that can't be changed." She folded her arms and looked to her shoes. "I'd be a hypocrite if I was upset about yours."

Like her past with the father of her baby? If he wanted her to tell him about that, he needed to earn her trust.

"Jacinda was never my lover."

She released a choked noise of disbelief. "Perhaps we have different definitions of that word. When I came out to the pool that day on the yacht, her boobs were in your face."

"I don't take something just because it's offered. I decide what I want, then I don't rest until I have it." He held her gaze, drilling the deeper meaning of his words into her.

He wanted her.

She swallowed and her lashes quivered.

Tension was creeping in around her eyes, though. A vulnerable tug pulled at the corners of her mouth, giving her a look of persecution.

Pregnant, he reminded himself. He couldn't take the high-handed, steamroller approach that was his preferred method of getting what he wanted. He eased the moment with humor instead.

"Her breasts were in *your* face, too," he reminded her. "She shows them to everyone."

After a beat, she muttered, "I felt like I'd stumbled into a nudist colony."

They were both chuckling as the doors opened, but her humor fell away very quickly.

She was still bothered by the interaction. He could tell. "Molly—"

"We have to meet Travis and Imogen, don't we?"

"Yes," he agreed, accepting that this conversation was too

important to have on the fly. He would wait until they were back at the villa, where there would be no interruptions.

He had the sense of walking up a dune of sand, though. Every footstep should have gained him ground, but it slipped away beneath his feet instead. The harder he tried to climb it, the slower his progress became.

He hated this feeling. This lack of surety. It took him back to a time when nothing in his life had been stable. When the people who were supposed to be constants in his world were only consistent in letting him down.

Marry her. Keep this one.

It wasn't his grandfather's voice this time. It was his own.

Otto was looking infinitely better when they returned. He was able to move into a chair for his meals and was in very bright spirits. He even dressed long enough to meet Travis and Imogen when they came for lunch before they flew back to Milan and their children.

"I think I'll be able to attend your wedding," Otto told Molly when he made it all the way to the terrace for breakfast the following morning. "Have you set a date?"

"Um…no." She silently pleaded for Gio to tell him.

They'd had a busy few days, fitting in playing tour guide with the other couple between the demands of work.

"I don't have much time left," Otto scolded with dark humor. He sent Gio an incisive stare that belied the fact that he was barely able to hold his espresso cup in one hand. "Plan a big reception if that suits you, but marry quickly. Before she changes her mind."

Oof. Apparently, Otto really was feeling stronger if he was throwing down gauntlets like that at his grandson.

"My mother is a midwife," Molly blurted. "It's hard for her to get away without a lot of notice. I couldn't possibly marry without her and my sister here." Patricia actually worked through a clinic to ensure they always had coverage for expecting mothers. She had also lightened her patient load this year so she could be responsive to Molly's potential needs.

Otto brushed off that excuse with blasé confidence. "Gio will find someone to step in for her. The two of you are already going through the motions of starting a family. Take it seriously."

"Nonno!" Molly covered her blush with her hands, not surprised he knew she wasn't using the bed in the room she'd been given, but not expecting him to be so brash about mentioning it.

"Since you seem back in fighting form, we'll go to the London office for a few days." Gio transferred his hooded look to Molly. "That will give you a chance to close your apartment. We'll discuss the wedding date while we're away."

Since she actually did need to close her flat, she didn't argue.

They arrived in London later that afternoon. Nelo had flown with them on Gio's private jet and Molly had been busy arranging for Nelo's counterpart from New York, Avigail, to meet them for an all-hands meeting with their London colleague, Yu. They were gelling as a squad, but she thought it would be good for all of them, including Gio, to work together for a few days.

"If you want a team-building exercise, have them close your apartment for you," Gio suggested after they dropped Nelo at his hotel.

"Ew. No." She had asked her neighbor to empty her refrigerator of perishables the day after she'd flown to Genoa.

"I already have a moving company arranged to put everything into storage. I need to collect a few personal items, though. Maybe I'll spend the night, so I can be sure I have everything."

She could use a night away from him, to recalibrate. The more time she spent with him, the more they made love, the more she wished this could be her life. She needed to remind herself that was not only impossible, but it also wasn't something *he* wanted. They had agreed this was an affair. Temporary.

"Drop me and I'll meet you at the office in the morning."

She was dreading the office. She had left with Gio very abruptly, before her promotion to being his executive assistant was even announced. Instead of that news, she had come out as his fiancée who was leaving the company. The coworkers who had reached out with congratulations had definitely been fishing for more information.

"I'll stay with you to help," Gio said, nodding for her to give the driver her address. "There can't be much? You gave Ilario a list of everything you wanted to be waiting at the town house."

Then Gio had added to it. Some poor maid was probably unpacking boutique deliveries as they spoke.

"I can manage. You don't have to come with me." A rush of inadequacy flooded through her. Her flat was very modest. She had chosen it for its minimal maintenance and excellent location, close to the tube. It was nothing like how he lived.

He didn't say anything more, only waited patiently for her to give the driver her details so they could pull away from the hotel entrance.

Molly gave in, but her tension ratcheted up when she led Gio up the two flights to her quirky, corner unit. Inviting him to enter her personal space felt a lot like opening her diary.

It was tidy and cheerful, at least. She liked it for its abundance of natural light and a decor that was a little too colorful to be sophisticated, but it was comfy and welcoming after a long day at the office.

Gio immediately began studying the photos on the wall, then picked up the snapshots of her with Libby and her mother that rested on a shelf and the end table.

He had already met her family over video chat, but he suddenly asked, "Who is this?" in a dangerous tone.

"Is that you being possessive, Gio?" She couldn't help throwing that pithy question at him as she took the framed photograph from him.

"It damned well is," he said without hesitation.

She couldn't help being flattered that he thought she could punch so far above her weight, but he didn't have anything to worry about.

"He was a child actor in America. I guess he's still an actor since he's doing a play in the West End. Libby watches reruns of his show and thinks he's dreamy. I happened to see him at a coffee shop so I asked him for a photo. This is her birthday present."

She stowed the photo in her laptop bag, then drew an overnight bag from the closet.

"You really were planning to leave." His gaze dropped to the boxes that were labeled and stacked in the closet, filled with off-season clothing that already didn't fit her.

"I *am* leaving," she confirmed, voice not as strong as she would have liked. A sting rose under her cheeks and arrived in the back of her throat. Chagrin? She didn't want to leave, especially when Otto was talking about attending their wedding. That wasn't on her, though. Gio was the one who had made this so difficult by faking this engagement of theirs.

She threw a handful of everyday items into the small suitcase along with her supplements and the historical romance novel she'd found at a café and hadn't finished yet.

When she picked up a thick hardcover off the bookshelf, Gio said, "Another gift for your sister?"

It was an iconic title about a wizard that Molly had defaced by carving a hole in the pages. She opened it to reveal the slender yellow envelope she stored there with her birth certificate and her company ID when she wasn't working.

"I'll empty my safe-deposit box tomorrow." She put the key in her purse. "I have custodial documents for Libby, in the event something happens to Mom, along with other papers I need access to if things go sideways." Like her surrogacy agreement.

She had volunteered to carry Sasha's baby knowing that an extreme outcome could include keeping the baby and raising it herself. This baby was the heir to the Zamos fortune, but Molly only cared about that in so far as that fortune was this baby's birthright. Between her savings and her mother's support, she could provide a good upbringing—not privileged, like Sasha's, but stable and rich in other ways.

It was still a daunting prospect. Was that what Sasha and Rafael wanted, though? Were they changing their mind about the baby? She didn't believe that, but it was hard to imagine anything else when they were ghosting her. Jacinda had shown little concern for her friend, but Molly was growing ulcers of anxiety in her stomach, wondering what was going on with the other couple.

With Sasha and Rafael top of mind, she felt compelled to be firm. "Gio, we can't keep leading Otto on. You have to tell him the truth when we get back."

"It's not that easy," he said testily. "Nonno has given me everything. Not just the wealth and position I enjoy, but everything that means anything to him." He pointed to the ring on her hand. "He saved my life when I could have died of neglect or turned out like my father. I can't bear to disappoint him."

"Neither can I, but…" She clenched her hand over the ring. The gem dug into her palm. It was an instinctual safe-guarding. She was always aware of the value it carried be-yond its carat or clarity. Now a pebble, hard and sharp as a diamond, arrived in her throat. "What do you mean…you could have died?"

"You've seen my parents," he muttered, scraping his hand over his hair as he tried to find a pathway in the tiny area between the coffee table and the love seat. "They are the poster children for why people ought to need a license to procreate."

She had never seen him so agitated. Well, not since he'd received the news that his grandfather was ill.

"Gio…" She tried to move to stand in front of him, but he turned away. "You don't have to tell me what they did if you don't want to talk about it." It was obviously a painful memory. "But you *can*."

"Nothing," he said starkly, slicing his hand through the air. "They did a lot of nothing. Which didn't make much impact while I was an infant. There was usually a nanny around to feed or change me. Occasionally, one was fired for insubordination or *intoxication*, because they would get her drunk or high with them. A new one would be hired within a day or two, so I survived it."

"Are you saying…?" She started to feel ill.

"Yes. They left me crying in a room, hungry and wet. I know this because Nonno hired investigators later, when he took guardianship. They interviewed dozens of people who had worked for them in those years. Staff and others who did what they could, taking a minute to give me a bottle out of pity. No one stayed working for them long, though. They were terrible employers. They bullied and sexually harassed their staff, ordered them to do things that weren't legal."

"Otto let that happen to you? How long did it go on?" she asked with sick dread.

"My father wouldn't let him see me. He was trying to take over as head of Casella, but when I was due to leave for boarding school, my father told Nonno to pay the tuition or he wouldn't send me. Nonno did, which meant the school sent their initial report to him. That's how he learned I was underweight and well behind my peers. I lacked basic social skills and had behavior problems."

"Gio, I'm so sorry." She took another step toward him, but stopped herself when he tensed up.

"He pulled me from school and brought me to his villa, hired specialists and nutritionists. Spent all day with me, bringing me to the office so we were together constantly. My father tried to take me back, but Nonno bought him off. My parents continued to use me as a pressure point for years, threatening public custody battles until I was old enough to tell them to go to hell."

"I can't understand how anyone could be so heartless." Her heart was aching. Her throat was hot, her eyes pressured by a force of tears she was fighting to hold back.

"Because they never cared about *me*. I was conceived to be a pawn," he said bitterly. "My father thought a son would secure his place as Nonno's heir, even though he'd proven himself inadequate time and again. Nonno didn't imagine how bad it was. It took a long time before we enjoyed the relationship we have today, but eventually I learned that he would always be there for me."

Not forever, though. Time, that inexorable thief, wanted him.

"Gio." She couldn't stand it any longer. She rushed across to him and hugged her arms tightly around his waist. "I'm so sorry that happened to you. So glad that you had Nonno to turn to."

"That's why I can't bear to hurt him, Molly." He cupped the back of her head, all of him stiff, as though trying to withstand great pain. "If I had been left at boarding school, I would be as profligate as my father. Worse, likely. I had a daredevil streak in my childhood that bordered on a death wish."

She hated to hear that. Hated to think of him alone and hungry and scared, or so angry he endangered himself.

"I would stay with you for Otto's sake if I could, Gio. But I *can't*." She clenched her eyes shut, feeling the tears press through her lashes. What would he think of her if he learned this baby wasn't hers? That she didn't plan to raise it herself?

Her heart juddered in her chest.

"Would you?" He closed his fist over the low ponytail she was wearing, gently pulling so she was forced to turn her tearstained face up to his.

She tried to nod, but his hand was too heavy on her hair. Her lips trembled as she tried to find the words to explain why she couldn't, but those words were on a document in her safe-deposit box. He would never see them.

Something seemed to break in him. He covered her mouth with his own, once, hard, as though physically trying to stamp himself onto her, then softened into a tender plea that dragged an ache from her chest and a moan from her throat.

I can't, though. I can't.

This needed to stop. She couldn't continue the charade of their engagement or the affair that had no future. She knew that, but when he would have drawn back, she pressed her hand to the back of his head, urging him to keep kissing her. To singe away all the angst and terror of the future. All the anguish that would come soon enough. Just not today. Not yet.

The moment her hand started to slide his jacket off his shoulder, the mood between them altered, becoming frenzied. They hurriedly raked at each other's clothes. He tore open his shirt, then hers just as ruthlessly.

It was one of her favorites, but she didn't care. She threw it off her shoulders with her bra and grasped at his waistband, yanking his belt free.

They didn't even go to the bedroom. As he dropped to his knees and dragged her pants down her legs, he elbowed the coffee table aside. She stepped out of them and sank to her knees, too, naked, and kissed him as she jerked at his fly and freed his erection.

His breath hissed in, then he was cupping her mound. Giving her equal pleasure, sweeping his tongue against hers before dragging his mouth across her skin, pressing her onto her back.

The carpet was rough and cool, the weight of him scorching. He was so intent, she should have been alarmed, but his control was not completely gone.

"Tell me," he demanded in a rasp as he clasped her breast and ran his tongue against the pulsing artery in her throat. "Say you want this."

"Always," she moaned, writhing at the way his mouth was straying down, down, down. A flagrant suck of her nipple, a scrape of teeth against the underside of the swell. Hot breath against her ribs and a lascivious lick into her navel.

He spread her legs and she arched in agonized ecstasy as he claimed her.

They knew how to do these things to each other now. She knew he liked the feel of her hands in his hair and her thighs twitching in pleasure. He knew when she was approaching her crisis and that she was flexible enough to let him keep her legs over his arms as he rose over her. She knew it only took the tiniest bit of guiding for him to arrow into her with one slow, implacable thrust and that they both loved that moment almost more than the finale.

Almost. Because then there was this. The act.

"Say you want this forever," he demanded, pinning her there on the floor with her legs splayed over his arms while he withdrew and returned in thrusts of careful power.

It wasn't a lie. "I do," she admitted, then closed her eyes, knowing they were words that shouldn't have been uttered. They felt too much like a vow.

Her statement was the button on a detonation, one that was as physical as emotional. After a few more heated thrusts, they were both exploding, clinging and shuddering and crying out with both exaltation and defeat.

CHAPTER EIGHT

"I SHOULD HAVE taken you to the bed," Gio said with less remorse than he should have been suffering.

He had managed not to crush her in the quivering aftermath, sinking beside her and pulling her into him, but sex on the floor was a poor example of how well he intended to take care of her. His knees were stinging with a friction burn and this flat was cold enough that he dragged her mostly on top of him to keep her warm.

It wasn't like him to cast off self-discipline, but he'd been talking about things he never revisited in his own mind, let alone spoke of aloud. He'd been feeling raw and, worse, threatened by the reality of her packed boxes.

If his grandfather's illness hadn't arisen to keep her with him that day two weeks ago, she would have given notice and be out of his life after next week. Perhaps she would have come back after the baby was born, but he would have missed this time with her.

Recognizing that had filled him with an urgency he wasn't expecting, making him greedy for her. More demanding than he should have been.

"Did I hurt you?" he asked, bracing himself for her response.

"No. I would have stopped you if I didn't like it." She was tracing a tickling pattern against his pec, but she sat up beside him. Her hair was falling out of its clasp and her eyelids were still heavy, her makeup smudged and her mouth sensually swollen. "I'm going to have a quick shower."

"I'll join you."

"Ha! Good luck."

The stall was a tiny corner unit without a tub. He squeezed himself in with her purely for the entertainment of rubbing their soapy bodies together while sharing a few wet, lingering kisses.

She kept her hair out of the spray, but washed her face. Afterward, she leaned over her dresser to reapply her makeup, providing a delightful view of her backside where her T-shirt rose to reveal the lace edge of the cheekies that cut across the globes of her spectacular ass.

He wore only a towel as he waited for his body to cool. Absently, he paced her small flat, liking the way she'd decorated it. Her possessions weren't abundant or extravagant, but they were arranged tastefully. The whole was an appealing mix of plain and bright colors with soft textures and inviting warmth.

He wanted to bring up marriage and had since Milan, but he was uncharacteristically unsure, despite what she had said while they were making love a little while ago. When Molly had talked about her parents' marriage, she had said she was holding out for love as a practical choice. Surely she would see that he offered an extremely comfortable life for her and her baby, though?

The baby.

He glanced over as she straightened to sort through her palettes of cosmetics. Her T-shirt fell to rest against her baby bump, something he saw every time she was naked, but for some reason, seeing it now caused a sledgehammer of emotion to hit him. Something between longing and anticipation.

For the first time in his life, he was enthused by the idea of fatherhood. The concept had shifted from being a role he felt obliged to take on, into one that he wanted. With Molly at his side, he felt ready for the challenge.

"I can feel you staring holes through me." She shakily pumped her mascara wand before applying it to her lashes, then said in a conciliatory tone, "I promised you three weeks and I'll honor that. I don't want to make the lie worse by giving Otto a date, but if he presses the issue, we could say we're looking at August, before Libby has to return to school."

He relaxed slightly and returned to his aimless pacing, mind turning to how he would use the next week to convince her to stay for a lifetime.

His gaze snagged on the only art hanging on her walls. It was a butterfly of pins strung with colored threads against a black background. The maker had taken great care with it, but it was the type of makeshift craft one expected from a preteen summer camp.

Was this why she felt she didn't belong in his world? Because she didn't have Renaissance oils? From what he could tell, her single mother had provided her a far superior upbringing than the dismal start he'd endured. That's what made her right for him. She didn't *care* about money or material possessions. She cared about that baby she carried. About her family.

He absently glanced at the white signature, expecting to see Libby's name. Maybe Molly's.

"Who's Sasha?" he asked.

"What?" She flung around from the mirror. "Oh." Her eyes widened as she realized what he was looking at. "I've had that so long, I forgot it was there. She's, um, a friend from my high-school days."

She dropped her makeup and moved to fetch a clean towel from the bathroom.

"I thought you homeschooled?" he asked.

"I still had friends." She took the artwork off the wall and wrapped it in the towel, then set it in her suitcase. Her hands were shaking. She was avoiding his eyes.

"Are you telling me the truth, Molly?"

"Yes." She snapped a look at him that was so surprised and unwavering that he dismissed his suspicion. It still seemed like a strong response to an idle question, though.

"She must be very special to you."

"She is. Are you hungry? There's a takeaway place around the corner that does an amazing rice bowl. I probably won't get to enjoy it again for a while so…" She picked up her phone to tap into an app. "I'll say thirty minutes and we'll pick it up on the way to your town house? I'm almost finished here."

He glanced once at the suitcase, still puzzled, but she asked him about his order. Then she was gathering up her last few items and he put the odd moment out of his mind, pleased that she was coming home with him, which was all that mattered.

Molly felt like the worst person alive. Even her mother gave her a fretful look when she had a private moment to catch up with her over the tablet.

"You can't stay into August, Molly. You're already showing."

"I know, but I had to tell him something." She understood Gio better now, and saw why he felt such an allegiance to his grandfather. Her heart went out to the neglected child he'd been and she was so filled with admiration for the man he'd become.

It made her crush all the more intense.

Oh, who was she kidding? She was way past crushes and infatuation. She was falling in love with Gio. Given his childhood, he could have turned out bitter and cold, but he was a man of strength and integrity, capable of kindness and even tenderness. If she hadn't been pregnant with Sasha's baby, she would stay with him as long as he wanted her to.

But her time in his world was evaporating.

"Still no word from Sasha?" her mother asked.

"We're going to Athens tomorrow. Gio is meeting with Rafael so I know they'll be there. If I have to walk up to their front door and ring the bell, I'll see Sasha. Once I know where I stand with them, I'll know whether..."

"What?"

"Whether I'm raising this baby myself." If that happened, everything would change, but she didn't let herself consider how. She would cross that bridge when she got to it.

"Do you think Sasha is having second thoughts?" Patricia asked with deep concern.

"*I don't know.* I've texted so many times, asking them to call, to tell me what's going on. She seemed extremely sure that she wanted this baby, when we were seeing that counselor in London, before the implant." Sasha had admitted things between her and Rafael had been strained at the time, but blamed herself. She was upset about her fertility issues and not an easy partner to live with. "Perhaps her parents are there? Or her injuries are more serious than they're letting on in the press?"

"That doesn't explain why Rafael isn't replying to you."

"I know," she murmured, disturbed by that. She couldn't understand why they would give her the silent treatment when she was *carrying their baby.*

"When you see her—" Her mother *tsked* with distress. "If

she seems open to it, let her know that Libby is curious about her. We would still love for her to be part of Libby's life."

"She knows, Mom." Molly had made that crystal-clear the day they'd talked on the yacht. "I'll tell her again, though. Oh, Gio's back," she said as she heard the door.

She smiled at him as he came into the sitting room.

"Would you like to say hi to Mom?" Gio popped into the frame behind Molly and her mother offered the smile of natural warmth that inspired such trust in pregnant mothers.

"Hello, Gio. Molly tells me your grandfather is improving. That's good to hear."

"He is, and he would love to meet you and Libby. Molly said you might have time before Libby goes back to school. Can I book you a flight? My treat."

Her mother was briefly taken aback, as was Molly.

"I would have to ensure my colleagues could cover for me. Let me get back to you," Patricia said, but Molly felt the pointedness in the way her gaze asked, *How long will you continue this farce?*

They ended the call a moment later.

"What was that?" Molly twisted around to ask with astonishment. "I'm only here until the twenty-first. I'm not taking that bonus you offered to double my time."

Gio moved around the end of the sofa so he faced her and pushed his hands into his pockets. He stared over her head a moment, seeming to be choosing his words, then dropped his gaze to hers.

The weight of his stare landed so hard, she instinctually braced herself.

"What's wrong?" she asked.

"Nothing. I'd like to make this engagement real."

"Real?" Molly pulse skipped so hard she heard it. "What do you mean?"

"I'm proposing marriage, Molly."

He had done that already. She actually looked at the ring she wore as if it had been made of sugar and had somehow dissolved. It was there, though.

"You don't mean… Like, have a wedding for your grandfather's sake? Gio, I can't." And why was he torturing her this way? Did he not realize she was falling in love with him?

Or was that precisely why he was asking? Did he feel the same? She drew in a breath and held it.

"We're good together," he said in the same voice he used when he was negotiating across a boardroom table. It was the furthest thing from tender and made her throat tighten. "I'm not just talking about in bed, either. We're well-matched intellectually. We have similar values. You understand my work demands and I'm supportive of your continuing to advance your career, if that's something you want to do. I would like a family. Obviously, you do as well."

No mention of love. The swell of hope in her chest shriveled.

"My grandfather likes you and I'd like him to have the reassurance of our being married."

"Oh, your *grandfather* likes me," she said facetiously. A semihysterical laugh was trapped behind the rock that was sitting inside her chest. She began to see how he had approached his first engagement, *like any other merger and acquisition*, and felt some sympathy for the woman who hadn't been able to go through with it. "What do you feel, Gio?"

His expression grew stoic. "Liking. Respect. *Desire*," he added in a tone that held a rasp.

"That's not enough!" She rose to pace, trapped in this impossible situation and longing for escape.

"I disagree. It's a strong foundation. We're both sensible people, Molly. We'll find a way to make it work. If it doesn't, we can divorce after Nonno's gone."

"I told you how I feel about divorce." She flung around to face him. "If you're already considering it, then why bring up marriage at all?"

"Because I'm confident we'll stay married," he said with exasperation.

"You genuinely believe you want to spend the rest of your life with me? *Me?*"

"And your baby. Yes."

Her chest knotted up. The baby. Oh, God.

"Whatever is going on with the baby's father, you can tell me." He came closer and tried to take her hands.

"I can't—" She pulled her hands away. "You don't understand."

"No, I don't," he said with instant frost, withdrawing. "But I want to."

She was hurting him with her rebuff. It went beyond the fact that no one ever said no to him. They were lovers. Close. He had told her about his childhood and why it was difficult for him to trust that people would be there for him.

She didn't want to reject him, but she didn't have a choice. She shook her head, filled with despair. What if she did wind up raising this baby? Would he understand? Would he still want her? Them?

"Can we talk about this in a few days? I need some time." She needed the weekend. She needed to see Sasha and Rafael.

When she warily lifted her gaze, she saw his cheeks were hollow, his mouth tight with dismay. He nodded curtly. "Fine. We'll revisit this after we get back from Athens."

"Thank you," she said through an arid throat, doubtful that she would have a better answer for him by then.

Her stomach was in knots when they landed in Athens the next day.

Yesterday, when she had worked out details with Rafael's assistant for a meeting between him and Gio to finalize their business agreement, the assistant had tacked on a personal message to the email.

Mr. and Mrs. Zamos are hoping to see Mr. Casella and his fiancée at the art museum benefit on Saturday night. They want to congratulate them on their recent engagement.

Was it a coded message meant for her?

Molly was on pins and needles as she dressed in a one-shouldered gown of gold. Ruched silk formed the bodice. Gold leaves decorated the shoulder and the high waist. The skirt fell in narrow pleats that hid the thickening at her waist.

"Is the serpentine necklace in the safe?" she asked Gio when the stylist had finished her makeup. She wore her hair up tonight, with a few long ringlets dangling to frame her face.

His admiring gaze took her in, making her skin warm under his regard.

She was warming and softening with more than that. She was fighting an urge to agree to his proposal and fold her life into his. He might not love her, but he loved his grandfather very much. He was *capable* of love, which filled her with hope that he could love her, given time and absolute honesty.

Sadly, she couldn't give him either of those things, which was cleaving her heart in two. She felt torn every minute of the day, but especially now, when she was preparing to confront the parents of the baby she carried.

Gio removed a velvet case from the hotel safe, one that was unfamiliar and pristine.

"I bought something else for you to wear." He nodded to dismiss the stylist and opened the case.

"Brought? Or b-bought?"

"Bought. I thought you might like to wear something of your own for a change."

No-o-o.

She swallowed as he revealed a stunning necklace in yellow gold with a dozen links made of pear-shaped yellow sapphires. Each was surrounded by white diamonds. A larger sapphire, also a pear surrounded by bigger diamonds, formed the pendant. The earrings matched.

"It's too much," she said weakly.

"It's an incentive. We both know that," he said impassively.

He really wanted her to marry him, she realized with a thudding sensation behind her heart. Why, though? For those dispassionate reasons he'd given her yesterday? For his grandfather? Or was he developing feelings for her?

She couldn't bear to slight him again by refusing the necklace, so she stood still while he circled behind her and set the weight of the pendant against her throat. He clasped the chain behind her neck before he set a kiss on her nape, exactly in the spot that weakened her knees.

"Surely this is an incentive, too?" He lingered to nuzzle and inhale.

Goose bumps rose on her skin and a moan of longing throbbed in her throat.

She couldn't resist turning to kiss him. To touch and hold on to him a little longer, a little harder. She was in Athens.

The last grains of their time together were falling into the bottom of the hourglass.

Since becoming lovers, they had been making love every chance they got. Each time she felt as though she lost a little piece of herself, and today, with this dark cloud looming, she felt an urgent need for one last act of intimacy.

She sank to her knees and worked to open the fly of his tuxedo pants.

"That's not what I was hoping to gain," he said in a voice that had turned gritty.

She paused in freeing him. "Is that a no?"

He swallowed. "You know I always want this."

She finished exposing his thickening flesh. A feral noise came out of him as she took him in her mouth. He grew harder against her tongue as she sucked flagrantly on his salty flavor, exploring his textures then tilting her head to take him deeper into her mouth.

His fingertips dug into her shoulder and he made a noise as though he was trying to withstand acute pain. His other hand cupped her cheek and he pumped a few times, saying something unintelligible.

His stomach tightened. All of him did as she caressed between his thighs and closed her fist around the base of his shaft, trying to give him every bit of pleasure she could.

Just when she thought he would lose it completely, he crushed his fist around her own and carefully withdrew from her mouth. He pulled her to stand before him.

She swayed drunkenly. "Don't you want…?"

"I want *you*," he said in a rasp. "All of you."

He brought her with him as he backed toward the bed and sat on the edge.

She wanted him, too. All of him. Forever. But she could only have this, so she gathered the delicate fabric of her skirt before she straddled his thighs. When he moved her underwear aside and caressed into the slippery heat that awaited him, she closed her eyes to savor the sensations.

"Take me," he growled as he dropped onto his back.

She was aching. Not just physically aroused, but aware of a hollowness in her heart, in her soul. She needed more than pleasure. She needed the indelible connection of their bodies.

She guided herself onto him, lowering and blinking away the rush of tears that had been prompted by the starkness of the moment. By the magnitude of it.

She loved him. She loved him with everything in her and, one way or another, she was going to lose him.

His wide hands slid up her thighs to bracket her hips beneath the skirt. He lifted his hips, urging her into moving on him.

She let her skirt spill around them and braced her hands on his shoulders while she rode the rhythm he set. The wool of his pants abraded her legs, but she embraced that discomfort in the greater frenzy of claiming him.

As the intensity of emotion and pleasure converged, she cried out what was in her heart. What couldn't be contained or denied anymore.

"I love you, Gio! I love you!"

Ecstasy shot through her like golden light, but even though he threw back his head and bared his teeth, releasing a shout of pure exaltation, he didn't say the words back to her.

Molly disappeared into the bathroom to put herself back together while Gio picked up the ringing phone.

"The car is waiting for us," he called to her, still tucking himself back into his trousers, titillated by the smudge of lipstick she'd left on him.

He moved to ensure he wasn't wearing that shade on his mouth. He was still perspiring and dull-witted from his powerful orgasm, but also off-kilter. Had she heard herself?

He wasn't sure how to take her confession. Was it an agreement to marry him?

Women had claimed to love him in the past, of course, including his mother. For Fridrika, the word *love* was a means of manipulation that had worked when he'd been young. She had used it to twist his feelings and impose a sense of obligation, which had made the words downright repulsive to him for a long time.

Not every woman was a sociopathic narcissist, however. Eventually, he had come to understand that *love* was something some people believed they were experiencing when enthusiasm and accord ran high. Hell, when he'd watched Molly's painted lips close around his aroused flesh with such erotic greed, he could have said he loved her and meant it. Context was everything.

Molly would have a definition of love that was deeper and more meaningful than his, though. She wouldn't say it to impose obligations on him, but she wouldn't say it superficially, either. She had said she wanted to marry for love, so...?

She joined him, makeup once again flawless, hair a tiny bit less polished than it had been, which was actually very sexy. The blush of orgasm still sat on her cheekbones, which was also sexy as hell. She sent a vague smile in his direction and hurried to put on the earrings that matched the pendant he'd given her.

Her hands were trembling, which distracted him from the thick tension coating the air. Was she waiting for an acknowledgement of what she'd said? Reciprocation?

"Shall we go?" Now she was looking into her clutch and moving to the door, making him realize she hadn't once met his eyes.

He'd been waiting for her to look at him so he could better read her mood, but she was opening the door herself and walking through it.

They made their way down to the lobby in weighted silence.

As the car took them the short distance to the museum, he reached across to take her hand, starting to say "thank you for earlier," but he stopped himself when he realized how ambiguous those words might sound.

Her fingers curled loosely around his, but she kept her focus out the window.

It wasn't until they walked into the gala, where Rafael Zamos and his wife were holding court, and he felt her stiffen beside him, that he realized she might be suffering nerves. Gio took his acceptance in any group of people for granted, but she was still finding her feet in his social circles. Plus, the last time she'd met this couple, Alexandra Zamos had been very condescending toward her.

"Don't worry," he murmured. "They'll be polite." They had damn well better be.

Thinking back to that day, however, Gio recalled that it was the first time he'd had to admit to himself that he had a personal interest in Molly, one that went deeper than sneaking glances at her figure. When she had appeared on deck, he'd been preoccupied with his negotiations with Rafael, irritated that lunch had turned into a swim and drinks. Precious time had been wasted and Jacinda had been circling like a shark. Despite her very pretty breasts, he'd been dead from the waist down...until Molly appeared.

She had been a wild rose among manufactured silk blossoms. Her beauty originated in the way that nature had put her together, not from any false adornments. She smelled fresh and moved fluidly, and smiled with shy warmth.

When Alexandra had been so offended that Molly had dared to show herself above her station, Gio had genuinely questioned whether he should be doing business with her husband.

That rush of hostility and protective aggression had been so ferocious, he'd almost missed that Alexandra was trying to smooth things over with Molly. She'd been clumsy about it, but she had invited Molly for breakfast and had seemed genuinely embarrassed by her own behavior. He'd left Molly to decide for herself whether she wanted to give the woman an opportunity to make up for her discourtesy.

Now, however, as they made their way toward the couple, he could feel tension coming off Molly in radioactive waves. It ignited a prickling need to guard, but he couldn't identify the threat.

Rafael spotted them and excused himself and his wife from their group. He glanced at Alexandra in a silent signal that she should accompany him as he began making his way toward them on a pair of crutches. Alexandra was frowning with tension. Her attention skimmed the room in a way that struck Gio as hunted.

Molly's grip tightened in his. Was her palm clammy?

He squeezed her hand in reassurance. Alexandra might have the arrogance of blue blood, but Rafael was the last man to portray any snobbish tendencies. He might wear a bespoke tuxedo and a Girard-Perregaux on his wrist, but he'd come from the humble roots of operating his father's marine repair business before turning it into a heavy player in marine manufacturing and technologies. Once they signed their agreement, they would expand container cargo transfers, so they would become one of the largest players in that industry. It was something Zamos needed more than Gio, but if Gio didn't leap on this partnership, someone else would, so he wanted to exploit it.

Rafael wore an even more inscrutable look than Gio was used to seeing on him, which subconsciously increased his own tension.

Gio had judged Rafael's marriage to be a practical one. Alexandra was an American heiress who had attended school in Switzerland. They taught haughtiness there, that was a fact, but she was enormously well-connected. Alexandra was capable of warmth and witticisms, but she had the conceit of exceptional beauty. Her superciliousness bordered on appearing spoiled, which Gio found off-putting, but he kept his opinions to himself.

As the couple arrived before them, Alexandra skimmed a blank, polite smile over Molly, one that dismissed her as unimportant. Her attention only landed on Gio because Rafael was tucking his crutch beneath is armpit and offering to shake his hand.

"Gio. Good to see you again. Gio was on the yacht with us late last year," Rafael told Alexandra. "And this must be your fiancée?"

"Molly, yes," Gio confirmed, disconcerted by the bland smile Alexandra offered them.

"I was on the yacht, too." Molly said, offering her hand to Rafael while looking to Alexandra. "We met briefly. You may not remember."

"I don't," Alexandra stated flatly. She turned her gaze up to the blue balloons and silver streamers in a rude lack of interest. "I have a concussion. I can't remember a damned thing. I don't even know why I'm here. None of this means anything to me."

Her husband's expression tightened. He shot Molly a look that might have been apologetic.

Molly's eyes were swallowing her face as she stared intently at Alexandra. Her lips parted and trembled with what looked like disbelief. Horror, even.

When her glance flashed to Rafael's, something passed between them that closed a fist around Gio's heart. It was gone in the next second as their eye contact broke, leaving him to believe he'd imagined it. Molly went back to studying Alexandra.

"That must be terribly confusing. I'm so sorry," Molly said with genuine concern. "It looks like you're both still recovering from the crash. Should we sit down?"

"No. I don't like these lights. They're giving me a headache." Alexandra touched her brow and winced. "Rafael insisted on my coming so people can see I'm only half there—"

"I never said that," he bit out.

"What else are they going to think when you parade me around, explaining my brain injury like I'm a circus attraction?"

"Would you excuse us?" Rafael said tightly. "I'll see you at the office tomorrow, Gio."

As the pair moved away, Gio said, "Here I was so confident she wouldn't be rude."

"She's injured," Molly defended quickly. Her face was still white. "Why did they even come out?"

"They didn't have a choice," Gio said in grim observation. "Rafael's growth was fast and furious. His success is new enough that he's vulnerable." Buzzards would be circling, sensing his weakness. "He's making it clear that he's not going anywhere." Crutches notwithstanding.

"You mean he could lose—"

"Everything. Yes."

"That seems…impossible." Her gaze fixated on the exit long after the couple went through it.

"Business is cutthroat. You know that. Rafael might have survived the car crash, but he's a stag with a broken leg. He and his wife were a very powerful team and she still seems feisty despite her injury, but I don't know that she's capable of taking over in his place if she's suffering memory issues. They're in trouble on many fronts. It would be different if they had a baby—"

A jolt seemed to go through Molly, one that was so electric, he felt it like a shock in his hand, as though he'd grasped a live wire.

"Wh-what do you mean?" She took her hand from his and rubbed it with the other.

He was so startled by her reaction, he almost forgot what they were talking about. He gave his head a slight shake, trying to dispel the strange vibes he was picking up.

"For all our marks of civilization, humans are still pack-mentality animals. We protect what we have so our young can thrive. That's why I've become so serious about putting the pieces in place for the next generation at Casella. Until recently, I didn't appreciate how important that was because I *was* the next generation. When I took the helm, I presumed that settled things, firmly bypassing my father. I naively believed that if something did happen to me, Nonno would step in." He ran his tongue over his teeth, feeling raw as he touched on brutal reality. "But he won't always be here."

Her worried gaze searched his. "A baby can't take over, either," she pointed out faintly.

"No, but those who are invested in an heir protect what belongs to him or her. I'd name you as my successor at Casella Corporation before I'd let my father so much as walk through its front doors. I know you would safeguard every brick and pencil in the place because that's the kind of person you are, but if your own child stood to inherit? You'd be relentless."

She blinked emotively. "I'm glad you see me that way, but…"

He ignored that *but* and closed his hand on hers again, trying to impress on her why their marrying was so important to him.

"Having an heir matters, Molly. Look how exposed Rafael is without one." He nodded toward the door.

She caught her breath, and her profile seemed to grow hollow with angst.

An acquaintance approached them. They had to circulate, but Molly was so quiet and withdrawn, he insisted they leave a short time later.

CHAPTER NINE

"I'LL GO TO the meeting alone," Gio said the following morning when Molly came to the breakfast table. Given both men's demanding lives, and Rafael's recent injuries, they'd had to reschedule this signing of the final agreement for a Sunday, but that didn't mean Molly had the day off. "Go back to bed. You barely slept."

"Did I bother you last night? You should have let me go to the other bed." Molly had had a tension headache by the time they got back to their hotel. She'd been awake much of the night, trying not to toss and turn.

When Gio had asked her why she couldn't sleep, she had tried to leave, but he had spooned her. His cradling hold had been such a comfort against her angst-ridden thoughts, she had stayed in his arms, still awake, trying to make sense of the incomprehensible. Then she'd felt a faint, fluttering sensation in her middle that had made her want to cry into her pillow with a mixture of elation and misery.

Would Sasha care that this baby was beginning to make itself known with those tiny movements? She didn't even remember Molly! Neither she nor Rafael had acknowledged that Molly was carrying their baby. Did she even remember that she had given birth to Libby eleven years ago?

The idea that she had forgotten Libby broke Molly's heart.

Libby would never know, but it was still tragic. Patricia would be equally upset to hear it.

It was tragic for Sasha, too. Maybe the suppression of the memory of her daughter was something her brain was doing to protect her, but it also meant she didn't remember how devastated she'd been over her recent fertility troubles. Or how she had seemed so jubilant when Molly's pregnancy had been confirmed.

"You look exhausted. That's not an insult. It's concern," Gio continued.

"It's one meeting," she mumbled, wishing she could skip it. Facing Rafael again, and pretending they didn't have a closer relationship, would be a difficult test of her acting skills. "Once I shower and put on makeup, you won't even notice how awful I look."

"I will always notice how you look and I will always be concerned if you don't look well," he assured her. "If your insomnia had anything to do with what you said to me yesterday, before we left for the museum—"

"Oh, God, please don't." She covered her face like a child, too mortified for him to continue. She had revealed her heart in the most glaring way, then had felt raw all the way to the museum, waiting for him to say something while praying he wouldn't.

That torture had been eclipsed by their encounter with Sasha and Rafael and everything Gio had said about how precarious Rafael's position was, but her mortification was still sitting under her skin like a splinter that wouldn't stop throbbing.

"Molly." Gio reached across to take her wrist, urging her to look at him while he tangled their fingers. "I hope you understand that any emotional reserve on my part is a result of my childhood. It took me a long time to accept that my grandfather genuinely cared about me. I was taught *not* to attach to people. The few who were kind to me, always left."

She clung to his hand, searching his expression for something more than concern. Tenderness. Affection. Something that would indicate that he returned her love.

"Hearing those words from you…" His expression flexed with anguish, but his eyes were burning flames. "I know you wouldn't say something like that lightly. It means a lot to me that you did."

She knew he was being sincere, but it was still a disappointing shortfall compared to what she longed for him to say. Her mouth began quivering and her eyes filled, which only made her feel transparent, increasing her agony.

Her personal phone, the one she had been carrying like a lifeline since Sasha's crash, pinged with an incoming message.

"That's early for Libby," Gio noted as she picked it up to glance at the screen.

It's R. When can we talk?

"What's wrong?" Gio asked sharply, making her realize she'd allowed her shock—and relief?—to show on her face. Finally she would have an explanation!

"Nothing. It's Mom. Late night with a client," she lied. "I will stay here while you go to the meeting," she decided, texting essentially the same thing to Rafael, asking him to come up as soon as Gio left. It took all her courage to lift her gaze and betray nothing of the way her nerves were screaming with tension. "If you don't mind."

Gio's brow furrowed as he searched her expression, but after an endless moment of silence, he nodded jerkily.

* * *

Gio left an hour later. She texted Rafael, then hurried to change from the pajamas she still wore, pulling on a pair of floral leggings and a belted shirtdress.

She clutched her roiling stomach as she waited.

The room phone rang and the concierge said, "You have a guest. Rafael Zamos?"

"Send him up, thank you."

"You got here fast," Molly said moments later, when she let Rafael in. Neither of them bothered with greetings.

"I was in my car on the street, waiting to see him leave." Rafael looked even worse than she did, wincing in pain as he came in on his crutches. He was still very handsome, wearing a suit for his meeting with Gio—the meeting for which he'd be late since he'd come to see her first.

"I don't imagine we have much time," Molly said. "Has she really lost her memory?"

"Yes. It's a bloody nightmare." He slouched on one crutch and pinched the bridge of his nose. "I hoped that when she saw you last night, something might be triggered. I should have talked to you sooner than this. I know that. It's been hell—"

"It's okay. I can imagine you've had a lot to deal with."

"Between the surgeries and painkillers, I can hardly work, let alone prepare for—" His tortured gaze struck her middle. "Forget about me. How are you? How is the baby?"

"Fine." She covered where the flutters had heartened her last night. "We're both fine. Gio knows I'm pregnant, though."

"You told him? *Why?* And why the hell are you two engaged?"

"I had morning sickness. He figured it out," she cried with exasperation. "Then I fainted when I heard you'd been in that crash. I didn't know what was going to happen to you! Gio has been going through some things. He needed me."

Did he, though? Or was she still using his grandfather's illness as an excuse to stay with a man who didn't love her?

"He doesn't know everything," she clarified. Heck, *Rafael* didn't know everything. He didn't know Sasha was Libby's birth mother. Tears of distress came into her eyes as she wondered what Sasha's memory loss meant. "Rafael, what are we going to do?"

"I don't *know*. I told her we're expecting a baby, but—"

A subtle beep was the only warning before the door was thrust open. Gio entered wearing exactly the thunderous expression that anyone might, when they walked in on what looked like brazen infidelity.

Molly's blood went cold. She hugged herself and stammered, "Wh-what are you doing back here?"

"There was a traffic snarl. My driver had to circle back. He turned the corner in time for me to see a man on crutches entering this hotel. *This* is why you refused to tell me who the father is? Because he's *married*?"

"No. Gio—" She held up a hand. "Rafael, tell him."

"No," Gio said coldly. "The only thing he has to do is go home and pack whatever he can carry because I am pulling our deal," he snapped at Rafael. "I know that knocks the legs out from under you. Think about that the next time you step out on your wife."

Rafael swore sharply and tried to speak, but Gio spoke louder.

"And *you*—" He pierced Molly with his severest look. "You could have told me the truth. I *asked* you if the father was married. I told you I wouldn't judge. Rather than be honest, you're still involved with him and sneaking behind my back to meet him? While wearing my family ring? That's unforgivable. Give it back." He held out his hand.

"I *can't* tell you the truth." She wanted to throw up as she gave the ring a tug. Her fingers were still morning-swollen. It wouldn't budge and only hurt her knuckle to wrench against it. "I'm bound by an NDA. *Tell him, Rafael.*"

Rafael's fists were clenched around the cross bars of his crutches. His features were carved from granite as he returned Gio's look of utter contempt.

"You're right. The baby she's carrying is mine," he said through gritted teeth.

Gio raked in a harsh breath, as though the words had been a knife into his lung.

"It's also *my wife's.*"

Shocked confusion made Gio's dark eyebrows crash together.

"I'm their surrogate," Molly clarified, still struggling with the ring, but exhaling with relief as she finally, *finally*, was able to tell the truth. "The embryo was implanted through IVF. I've never had sex with Rafael. I told you I wasn't romantically involved with the father."

Gio looked between them with astonished disbelief.

"I would have my wife confirm all of this, but she's lost her memory," Rafael said with bitter humor. "Perhaps the word of the specialist in London will suffice?"

"Why would you agree to this?" Gio asked Molly with utter bafflement.

Here came the lie she had cooked up for Rafael's sake, to protect Sasha from having to confess she'd given birth as a teen. Even now, she couldn't reveal her true connection to Sasha.

"You know that my mom is a midwife," she said with a tremor in her voice. "I've always been very aware of the difficulties some women face with pregnancy. I was moved by their situation and…" This was so hard to dance this close to the truth, yet tell him something she knew would be hard for him to accept. "You know how close I am to Libby. My dad helped with my college fund, but he's not Libby's father. Her future is all on Mom. I want to ensure Libby has every advantage I had."

Libby already had more than Molly ever would. A trust had been set up through an intermediary that Libby would access when she was old enough, but only Molly and her mother knew about it.

"You're doing this for *money*?" Gio recoiled the way he had when his mother had tried to kiss him. "If you needed a raise, you should have said," he growled.

"It's not for *me*." Her argument was futile. She could see Gio shutting down, closing every door and window to his soul against her.

"Along with taking time away from her career, Molly is putting her body through significant stress," Rafael pointed out. "Professional athletes are paid to treat their body well and make every effort to produce a desired result. Why shouldn't she be compensated for doing the same?"

Gio released a choked noise. "You're going to carry this baby for nine months, then give it away to strangers?" He shook his head at her as though he didn't recognize her.

Not strangers. Sasha was *family*. But she couldn't say that.

This was what she had dreaded, that he would think he was seeing her through clear eyes when he had a more distorted view of her than ever.

"Pull our deal. I don't care," Rafael said grimly. "Destroy me if your ego demands it, but leave my wife alone. She hasn't done anything except try to give us a baby the only way she can."

Fresh tears sprang into Molly's eyes as she heard that. Poor Sasha. She'd been so piteous that day on the yacht. So ground down by the harsh realities of her life.

"Don't make Molly a target, either," Rafael continued in warning. "People like you, born to this kind of wealth—" He sent a disparaging look around the luxurious sitting room. "You don't understand why some of us have to do whatever the hell we can to get ahead. And even if you have nothing but disgust for her—"

A sob of anguish caught in Molly's throat at that thought. She instinctually covered the swell in her middle.

"She's carrying an innocent baby. Exposing what she's doing could impact that baby, and I promise you, if you do anything that causes harm to my child, my retribution will be swift and very final."

Gio's cheek ticked with insult.

Lethal tension was so thick in the air, Molly could hardly draw a breath.

"He wouldn't," she stated, feeling compelled to say it. "Gio would never hurt me or anyone's baby. I don't blame him for being angry, but he won't retaliate against the baby. I *know* that."

"I don't need you to defend me," Gio said with a curl of his lip.

"Let's not take chances," Rafael said, still using that stark tone. "Get your things."

Molly's heart stopped. "But—"

"You'll go to the villa with Alexandra. She needs time to get used to the idea she's going to become a mother."

"Are you saying she doesn't want this baby anymore?" Molly asked numbly.

"*I* want it," Rafael said fiercely, then scraped his hand

over his face. "You need to give her a chance to…get used to the idea again." Desperation edged into his tone.

Molly's heart lurched. All she could think of was a teen-aged Sasha, so determined to say goodbye to an infant she clearly loved. And later, Sasha refusing to hear about her daughter because leaving her had hurt too much for her to bear.

When Molly looked to Gio, she saw a man made of granite, but there were fissures running through him. Cracks of anger and resentment and disbelief. Beneath it all was an underpinning of acute pain.

I was taught not to attach to people. They always left.

"I told you I couldn't marry you," she said, pleading for his understanding. "I *told* you I couldn't stay. That this pregnancy made it impossible for us to be together. I told you…" *I love you.* "I told you as much of the truth as I could."

It didn't matter. He turned his face away in rejection.

She jammed her knuckle into the butter on the table and was finally able to work the ring off her finger. She had to pick up his hand to make him accept it.

"Where's Molly?" It was Nonno's first question when Gio returned.

"Gone," Gio said flatly. "We're not marrying."

Gio was blissfully numb, still in shock, but also wearing the insulated cloak of disinterest that had allowed him to survive the emptiness of his early years.

She had said she loved him and he had believed it, but she had known they were on their way to see the Zamos couple when she'd said it. She had been hiding such an explosive secret at that point, he found himself replaying every single thing she'd ever said to him, uncertain what to believe anymore.

Walking in on what had looked like an affair had shocked the hell out of him. Discovering she was carrying Rafael's baby, but that the baby wasn't actually hers…? He still couldn't wrap his head around that.

All of the twists and developments left him wondering if her version of *love* was as manipulative as his mother's.

That thought sliced through his chest like an electrified knife, leaving him so disturbed, he could only think that he was glad she was gone. Glad the ruse was over.

His life was simple again. Clean, if bleak and empty.

"I lied to you," Gio admitted to his grandfather. "Molly was my assistant. Valentina's assistant, actually. I was worried about you when we arrived so I asked her to pretend we were marrying."

"I know."

Gio shot Nonno a sharp look.

His grandfather was still convalescing, not leaving home, but his color was much improved and he dressed every day. He ate well and Gio had come to him where he was seated on a bench in the garden, soaking up the late-afternoon sunshine.

"I was sick, not stupid," Nonno said with an impatient *tsk*.

"You told me to keep her."

"I meant it. Why didn't you?"

"Because—" Gio squeezed the back of his neck, forestalling his impulse to blurt out her pregnancy.

Rafael had gotten under his skin, though, warning him not to attack his injured wife or a helpless baby. *Molly* had got under his skin, sounding so confident when she had said he would never hurt her. He'd been furious in those moments of finding her with Rafael. Scorned and, yes, feeling attacked by her secrets and prevarications, and her *de-*

parture. He'd been deeply tempted to say terrible things to her. Unforgivable things.

Agonizing fissures were still extending their way through him, breaking through his cloak of shock. His entire world had been overturned in twenty short minutes, from the moment he had caught sight of Rafael entering his hotel, when suspicions had skyrocketed inside him, to watching Molly gather a handful of things and leave.

"Because?" Nonno prompted.

"Because she's not who I thought she was. She's like *them.*" His parents, he meant. "Motivated by money."

"Pah." Nonno refused to believe that. "Did she keep the ring? The necklace?"

"No." Perversely, Gio was insulted that she had not only handed him the heirloom ring, but she also hadn't taken anything he'd given her, just the modest clothes she'd been wearing. The electronics she'd shoved into her laptop bag were her own. She'd left all the jewelry and clothes, the company tablet and phone. Even her ID badge, which had felt very final.

Apparently, she would rather Rafael support her than take one thing from Gio.

"I thought she would make a good mother for our children, but she's actually very dispassionate about family." Despite his anger and sense of betrayal, he was trying to give her the benefit of the doubt. Molly had likely been moved emotionally. It was her body, her choice, but it seemed very out of character that she would carry a pregnancy for money.

That was the part that kept smacking him in the face—that he hadn't really known her or understood her circumstances or what motivated her.

Was it really as Rafael had said? Was she trying to get

ahead via the only means open to her? That didn't ring true. She *had* been getting ahead. Maybe she hadn't known she was in line to be promoted to his executive assistant, but she had held a very prestigious position under Valentina and enjoyed a generous salary.

He'd been shocked at how modest her flat was, though, given how well she was paid. It was in a good neighborhood and the building itself had been upscale. She'd told him she liked to live below her means so she could send money to her mother. "I'm helping Mom pay off her mortgage since the house will come to me one day," she'd said. "Real estate is always a good investment."

"You're mistaken, Gio," Nonno chided. "She has very strong feelings around family. She's close with her mother and sister. I would swear on my life that she's in love with you."

She had said she was, but it hadn't kept her with him, had it? She had walked away with another man.

Angry words burned on his tongue. He wanted to malign her because, if she felt love, if her feelings were strong and true, he would expect her to have been honest with him. She wouldn't have walked out without a backward look.

Maybe she had looked back. He would never know because he had turned his back on her, refusing to watch her leave.

"You pushed her into the engagement," Nonno said pensively. "And I pushed marriage. I thought…" He sighed heavily. "I thought if she was tied to you, you would begin to open up to her. Women need more reassurance up front that a man's heart is available to her. A lifetime is a long time to live without love."

"I've lived without it. It's not that bad."

Such a heavy silence crashed down upon the garden, the bees seemed to stop buzzing in the flowers.

"I love you, Gio." Nonno's eyes grew damp. "I have loved you since the moment I learned you were on the way. I failed you by not letting you know that. By allowing you to believe for a long time that no one loved you. That is a cross I will bear all the rest of my days. Don't do that to Molly. Don't withhold your heart because you're angry or hurt. Don't leave her wondering and feeling that emptiness you suffered."

"She's fine," he said through his teeth. She had her mother. Her sister.

She wouldn't have the baby she was carrying, though.

How did she imagine she could give it up? That was the real question that was pounding like a rusty nail behind his eyes. Her attachment to her sister and mother was indisputable. He had seen her with his own eyes looking for signs of the baby in her body—not with a critical eye, but with a tender look and a shaping touch of her hand, revealing anticipation. If he wasn't so confused by her and her motives, he would have called *that* love.

How did she think she could walk away from the baby after carrying it so close to her heart? Why would she put herself through such an agonizing ordeal?

"I'm not the one who walked out," he said. "If she wants to talk to me, she knows how to reach me."

He went into the villa and tried to put her out of his mind, but reminders cropped up over the next days and weeks. If it wasn't the cautious way people spoke to him at the Genoa office, it was a visit to New York, where he kept thinking about how near he was to her mother and sister. He had fully expected to meet them the next time he was here.

After a few hollow days in that city, where he worked

nonstop, trying to shorten his trip, he found himself staring out a window. Far below, a woman pushed her baby in a stroller. How far along was Molly? Was she well? He couldn't help thinking of the morning she had fainted. He'd been so worried—

Damn it! That had been the morning he'd told her about the Zamos car crash, he realized. No wonder she had passed out with shock. What if they had died? Would that have prompted her to tell him everything? Would she still be engaged to him?

Not that he wished the Zamos couple dead. He hadn't even pulled his deal with Rafael, only left it in limbo. Rafael wasn't reaching out, either, and that suited Gio fine.

When he found himself pacing that evening, still brooding, he impulsively texted her mother.

I'd like to speak to you.

Her response came promptly.

Tomorrow would be better. Libby will be at school.

He wasn't sure why he was surprised by her willingness to see him, but he replied, I'll come to you. If this was a conversation he wanted to have over a video chat, he would have had it already.

The next morning, he drove himself into New Jersey, halfway to Pennsylvania, turned up a country road, then climbed a short, private driveway. The lawn was mowed, but the house was surrounded by encroaching woods and shrubs that could have used some aggressive pruning. The garden was in need of weeding, but it was filled with vibrant color. The house was modest and quaint, with a gable over the porch and a pot of flowers next to the front door.

"Gio." Patricia opened the door before he knocked. "Come in. I just made coffee. Have a seat." She waved at the overstuffed blue sofa that faced the television.

He stayed on his feet, glancing over the home office tucked into the corner next to the wood fireplace, then at the floor-to-ceiling bookshelves filled with both fiction and what looked like medical textbooks.

"How do you take it?" she called from the kitchen.

"Black is fine."

She came out a moment later and set his mug on the coffee table. She was an older version of Molly with silver strands in her brunette hair and a similar build encased in comfortable jeans and a T-shirt. She turned the chair from the desk to face the sofa.

"I'm going to sit and drink mine, if you don't mind," she said as she sank into the chair. "I had a late delivery last night. I've only slept a few hours."

"You should have said. I could have come at another time."

"Do you mean that?" she asked against the rim of her cup.

"No," he admitted. "Thank you for seeing me, even though it's not convenient." He was still on his feet, too restless to sit. "Is Molly well? Do you know?"

"As a rule, I take confidentiality very seriously." She lowered her mug. "But I'll put your mind at ease and say that I have no concerns around her health."

He leaped on that comment. "But you have concerns."

"She just ended a relationship that was very important to her. She's in a situation that is very complicated and makes it awkward for her to come home. I wish she was here, so

I could feed her chicken soup and watch rom-coms with her, but I can't." She shrugged and sipped her coffee again.

"Your concerns don't extend to…" He was distracted, still turning over "a relationship that was very important to her." "Do you condone what she's done? Offering to surrogate?"

"I'm also under an NDA," she said with a pained smile. "But I can tell you that I counseled Molly exactly as I would anyone considering pregnancy. We talked extensively about the risks. Ultimately, the decision was hers. As a midwife and her mother, my role is to support her however I can. This wasn't a decision she made lightly."

"I should hope not," he muttered, turning to pace again.

There were photos on the small space of wall that wasn't taken up by bookshelves. One showed Molly as an infant in Patricia's younger arms. Another showed Molly grinning widely, showing her missing front teeth. There she was winning an award at eleven or twelve, then dressed in a pretty gown for what he imagined was prom.

Here she was proudly feeding a bottle to Libby, he presumed. There she had the toddler in her lap while they read a book. There the two of them were asleep and there they were with Santa.

"How is your grandfather?" Patricia asked.

"Much better," he said absently, still studying the photos.

"Was that why you wanted to see me?" Patricia asked, tugging at his attention. "To ask whether I approve of what Molly is doing?"

"Yes." He turned in time to see her tense expression ease into an attentive smile.

"I didn't quite approve of your engagement, given the circumstances, but Molly has a big heart. She wanted to ease your grandfather's mind. It got out of hand."

"I know. I backed her into a corner. And I understand

that she couldn't talk about the surrogacy. That part I can get over. What doesn't make any sense to me is *why* she's doing it. She's the least materialistic person I know, and this is not poverty." He waved at the home. It was rustic, but cozy and in good repair. The laptop on the desk was a recent model. The car outside the window wasn't sporty, but it was newish and a top brand for safety.

"She said she was doing it for Libby," he said. "To pay for college and give her a strong start like you and her father were able to give her."

Patricia's face blanked, then she looked into her mug as she sipped.

"Is it not?" Gio asked with sharp suspicion.

"It's true that I don't have the same type of college fund set up for Libby as I had for Molly. As I said, Molly has a big heart. She would absolutely want Libby to have everything and more than she has been able to enjoy."

That struck him as a prevarication, especially since she wasn't meeting his eyes, leaving him at a loss. Suspicious.

"Did Molly give birth to her?"

"Who? Libby? No!" she said with genuine shock. "Why on earth would you think that?"

"Because this doesn't make sense!" As he turned his head, he spotted a pin-and-thread craft like the one Molly had had in London. Two of them.

One was a turtle and quite clumsily done. The other was a hummingbird, made with beautiful finesse in the way the strings crossed to produce different intensities of color. The turtle was signed by Libby, the hummingbird by Molly.

Next to it hung a recent photo of the sisters. They sat on a rock overlooking a river.

The sunlight struck golden lights into Libby's dirty blond hair. At eleven, her profile was only starting to hint at the mature features she would carry into womanhood, but it was obvious she would be beautiful. She was caught in a moment of solemn contemplation, looking toward the sky, but squinting against the reflection off the water.

A sense of recognition, almost déjà vu, accosted Gio. He heard a woman's voice say *These lights are giving me a headache.*

That same voice had asked with profound shock last November, *What are you doing here?* He'd been so focused on Molly that day, he hadn't heard the small, but significant inflection in Alexandra's voice, the one that had stressed, "What are *you* doing here?"

Molly had been shaking. He'd put it down to nervousness at being the center of attention, but the women had recognized each other. That's why Alexandra had invited Molly for breakfast. At the time, he'd dismissed it as the whim of a spoiled socialite.

As he put all of this together, the colored threads on the pin art were stretching like red yarn in a blockbuster mystery, joining to the photo of the women at the river, reaching across an ocean to connect to the butterfly he'd seen on Molly's wall.

"Who is Sasha?" He turned slowly, but felt as though the floor was falling away beneath his feet. He had detached from earth and was drifting through space.

"I beg your pardon?" Patricia went ghostly white.

"It's a sobriquet—" No, that wasn't right. He searched for the English word and couldn't find it. "Sasha is short for Alexandra, isn't it?"

My wife hasn't done anything except try to give us a baby the only way she can. Molly has a big heart.

"That's why Molly is having this baby," he said in realization. "She wants to give her sister's mother a child."

CHAPTER TEN

IT HAD BEEN eight weeks since he'd seen her.

At first, Gio had walked through a noxious fog every day, unable to see colors or feel anything but the weight of existence.

After meeting with her mother, and learning Molly's real reason for agreeing to surrogate, things had changed. He had clarity, but that only brought the world back into focus, so everything felt sharp now. Painful. He wasn't sure why. Perhaps because, when he'd thought Molly's motivates were mercenary, he'd been able to put up a wall between himself and the things they'd shared. He'd dismissed his attraction and affection as something he'd felt for a woman who was an illusion.

Now he knew it had all been real. When she had promised to keep her friend's pregnancy a secret, she had meant it. When she told him she couldn't marry him, she had meant it.

When she had said that she loved him, she had meant it. And then she had left.

The pain of her absence was both fresh and agonizingly familiar. No one should have this effect on him. He simply couldn't allow it. It was too debilitating.

He continued to use Genoa as his home base because his time with his grandfather was finite. He curtailed some of his travel for the same reason, but otherwise, he became the man he'd been before Molly had entered his life. He attended benefits and forced himself to at least go through the motions of taking a date with him. He had zero interest in starting a relationship of any kind with anyone, but he still had to legacy to secure.

He tried to convince himself that Molly was a chapter in his past. Not even a whole chapter. A footnote.

"*Signor*, the lawyers are asking again if we're scratching the Athens deal or…?" Nelo ventured warily.

"Enough," Gio said aloud. He refused to have that ever-present reminder hanging over him any longer. "Set up a meeting with Zamos. Tell him my last offer stands. I'm not interested in negotiating. Take it or leave it."

Two days later, Rafael came to him, walking into Gio's office without so much as a trace of a limp. He was completely alone.

"No lawyers or assistants?" Gio asked, jerking his head for Nelo to leave and shut the door so it was only the two of them.

"Legal has read through everything. We both know I need this deal to close and I don't have room to negotiate, especially given all you know about my personal business." He didn't bother to sit, staying in the middle of the room. The leather portfolio he'd brought dangled from one hand.

"I'm not extorting you," Gio snarled. "All of this was negotiated in good faith before your crash and the rest."

Gio did know things, though. Things even Rafael didn't know about his wife. It was a startling moment of comprehending exactly how much power he wielded over the other man. On the other hand, Rafael knew things Gio didn't.

Gio bit the inside of his cheek, refusing to ask… *How is she? Where is she?*

Presumably Rafael saw her every day. He wanted to hate him for that, but he couldn't seem to.

If you do anything that causes harm to my child, my retribution will be swift and very final.

Rafael was protecting his unborn child and had stood up for Molly, too. Gio couldn't help but respect him.

"Let's sign it and I'll get out of here," Rafael muttered.

Gio rose and they both sat down at the small table. Rafael opened the folder and, aside from initialing a handful of adjusted dates, they made no changes. It was completed with silence and a final flourish of their signatures.

If Rafael was relieved, he didn't show it. He ought to be relieved, considering this would take a lot of pressure off his cash flow and signal to his investors that if Gio had faith in his operations, they could, too. It also made an attack on Rafael's company an attack on Casella Corporation. Most would think twice before embarking down that road.

"She's well, by the way," Rafael said as he rose and secured the contract in the portfolio.

"I didn't ask."

"I know. I wanted to know if you were serious about her or just using her for your own purpose. Now I do." His lip curled with contempt.

"*I'm* using her?" Gio said with outrage.

"At least I care whether she's well, Gio."

I care, he wanted to shout, but his throat was too dry. He did care. Too much. If this was a taste of what it was like to be loved by her, to have had her and then to lose her, he couldn't bear a lifetime of fearing it could happen again. Better to heal this sense of having a limb amputated and be done with it.

Molly's hands had been clammy for weeks, ever since her mother had told her about Gio's visit.

"I told him Sasha's story is not mine to tell and neither is it his," her mother had stressed. "I pointed out that it's not up to him to reveal Libby's birth mother to her or anyone else, but I don't know what he'll do with what he knows."

Molly had relayed everything to Sasha.

Sasha was still dealing with headaches, real and proverbial. Her parents were pestering her and her marriage was foundering against the many rocks between her and Rafael.

Those things were to be expected, but the minute she and Molly had been left alone at this villa on a remote island south of Athens, Sasha had confided, "I didn't really lose my memory, Moll."

"Oh, my God, Sasha. *Why* are you faking amnesia?" Molly had cried.

"It got out of hand! I was trying to get my parents out of my hospital room. Out of my *life*. Then it helped me avoid dealing with how hard things had become with Rafael, but it turned into this…" She waved helplessly. "I wanted to text you, but then Rafael might have figured out I knew everything. *Please* don't tell him."

Molly groaned with mental agony.

"You know I'll always have your back, but I also know how these things snowball into something that becomes bigger than you can handle." Before you knew it, you were fathoms deep in love with the man of your dreams and he was shutting you out of his life. "The sooner you come clean to him, the sooner you can get past it."

"I know, but…" She blinked damp lashes.

Compassion overwhelmed Molly. She couldn't blame Sasha for trying to protect herself when she was genuinely suffering from crippling headaches.

"Will you tell me one thing?" Molly prodded her gently. "I need to know. Do you want this baby?"

"Yes! So much." A thicker sheen of tears came into her eyes. "But I'm really s-scared that I'll be a terrible mother."

"No. You'll be wonderful."

"You don't know that!"

"I do. I have every faith in you." Then, they had hugged it out. "But let's both have a rest. We can talk more later."

It became a time of healing for both of them.

A nurse came weekly to monitor Molly's pregnancy and Sasha's concussion, but for the most part, it was just the two of them in the modern home built on the ruins of an ancient villa. Crumbled walls formed the garden fence and were covered by hibiscus and wisteria. Fragrant thyme and sage bloomed in the corners of the yard and bright pink bougainvillea flowered against the white walls of the house.

If they followed the path around to the back, there was a vegetable garden filled with tomatoes, peppers, eggplants and herbs. Beyond the arched gate in the wall were arid hills and barley fields, groves of fig and fruit trees, and rows and rows of grapes.

In the mornings, they wandered the olive groves and the acres of vineyards, breathing in the serene ambience and breathtaking views of the Aegean. Then they ate breakfast on the terrace by the pool and swam when the day grew hot. They had naps in the afternoon and spent the evenings reading or watching television, if Sasha's head could stand it. Sometimes they did very little at all.

It was not unlike the time Sasha had spent living with them as a teenager, when they would find silly things to amuse themselves, such as completing jigsaw puzzles or collaging a dream board while they waited for the baby to grow.

Sasha didn't want to talk about her marriage, but she did let Molly tell her about Libby. Sometimes Molly talked about Gio. Her heart was cracked in half over the way things had ended with him. She missed him constantly. She felt as though she'd lost a lifetime with him and it made her sick with regret.

Not that she blamed this baby, though. In the weeks she'd been here, her baby bump had become pronounced and its subtle kicks put a gleam of happy tears into Sasha's eyes. Every week, after the nurse left, Sasha said, "Thank you for doing this, Molly."

Thankfully, Rafael had business in Asia for several weeks. He often asked Molly how she was feeling when he chatted with Sasha, but it was awkward for her, since she knew Sasha was lying to him about her memory loss.

At one point, Molly said to Sasha, "I might have had second thoughts about this if I'd known you two weren't in love."

"I'm in love with him," Sasha said with quick defensiveness. "He's the one who—"

She didn't finish the sentence and Molly decided it wasn't her place to judge. She knew what it was like to be in love with a man who didn't love you back. All too well.

Which was why, as she was closing in on her twenty-fifth week, when everything should have been sunshine and roses, Sasha came upon her crying on the couch.

"I thought we agreed that only one of us is allowed to cry at a time," Sasha said.

"Was it your turn? I didn't realize." Molly grabbed a few tissues and tried to mop up.

"Why are we even crying over them, anyway? Should I order a hit? I can afford it and I'm not afraid to go to jail again."

"You've never—*tsk*." Molly chuckled as she blew her nose.

"Made you laugh, though." Sasha sat down beside her and nudged her shoulder into Molly's.

They leaned on each other for a bolstering moment.

"Here's what I think we should do," Sasha proposed. "We'll hang a sign on the door that says No Boys Allowed. Then we'll stay here forever, raising our little peanut, just the two of us."

"That's very tempting," she said truthfully.

Can Libby join us? She didn't ask, though.

Sasha was making progress at her own pace. She had reconnected with their counselor in London and had said, after yesterday's chat with her, "I want Libby to know she has a sibling, but I don't know how to tell Rafael about her."

The same cheerful woman had checked in with Molly about how she was feeling about the inevitable separation after she delivered.

Molly expected it was going to be hard emotionally, but now that she had this time to reconnect with Sasha and knew they would continue to have a relationship after the baby was born, her anxiety on that front was manageable. From the beginning, Sasha had assured Molly she would have an auntlike relationship to the baby. That would go a long way to softening her sense of loss. Now she was even talking about opening herself to Libby, which made Molly even happier that she was doing this.

No, she wasn't particularly worried about the aftermath of the delivery. It was the emptiness in the other corners of her life that loomed like ghouls. She wouldn't have her job. She had planned to live with her mom and Libby while she looked for a new position, but already knew her life would feel desolate because it already did. Gio wouldn't be in it.

"I think I expected that if Gio knew you were Libby's mom, and that I'm just trying to give you what you gave us, it would make a difference. That he would understand." She started to choke up again.

"Oh, Moll. Let's both have a good cry and get it over with for a few days. Shall we?"

"I'd love to, but now I have use the bathroom again," she said with a beleaguered sigh as she rose. "Maybe we should go back to bed and start over tomorrow."

"Sounds like a pl— Oh, my God. Moll."

Molly looked over her shoulder. Sasha was staring with horror at a bright red stain on the sofa.

Gio was in New York, heading to one of a dozen quarterly meetings, when Avigail walked in, wide-eyed with alarm. She held out her phone.

"My grandfather?" Gio asked with a lurch of his stomach.

"No, but she says it's urgent. Alexandra Zamos."

Gio jolted as though struck by lightning. His heart nearly came out his mouth.

In every way, he had tried to cut Molly from his consciousness, but she was still there, every single hour of every single day. The most coldly pragmatic side of himself told him that accepting the call was prolonging a weakness he needed to conquer, but another part grasped at this delicate thread of connection to her.

He walked from the room, then said gruffly into the phone, "Alexandra?"

"I'm evacuating Molly to the hospital in Athens." She sounded as though she was crying. "She's bleeding. Will you—"

"What happened? Does her mother know?"

"No. That's why I'm calling. Can you tell Patty? I can't ask Rafael. He's never even spoken to her and he doesn't know—" Her choked voice was almost drowned out by the growing sound of helicopter blades thumping the air. "Can you arrange to get them here?" she shouted. "Tell Patty—

Tell her that she should tell Libby anything she needs to know. Tell her about me. *Everything.*"

She didn't sound like the spoiled heiress he had met in the past. She could barely speak through palpable anguish that was causing the blood to drain from his head into his shoes. He had to lean on the wall for support.

"I know this is a lot to ask when you and Molly are on the outs, but Rafael—"

"It's done. I'll handle it." Gio didn't know how he would have that conversation with Molly's mother. He didn't know how he would speak or breathe or function if Molly didn't survive this. "Keep me posted," he said, but he wasn't sure she heard him.

Molly blinked awake to the dimly lit private hospital room. She sensed it was the middle of the night and wasn't certain what had pulled her from sleep except lingering anxiety over all that had happened today.

First there'd been the shock of realizing she was bleeding, then the drama of a helicopter evacuation to the mainland. A scan had revealed a placental abruption. For the moment, the baby was getting enough oxygen, but they had given Molly steroids and put her on strict bed rest, hoping to buy the baby at least one more week of development. She would definitely deliver early, probably within the next two weeks.

She touched her belly with concern. Her hand still held the IV tube and the firm swell of her bump wore the monitor, reassuring her that the baby was safe inside her, but she was not quite twenty-five weeks along. Far too early.

"The baby's okay. You're stable," Gio said in a quiet rumble, coming to her side from the darkened corner by the window.

Her heart soared, then plummeted as she tried to read his expression and found it deeply guarded.

"When did you get here?" she asked with shock.

Why are you here?

He touched a finger to his lips and nodded at the sofa. She lifted her head to see Libby sleeping under a draped blanket.

"Your mother is here," he said in an undertone. "She's down the hall with Alexandra. Libby wanted to stay here with you. It was a long flight and…" He hitched a shoulder. "A lot for her to process. She's worried about you."

Oh, kiddo. Molly dropped her head back onto the pillow.

"Thank you for bringing them," she whispered.

Rafael had been Sasha's first call after ordering the helicopter, when they realized Molly was hemorrhaging. In her panic, Sasha had said all the wrong things, including "Of course, I remember everything!"

She had blown up her marriage in a way that was inevitable and possibly irrevocable. Rafael had promised to meet them here at the hospital, then hung up on her. At that point, Sasha had had no choice but to involve Gio.

Sasha had said that Gio had promised to handle everything, but Molly hadn't expected him to escort her mother and sister to her side himself.

"I really appreciate this. I need Mom and Lib here, but…" She couldn't keep her mouth from quivering. "You don't have to stay if you don't want to."

His cheek ticked. "If you don't want me here then say so."

"I want you here." Her voice was a mere scuff in the back of her throat.

He started to reach for her hand, but there was a rustle of noise behind him.

"Moll?" Libby asked sleepily.

"Hi, pumpkin. I'm awake. I'm okay."

Gio stepped back so she could see her sister sit up and throw off her blanket.

"That's good, because I need to tell you that I'm really mad at you," Libby informed her.

Ten days passed. Ten precious days of consistently lying on her left side, playing cards with Libby as they talked out secrets and lies. Ten days of letting her mother check her pulse and smooth her hair while they exchanged suggestions on what to read next on their e-readers.

Ten days of seeing Sasha and Rafael separately, both concerned about her and the baby, but not bringing any of their marital issues into her room.

That was her mother's doing. Patricia had read a riot act that Molly needed to remain calm and keep her blood pressure down. Conflicts should be taken down the hall and preferably kept from the hospital altogether.

Thus, Libby wasn't saying much to her birth mother, either.

"I just wonder why she didn't come and see me if she wanted a baby?" Libby had said to Molly one day, voice ringing with confusion and hurt.

Molly had a feeling that Patricia was spending a lot of time stroking Libby's hair, too. Maybe even Sasha's.

Then there was Gio. He was the first person Molly saw every morning and the last person at night. He usually stepped out when someone else arrived, but he never went far, because once they left, he flowed back into the room like a loyal sentry.

He brought flowers, which he insisted were from Otto.

"Does he know why I'm here?" she asked with alarm. It was her fourth day in hospital. They were all doing their best to continue keeping her surrogacy confidential. The last thing Sasha wanted was for her parents to catch wind of this and turn up. "How is he?"

"He's back to his old self. He only knows that you're receiving necessary treatment and that's why I'm here."

"What about work? I feel like I'm keeping you."

"I'm working." He held up his phone. "Valentina is overseeing our three musketeers. We're managing."

He could have at least pretended the place was falling apart without her.

"Gio—" She hesitated, not sure she wanted the answer, but she had to ask. "Why are you here?"

"If I were in hospital, where would you be?"

By his side, if he would let her, but that was because she loved him. Did that mean...?

"You heard your mother. I'm only allowed to stay if I let you nap. Go to sleep." He'd patted her calf and moved to the chair in the corner.

A few days later, he came in after Alexandra had left and said, "I keep thinking about that day on the yacht, when she was so shocked to see you. You never kept in touch after she placed Libby with you?"

"No. I was sad about that, but it was a painful time for her. Please don't judge her for pretending she lost her memory. If I had some of her memories, I'd want to forget them, too."

"I don't." He pushed his hands into his pockets, cheeks hollowed with reflection. "When we were on the plane, I overheard your mother tell Libby that Alexandra's parents are very wealthy and influential. That if they learned about her, they might destroy Patricia's career and make an attempt to take custody of Libby."

"They wouldn't win. Libby's birth father agreed to the adoption and even set up a trust for her, but they would put everyone through hell. Mom's practice would be impacted, which would be the point, given what I know of them," Molly said dourly.

"They sound delightful. We should introduce them to my parents." Gio curled his lip in contempt.

"When Sasha came to stay with us, I was really jealous of her. She was like you. She never had to think about money. That's not an insult," she said as his expression stiffened. "It's a fact. But as I got to know her, I realized she was deeply unhappy. She made me realize that having enough is enough and that I was lucky to have a mother who loved me. That's why she wanted to place Libby with us. She knew we would love her in a way she had never been loved herself. And we love Libby *so* much." Hot tears pressed into her eyes, her love for her sister was so big inside her.

"I know." He caressed her arm. "You don't owe me explanations. We can talk about this another time if it's upsetting you."

"No, I really need it off my chest because I couldn't tell you before." She covered where his hand sat on her upper arm. "I always believed that Sasha had had this one dark spell in her life and that she had made the best of it by giving both her baby and herself the best chance at a fulfilling life. Then I saw her on the yacht and she was miserable. She wanted a baby so badly and her body was betraying her. She had given us such a precious gift. I had to do the same for her. *I had to.*"

"I won't pretend I didn't struggle to understand it," he acknowledged somberly. "Especially when I thought you were doing it for money. My baggage put a dark spin on that."

"I know." She swallowed a lump in her throat. "I hated lying to you about that."

"It didn't fit with who I believed you were. You're ambitious, but if money motivated you, you'd be married to me right now. You have a soft heart, but you're not so soft you don't know how to say no. I spent a lot of time questioning whether I could even trust my own judgment. That's why I went to see your mother. I was certain I was missing something and I was."

He hadn't come to see her afterward, though, once he knew the truth. Why not?

Rafael had arrived at that point and Gio stepped out.

Rafael never stayed long. He only asked how she was feeling and glanced at the reports on the baby's vitals, then offered to bring anything she needed.

"Rafael, I'm worried about you and Sasha," Molly blurted, because it was genuinely eating at her.

"You're forbidden to worry," he reminded her dryly. "Alexandra and I want this baby very much. We'll do whatever we have to, to give our child a good life, including reconcile our differences. I know I speak for her when I say we're equally sorry this pregnancy is costing you so much. I don't know how I'll ever make that up to you. It eats at me every day, so, please, don't worry about me on top of it. I'll expire from guilt."

Until these daily visits, she hadn't really gotten to know Rafael. He was still aloof, but he sometimes offered these small glimpses that reassured her a human lurked behind the iron wall he presented to the world. That helped her see why Sasha had fallen for him. Molly only wished the pair would find their way back to each other before this baby arrived.

Who was she to talk, though? She was terrified to ask Gio point-blank what his feelings for her really were.

When Rafael left a few minutes later, she heard him speak to Gio in the hall. It sounded like Rafael had said, "So you do care."

Gio's response had been too low for her to hear. By the time he came back into her room, he was on the phone with Nelo and asked her if she recalled some detail about a contract. From there, the day wore on in its glacial fashion.

Every day was one minute at a time. For those ten days, Molly felt as though her life had stopped altogether. Or rather, that her life became focused on "life" in its most elemental sense—on the life inside her.

Then the decision was made for both of their sakes that the baby should be delivered by cesarean section. Molly was prepped for surgery and everyone gathered in her room. Since she was having a full anesthetic, no one would go into the theater with her.

"It's going to be fine," Sasha insisted with a strain in her voice. Her lips were white.

"I have every confidence in these doctors," Patricia assured her, which bolstered Molly a little.

Libby put on a brave face, smiling through her tears while Rafael was at his most stoic.

So was Gio, until they started to wheel her out.

"Molly!" He lurched into the hall and stopped the gurney to lean over her. His expression was tortured as he cupped her cheek. "Make sure you come back to me."

It was hardly in her power, but she promised, "I will."

He pressed one hard kiss on her dry lips, then she was on her way again, heart pounding.

CHAPTER ELEVEN

ATTICUS BROOKS ZAMOS was tiny, but utterly perfect. He was in neonatal intensive care, requiring extra oxygen and accepting his nutrition from an IV, but his lungs were working and his heart duct had closed. He needed time and a lot of close watching, but he was as healthy as could be expected for a baby born so early.

When Molly was wheeled down to visit him, and she saw his naked brow bunched with stern determination to stay alive, she knew she would love him for her whole life. She would have kept him as her own in a heartbeat, but as she watched Sasha shakily cradle his achingly small form against her bare chest, crying with love for him while Rafael stood over them like a wolf guarding his mate and cub, she knew she had done the right thing.

Which wasn't to say the baby blues didn't hit her like a ton of bricks. She was kept in hospital a few days to ensure she was recovering from the surgery, and she expressed a little colostrum to give Atticus his best start, but she was planning to go home to New Jersey with her mom and Libby, so she only pumped to keep herself comfortable, not to encourage more milk.

That caused a hormone roller coaster that had her unable to stop crying the day she was discharged. It felt wrong to leave Atticus here, but even Sasha couldn't bring him home yet. He would be in hospital for several weeks, likely until what would have been his due date if he'd gone to term.

"We'll stay at the apartment. It's just a few streets over," her mother said to console her, pacing alongside the wheelchair as Molly was brought to the exit. "We can visit him every day."

"I thought you were at a hotel?" Molly said with confusion.

"Gio moved us into his penthouse the second day we were here. It's closer and has a pool. Libby loves it. I thought it was too much of an imposition, but he's very persuasive," Patricia said ruefully.

"Oh, you've met him," Molly said, brightening with humor for a moment, then wondered why Gio hadn't come to fetch her if he was still here. Was he? Or had he left, now that he knew she had safely delivered and was on the mend?

"It's been nice getting to know him," her mother said. "And I won't pry, but…" She swept her hand over Molly's hair. "I like him. I hope things work out between you."

A nurse had helped Molly shower this morning. At least her hair was clean, if damp, but between that and the surgery, and the activity after so many days of bed rest, then the shuffle from the car into the apartment building, then into the penthouse, Molly was exhausted by the time she found Libby playing a lively hand of cards with Gio.

"Oh, no," Libby said with guilty horror when she saw her. "I was supposed to move my stuff into Mom's room so you could have mine. I'll do it now."

"Rest in my room while she does that," Gio said, rising to help Molly down the long, marble hallway into the sprawling bedroom where wide windows offered a stunning view of the Parthenon. "Can I get you anything?"

"No. I'm f-fine." She wasn't, though. Tears started to leak down her cheeks.

"Molly. Do you want me to get your mom?" he asked with concern.

"No," she sniffed. "I want to lay down."

He closed the door and came to help her sink onto the bed, then picked up her feet for her. She habitually rolled onto her left side.

"The counselor told me I should expect to be sad, but I don't want to cry. It hurts my stomach."

"Ah, *cuore mio*." He moved around the bed and lay facing her. "Of course, you're sad." Very gently, he drew her closer, arranging her against his warmth in a way that brought fresh tears to her eyes, but of a completely different sort. "I imagine you'll feel sad for a long time, but I hope you're proud, too? That was quite a gift you have given them."

She hitched back her sob, fighting to control herself, and adjusted how her head was pillowed on his shoulder, then relaxed with her arm across his waist.

"Thank you for saying that. I don't have any regrets about doing it. I really don't. Except…" She swallowed.

"Hmm?" he prompted, dipping his chin.

"I'm sorry I hurt you."

"You did hurt me." The admission sent a slicing pain through Gio's chest. He looked to the ceiling and blinked to hold the dampness in his eyes. "And I hurt you. I shouldn't have stayed away all those weeks." He tried to swallow away his regret for that lost time, but it would be with him forever. "Having that much power over each other felt dangerous. It was something I wanted to put back in the box, but I couldn't, no matter how hard I tried."

She brought her hand off his chest and into the nook of

her throat, but he caught it, prickled by that small with-drawal. Her desire to self-protect was his fault, he knew that, but he didn't know how to open himself to her. How to keep her feeling safe while he told her the truth.

They needed the truth, though. There had been too many secrets and prevarications. Only complete honesty would move them forward and that's what he wanted above all—a future with her.

He drew a deep breath that felt as though it was nothing but powdered glass, trying to find the words to make things right between them.

"I need you to remember two things, Molly. That I was taught not to expect love and that I wanted you from the first time I saw you."

She went very still. A discernible tension remained in her, but it told him she was listening very attentively.

He played with her fingers and caressed her upper arm.

"Given my history, you and I would have struggled whether you were carrying your friend's baby or not, but that certainly didn't help," he said with a humorless choke.

She coughed a similar dry chuckle.

"I knew you were different the first time I saw you. I knew you affected me in a way that was deeper than any-one else ever had. That's why I liked having you on the other side of Valentina. I could see you, but there was no emotional risk. Did I want to have sex with you? All the damned time."

She released another small sniff of laughter and snug-gled her head deeper into his chest, which encouraged him to continue.

"The fact you were my employee was a convenient fire-wall. When I promoted you into Valentina's position, I was looking forward to getting to know you better, but I was confident I could keep it professional. That didn't turn out as well as I'd hoped."

"You were going through a lot," she said, vouching for him, because she was far too generous. Her lashes lifted and the way she tilted her face up invited him to kiss her, but he made himself resist the urge and finish saying what he needed to say.

"I was devasted by the thought of losing Nonno, that's true. But I was just as troubled that you were talking of leaving. I could barely admit that to myself at the time. Saying all of this aloud here and now is still very hard."

She splayed her hand on his chest with such empathy, such care, he would swear she was leaving fingerprints against his heart, ones he would happily wear forever.

"Nonno's illness gave me the excuse to do what I wanted to do, which was shift our relationship into a personal one, but in a way that demanded very little emotional exposure."

A skeptical shadow entered her gaze.

"You don't believe that? Molly," he chided. "I hold Valentina in the highest esteem and she is loyal enough she would have gone along with a similar pretense. Frankly, it would have been an easier sell that she and I were spontaneously deciding to marry given our long association, but that subterfuge wouldn't have occurred to me if she'd still been with me. Engaging myself to you was about me hanging on to you in the most expedient way I could without admitting to anyone, especially myself, that I was afraid of losing you. I'm not proud of that. It was dishonest and I shouldn't have pressured you that way."

"I wouldn't have let it happen if I didn't already care for you," she chided, moving her hand so it became a pillow for the sharp weight of her chin on his chest. "I knew where the door was. I had credit cards and people I could call. I could have told Otto at any time that it was a lie. I let the engagement happen because it was *my* only chance to have a personal relationship with *you*."

"I wanted to believe you were with me by choice, but thank you. I needed to hear that." He combed his fingers into her soft, sweet-smelling hair.

"I shouldn't have let it go so far, though," she said with remorse.

"In what way? Sleeping with me? Telling me you love me?"

She bit her bottom lip and nodded.

"I've seen the lengths you'll go to when you love someone, Molly." He tried to swallow the lump in his throat, but it stubbornly stayed there. "Would you have *my* baby if I asked you to?"

"As a *surrogate*?" She picked up her head.

"As my *wife*."

She withdrew, rolling onto her back with a sharp wince.

"I'm handling this badly." He came up on an elbow, still loathe to fully expose his heart because it was so damn frightening.

On the other hand, he'd walked through the cold shadows of all the ways he could lose her. He knew now that even if she cheated on him or revealed some venality of character, if she abandoned him or lied or if death stalked her, he would still feel the same about her. He would carry this want, this need, to have her near.

It was terrifying and humbling to be this susceptible to someone, but he was beginning to understand that that was what love was. It was this horribly exposed sensation of having a hole in your soul, one that also let in an abundance of joy and light, passion and harmony. Belonging. It sounded too sentimental to call it "completion," but it was an end to feeling as though something was missing.

"You know that I'm at a higher risk to have the same complication with a future pregnancy?" Her brow angled into worry.

"Is that what you took from what I just said? *Bella*, we can find our own surrogate. We can adopt. That is a discussion for a year from now, when you're fully recovered and want to think about children. I was asking if you still love me. I want to say it to you, but—" He closed his eyes, hardly able to breathe, he stood on such a high precipice.

He knew he had to step off and trust that she would catch him. He knew that's how it was done. He knew she *would* catch him, but, *mio Dio*, it was hard.

"Gio," she whispered. Her hand came to his cheek.

"No. Shh. Let me do this," he urged her softly. "I can."

He opened his eyes and saw such a glow in her expression, it brought tears to his eyes and a swelling elation into his chest.

"I love you, Molly. I don't want you to go home with your mother. I want you to come home with me. I want you to be my wife and make a family with me however we can. I want you to be beside me for as long as we both shall live."

Her mouth trembled and tears flooded into her eyes. "I want that, too," she choked. "I love you so much."

How could something so hard be so easy in the end? He brought her hand back to his chest and gently, gently brought them into full contact so he could feel every curve and muscle and twitch and sigh. He covered her mouth with a hungry kiss and dragged her an inch closer, being careful, so very careful, because she was infinitely precious to him.

She was his heart. He understood that, now. But that was okay, because he was hers.

* * *

Two hours later, Molly woke cotton-headed from her nap. Gio was still holding her.

"Did you sleep?" she asked as she stretched and winced.

"No. But I didn't want to disturb you. It was nice to hold you again. I missed you." He rolled onto his back, moving with enviable lack of discomfort.

"I missed you, too." She was touched that he was so unabashed in saying it. Even so, she experienced a stab of shyness and asked, "Did I dream that we're in love and getting married or...?"

His mouth kicked sideways. "If it was a dream, I would like to make it real." He fished into his trouser pocket and brought out Nonna's ring. "Let's hope three times is the charm. Will you marry me, Molly?"

"Yes!" Here came the tears again, but they were happy ones.

After a dab of hand cream, the ring went on and they went out to tell her mother and Libby.

Patricia gave her a heartfelt hug, but Libby, being on the verge of twelve and still stung by all the secrets that had been kept from her, asked skeptically, "Do you mean it this time?"

"We do," Molly insisted, and tucked her hand into Gio's.

"All right, then." Libby hugged her, then hugged Gio. "You don't mind if I come live with you guys, right?"

"I'm sure your mother would mind, but I would not," Gio said with good humor, then he winked at Patricia. "Why don't we visit my grandfather before you fly home, so you'll know where to find her if she runs away?"

They married at Nonno's villa that December, when Libby was off school for Christmas holidays.

It was a beautiful, intimate ceremony with only Otto, her mother and sister, Sasha and Rafael, and the sweet and mighty Atticus. He had been out of hospital more than a month and Molly saw him as frequently as she could. He was still small, but he ate nonstop and had a terrifically demanding cry, one that cut off with comical abruptness when Libby gathered him into her arms.

"Do you remember me?" Libby asked him with quiet joy. "I'm your sister." She leaned close and whispered, "I'm also kind of your aunt."

They had confided the surrogacy arrangement to Otto, so he knew Molly was only a few months postpartum, but he still gently chided Molly. "When will you give me one of those?"

Her doctor had pronounced her fully healed from the surgery, but suggested she wait a little longer before attempting pregnancy, to give any potential baby its best chance for success.

She didn't mind waiting. She had a passionate husband who tumbled her to the bed in his jet when they left the villa for their honeymoon in Australia.

"We have twenty-something hours in the air," he informed her. "I intend to take advantage of you for every one of those hours."

"Show me."

He did, stripping her without ceremony. They knew each other very well now and flagrantly ran their hands over each other, enticing and caressing, trying to see who would break first.

It was her. It was always her. He loved making her shudder and cry out and weakly succumb to whatever he wanted. Today, after two shattering orgasms, he left a final damp kiss between her thighs, then rolled her stomach onto a pillow and guided himself to the still sensitized flesh he had pleasured so mercilessly.

"Ready, *cuore mio*?" he asked against her nape, sending shivers of fresh anticipation down her spine.

"Yes," she moaned, arching with invitation, longing for his thick length to fill her.

He did, then he roamed his hands over her cheeks and grasped her hips and unleashed his full power, claiming her with proprietary thoroughness.

She loved it. Loved him. It was the randy, earthy lovemaking they hadn't been able to enjoy when she'd been pregnant and still healing. It was rough, yes, but it was a joyous, carnal experience, one that reinforced the trust between them. The fierce bond that had already withstood so much.

When they peaked together, they were together in the most elemental, indelible way. It was pure and perfect. Eternal.

But as their skin cooled and their hearts returned to a resting rate, she noticed he wore a slight frown.

"What's wrong?"

"Nothing." He closed one eye, rueful at not being immediately honest. "I'm envious of Sasha and Rafael," he admitted. "Every time I see them with Atticus, I'm impatient for us to have a baby of our own, but I don't want to give this up yet, either." He brought her hand to his lips. "I don't know if you noticed, but I *love* having wild sex with you."

"You don't want to give that up and go back to visiting me in the hospital while I'm on strict bed rest? That's weird."

"I do not," he said somberly. "Perhaps we should consider other options."

"I'd like to try getting pregnant first. Not yet," she added quickly. "But soon. If we run into complications, I won't put myself through a lot of procedures. We'll look at other options right away, but for now…" She rolled atop him, reveling in the fact she could push her own body to its limits while testing his. "You made a certain promise about this flight. Have we crossed the equator? Because I'm about to." She began kissing her way south.

He made a noise of agony when she took him in her mouth, then said on a sigh of bliss, "I love you so very much, *mia amata*."

She smiled, not surprised that he would say that to her when she was anointing him in this very intimate way, but later, when they were both sated and falling asleep in each other's arms, he said it again with deep sincerity.

"I do love you, you know."

"I know," she assured him. It was as real inside her as breath and blood. "I love you, too."

EPILOGUE

TWO DAYS BEFORE their second anniversary, Molly gave birth at the villa in Genoa to a boy with brown hair like his mother and blue eyes like his father. Patricia had monitored her very healthy pregnancy, then attended her through the labor and caught the baby. Libby brought ice chips and texted reports to Sasha. Gio cut the cord.

Otto came in the moment he was invited, then wept when they told him he was holding his namesake.

Everything about the experience was as perfect as Molly could have imagined it, but when she woke in the night, Gio was awake, holding baby Otto and wearing a pensive frown.

"What's wrong?" she asked with a skip of alarm, starting to sit up.

He lifted his face to reveal damp eyes. "I was so afraid I wouldn't have this feeling," he choked. "Now it's here and it's so fierce, I don't know what to do with it."

"Love?" She tucked her chin, absolutely undone when he showed her his heart like this.

Gio was a man of great affection and generosity. He spoiled Libby, which she did not need, given everything Sasha and Rafael did for her. He was constantly trying to soften Patricia's life any way she would allow, too, coaxing her to let him buy her a new car and book her vacations. He wanted to buy her a home in Genoa so they could all see each other more. Now that her first grandchild was here, Patricia was coming around to the idea.

Gio had proven himself a doting husband and family man even before he had refused to travel farther than the office here in Genoa for the duration of Molly's pregnancy. She and their son were his top priority and always would be. She knew that.

"It's okay to love him that hard. He won't break," she reassured him, then teased, "Look at me. I'm alive and well and you love me a *lot*."

"*I* might break, I carry so much love for you." He came to sit on the edge of the bed with Otto still in the crook of his arm. He cupped the side of her neck and leaned down to drop a kiss on her lips. "*Ti amo, cuore mio.* Thank you for all that you've given me. Not just our beautiful son, but the ability to love you both with all my strength."

Her mouth started to quiver. "I don't know where I would have put my love for you if you hadn't opened your heart to take it." They shared a longer kiss, one so ripe with emotion, it brought tears to her eyes.

She peeked at their son, who was fast asleep. Her heart swelled a dozen sizes. What an astonishing little miracle.

"Have you slept at all?" she asked, recalling that Gio had been awake since her first labor pain in the early hours of yesterday.

"I will soon, but I want to hold him." He rose and came around the bed so he could sit against the pillows beside her. "I want him to know I'm here. I'll always be here," he vowed to their boy, kissing the infant's cheek. "For both of you."

She believed him. With a smile on her lips, and the weight of her husband's hand over hers where she rested it on his thigh, she drifted to sleep.

* * * * *

THE ITALIAN'S
PREGNANT ENEMY

MAISEY YATES

MILLS & BOON

CHAPTER ONE

LYSSIA ANDERSON HAD a plan. Pink boots, and extremely racy underwear. The boots were useful in the current climate—the ski fields at her father's Alpine resort were freezing. The underwear was not, but that was fine. It wasn't related to the weather. It was related to her plan.

To Carter Westfield, and the growing connection between them.

Her father's new assistant was just…the best. Endlessly caring, so in touch with his feelings, so…sweet. And he was so cute.

Just so cute.

She had never lost her head over a guy before. Not once. And Carter was…

Well, her father sending them on this mission to audit the goings-on at the ski resort was just perfect.

She was thrilled her dad was involving her with the company to begin with. She was at a weird crossroads—one where she was trying to decide what to do with her own company, and what she would do if she did let it go, and she'd finally told her father that it would be nice if there was a space for her at Anderson Luxury Brand Group because she had interned there after all.

He'd listened. He'd told her he would value her input on

the condition of the Swiss ski property and that was almost as exciting as the prospect of hooking up with Carter.

They both felt linked, in some ways. She was starting to feel stagnant and there was an underlying discomfort in that stagnation. A feeling that she was treading water when she didn't believe people had that kind of time.

Her mother had died in her twenties. Life wasn't infinite, time wasn't guaranteed.

Onward!

She tightened her parka more firmly around her body—the underwear was beneath layers of warmth, obviously—and pushed open the doors of the lobby. The wind bit into her skin and she fought to keep from reacting to it. She didn't need to go shrieking about the cold in front of the locals.

People already thought of her as a soft heiress, she knew that. A nepo baby. She frequently made online lists of *Twenty-Five Nepo Babies Who Got It All from Their Daddy*, or whatever.

Some nepo baby she was. Her father's luxury vacation empire wasn't even ever going to her. Which was why she'd started her own business three years ago. Which landed her on other, even meaner online lists: *The Least Successful Nepo Babies Squandering Daddy's Money*.

Lyssia Anderson, of the Anderson Luxury Brand Group, runs a tiny boutique interiors business, making furniture and tchotchkes no one asked for.

One has to wonder what a little rich girl who grew up with a pony and an indoor pool knows about what the poor want in their houses. One of her pink couches, which professes to have "custom premium fabrics," retails for over ten thousand dollars.

No wonder she hasn't taken the world by storm.

Not that Lyssia had articles like that memorized.

She was damned if she did and if she didn't. She'd started her own business and it was a source of mockery and disappointment, but if she did nothing she'd be a leech, and if she worked for her father she would just be folded into his dynasty and on and on and on.

She was twenty-three. It wasn't like she was lagging hideously behind. Her company was solvent. It was just that people thought she should be *successful*, so that they could tell her she didn't deserve the success. And until she was, they were going to sneer about how she was losing at life on the easiest setting.

Blah-blah-blah. So many people tore down the achievements of others, but what did they build? Nothing. She'd built something at least.

And she had options.

The problem was, maybe it was true. The business hadn't grown very much in the last few years, and at a certain point she had to wonder if there was truth to what was being said. If she had the backing of her father's name, why was she so mid?

But then her dad seemed to think she was mid too, since she had never been the potential heir to his empire, despite being his only child.

Not when there was Dario.

Something hot churned in her stomach when she thought of him. Dario Rivelli, the antithesis of a nep baby. He'd clawed his way up from nothing, had been taken under her father's wing when he was twenty and making waves in the business world.

He'd gone out on his own, had taken the green housing industry by storm, with groundbreaking build techniques that had quite literally changed the world. Then he'd pivoted into eco-tourism, which had brought him back into her father's life. And her father had…promised him everything.

"Dario Rivelli is the future."

Her father said it like Dario was a god.

But then, her father had always treated Dario like a god. Or perhaps just the son he'd always wanted and never had.

But seriously, he was. Her mom died before her parents could have more kids, and had left this space that contained so many possibilities and no answers. Her dad had been lost in grief, unable to parent, unable to handle Lyssia's emotions and by the time he emerged…

Dario had appeared. Tall and bronze and eminently golden from the inside out.

Lyssia had been keenly away of Dario as competition from the time she was twelve years old. He'd been a grown man and she'd been…jealous of him. Not even mentioning that his dark gaze had always made her feel like something had gone haywire inside of her.

That was how she'd thought of it then. It was how she thought of it now.

The problem was, Lyssia tried. It was only that she wasn't Dario, so what could she do?

Dario might be like a son to her father, but he wasn't like a brother to her. Granted, she did delight in irritating, infuriating and otherwise refusing to be impressed by him. Dario seemed to pride himself on his people management skills. Consequentially, Lyssia refused to be manageable when in his presence.

She'd watched Dario work a room—many times. He was excellent at reading people and figuring out exactly how to behave with them. Lyssia refused to be known. When he looked at her with his cool, dark eyes, she responded with fire. When he treated her to dry, scathing commentary, she responded with spiky words and a placid expression. She knew Dario couldn't tell if she was toying with him, if she was incompetent or an airhead.

When she'd interned at Anderson after she graduated high school she'd been installed as Dario's assistant when he was present at the office and she had absolutely delighted in acting the most unserious person imaginable, much to his irritation.

Of course, in hindsight she could see that hadn't done her many favors.

Act unserious long enough and people believed it.

She wasn't unserious.

She sniffed against the wind—her nose was running—and looked out at the snow, trying to see if there was a vehicle coming for her yet. It was clear and pristine out there. The sky was blue, but there was a band of dark gray clouds looming over the mountains that looked portentous.

Finally, a sleek, black Land Rover pulled up to the curb and Lyssia got inside, her stomach tightening. Carter would be at the chalet she was staying in.

The driver loaded her bags into the back and Lyssia thanked him, even though she could barely hear her voice over the sound of her heart pounding in her head.

She wondered if Carter was expecting this? For her to say it was time for them to take things to the next level. They'd kissed. Like, twice but still. But she wasn't a *child*. And no, she didn't have a lot of physical experience with men, but she was sophisticated enough to know no one was *making out* these days and ending it there.

People were sex positive and liberated. And she was also those things, she had just never been positive she wanted to have sex with anyone, so she hadn't done it. Which was liberation in and of itself, wasn't it?

She wanted to have sex with Carter, though. He made her feel warm and happy, and seen, and wasn't that the thing that was worth waiting for? She thought it might be.

The truth was, he made her feel happy. He made her feel good about herself. That was what she wanted. Someone who made her feel good.

There were just so many hard things. Carter felt easy.

She had been so tempted to text him the whole day but then she'd kept reminding herself to try and be cool. To try and just let it happen. It was very hard to be cool.

As the chalet came into view, her palms got sweaty. Great. No one wanted to be seduced by a woman with sweaty palms. Only then did she think perhaps she should take her mittens off.

But then they stopped and she knew she'd be headed outside again, so the mittens stayed on.

She got out of the car, and the driver handled her bags, bringing them up to the front of the chalet.

Pure adrenaline spiked in her veins. She was going to do it. She wouldn't even wait for it to get dark. That's how sex positive she was.

She went through the door of the chalet, expecting to see Carter there with his laptop. But he wasn't in the grand living area. Nor did he have anything set up in the kitchen. No milk frother. No French press. He kept both on his desk back in Manhattan.

Well, then she could go and take her clothes off. Strip down to her underwear…greet him that way when he arrived.

She laughed out loud in the empty house. No. That was her hard limit.

Still the thought made her feel edgy and a bit…aroused. She didn't hate that.

She went back to the front of the chalet and dragged her bags inside, then began to try and ferret them up the stairs.

She never saw the point in packing light until moments like this, when there wasn't someone around to help her with the heavy lifting.

She grabbed the largest bag first and began to try and drag it up the steep staircase. She struggled, grunted and otherwise made all sorts of very uncute sounds, but finally managed to get it to the top of the stairs.

Then she raced down the stairs and grabbed her other bag, thunking up three steps, then a fourth.

"Trouble, *cara*?"

She shrieked, and released the bag, which slid forward like a sled on the snowy hillside outside, and hit the elegant, gray wood floor below and popped open like a plastic Easter egg, spilling lingerie all over like fruity candy.

Then she looked up and her eyes met *his*.

No.

No this was not happening.

Her heart beat rapidly, like she was a frightened rodent cornered at the edge of her burrow. But she wasn't frightened of Dario Rivelli.

She was *nothing* of him.

So her heart needed to calm the hell down.

"What the…actual…f… What are you doing here?" she asked, hoping she didn't look as red-faced and undone as she felt. As her suitcase looked.

All her underwear.

Her *seduction* underwear.

That Dario was now looking at dispassionately.

He had a cup of coffee in his hand, his white shirtsleeves pushed up to his elbows. The large watch on his wrist somehow served to highlight the muscles on his forearms. She declined to figure out how that worked.

His shoulders were broad and his white shirt rested perfectly over the broad muscles of his chest. It didn't tug at the buttons or anything half so unseemly, yet still seemed far too tight because she shouldn't be able to like, see his muscles? No.

His dark pants were also tailored in a manner she felt to be borderline obscene. She ought not to notice his thigh muscles or…

She forced her gaze back to his face. It was no better. He was practically sneering at her. His dark eyes carrying that hint of mocking humor—as ever. His jaw square, his nose straight as a blade, his lips…

Did not bear reporting on.

At all.

She wasn't looking at his mouth and she never would.

She gathered herself up and walked slowly, very slowly, down the stairs.

"How long have you been standing there?"

He ostentatiously checked his watch. "A couple of minutes."

"You didn't think to announce your presence?" she asked. "Or…help me?"

He lifted one dark brow. "I am a feminist, *cara*. I would never assume you were in need of help without your asking for it."

A feminist her ass.

But she refused to give him a reaction. She outright did. She kept her chin tilted up, her body straight. "Perhaps, once I return my things to their rightful place, you could help."

He moved nearer to her detritus and brushed his foot

against the corner of one of her lace nightgown sets as if he was checking a small, limp animal for signs of life.

No dead animals here. It was only her pride that was in danger of dying. That was all.

She slowly—very slowly so as not to seem eager or rushed—bent at the knees and began to shovel her things back into her bag.

He watched her do that, sipping his coffee as if he had all the time in the world. As if he wasn't a very busy, very important billionaire man who had no business being at this chalet when it was a job her father had sent his daughter and his assistant to do. So. Beneath. Him.

But there he was. As if he didn't have a full calendar, demands for interviews every second of the day, and didn't appear in online articles with titles like "Billionaires You'd Actually Like to F—"

"Now, you would like help?" he asked, as soon as she got the zipper down.

"Yes," she said, feeling breathless from exertion and absolutely nothing else. "If you don't mind."

"Not at all. I live to serve you, Lyssia."

She nearly wretched.

He picked up the bag, hefted it over his shoulder, while still holding his coffee in his other hand, and carried it easily up the stairs. Lyssia sniffed and began to trudge up behind him.

She didn't want to sound too interested or eager when she asked her next question. "When are you leaving, Dario?"

Oops.

"I have only just arrived," he said, as he stopped just in front of her bedroom door.

She stopped. "What?"

"I am here for the inspection of the resort."

"What?"

"Your father asked that I come and oversee."

"But Carter and I were supposed to—"

"Your father wanted someone with more seniority to come and inspect, and I offered to do it."

So. She wasn't actually good enough as an inspector for the resort. Of course not. Dario would need to consult and Dario didn't even work for her father anymore. But he was looming about, poised on the brink of an "acquisition" that was really just inheritance, and so his opinion mattered most of all.

All that and Dario was now staying in the same house as her and Carter? Like a big, brooding chaperone?

She could see it now. The real problem wouldn't even be Dario supervising them, it would be the feral monster Dario brought out of her every time they had to share space. She would spend the whole week fighting with him, picking at him, while he sipped his espresso and looked unbothered until he wasn't, until she won her victory. And she'd forget to even kiss Carter, let along bang him.

No. No. She wouldn't let that happen. Dario didn't have to be a barrier. They had their own…whole thing. Whatever it was. It had nothing to do with what she and Carter had.

"Carter is coming, right?" They could find another room.

Dario lifted a dark brow. "No. He stayed behind. Is that an issue for you, *cara*?"

It felt like a black hole had opened up under her feet. But it refused to swallow her. What was the point of a black hole if it wouldn't even swallow you whole when you were faced with the most horrifying scenario possible?

"Stop calling me *cara*," she snapped. "You don't even like me."

"It's said with irony, are you unaware of irony?"

"A feminist and a comedian, Dario. How did the world get so lucky?"

Here they were. Right in the pocket. Lyssia and Dario and their epic need to go back and forth until one of them broke. It made her forget everything. And everyone. And often the point of what the initial conversation was. Like the whole world fell away and it was just the two of them.

Dario lifted one dark brow and something came alive within her. "Some have said I am a creation of all that the world required. I spontaneously appeared when it was in its darkest hour. And lo."

"The anti-Christ came forth to usher in the end of days?" she asked, sweetly. She thought. A joke, obviously.

"I have not seen any locusts about recently. Though, it may be because of the weather."

"Hmm. Indeed. Locusts are notoriously snow-shy." They stood there in the hall, regarding each other.

Her stomach tightened, her chest getting heavy. It was almost impossible to breathe. Because she hated him so much. So, so much. It was always like this and it never got better. If anything, he had gotten worse in the last couple years.

He was so arrogant.

So tall. It was infuriating. His shoulders were so…so broad and his hands were so big. And she didn't like any of it.

"Thank you," she said, pointedly.

"You do not wish me to place the bag in your room? I know you're accustomed to a full-service life."

She scoffed. "As if you aren't at this point."

It had probably been years since he'd had to see to his own needs. He probably had a driver to drive him in a car and a butler to brush his teeth and a woman to…

Well.

Whatever. She wasn't going to follow that thought up.

She knew full well what women thought of Dario. If there was an event, and he was there, he was sure to have a beautifully polished woman on his arm. A model, an actress, an influencer, a high-society maven, as long as she looked nice in couture.

He didn't have any trouble pulling the kind of woman who looked effortlessly at ease on his arm.

He didn't respond to her jab, which was annoying. They'd had a pretty good streak going. Instead he opened the bedroom door without her permission and brought her bags inside.

She slipped into the room and realized her mistake immediately. The feeling that had been throbbing between them in the hall—the hatred, that's what it was—seemed to expand in here, making it impossible to think, let alone breathe or make a normal facial expression.

He said nothing. He only looked at her. The stark lines of his chiseled face seeming more pronounced just suddenly. Like he was taller, suddenly. Broader, suddenly.

Closer, suddenly.

"All right, *cara*?"

"Yes," she said, her throat scratchy.

Suddenly, she didn't even want to needle him. She just wanted him out of her space.

And she would have it. Tomorrow, she would arrange to have herself moved to a room in the chalet. She was going to finish this job, because as much as she wanted to fly back to Manhattan so she could go ahead and complete her Carter mission, she couldn't let her father think she was putting her personal life over her work. Even if sending Dario to supervise her was an insult.

If she wanted to girl boss her way out of mediocrity, she had to prioritize work when the opportunities came her way.

But she would get in touch with him and make a date for when she got away from here.

"Thanks, Dario," she said.

She hoped the definitive thanks would give him the hint to get on his way.

"Anything for you, of course, Lyssia."

He was mocking her, obviously.

She didn't return volley.

He turned and walked out of the room and left her there to look around the space. It was a lovely room. Big picture windows looked out over the snow. The bright white reflecting beautiful, clean light all around. The bed was modern, low and on a platform, with a white bedspread. The rug right next to a modern, glass fireplace was white reindeer hide, with pale bamboo flooring beneath.

She kicked her shoes off and sighed. The floor was warmed from radiant heat beneath and it felt like luxury. The bathroom was lovely, with a big, deep white tub and slate-gray floating counter.

This would have been a great place to take a bath with Carter.

She sighed wistfully, the romantic scene in her mind feeling cruel now that it wasn't happening. She could so easily imagine sitting with him in the tub, covered in bubbles, sipping champagne.

They would talk about the day they'd had and it would be so…sweet.

She frowned.

And for some reason her brain glitched right then and the picture in her mind tore in two. Behind that image, of herself and Carter with all his golden handsomeness…was Dario.

But in that picture there was no champagne. There were no smiles. No bubbles.

She was across from Dario, naked in the water, his broad chest muscular and covered with dark hair. The look on his face was…angry. Intense. His dark eyes never left her as he moved in to—

"No!" she shouted and leaped back from the empty tub.

What the ever-loving hell was wrong with her?

She needed to get out of this house.

She needed to get away from Dario Rivelli.

The man was her nemesis. And nothing more.

CHAPTER TWO

LYSSIA ANDERSON WAS the most beautiful pain in his ass.

Dario sat in front of the fireplace in the expansive living area of the chalet and pondered his present situation. He shouldn't have agreed to do this. But Nathan Anderson was the closest thing he had to a father—that he acknowledged—in this world, and when the man asked him to do things, he found himself doing them.

No one else on earth could compel Dario to interrupt his schedule to do them a favor.

He thought of Lyssia. Blonde, wide-eyed and hapless, staring at a pile of lingerie at the bottom of the stairs.

A reluctant growl rose in his throat.

The problem with Lyssia was that he could see her. More clearly than she saw herself at times, he had a feeling. She thought he enraged her because she hated him. And perhaps she did. But that wasn't the real reason she puffed up like an angry kitten every time he got too close to her.

Ten years her senior, and vastly more experienced, Dario did not have a life that lent itself to the sorts of blind spots Lyssia still possessed.

She had clearly imagined she would be having a dirty weekend with her father's pet of a PA. He was the most pathetic puppy of a boy Dario had ever met. Lyssia was obviously besotted with him.

She could control him. That was why.

That was not what Lyssia needed, though. And sadly for her, not what she wanted. Not really. She thought she did, and she might even have some fun with him, but he would never be enough to satisfy her.

He wondered how long it would take her to realize.

That while he truly did find her to be an annoying brat, and he had a feeling she thought he was the most arrogant bastard on the planet, the thing that pulsed between them whenever they clashed was not merely hatred, but desire.

He could remember the moment she'd become a problem.

He'd known Lyssia since she was a child. But he'd only had a vague concept of her. She'd been the little creature running around Nathan's home on his rare visits there, but he'd only ever seen her in passing. After her mother's death, Lyssia had begun to spend more time in the office. A sullen teen with questionable fashion sense, she'd often been found lying upside down on a couch in the lobby of her father's multibillion-dollar company, like an insolent throw pillow, or sitting in her father's office chair while he was in a meeting.

At eighteen, she'd started an internship there, and he'd been forced to interact with her. At that point, Dario no longer worked at Anderson's. In fact, his company had acquired it under the umbrella of his other interests, as part of Nathan's retirement plan. They had a ten-year contract that would slowly begin to turn the operation over to Rivelli Holdings, integrating financial systems and other areas of the company over time while trying to retain as much staff as possible.

Nathan was very conscientious about such things, and Dario appreciated it because he wasn't certain if he would have been.

He'd come to Manhattan an angry thirteen-year-old who'd lied about his age to get a contract on a cruise ship sailing between Europe and the US. He'd seen it as a way out of Rome, and he'd wanted out badly.

And he'd gotten what he wanted. He'd spent the first years of his life helpless. After the worst had happened, he'd realized he had two choices. To sit down and die, or to use the breath he had in his body to ensure he would never be helpless again.

He hadn't been. He'd gotten off the ship and disappeared into the city. He'd fashioned a new identity for himself. Gotten papers. Gotten work. In kitchens, in restaurants. Finally, in hotels. He had been tall for his age, handsome and in possession of natural charisma.

Lyssia might disagree, but most other people found him charming.

He'd used that to his advantage. He was an expert at reading people. At mimicking manners and voices. He'd worked to leave most of his accent behind. He had just enough to sound delightfully foreign when it suited him. He'd educated himself by speaking to the people around him. He'd learned to talk, dress, act and comport himself as a member of the upper class he saw come into the hotels he worked in.

He'd gotten a job at the Anderson's on Fifth Avenue when he was seventeen. By the time he was nineteen, he was the manager. At twenty-one he was managing all of the hotels in North American. At twenty-four he'd been the global strategist for the brand and had grown the company astronomically, earning himself a reputation and a vast fortune.

At twenty-five he'd gone out on his own, with his mentor's blessing. He'd bought a struggling hotel chain and had turned it around, had made it a business, rehabbing old resorts, before beginning to build new resorts that catered to eco tourists.

He'd been a billionaire before his thirtieth birthday.

It was then that Nathan asked him to consult on making his resorts as close to net zero as possible, and they'd come up with the idea of his eventual takeover.

It was the closest thing to family Dario had ever known.

The closest thing to an inheritance he could have imagined. It wasn't the value that mattered. It was the trust.

He'd never had anything like that before, and he would never take it for granted.

But that had meant that even though he was not an employee of Anderson, he still had a lot of business to do with Anderson. Which meant he was exposed to Lyssia. Often.

At the time he'd had an office in the Anderson Group building in Manhattan and Lyssia was his assistant when he was in the office.

He'd lost track of the amount of coffees he'd been delivered with her patented pout.

She had the most beautiful mouth. Her top lip was fuller than the bottom lip, pale pink. Her lips curved down at the corners. It was an eternal sulk.

She would bring it in and bend over his desk, smelling like sunshine and something sweet, and very expensive.

He'd been twenty-eight at the time and not interested in teenagers, even if they were technically adults in the eyes of the law.

Until one day she'd brought a coffee, and she'd tripped.

He'd jumped up out of his chair and grabbed her forearm, preventing her from crashing headfirst into the carpet, and the coffee had gone all over the front of his shirt.

She'd paused for a moment, frozen.

Then she'd looked up at him, and the sulky corners of

her mouth had turned upward. She'd smiled. And then she had laughed.

Loud and long, like music, as he'd held her, wearing a sodden shirt.

He'd set her back on her feet. It felt as if the room had turned, while they'd stayed standing right in the same place they'd been at before.

But it had forced him to see her from a new angle and he had never been able to unsee it. For five years, he'd been held captive by her beauty.

But Lyssia was the only woman in the world who didn't find him charming.

Even if she did, she was the daughter of his mentor and he had no desire to negatively impact that relationship by touching his baby girl. God forbid.

Dario wanted neither marriage, nor children.

Lyssia would want both. And a golden retriever. As her husband and her pet.

He stood up from his place by the fire and walked into the kitchen, getting a pot of soup out and putting it on the burner. Then he found a boule of bread and sliced it, taking out a large block of butter as well. A simple dinner, but fine for him.

He loved luxury, he could not deny it. Excess would never fail to make the streets feel farther and farther behind him. But he also didn't mind simple food, simple evenings.

He took his bowl of soup to the table by the window and looked out at the scene. It was twilight, and all the snow was brilliant blue.

Silence was a luxury. In Rome a man could scarcely achieve it, even with millions. It had been far beneath a boy who lived on the streets.

Silence was his favorite indulgence.

"Dario."

He lifted his head and saw his little blonde problem standing in the doorway. She had shattered his silence. Her hair was wet and she was wearing a white T-shirt that fell down to her knees, with a pair of sweatpants underneath.

"Did you have a bath, Lyssia?"

Her blue eyes widened, her cheeks going pink. "No. A shower. Why?"

Why indeed? Because he'd asked the first question that had come to his mind. Never a good idea. "Just concerned you were engaged in some sort of social media challenge where you stuck your head in a snowbank for clout."

"As I'm known to do," she said, dryly. "Is there dinner?"

She expected him to have handled dinner, of course. And he had. She was very spoiled, and he had a feeling she had no real idea that she was. But watching her careen about with her luggage she couldn't manage, only to emerge hours after he'd left her in her room looking hungry and fragile, he wondered if the child could survive for five minutes on her own, even if she was in a luxury chalet.

"Yes, of course. Soup and bread. Feel free to avail yourself."

He should leave. He didn't.

Lyssia returned a moment later with a bowl of soup and a stack of bread on a plate.

She sat at the table across from him and she looked... disappointed to see him there.

"Sad that I'm not your boyfriend?" he asked.

Her cheeks turned pinker still. "Carter isn't my boyfriend."

"But you expected to meet him here and stay with him."

"Yes," she said.

"He didn't tell you about the change?"

She opened her mouth, then closed it, and opened it again. Like a very small guppy. "Well, in fairness to him, I don't think he knew I was hoping for this to be more than business."

A funny thing about Lyssia. She didn't lie to him. She might jab at him verbally, she might fight and hiss and spit, but she didn't lie. Then, he didn't lie to her either. Why? They drove each other mad. He had no reputation to preserve with her, and she none with him. Dropping bombs was more fun than crafting narratives. And they both seemed to take that tactic.

"How long does it take to send a text?" he asked.

"He's busy," she said, her teeth clenched.

"Have you spoken to him?"

"Not yet. But I haven't texted him either."

"You could call."

"I will tomorrow," she said.

Interesting. He would have thought that thwarted young lovers wouldn't be able to spend even a moment apart. Unless they were not lovers yet. That could very well be.

She'd obviously intended for this week to change things, in that case.

"It seems poor form to leave a woman guessing."

"Maybe people in your generation need to be in constant contact."

His generation. He couldn't help himself. He laughed. "*Cara*, a man who wants a woman makes it plain, regardless of his generation. If he does not, then he is not a man, and he does not want you."

"First of all that's very gender essentialist, and second of all, that isn't true. People's lives don't revolve around romance, you know. They have to prioritize themselves too. Carter has likely had a long day dealing with my father—

I used to assist both him and you so I know how blessedly annoying it can be."

"Yes, I'm known for that."

"And," she continued, "he probably has to engage in some self-care before going to bed and preparing for work tomorrow."

"Self…care?"

"Yes. Lighting a candle, listening to Enya, doing a sheet mask."

Her expression was entirely bland. He couldn't tell if she was being serious or not.

"I do not understand how this is care?"

"OMG, of course you don't."

She was goading him. He could do one better.

"Lyssia, if I had a beautiful woman waiting for my call I would call her. What is a lit candle for if not to gaze at your lover in firelight?" Her eyelashes fluttered. She looked away from him. He felt something wicked tighten his gut. Something he knew full well he shouldn't indulge. "What is music for, if not a soundtrack to which you might seduce your lover?"

Her eyes had gone glassy and she was looking at him now. "And the sheet mask?"

"I do not know what that is."

"It's for your skin."

"I still don't know what it is."

"It makes your skin look…glowy."

He laughed. "Now that really is useless. Nothing makes a woman's skin glow better than the aftereffects of lovemaking. A man who needs a *sheet mask* is not an accomplished lover."

She sounded like she was wheezing. "In this case it's for his skin, not mine."

"Either way."

"Well, that's how you see things," she said. "People now might argue that's toxic."

"To be thought of at all times? Desired at all times?"

"Yes. It's not that deep."

He huffed a laugh. "Then why bother with it?"

It was a disingenuous question. His relationships were never deep. But she didn't seem like she would be that sort of person. She was...

It was difficult to describe Lyssia, who seemed to take many of life's luxuries for granted, but was also emotional, passionate and compassionate...in certain ways.

She could also be scathing, sharp and sarcastic. With him. Only ever with him.

"You're indoctrinated by Fairy-Tale Culture," she said. "Entertainment aimed at children that centers on romantic relationships and only depicts happy endings containing conventional romances have poisoned you."

He did not bother to ask her why she thought he might have consumed such media. "Yes, Lyssia, that is my Achilles' heel. I am an old-fashioned romantic."

He stared at her, his face perfectly blank.

She stared back and frowned. "Are...you?"

She thought him humorless, and as a result could never really tell when he was simply being dry.

He did wonder how much of that she turned back on him.

"I've been planning my wedding since I was a small boy."

"You...have?"

He declined to answer.

"My point is," she said. "Just because you don't understand something doesn't mean it's *less than*."

"Ah. A good thing you told me since you did not, in fact,

make your point. My point, *cara*, is that just because you have an internet connection it does not make you an expert."

"I think I can claim to be the expert on the situationship that I'm in."

He frowned. "What is that word?"

"It's like a relationship but not as binding." She lifted her spoon out of her bowl and swirled it in the air. "A situation that is relationship adjacent."

"I should have invested in space travel so I could leave this planet."

"So pressed," she said, putting her spoon back down into her soup.

"If I seem *pressed* to you it is merely because I'm trying to explain to a spoiled rich girl why she should value herself a bit more, when from my perspective you should value yourself innately, given the advantages you have."

She frowned. "You think by being with Carter I'm not valuing myself?"

"It seems like it to me."

"And also, why should I innately value myself exactly? Because my dad loves some random dude more than he loves me, so much so that he's sold off my inheritance to said man?"

He was the random man, he realized. And this was the first he'd heard of her feeling...angry about him taking over Anderson. Also, she was being well provided for. So he knew she was being over the top by saying this; he just wasn't certain how much of it was true and how much was part of her brand of drama. "I was unaware your father was leaving you penniless."

She scoffed. "He isn't. But he's turning the company over to you and he never once asked me if I wanted…"

"Are you an accomplished businessperson in the hospitality industry?"

"Well...no."

"Did you work your way up from nothing through every level of hotel work?"

"I...no."

"Have you ever had an hourly wage job in your entire, privileged life?"

"No. But."

"I am more qualified than you are. If you had ever been interested in taking over your father's empire, then you would have worked for it, wouldn't you?"

"I was eighteen when he made the decision to give it to you. I barely had a chance. And anyway, it isn't about whether or not I should be in charge, or if you're more... qualified. It's just... If I were his son would he have done this?"

It was a fair question, he supposed. But as his relationship with his own father was so much more toxic than she could ever imagine, he'd never once turned over this sort of philosophical ridiculousness.

"I was on a ship bound for America when I was *thirteen*."

"With the pilgrims?" she asked.

He laughed. "Very funny. I was working in hospitality then, and I continued to do so. My course was set by the time I was eighteen. I don't view age as an excuse."

He wasn't entirely sure how much of his personal biography she knew. It would be entirely on brand for her to be completely studied in it, yet look at him with wide eyes and say she'd had no idea.

"Have you not read my biography?"

"The one where you had a literal sea monster's baby?

Oh, sorry, I think that was some weird fanfic I found on the internet."

"Did you write it?"

She smiled. "I did write you into a story of mine when I was twelve or so."

"The handsome prince."

"No. You were the villain."

He smiled. Slowly. "Sadly for you, Lyssia, I think you're drawn to a villain."

She laughed, and then inhaled her bread on accident and began hacking while laughing. "Please! *Please.* I do not like villains. I like nice men with nice hair and French presses on their desks. Who ask how my day is and who kiss like summer rain. And who will appreciate my underwear, not stare at them like they're flat animals."

And just like that his mind went back to that underwear, scattered about the floor, not like *flat animals*, whatever the hell that meant, but like forbidden confetti for a party he had no business wanting to attend.

And yet she vexed him. Tormented him. When nothing else on the earth dared to.

"Has he called?" he asked.

Lyssia's mouth dropped. Her cheeks went scarlet. "I've already told you…"

"Careful, your mask is slipping."

Her eyes narrowed. "There is no mask, Dario. We aren't all committed to facades."

"So this is you, then."

"This is me," she said, standing from the table. "I am exactly what you see here. I am the ever-underestimated Lyssia Anderson."

"Sheet masks and self-care."

"If that's all you got out of the last couple hours, the problem is you, not me."

It wasn't. She was smart and funny, and angry. Very angry. At him, he thought, but also at her father. He knew she felt undermined by his presence. But the truth was, Dario felt like Nathan was taking care of Lyssia by ensuring the business went on, and healthily. Lyssia had many shares in the company in her name, and she would be getting money when the acquisition went through. Her pride was wounded, perhaps, but he couldn't see Lyssia seriously wanting to run a major corporation.

The problem with Lyssia was she didn't know herself.

"You are the most committed to facades, Lyssia. You don't even know what's beneath your own mask."

"That is some impressive arrogance."

"Let me impress you further. You don't want a nice man. You want a man who will tell you when you're being a brat. You want a man who will ask you how your day has been, and if it's been bad, he'll do something about it. Even unto turning the city upside down to right a wrong against you. You want a man who will call you. You don't want warm summer rain. You want a hurricane. You don't want a job at your father's company because you want to make a name for yourself, but you have to stop being so stubborn about how you want that success to look. And until you can admit that to yourself you'll be stuck in this insipid in-between space with an insipid in-between man. And you deserve more, Lyssia."

He had moved nearer to her while he was talking and the space between them was charged. Lyssia's breathing changed. It was short and sharp, her eyes searching his face as if she might find answers there.

"You don't…you don't know me," she said.

"But I do. I've known you for a very long time."

She shook her head. "You know what you think you see, and nothing more."

"No, Lyssia. I see you. The you not even you see."

She took a step toward him and all went silent. "Does that mean I see you? Am I the only one who sees that you're more arrogance than substance?"

He reached out and gripped her arm and the touch was like an electric shock. He released her, as instantly as he took hold.

She was stunned into silence.

The truth was, Lyssia Anderson was a brat.

And he should not struggle with the desire to take her in hand and turn her tantrums into sighs of pleasure.

But even now, he did.

"I'm going to bed," she said, her voice thin.

"Yes," he said. "A good idea."

Tomorrow she would move back to the main hotel and she wouldn't be his problem. He could do his work without distraction.

That was all he really wanted.

CHAPTER THREE

WHEN LYSSIA WOKE up the next morning, all was quiet. The kind that felt like a weighted blanket, settling over her all warm and comforting.

She didn't want to move. Didn't want to disturb her own relaxation. But then she remembered. Dario.

Her eyes popped open. She needed to get out of here. She was stuck in this house with that man.

She needed to call Carter, and she needed to get a room at the main lodge. Wouldn't be an issue. Easily solved.

She tumbled out of bed and looked at the clock. She was jet-lagged, so it was an odd time, and not a good one to call Carter. Too bad.

She picked up the phone on the nightstand, a landline that was connected to the front desk. There was no tone.

That was weird.

She pushed a button to try and wake the phone up. If that was how such things worked. It didn't seem to be.

She pushed a button again. And then again.

Nothing seemed to work.

She growled. Well, she would use her phone to look up the number to the front desk, then.

She would take some coffee first, though. She hoped that there was space available for her. Because while she was keen to get the overview of the property done, she was even more keen to get out of the presence of Dario.

He just…

He got under her skin. He had been so rude and condescending last night. Lecturing her about her relationship with Carter.

And all right, maybe they hadn't given their relationship rules or parameters or a title. But it was there. She knew it.

She let herself think, for just a minute, that he might even be the one. That he was actually Prince Charming.

It made her heart lift.

Maybe he was the one who would see her for who she was. The one who would put the slipper on her foot…

She was a product of society. She might know full well that fairy-tale syndrome was a problem, but that didn't mean she hadn't taken some of the motifs on board and internalized them. And sometimes, just a little bit, she indulged in a fantasy or two that was maybe a bit more sweeping and romantic than she had pretended while talking to Dario.

You want the villain…

She didn't.

And, oh, how she hated Dario.

She really did.

She'd been speechless with it last night when he'd reached out and grabbed her arm…

How dare he?

How dare he criticize sweet, lovely Carter and…and…

She looked at herself in the mirror and frowned. What she had ended up wearing to bed last night was not cute. It was not like any of the gorgeous things in her suitcase.

All those beautiful, sexy things. She had been so intent on having that… On playing the role of seductress.

She had so looked forward to being wanted.

Because at least with Carter she felt like something was there. Like he enjoyed having her around. At least with him she didn't feel like she was fitting through cracks. Her father's daughter, but only a little bit. Because somehow Dario was more his child than she was in many ways. Or perhaps the child he wished he'd had.

And he certainly wasn't like a brother to her.

No. Not in the least.

He didn't even *like* her. He didn't even…

Right then, her eyes went past the mirror, into the bathroom and landed on the baths.

Lord.

She was not going to think about that again. It had been an aberration. Dario was… He was attractive. She supposed. If you were into that kind of thing. To that macho, old-school, extremely masculine sort of beauty.

He was also a brick wall.

And anyone who was with him was going to spend most of her life flinging herself at that wall. No thanks.

She already felt unwanted and invisible half the time.

Of course, the truth was, when she thought about seducing Carter she thought about what she would wear. What she would do. How beautiful she would feel.

She hadn't spent much time thinking about what he might do to her. Even when she had tried to have a fantasy about being in the tub with him, it had been about companionship.

That image of Dario hadn't been companionable at all. It had been about his hands on her skin, his lips on her neck…

She squeezed her thighs together and made a short, frustrated sound as a lightning bolt of sensation centered there. She did not need that.

In any variation.

Even though she was not fond of her pajama situation,

she decided it didn't matter what she looked like, and went downstairs on the hunt for caffeine. That way, she could actually think, and not hallucinate about things she absolutely did not want to hallucinate about. Her imagination did not have her consent to go putting images like that in her brain.

She stood in front of the coffee maker, and saw it was much more complicated than she had anticipated. A manual espresso machine.

Great.

"Need some help, *cara*?"

She turned around, her heart thundering. "I don't need any help."

"You look as if you do."

The bath images came to her mind again.

He did not have the right to look so good this early in the morning. He was wearing a tight white T-shirt and black sweatpants and she could see every muscle through that T-shirt.

She would do well to remember that he was an asshole, and just because she had noticed that he was attractive did not mean that she needed to focus on him being attractive.

It mattered much more how somebody was on the inside, anyway. Every child knew that.

That was kindergarten stuff.

Sadly, when she looked at him she did not feel kindergarten stuff.

But on the inside, he was mean. So it didn't matter how beautiful he was. It didn't matter that his abs were visible through a T-shirt. Abs couldn't talk to you about your day. Couldn't offer you emotional support.

"I'm good."

He shifted, and her eyes went to his muscular thighs.

They could not listen to her talk about her day either,

but would probably be useful in lifting her up and carrying her around. She imagined the way that he had thrown her suitcase over his shoulder last night. How much more easily could he pick her up and…

What was that about? She was not that woman. She was not the kind of woman who lost her head over raw masculinity. She wasn't… The truth was, she wanted to be close to Carter. It wasn't really about sex. It was, but it wasn't. For some reason, her thoughts of Dario seemed to be a bit too much about sex.

She needed to get out of here.

"The phone in my room wasn't working."

"No," he said. "It wouldn't be."

"Why wouldn't it be?"

"Have you looked out your window?"

"No."

"You might want to do that."

She scampered from the room and went into the dining area, where there was a large set of corner windows. She looked out and she saw nothing but white.

"Um… What?"

"We are snowed in," he said.

"No," she said. "How could that be? This is a modern luxury resort!"

"Yes, and it exists in a world with weather," he said, his tone maddeningly dry.

"But this wasn't called for."

"Apparently there was a major event last night. A wind change that blew a storm front this direction. It dumped an unprecedented amount of snow by here."

"You can't mean that we're actually snowed in in this house. You mean like onto the mountain."

"I do not," he said. He strode from the room, without

saying anything, and she followed him. As fast as her legs could take her.

He opened the front door to the outside, and there it was. An absolute wall of snow. Blocking the way out.

"We're going to die!" she shouted.

She was maybe being overdramatic, but she was doing it to try and make herself feel like it was a performance and not…a very real fear and oh, she was going to die a virgin.

She looked up at Dario and decided that was a very bad line of thinking.

But also her mother really had died in her twenties. Young and beautiful and with a whole life ahead of her…except she hadn't had anything ahead of her at all.

"I don't think we will," Dario said. "Die that is. Considering we are on a powerful backup generator that has stored enough solar power to run for a week, and there are food stores not just in the fridge, but in a basement area. I have already made sure that we are fine. We are still able to use satellite internet. Though, wired services are down in the area."

"This is… This is unreal. Unbelievable. There's no way. I can't be snowed in here with you."

"But you are," he said.

"No," she said. "I won't have it. I was supposed to be here with Carter."

"Alas," he said. "I can see how you would've found him to be a more agreeable roommate. But it is not to be."

"I…"

She suddenly felt overwhelmed. By everything. By the betrayal of the weather, her own imagination and Dario himself.

"If you weren't such an unpleasant bastard," she said. "Perhaps this wouldn't be so upsetting."

"I'm sorry that you find me to be so trying," he said. "But the truth of the matter is, we are adults, and we will figure out how to weather the situation. As soon as the sun rises in New York I will call your father and let him know that you're safe."

"He will be much more concerned about your safety, Dario. And I think you know that. I'm not the heir apparent to his empire."

"Neither am I. I'm the man who acquired it. You seem very fixated on the idea that I inherited something. I bought it."

"It's all the same, isn't it?"

"It isn't. Because your father was given money in exchange for the business, and who do you think is going to get that money?"

She felt like she had been slapped.

"It doesn't…"

"It does," he said. "Your father gave you freedom. You have never shown the slightest bit of interest in running the company, and he knows that. Imagine, walking around feeling so wounded when your father cares for you so very clearly. I cannot imagine such a thing. Your father is one of the best men that I have ever known. Your determination to see him as an enemy is ridiculous."

"Is it? He has certainly never given me any reassurance about the situation. I am obviously of the lowest priority to him."

"He has given you…"

"Do you not understand that there is…more to being someone's family, to being their father, than giving them money? I thought when he sent Carter and I here this week it was a gesture. That it was him finally acting like I had a brain and that I was capable, but it isn't. Because here you are. You, his golden boy."

"You are of the highest priority to him. Why do you think my intention is to let him know of your safety the minute he awakens?"

"You're unknowable."

"Am I? I think that actually I've made myself fairly clear. You're the one having a tantrum because you are stuck with someone that you have known all of your life, as if you have been thrown in a prison cell with a stranger."

"My week is ruined," she said.

"What a trial for you. To be stuck in a luxury chalet. Thank you for reinforcing my opinion of you, Lyssia."

She felt stung by that. She was upset. Did she have a right to be? She was supposed to be here with someone she actually cared about, someone who cared about her. And instead she was stuck with a man who disdained her. It was fair to be upset about that. It was fair to be upset about the fact that she was having intrusive thoughts about being naked with him when she wanted to punch him in the face. He didn't listen. He was so arrogant his ego practically needed its own chalet.

"They'll come and fix it, right?" she asked.

"I'm sorry, what do you mean by they will come and fix it?" he asked.

"Snowplows," she said.

"I have a feeling that this is a bit beyond just calling in a snowplow."

"Why… Then I'll dig out myself."

He looked at her and said nothing. Then he turned and walked away, leaving her standing there in front of the wall of light, the cold radiating off of it sending chills through her body. He returned a moment later, with a gleaming silver spoon in his hand.

"I know that normally you keep this in your mouth. But perhaps you might make use of it as a tool to tunnel out?"

She grabbed the spoon and threw it across the room. "You're unbelievable," she said. "You're making fun of me."

"Yes, I am. I have been since you arrived, in fact." He shrugged. "Actually, I've been making fun of you for several years, it's only that you don't think I have a sense of humor."

"Because you're unpleasant. Because you're ridiculous and…"

"Please, save your energy," he said, closing the door. "All is well here. And I do not foresee there being any problems."

The adrenaline of the situation was beginning to wear off and she was starting to think a little bit more clearly. He was speaking very confidently, but the truth was… He didn't know any of those things. What if they did lose power? What if the generator wasn't sufficient? What would happen to them then?

"Lyssia," he said softly. "Do not work yourself up. You're fine. You will be all right. Nothing bad is going to happen to you."

He was being nice now and that was almost worse. Because he really didn't get her. And she shouldn't be upset by that.

He didn't understand that she was frightened because the world was unforgivably random and violent. He didn't understand she was hurt by her father because she had never, not once, been the number one person in his life. It was her mother, and then Dario, and never her.

"You don't know that," she said. "You don't know that nothing bad will happen. But if the power goes out…"

"We will make a fire."

"Do you know how to do that? Can you actually get to any wood?"

"I grew up on the streets of Rome," he said. "And no, I was not often caught in blizzards, but I know how to survive. This will be no different. It is not even a challenge. We are in a luxury chalet."

She knew that. She knew it as part of the legend of Dario Rivelli. Up from the streets! A tale of survival and hardscrabble work ethic. Bootstraps, bootstraps, etcetera. But the problem was, she had never really sat and pictured the Dario she knew living that life. He felt so removed from it. But when he'd said that just now she had pictured him on the streets. Alone. Dario, a small boy out fending for himself. Was that really what that meant? How long had he been on the streets?

"How many years?"

"I'm sorry?" he asked. "It's pretty well stocked but I doubt we have years."

"No. How many years were you on the streets of Rome?" He stared at her and she stared back. "It gets tossed around like…like it's just evidence of your survival skills or your exceptionalism but I'm…absolutely freaked out about spending five minutes in this place and you're right. It's heated and safe and fine. How many years?"

Something shifted in his gaze and it physically hurt her to see it. "Perhaps only a year or so on the actual streets?"

He was lying. He knew how many nights. Down to the exact number of them, she was certain. "I eventually got work, which allowed me shelter, even if it would be considered subpar by many. Once I could work I could live. It saved me."

"Were you… Were you afraid?" She would have been.

"Of course."

"Did you have a house before that? What happened?"

"Is this twenty questions about tragic backstories now, Lyssia?"

She shrugged. "We're snowed in."

"Aren't you afraid of the snow?"

"Yes, but I want to know."

Anyway, his confidence had soothed her. She felt slightly calmer now, but also a bit rueful, because he was the one who had calmed her.

She hadn't ever appreciated before that it was an asset to be near a man like him who had experienced certain things. The truth was, she didn't have experience with much.

She hadn't really been conscious of that until now. She had never thought of it as a lack, or something that would give her a deficit. She did feel young then. Next to him. She did feel sheltered and cosseted and unaware. In a way she never had before.

It made her... Feel respectful of him. It was a strange experience, and she didn't like it. And yet she was in no real position to push back and be bratty. Mostly because she had already overplayed her hand quite a bit. But also, because he was the person offering to keep her alive during this unexpected blizzard.

"Yes, I had a house. A normal house. And then things changed. As I think you know life often does."

"What happened?"

"The usual sorts of sad things," he said, his tone clipped.

He wasn't being honest. Because Dario was always honest. It wasn't a lie, necessarily, she had a feeling it was all very sad, but she also had the sense that there was something underlying it.

"Come," he said. "I'll make you coffee."

"Why are you being nice?"

"Who said I was being nice? Perhaps I simply want you quiet."

That was how she found herself hooked up on a fluffy round white chair in the living room, waiting for him to deliver her a hot cup of coffee.

He bestowed it upon her and she was struck by the strange irony of the moment. How many times had she brought him coffee in his office?

She looked up at him, and decided that was a mistake. There was something in his dark eyes that made her stomach feel tight.

Then she reached out and took the cup of coffee from his hand. Their fingertips brushed. In spite of herself, she felt that same arrow of pleasure right there between her thighs that she felt when she thought about being in the bathtub with him up in her room. Correction, she hadn't thought about it. Her brain had implanted the thought into her consciousness. She had not thought of it on her own. No way.

And now something was happening to her here.

"Thank you," she said.

She sat there in the living room brooding for the next couple of hours, and then she heard his deep voice coming from the other room. He was talking to her father. Assuring him that everything was all right.

She couldn't hear the exact words, but she could hear the melody of his voice.

It was deep, and reassuring.

She felt bad he'd called her dad first, actually. She should have done it but she was all tangled up in hurt over him sending Dario in the first place.

You're glad Dario is here now...

And that was when she realized that she should probably give Carter a video call.

She also realized that she was hungry.

And she wanted to talk to him, so why shouldn't she?

She pushed aside all of the things that Dario had said to her last night.

It wasn't Dario's business what she was doing. A side effect of being snowed in was that she happened to be in his vicinity. But that was not her choice. She grabbed her phone and walked into the kitchen, setting it on the counter as she pushed in the numbers to make a video call, reaching for some bread from the cupboard as the phone rang.

She heard the tone that indicated he had picked up, and she looked down at the screen, smiling. He had his phone sitting on his desk, but she could tell that he looked happy to hear from her.

"Hi, Carter," she said.

"Hi. How is Italy?"

"Snowy," she said. "Actually, I'm snowed in at the chalet with Dario."

"Oh," he said, sounding… She couldn't quite pinpoint it. Was he regretful because he wasn't here? Because if he had come, then they would be snowed in together.

"I know, right? So insane."

"Was it even in the forecast?"

"No," she said, getting down a jar of peanut butter. She began to make a sandwich, standing above her phone. "Dario says that the generator should work? But it's honestly a bit unnerving. There's snow all the way up the windows."

"You're completely trapped with…"

He didn't say Dario's name, he only made a face.

"Don't worry," said Lyssia. "I think he only eats children and small animals. I should be safe."

"Perhaps." She jumped, then turned around sharply and saw Dario standing in the doorway.

"I'm on the phone," she said.

His eyes flicked down to where her phone rested on the counter.

"Is that… Being on the phone?"

"Yes," she and Carter said at the same time.

Dario walked over and peered down into her screen. "Who wishes to speak to someone by talking up their nostrils?"

"It's… It's called making face-to-face connections and being authentic," she said.

Then she picked the phone up and grabbed her newly assembled peanut butter and jelly sandwich. Then she hopped out of the room past Dario.

"I wish you were here," she said.

Because she did decide to go ahead and put herself out there, even though Carter hadn't said anything to the effect of being sorry he wasn't there.

She had thought that she would be losing her virginity this week. Not that virginity mattered. It was a social construct. But a person was allowed to think it was a little bit momentous that if they had never driven a car before they were going to drive a car for the first time. It wasn't like it fundamentally changed you or anything, but still. It was okay to have nerves and excitement and anticipation about something like that.

So too, with the virginity.

"I'm sorry that you're stuck there with Dario."

She realized that he didn't say that he was wishing he was there.

And she wouldn't have worried about that, she wouldn't have worried about that at all if it wasn't for what Dario had said last night. The way that he had made a big deal out of whether or not a man was indicating he wanted her as much as she wanted him.

But that didn't matter. It was a fundamentally uninteresting thing.

Because the way that she felt about Carter was about her. About what she wanted. It didn't need to be twisted up in a competition for who felt the most deeply. If she wanted him, then that was what mattered, right?

She wasn't needy.

"Well, it's a good thing you have power," said Carter.

"I know, right? The phone lines are down, and if we didn't have power then we wouldn't have internet of any kind. Well, I suppose we would be able to hook up cell towers for a few hours, but then the phone would die."

"A definite problem."

"For sure."

She took a bite of her sandwich, and right then, all the lights around her went out.

Her phone call kept going, owed to the satellites, certainly, but it was very clear the power was… Out.

Now, not only was she trapped in a snowstorm with Dario, she was trapped in a snowstorm with Dario without *power*.

And right then, it wasn't the darkness, or the potential cold that frightened her.

It was herself.

CHAPTER FOUR

"That can't be. He said that there was enough battery backup to last."

"Do you need me to call somebody?" Carter asked.

"I mean, maybe. You can call my dad and let him know that now we're stuck here with the power out."

"Yeah, I'll definitely do that. You should save your phone battery."

"Okay."

She hung up. Now she was standing in total darkness. And after leaving the kitchen in a huff because Dario had annoyed her, it felt absolutely irritating to stalk back in there to find him. But the problem was, she felt... Afraid.

She didn't like this at all.

She didn't want to think that she was naturally seeking out a man because she felt nervous. But the truth was, what Dario had said to her earlier had felt reassuring. He had been through a lot. He had survived a lot.

And what she tended to write off as him just being overly grand was actually a testament to all that he'd been through and all that he had accomplished.

It was easy for her to be defensive about that. Because she always felt like when he talked about his experience he was actually talking about the lack of hers.

But that was… Perhaps a limited perspective. It was perhaps selfish. Or at least self-centered.

"You said that the generator was going to work," she accused.

"Because it should," said Dario. "There was an official guide to the house and I read it."

Of course he had.

"Well, what are we going to do?"

"We're fine," he said. "We are able to have heat, and the stove is gas, so we should be able to melt snow in a pan. There's plenty of dry goods. It's hardly a difficult survival situation, and I would say at most it will only be a couple of days."

"*A couple of days*," she said.

"Yes," he said. "A couple of days. And all will be well."

"Our phones aren't going to last that long."

He lifted a brow. "Perhaps don't make video calls."

"But…"

"In fact, you should probably turn your phone off. It would be best if we made sure to conserve the battery in case we have an emergency."

"You said it wasn't an emergency. You said everything would be fine."

"I also said that the generator would work. Why are you taking everything I say as a clairvoyant prediction?"

She huffed, and looked down at her phone screen one last time. She had a text from Carter.

"Carter told my dad that the power went off."

"Excellent. I imagine he will be working to get us out of here. Text Carter and tell him you're turning your phone off to conserve battery and I'm doing the same. Tell him all is well."

She did, but put knife and gun emojis afterward, along with a skull. Then she turned the phone off.

"Do you feel better for having added drama?" Dario asked.

"Yes. Much better. A little bit of drama often makes things bearable."

"How so?"

"I just… Don't you ever feel like that? Like if you totally freak out you've sort of shown yourself the worst of it and then you can just breathe and deal with it?"

"I can't say that I do." But he almost looked like he wished he did, and that did something to her.

"I… I've never been in a situation like this before."

"You'll be just fine." He began to walk out of the kitchen.

"Where are you going?"

"Down to the basement. There's firewood down there, matches, lighters. And lanterns. I'm going to get everything that we might need to manage this."

"Oh… I don't want to go in a basement."

"Then feel free to stay up here."

He walked away, and she moved quickly after him.

"I don't want to be stuck up here without you either."

"You cannot be pleased."

"No," she said. "When snowed in with a man who drives me insane, with absolutely no electricity, I cannot be pleased."

"Perhaps go throw yourself in a snowdrift, then."

She hissed and spit the whole way down to the basement.

"For a creature who has never lived on the streets you are quite feral," he said.

"That's very infantilizing," she said, sniffing. "I am not feral, neither am I a creature."

"Then don't act like one."

There were stacks of wood in the corner, and he moved to them, taking hold of the logs with ease.

She felt like she was meeting him for the first time and it was a bit disconcerting. She knew that Dario had grown up on the streets. But it was quite another thing to see him being so calmly capable in what could be argued was a survival situation. She saw him often as a roadblock to fling herself against. A representative of all the ways in which she didn't live up to her father's expectations. Because if she did, why would he need Dario? And in this moment, she saw him as a man. Capable. Calm in a crisis.

Exactly the sort of man she should be glad she was stuck with, and that made her feel even more annoyed, because the truth was, right now it would be better to be stuck with Dario than Carter, and she didn't even need to know what Carter's hunting and gathering skills were to know that.

Dario had legitimately spent time in survival situations. It wasn't like Boy Scout camp or watching videos on YouTube.

And if pressed, that was what she needed.

Someone who could actually guide this situation, because Lord knew she couldn't. Galling to have to admit even internally, but she wouldn't have thought to go down into the basement in the first place. She hadn't known there was a basement. She hadn't read up on the house she was staying in. Because she just expected…

She was so worried about herself right now, and about how Dario's skills were benefiting her but…he'd gotten them by suffering and that was a stark, painful realization.

"Grab some of the lanterns," he said, gesturing to a shelf that had an array of camping equipment.

She picked up a few lanterns, and also some extra blankets. Fleece and reindeer hide. Because staying cozy was very high on her list.

She followed him up the stairs carrying all of the various supplies.

"It would be best if we chose a room to make warm. I would say likely best my bedroom."

"What?" Her heart slammed against her chest.

"The living room is too open. The ceiling is high. The bedroom has a fireplace, but it is much more closed off."

"What are we… Supposed to do in there?"

As soon as she said that she regretted it. Because she felt her face and body get very hot. And she knew that she had just implanted that very same image that had been living in her head the last couple of days right into his.

He looked at her, and there was something simmering in his eyes that nearly made her heart stop. "I'm sure we'll think of something."

She was imagining that. She had to be. He was Dario Rivelli. He didn't like her. And more than that, he thought of her as a child.

The truth was, she had always seen Dario as a man. He had been a man as far as she was concerned from the first moment she had met him. It was just that his being a man didn't seem appealing to her. Until… Maybe until recently.

Liar.

All right. So there had always been tension inside of her when dealing with him. Always. And if maybe she was extra sulky when she brought him his coffee because looking at him felt uncomfortable, and made her feel awkward and like she didn't know what to do with her hands when no one and nothing else did, then… Well.

She would never have called it attraction, though.

Not until now.

She had always thought of it is resentment.

But suddenly, looking at that starkly handsome face, with

all the snow piled up outside and the promise of being holed up in his bedroom in front of the fireplace, she felt like she couldn't deny anymore what it was.

It wasn't an aberration that she had imagined being in the bathtub with him.

It was her true heart.

How could that be? She liked Carter. She had just talked to him on the phone and she was thrilled to hear his voice. She had imagined sitting in naked companionship with him and it had been nice. When she thought of being naked with Dario it was anything but nice. It made her feel like someone had forced a fistful of butterflies down her throat and into her stomach. It made her feel like she was being victimized by hormones.

She felt hot and cold all at once. She felt like she might be dying.

Was that how it was supposed to be?

"Lyssia," he said, the warning note in his voice doing something strange to her.

"What?"

"You know exactly what."

"I don't," she said. "I just want to know where to put the lanterns."

"My room," he said.

And that was how she found herself marching up the stairs with him. The bedroom he was staying in was large, with a huge, imposing four-poster bed in the corner.

There was a fireplace at the back wall, and because they were on the second floor, the window looked out over the mountain of snow.

She went over and peered down.

"This is… Unbelievable."

"Indeed."

He settled down in front of the fireplace and put the logs in, working at lighting the fire. He accomplished it quickly, and she could only be grateful, yet again, that she was with Dario.

Except then a moment later the realization that she was attracted to him crashed back into her. Her eyes went to his thighs. Covered by the fine wool of the pants he was wearing. He had changed since early this morning, into the regular suit pants she was used to seeing him in, and a white shirt.

The sleeves were rolled up, and she watched the play of muscles in his forearms as he moved logs into the fireplace, his motions calm and expert.

The absolute certainty in everything he did was something she had never seen in anyone else.

Dario wore excellence as a second skin.

It was something quite unlike anyone else she had ever encountered.

Many men were overconfident. Brash. Arrogant. And she would easily characterize Dario is arrogant, but the difference between him and other men was that he actually had a right to the arrogance. If he said that he could do something, then he did it. If he professed to know about something, then he did.

It made her feel safe yet again, but at the same time, she felt on edge.

What was she supposed to do with this realization that she was attracted to the man. That made her feel just a small sliver of uncertainty. Of fear.

Like she had walked into a lion's cage, and anything could happen.

His movements fluid, he moved away from the lit fire. No. He wasn't a lion. He was a panther. She didn't know why that mattered. Except in that moment, she could think of little that mattered more. Then taking in the details of him. That dark hair, black and swept off his forehead. The perfect, sculpted cheekbones and square jaw.

It was like really seeing him for the first time. She didn't want to be having this moment, and yet she was.

She was like a child. A schoolgirl. Who had been antagonizing a boy because she thought he was cute.

Except he wasn't a boy, and *cute* was an offensive term for his sophisticated looks.

She wanted to fling herself out that window right into a snowbank, as he had suggested earlier.

Except part of her was… More interested than she should be.

Is this just because you wanted to have sex this weekend?

Her stomach twisted. The hard pain more intense than anything she had felt when she had been considering sleeping with Carter.

She couldn't even fathom the fallout of sleeping with Dario.

He was always around. Brooding and dark. He was older, he was… "Is there something I can help you with?" he asked. Because of course she was staring at him, and she hadn't realized she was.

"No," she said. "Sorry."

"I have an idea. I believe there were sausages in the fridge downstairs. For now, all the things in the fridge will still be all right. But they won't be for long. We can take certain things out and shove them into the snow that's butted up against the door. And we can bring the sausages upstairs and roast them in the fire."

"Okay," she said, grateful for the break in tension.

Though sausages weren't the most nonsexual food.

The task of stuffing things into the snowbank was so amusing that she forgot for a moment that she had been awash in attraction just a few moments before. She took a jar of jam and shoved it into the snow.

"This is hilarious," she said.

"But practical," he responded. "It will keep us fed. And that way we can save the dry goods."

"True."

"How are we going to grill sausages?"

"I have an idea," he said.

He took a rack out of the oven, and a large skillet, and they went upstairs where he was able to, at great personal risk, shove the rack into the fireplace and place it on a ledge. Then he put the skillet on top and put the sausages in there.

"This is almost civilized," she said.

"Very nearly," he agreed.

They sat for a moment, regarding the food. Her stomach growled. She had that peanut butter and jelly not that long ago, but she felt like the sense that she was in a survival situation had created a bit of a psychosomatic sense that she might be starving.

Maybe she wasn't great in a crisis. She had never really thought about it one way or the other before. But now it mattered. She felt somewhat galled by the realization. That many of the things Dario had said to her over the years that felt mean were a little bit true. She had been sheltered. A little bit cosseted even, and while she had gone out on her own and done a certain number of things, she had a very large safety net. Always and ever. A big backup generator, as it were. And it had never failed her, unlike the one here.

She had felt like it did, because it had felt like her father was being unkind to her by selling the company to Dario.

Which maybe wasn't fair. She didn't actually want the company. She wanted her father to…be proud.

She had tried. She had tried to be… Dario. But she wasn't.

"Is something wrong?"

His voice was dark as velvet. Just as soft. It scraped over her skin in the most deliciously uncomfortable way, and she felt like a different person, here in the silence of this house. Surrounded by snow, surrounded by him.

Normally, she would be sharp with him. Normally, she wouldn't try to see him as a person. She had seen him primarily as an obstacle, and then as an obstacle that made her feel prickly and uncomfortable as she had gotten older.

But not now. He wasn't an obstacle now. He was helping her, and unfortunately, she was also seeing new things about herself thanks to him.

It was not comfortable.

"What if I'm not as good at all of this as you and my father are? What does that say about me? And what does it say about my representation of *feminism*?"

"Who says you have to represent anything? You are not all women. You are simply you. And also, it is not about being good enough. Perhaps it is only that you are different. I couldn't design furniture. I wouldn't know where to begin."

"Well, my father doesn't esteem my ability to do that, maybe that's the problem."

He paused for a moment. "And yet what you do is esteemed, appreciated, or you wouldn't have clients."

"I don't have enough clients."

"For what?"

"For…for anyone to take me seriously." It sounded so small. But it felt so big.

"There are many people on the streets who want what

I have. The truth is, I was bound and determined to make a certain thing of myself. I believe that I had advantages, even in my disadvantages. I am not a vain man, Lyssia, but I am not unaware of the fact that I'm handsome. And that I have used that as a tool. I have an easy time connecting with people, telling them exactly what they want to hear in the voice they want to hear it in. It is not a moral failure if you have not risen from the streets to have a billion dollars."

"What about rising from one billion dollars to having something of your own."

"That isn't a moral failure either."

"It feels like it."

"Your father was born rich. He built on what he had, and it is well done. You are not the same person that he is, that doesn't mean you aren't as good. It doesn't mean that you aren't successful. You're twenty-three years old. You're allowed to take some time to figure out which path you want to walk."

"There are literal chat forums on the internet about how I'm losing at the easiest setting of life."

"And what does it matter if strangers think you've failed when you haven't?"

"I… I don't know, Dario. Maybe this is the really stupid problem with having the safety net. I could never work a day in my life and I wouldn't be fighting for survival, so why am I doing it? For a feeling, I guess. For a sense that what I do matters, that my being alive matters. That I'm important and smart and… I do want people to see it. That I care. That I'm trying. And they don't. My father doesn't or he wouldn't have sent you this week. It would be me and Carter. Snowed in."

"Right."

"Having sex."

"So you say."

The silence between them lapsed. "I'm not in love with Carter. I never thought it was love or anything. But he made me feel pretty. He made me feel…"

"He made you feel good about yourself. Perhaps in part because he is not as successful as you are."

She winced. "Perhaps. That makes me sound very shallow."

"Many people cannot handle having a partner who is more successful than they are. Though, particularly, men cannot."

"Well, points for Carter, then. Because I don't think that he cared. Or maybe like everybody else he simply doesn't think I'm all that successful."

"Why have you not used your connection with your father to get more accounts?"

"I'm trying to succeed on my own."

"But that's foolishness. Nobody succeeds in business on their own. If you have connections and you don't exploit them, then what is the point? You have the advantages, and you should use them. Your real problem, Lyssia, is that you're not trying to succeed for the sake of it. You're trying to prove something. And you are doing so at the expense of yourself."

She had never thought of it that way. She thought of it as trying to be independent. "But you didn't have any connections."

"That isn't true. I started working in a kitchen with no connections, but everywhere that I worked, every customer that I came into contact with, every room that I walked into I was building connections. When you are climbing a rope up from the gutter, you realize that you need handholds. And

I made handholds everywhere that I went. That is perhaps my greatest strength."

"It's different, though. When it's your father, versus…"

"It isn't. You were working with what you have, the same that I was working with what I had. I have been very hard on you," he said. "I fear that perhaps I have undermined you at certain points when I did not intend to."

Their eyes met. She found it hard just then to breathe. Her eyes suddenly stung, the pressure in her chest unbearable. She cleared her throat.

"You're not my father," she said. "So, it's not really up to you to fix all that."

He chuckled. "I know that I'm not your father."

The air between them seemed to crackle. She decided that it was just the sausages in the pan. Because she didn't want to acknowledge that crackle. Didn't want to find herself at the mercy of it. Because it was far too much.

Or perhaps it wasn't. Perhaps it was what she needed.

No. You know you can't. Can you imagine how scathing he would be?

She wasn't sure she could withstand that level of rejection. Flinging herself at the beautiful and condescending Dario only to find herself laid low.

No. That would be an indignity too far.

"I think the food is ready," he said, his tone mild, and she wondered if he felt the same thing that she did. She wondered if that moment had just been in her head.

He speared the sausages with a fork and put them onto a plate. Then he took out a bottle of wine and poured them each a glass. They were sitting on the floor in front of the fireplace, and it was like a picnic. It might have been romantic if he were anyone else.

She felt her face growing hot as she let that thought pass through her. As she tried to let it go.

"Thank you," she said softly. Because she never really was all that nice to him. "I'm…quite certain that I would've panicked and run into a snowdrift without you here."

"I don't think you would have. You're not a stupid woman. You consistently think the worst of yourself."

She frowned. "No, I don't."

"You do. I am realizing these past days that you do. Why do you think you need to be with a partner who is less successful than you? Why do you think that you're a failure, when in fact you're simply young? You do not trust herself. You are the one who looks down on you."

"Also you, sometimes," she said.

"Yes. Sometimes." But there was something unreadable in his dark eyes. Like there was more that he wanted to say, but wouldn't. But didn't.

She felt tension growing in the space between them. Expanding.

She felt herself growing hot beneath the intensity of that gaze.

"Why?" she asked softly. "Why have you always been so hard on me?"

He said nothing, but regarded her closely. She felt his gaze like a physical touch, as it moved from her face, down her throat, to her breasts, down her thighs.

The open masculine appreciation nearly undid her. From Dario. Dario, who she would've said hated her. Dario, whom she would've said she hated.

But nothing that was passing between them right now felt like hatred. It felt like something much more dangerous. Something she didn't fully understand. Something she didn't have full access to. But she wanted it. It felt like something entirely different from what she had imagined she might find with Carter. But then, on some level she had known that. She had.

But… She couldn't be right about this.

"It is safer," he said finally. "To allow myself to believe that you are young. Foolish. That you do not know your own mind. And you believe that as well."

"No, I don't," she said.

"You do. It keeps you safe. In many ways, it keeps you safe."

"From?"

She knew that asking the question was dangerous. And yet, she was so close to the flame, in every way.

It made her want to reach out and touch.

In spite of it all.

She didn't move forward, but she didn't move away either. And everything in her was screaming that it would be better if she did.

But she sat, rooted to the spot. Protected, somewhat, by the way that her plate sat on top of her knees. Acting as a barrier. Sort of.

"From myself, Lyssia."

He was dangerous. That was something she knew instinctively. A truth that radiated through her. She had never been drawn to danger, not even once. She had always valued her safety. She wasn't brave. She wasn't adventurous. She wasn't…

She had chosen Carter because he represented safety. Not because she wanted him. She had told herself all kinds of stories about why she wanted something that felt easy and fun. Something that lacked intensity and consequence.

At every turn, she downplayed the deepest of her own emotions, and denied herself anything with real resonance.

Was he right? Was it because she didn't trust herself? Because she didn't pay heed to herself?

She told herself so definitively all the things that she wanted, and in some ways, when she was telling Dario what she wanted it was like she was trying to reinforce all of those truths inside of herself.

But they started to feel thin now. For and in the face of what he had just said. That he was trying to protect her from himself.

And more than that, it was the way those words unfurled inside of her.

It was more appealing than it ought to be. And it was… Was she really understanding it right?

This was where she suddenly felt woefully inadequate next to him. He knew how to survive. He knew how to build something from nothing.

And he knew about sex. In a way that she simply didn't. It felt unbelievable that a man of his prowess would be interested in her. That he would've had to try to hold himself back from her in any capacity, and yet reading between the lines that seemed to be what he was saying.

Be brave.

"Why would I be in danger from you?"

She set her plate down. She removed the barrier.

"Lyssia…"

"Why?"

He looked pained then, as if he was on the verge of something he actually feared. And then he spoke.

"Because you are as stubborn as you are beautiful. Because you are my mentor's daughter, and far too young for me to have the thoughts that I have toward you."

Her heart jumped. Hit square against her breastbone.

"You don't like me," she whispered.

His gaze was impenetrable obsidian.

"Like and dislike have little to do with chemistry, or have you not noticed that chemistry is what we have?"

"We fight all the time."

"Why do you think that is?"

He didn't call her *child*, but she felt it was implied.

But it was also not as infuriating as it might've been. She expected it to be. It was fascinating. Like the rest of him. Like this moment. Like the fantasy that she had, unbidden, of the two of them in the tub. It had felt intrusive at the time, but now it felt... Intoxicating. It felt like it had potential. To be something. To be something that she wanted.

"I don't know. I..."

"Because you have trafficked in boys. And I am a man. As I told you, if Carter truly wanted you, then he would have spoken to you from the beginning. He would never have allowed me to take his place. He would've made alternative arrangements. You were not in the forefront of his mind. And in my opinion, when a man does not make you the beginning and end of everything, he does not deserve to have you. Why should he have access to your body? Why? If he does not make having you, cherishing you, the focus of the moment, then why give him all of you?"

"It's just that that's a very outdated—"

"Is it? Do women not surrender more during sex? Risk more?"

"I guess we do," she said. That she was unwilling to tell him that she actually didn't know firsthand.

He already thought her to be so much younger, so much less experienced, she didn't want to compound matters by letting him know just how much that was true.

"You can't possibly be saying that you're attracted to me," she said.

"Perhaps that is the problem. I am trying to say it. Perhaps it would be better if I showed you."

CHAPTER FIVE

DARIO KNEW THAT he had made a very bad deal with the devil just now. Sold a piece of his soul, and he didn't have all that many left. What he had said to Lyssia was true. He was a man who had done a very good job of making connections and then using those connections to his advantage whenever possible.

He was a man who had endured some very dark things. And he had very few connections in this world that were not about business. Her father was one of them. She was the other.

For that reason alone she had always been sacred to him. The connection had been sacred. They were fire and flame, and honesty—except in this. And now he had done it. He'd forced this truth into the open between them. And here they were, in the snow, the power out. And somehow, he had taken that connection and twisted inside of himself. He was telling himself now that she needed to know. That she needed to know what it was like to be with a man.

A man who wanted her.

A man who would not give her insipid sex and a wishy-washy petering out, or worse still, a ghosting. Dario was definitive.

No, he could not give her a relationship, but he would

give her honesty. He would give her good sex, and worship her the way she should be.

She needed to know what it was to have her body cherished. Lavished with pleasure.

And that, that rationalization, that was straight from Satan himself. But it was not the first deal that Dario had made with the dark Lord, and wouldn't be the last. And so, he found himself moving toward her, cupping the back of her head and bringing her in to kiss her mouth.

The sound she made was shocked and short.

And for a moment, she was still beneath his mouth, but then, she surrendered. Like a flower beginning to open. Her lips softened, parted, and when he slid his tongue against hers she responded in kind.

Suddenly, her hand came up to grip his shoulders, and she was moving toward him, leaning against him, her whole body pressed to his.

She was behaving as if she had never experienced anything like this before, and he knew that he hadn't.

The softness of her mouth, the sweetness of it, was a sucker punch. It was beyond. He always liked women, but he had known from the moment he had begun to feel attraction for Lyssia that the real danger with her was a chemistry that existed between them that she wasn't even aware of. Her whimper was one of helplessness, and as she clung to him, her kiss became bolder.

And that was when he moved. He pressed her down to the floor in front of the fireplace, licking his way into her mouth as he gave himself over to the clawing need between them.

It had always been this. Burning between them. What he had attempted to handle with indifference could no longer be contained, because he could not find a shred of indifference left in his soul.

He was jaded.

And from the beginning, the way that he felt for Lyssia challenged that jadedness.

It was dangerous.

It always had been.

He heard stories about such things, and he had always doubted them. That there was the potential for chemistry to overwhelm everything. Good sense and the whole of a man's nature.

He had never believed it. He had always thought that it was an excuse for weakness. Perhaps this was weakness now.

No. It was not a weakness. He had made a decision. He had made a bargain. And he had followed through with it.

It was no less than he did with a business deal. With anything. They were here, they were snowed in. It was an opportunity. A connection. And it had to be managed.

And managed it would be.

He stripped her sweatshirt from her body, followed by her shirt. She had a fine, white lace bra underneath that showed the pale shadow of her nipples.

She was beautiful.

So far beyond anything he had imagined she might be.

Beneath the cups of the bra was a delicate gold chain, linked in lovely intervals to the delicate fabric, creating a seductive design.

"What is this?" he asked, moving his thumb across one of the gold chains.

"It's… I had… I mean, you saw my suitcase," she said, breathless.

"Yes. I did. Was this for you to seduce him?"

"Yes. But obviously, I thought that maybe I would wear it because…"

"Were you going to seduce me, Lyssia?"

She laughed. "No. I wasn't that brave."

He looked down at her face, those glorious, glittering blue eyes. "Why do you not think you're brave?"

"I'm not. I…"

He gripped her chin and held her gaze. "You are brave. You have not been put to the test, but that does not mean that you aren't brave. I know you feel as if you were not strong today, but if you were by yourself, you would have done well. You would have figured it out. Let me show you how brave you are."

He knew this because of her spirit. He knew this because she tested him, tried him. He knew because she was Lyssia. And that had been all-consuming for quite some time.

He kissed her again, capturing her beautiful pink mouth and plunging his tongue deep. She gasped, arching against him. Her delicate hands moved over his shoulders, down his back. He growled and flexed his hips against her.

She moaned, unable to keep herself from trembling. She wanted him. As much as he wanted her.

"Did you want to seduce me?" he asked.

She looked down. "I was… I was beginning to come around to the idea."

"Look at me," he said. She obeyed, her blue eyes meeting his. "Tell me," he growled, as he kissed his way down her neck, over the plump, delicate curve of her breasts and down her stomach.

He gripped the waistband of her soft, cashmere sweatpants and dragged them down her legs, revealing a matching pair of underwear beneath. Lace and see-through with a keyhole just above the most intimate part of her, a gold chain creating a delicate web there.

"Tell me," he commanded.

"I… When I got here, I looked at the tub, and I imagined being in the tub with you. And it shook me, because I… I have pretended all this time that what I feel for you is nothing short of animosity. Because it's easier. It's so much easier. Because there's no point in having a wild, sexual need for a much older man, is there? Especially when he just thinks that you're a silly girl."

"I don't think you're a silly girl," he said. He moved his fingertips beneath the waistband of her panties. "You are beautiful. And you are smart, and you are brave. And you will find your way."

"Is this a motivational speech or are we about to have sex?"

There was Lyssia. Dry and spiky as ever. And of course when she put it like that, in such bland terminology, he knew that it should make him want to pull away from her, but he found that he didn't. He just didn't. He had made his devil's bargain. His mind was made up.

"Oh, we're going to have sex," he said. "You have no idea how long I've waited for this."

Her cheeks turned pink. "You have?"

"You are a problem," he ground out. "One that I have done my best not to take in hand. To not solve the way that I wanted to. Because I knew it would create only difficulty for me. If your father were to find out…"

"He would kill you."

"Very likely."

"He doesn't have to find out."

"No. He doesn't. You should know what it feels like when a man wants you. When he really wants you."

He took her delicate hand and guided it to the front of his pants. He let her feel him. How hard he was.

Her eyes went wide. She caressed him, slowly and deliberately through the fabric of the pants.

"What are you thinking?" he asked as he watched her breathing increase, as he watched her eyes go wide.

"Well, you are rather substantial."

He chuckled. "I do well enough."

"That is the kind of thing that men who are well endowed say. Because men who are not well endowed cannot joke about... Such things."

"The voice of experience?"

"I have been in the world."

"The world is often a disappointing place," he said. "But I will endeavor to not disappoint."

"I'm not concerned," she said, her breathing becoming ragged.

He pushed his hand down the rest of the way, into her panties, between her legs. He found her slick there, hot and clearly needy.

She gasped, arching her hips upward, and he began to stroke her slowly.

He watched her face, that beautiful, familiar face, flushed with pleasure.

He did not often make love to women he knew. In fact, he didn't think he ever had.

Yes, he had associations with women that lasted through multiple trysts, but he never got to know the woman. He knew Lyssia. He knew where she came from. He knew how she had grown up. He'd been in her childhood home. He had watched her grow from a quiet child to a sulky teenager, to a beautiful woman.

He knew her.

He knew her father, he respected her father. He knew that if her father were to find out about this that… It would compromise the only real relationship that he had in his life, and here he was.

This was sweeter for knowing her. And he would never have said that that was the case when it came to sex, but now it was.

He stroked her, and she removed her hand from him, clenching those fingers into fists and letting her head fall back as she continued to roll her hips in time with the movement.

"Do you like my touch?" he asked.

"Yes," she panted.

"What do you want?"

"You," she said.

"Be brave," he ground out.

He was poised on the brink of destruction. Past his own breaking point, for if he had not broken he wouldn't be here. He would not have sold himself for this.

But what a prize. Worth the cost.

He could think of nothing but this. Of how much he wanted her.

There was nothing outside this space. No consequence, nothing.

"You inside of me," she panted. "Please. *Please*."

He growled, pushing a finger deep inside of her, and she moaned with pleasure, throwing her forearm over her eyes as the beginnings of an orgasm began to ripple through her.

He pushed a second finger inside her and pushed her over

the edge. She gasped, then cried out, biting her lip, her eyes still covered by her forearm.

"Dario," she whispered.

"Yes," he ground out.

And when she shattered, it was complete. When she shattered, he felt himself lose his tether on his control.

He wanted Lyssia Anderson, and he was going to have her.

CHAPTER SIX

LYSSIA COULDN'T BELIEVE this was happening. She couldn't believe that Dario had just touched her to orgasm, that she had demanded he do so.

What was wrong with her?

She didn't know herself. Or perhaps what was worse was she did. She felt like there had been a great veil ripped away. She felt like all of the lies that she had told herself for all of this time had been burned to the ground. Sizzled over an open flame like a bunch of emergency sausages.

She was at sea.

Or perhaps just buried in a snowdrift.

She wanted him. She was certain of that. And as she looked into his blazing, dark eyes she knew with absolute certainty that she had wanted him all this time.

That the edge beneath her skin when she looked at him was desire.

But the absolute pull of need that wound its way through her like a live wire was deeper and more consequential than she would have ever wanted to admit.

It was not simple aesthetic appreciation for his perfectly formed features. It was not just an acknowledgment that he was a handsome enough man.

No. She wanted him.

Every time she had been tempted to misbehave to get his

attention when she had been his assistant, every time she had snapped at him rather than being civil or sane.

When she had come here and he had arrived, she hadn't been angry that he was here. She was angry because what she wanted was to want another man, and she simply didn't. Simply couldn't.

Not in the way that she wanted him. Being irritated with Dario Rivelli was more exciting than being attracted to Carter had ever been, and now that she saw it through this perfect lens, she knew that it had always been need.

She had been angry about it.

She had been resentful of it, but it was very much the truth. She wanted him.

Oh, how she wanted him.

"Make love to me," she whispered, wondering who belonged to that husky voice that had come out of her mouth.

She felt like an entirely different creature. But she wanted to be brave.

He had told her that she was, and now she wanted to rise to the occasion. She wanted to demand all the things she wanted, she just needed to know what they were. It wasn't that she was totally innocent, it was just that when she had imagined being with somebody finally, she hadn't really imagined it in a detailed way. She hadn't really imagined it in a graphic way. And she could already tell that this was going to be rawer, more physical than she had given space for it to be.

She had never been a raw or physical person. She had not been especially brave in her life.

She had been hampered by a desire to please. Oh, how she had wanted to make her father proud. She wanted to be acceptable. Not good, because it wasn't like she was a robot. She had been sulky as an assistant. She had not been perfect.

She had not been enough, trying to live in the space where she could fill the hold her mother had left. Fearing the world, knowing how fragile life was, grieving and stagnating while trying to push forward and heal.

She had wanted to carve out a system of success for herself, but she had been afraid to push too far out because what she really wanted was to be wholly approved of.

She wasn't sure that was possible. But she had tried.

Oh, she had tried.

But this wasn't about pleasing anybody. Not anybody but herself. She wanted him. And she was going to have him.

Outside of this room it wouldn't make any sense. Outside of this moment. It would be desire as a spark, and nothing more. But here, it raged. Here it became an unstoppable force. A wildfire.

And she was happy to let it burn.

Nobody else ever had to know. It could just be a secret between them. Just tonight. Just this moment.

That made her feel alive. Invigorated. If this was her night with Dario, the one and only night ever, then she could be whoever she wanted to be. And when they were free of this place they would go back to being the way they had been. He was experienced. It would mean nothing overly significant to him. And she was realistic.

"Take your clothes off," she commanded.

He arched a dark brow. "Giving orders?"

"I want to see you," she said.

"Do you?"

"Yes. You're beautiful. The most beautiful man that I've ever seen. And I have found that confronting all this time. You're right. I did want control."

"And now you'll surrender it," he said. "I don't think I'll

take my clothes off. Not now. Now, I think you have to wait. But I think you will get naked for me."

His high-handed tone should irritate her, but instead she felt herself growing even wetter with her need for him. She'd already had an orgasm, but she could feel another one building. He wasn't even touching her, it was just because of the way he was looking at her. And suddenly, her body felt more beautiful than it ever had. Felt powerful. Because she could see the need in his eyes, the need to see her. The need to touch her.

She moved into a sitting position, reached behind herself and took off her bra. The chains made a soft sound as she flung it to the floor. She watched as his gaze fell to her breasts, and then she stood up, pushing her underwear down her legs, all the way to the floor, stepping out of them. "Is this what you had in mind?"

He got up on his knees and growled. Then he cupped her ass with his hands, and brought her forward, taking a long, slow stroke of the cleft between her thighs, tasting her like she was ice cream.

She let out a shocked sound, forking her fingers into his hair as she widened her stance so that he could have greater access to the most intimate part of her.

He stroked her, the witness there easing his passage.

She was almost embarrassed by it, but... This was her night.

So instead she held his face there, moving her hips in time with the stroke from his tongue.

"Come," he commanded.

"I just did," she panted.

"Come again," he growled, his teeth scraping against her sensitive skin before he slicked his tongue over her body one more time and she came apart.

She shuddered and shattered, her whole world reduced to sparkling shards.

She was remade beneath that mouth. That beautiful, glorious mouth.

If she had the potential to be shocked by it, it wasn't here. Not in this moment.

"Dario," she whispered.

He rose to his feet and picked her up off the ground, moving his hands down her thighs and lifting her and encouraging her to put her legs around his waist.

She moaned, and he laid her down on his bed, rising up over her, and leaning down to kiss her mouth. She could taste her own desire there, the force of her own need.

She felt like perhaps that should embarrass her also. But there just was no embarrassment here. There was nothing but want. Nothing but need.

It was cascading glory, and she wanted to capture each and every glimmer.

He moved away from her, and stripped his shirt up over his head, revealing his glorious body. His dark, heavily muscled chest with dark hair sprinkled across. She watched the shift and bunch of his muscles, the glory of his abs.

Then he pushed his sweats and underwear down his legs, leaving him entirely exposed to her gaze. She had never seen a naked man in person before.

He was… He was incredible. Just beautiful.

If they wanted to make a real, impressive classical statue, then Dario would be the perfect model.

But he would leave all those other Italian sculptures shamed in his wake.

"I'm on the pill," she blurted out.

She took a low-dose birth control pill to help with her periods. And she had thought that it was probably a handy thing, for when she did become sexually active. And, she had always intended to use it in conjunction with condoms, since that was responsible. But she was stuck in a house with Dario, and she imagined he hadn't brought any. She was not about to let that disrupt the moment.

"Good," he said, short and sharp.

He moved back to the bed, back to her, kissing her deeply, pressed against her body, the heat of his skin, all that bare skin, leaving her breathless.

"Dario," she whispered.

"Beautiful," he said against her mouth. *"Bellissima."*

She shivered. She would've told anyone who asked that she wasn't the kind of woman to get silly over accents and foreign endearments, but here she was. Melting.

He gripped her thigh and hooked it up over his narrow hip, moved his hardness through her slick folds, ramping up her desire.

She'd already come twice, but this was… Waiting was killing her. She needed him. Needed to know what it was like to be filled by him. She ached. She felt hollow with her need for him.

His name was a drumbeat on her lips, a rhythm in her soul.

And finally, he pressed himself to the entrance of her body, and pushed home.

She gripped his shoulders. "Ouch!"

"Lyssia?"

A litany of curses went through her head and she tried to collect herself. She hadn't expected it to *hurt*. Not *really*.

She hadn't had anyone to talk to deeply about this and everyone around her acted like sex just wasn't a big deal, and so she'd imagined it must not be.

"I thought hymens were a societal construct," she said,

trying to deny the pain and the rising tide of emotion inside her.

"What?"

"It's just that… I thought that virginity was a completely social construct and the myth of the hymen was…"

He started to withdraw from her and she put her hands on his shoulder. "Don't," she said.

"You're not telling me that you were a virgin," he said fiercely.

"I guess so, but I didn't really ever think of it—" except when she did "—because, you know, that's all patriarchal nonsense designed to scare women. To control them. I didn't really think that it hurt the first time."

"Did you think women were lying to you?" He had never even been with a virgin and he knew that it hurt the first time.

"I didn't think they were lying, I just thought that… I don't know…the idea was implanted there ahead by the patriarchy, and then…"

"If you had told me I would have eased the way."

"You kind of tried to do that. But you… You're substantial."

"If you're a virgin, how would you even know?"

"It's not like I've never seen a naked man. On the computer."

"Lyssia," he said. "You cannot tell me that I just deflowered you."

She sniffed and tried to play unbothered. With him over her. In her. Talking to her. "I won't, because that is a vile term."

She was trying to be cool, but in reality she felt panicky, and upset. Because she didn't want that to be her only experience of sex. She wanted *him*.

But it had hurt and she hadn't been able to hold back.

She had no defenses. Nothing. It felt like being hit, square on by life, except she'd jumped into this feet-first.

He started to move away from her again and this time, she gripped him more gently. But more urgently. "Please don't leave me," she said.

"Lyssia… I won't."

"I just need a minute."

She acclimated to the feel of him. Hard and pulsing inside of her. It was different. Different from anything she'd ever experienced before.

It felt good. Amazing even. But it was definitely not what she'd anticipated.

And then, as the pain slowly subsided, desire began to return. And he began to move. So deep inside of her, and she realized that it wasn't what she had expected in many, many ways.

She had thought that she would have some control over this. She thought that she would be able to have sex and walk away without an emotional connection.

But it wasn't what she was experiencing. Not now. Not with him.

Not with him, she said to herself.

Because she couldn't be feeling this for him.

But then, his strokes turned from pain all the way to pleasure, and she could no longer think. She could only feel. That deep need within her driving her now. Urging her on.

She moaned as he thrust inside of her, as her internal muscles gripped him tight.

He held her hips, looking into her eyes as he built need within her with every movement of his body within hers.

She answered each thrust in kind, and when her climax

broke over her, he gave himself up to it as well, on a growl, and she felt him pulse deep within her.

She clung to him, shuttering as wave after wave of need overtook her.

As he poured himself inside of her.

And when it was done, she clung to his shoulders. And she didn't cry, only because she couldn't. Because she couldn't let her guard down quite so much. Because she couldn't admit that it had been quite so intense.

"You should've told me," he said.

It hurt that he was being so curt and cold now. But she shouldn't be needy. She shouldn't be looking for affirmations.

She'd been so sure she'd be okay with this. That it wouldn't matter. Because she knew better than to be needy. She knew that you couldn't count on life to not pull the rug out from under you.

But she felt needy for him. And she knew she shouldn't. She'd wanted sex to be a nice thing she could have. Something that made her feel special or cherished, maybe even the most of something. To someone like Carter, even. It had seemed possible.

She hadn't wanted to be torn asunder by it emotionally. Hadn't wanted to feel scorched.

She'd been a little girl when her mother had died, so of course she'd depended on her mother, and the loss had been crippling.

She knew better now, though.

Knew better than to want to cling to a man who'd only had sex with her.

Because sex was nothing really all that deep, was it?

"Well, I didn't," she said. "I didn't think that it mattered.

I didn't think it was your business. Also, I didn't know that you would assume anything about my sexual status."

"You were ready to seduce Carter. That was how you were going to lose your virginity?"

"Virginity doesn't mean anything," she said, ignoring her throat going tight. "Please don't yell at me. We just… We've just been together and I can't… I can't…"

And suddenly, his strong arms went around her, and she wanted to stop with relief. She buried her head in his bare chest, her palms pressed against his muscles. She relished the feel of his chest hair. The feel of his body against hers.

"I'm sorry," he said. "I did not mean to be harsh with you. But you must know that I…"

"I know," she said. "It's just for this. Just for now. We are snowed in together, so let's just… Be together for this. Only for this."

"It could be tonight. It could be tomorrow."

"I know," she said softly. "I know that's all it might be. I'm okay with that."

She wasn't sure what she was okay with. She didn't feel okay now at all. She wasn't sure why she was speaking with such authority when she wasn't entirely sure there was a name for the emotions that were rioting through her.

Maybe because she needed to believe it herself, far more than she needed him to believe it.

"All right. If that's what you want."

"It's what I want."

"Then that's what shall be."

She could have made fun of him. For acting like having sex with her was such a big, arduous task. But she felt far too raw.

They slept on the same bed but didn't cuddle. But then,

he reached over and found her, and took her again. And after that, he held her.

After that, they didn't talk about her past experience—or lack of it. They didn't talk about anything. They also didn't wear clothes. They stayed in his room unless they had to go forage for food. They made love, and they slept. For three days. It was all there was. There was no world beyond Lyssia and Dario.

She forgot why it was improbable. She forgot why they were unlikely. She could barely remember a time when she hadn't known Dario's body.

She couldn't imagine going back.

She couldn't.

But on the third day, Dario came back to his bedroom wearing sweatpants, looking grim.

"Your father has just arrived. Or rather, he is about to. The helicopter has landed out the front.

"Oh."

"Get dressed," he said, sharp and curt.

And she obeyed, because what else was there to do.

She looked out the window, and saw not just her father, but a snowplow. Along with a team of people. And that was when the attempt to free them began in earnest. It took several hours, and the entire time, she sat there with Dario, not speaking, not touching. By the time the door opened and her father appeared, the mask that Dario wore was so convincing that even she wouldn't have guessed at everything behind it.

Even she would never have known that they had ever been lovers.

He was as he'd ever been.

And she tried to be too.

"I'm so glad you survived," her father said, half joking, she could tell by his tone. But not entirely.

"And then, they were whisked outside, and to the helicopter. And when they left that cocoon, she knew that they would never be able to go back.

And part of her broke in half.

CHAPTER SEVEN

IN THE SIX weeks since they'd returned from being snowed in, Dario hadn't seen Lyssia at all. She had been completely scarce around the office, and she hadn't contacted him.

He didn't know why she would have.

He was the one that had made it clear that they needed to keep what was between them at the chalet. But he thought about her. All the time. He woke up having dreamed about her.

He had no interest in other women. It was grim and unprecedented. And it was beginning to affect his work.

But he felt like something had changed within him, and so it all felt… Wrong.

He did not like things to feel wrong, and he did not like marinating in feelings. He didn't like feelings at all.

He opened up his computer and saw he had an email. He clicked on it, and saw that it was a newsletter from Anderson Group, and announcing a partnership with Lyssia's brand.

"Well, it's about time," he said.

He knew that she had resisted that. But it was good business, and it was going to save her interiors company.

He thought, for a moment, that it might be because of the time they had spent together. He wanted to believe it was.

Why is that? It doesn't matter if you affected her in some way.

His phone rang then, and he answered it.

"Mr. Rivelli, Lyssia Anderson's office called. She has requested an appointment with you in the morning."

"I'm busy," he said, the words as a reflex when they tumbled from his mouth.

"She thought you might say that, but she said she has an offer to make you, and also some information."

"Information?" He was trying to imagine what Lyssia could possibly have to tell him.

"I have meetings."

"She knew that you would say that. She wondered if there was any possible way that you could take a drop-in now."

"Now?"

"She's at the front desk."

He had a meeting at ten minutes. He was going to cancel it. Because Lyssia was here, and he wanted to know what she was going to tell him.

He looked back at the email with the announcement. He had a feeling it was to do with her business. Perhaps she was going to try to get him to use her interiors in his properties. It would be the smart thing for her to do.

So yes. He would see her. It would be good. For both of them, perhaps. A unifying theme throughout the resorts, since Anderson was on the cusp of becoming his.

"Yes," he said. "Move my three thirty and send her in."

He sat down behind his desk and looked at the room.

It was large, with windows that overlooked the city below. He had always loved that view. Especially of Central Park in the fall. When the colors shifted.

Coming to New York for the first time had felt like stepping into another life. It had been.

He had been overawed by the place. And he had felt small in it. Gazing up at the buildings.

Now he gazed down at them from a building of his own.

What would Lyssia say when she came in?

It was the last thought he had before the door to the office opened.

He felt like his heart was going to burst through his chest when he saw her. She looked amazing. Her blond hair was pulled back into a low bun, her curves highlighted beautifully by the white sheath dress she wore.

There was a delicate golden locket hanging around her neck. And her shoes were bright pink.

She looked like a more polished version of herself. And just as glorious.

"Thank you for seeing me the last minute," she said. She had a folder held to her chest, and he nearly laughed at the way she was addressing him. Cold and professional. When only weeks ago he'd had her naked and undone in his bed.

"Of course. You know you don't need a business meeting to see me."

"This is business. I have two important matters to discuss with you. I assume you saw the announcement about Anderson."

"Yes. I assume that explains your timing."

She nodded. "Correct. I worked with my father on the press release. I knew exactly when it was going to go out."

"Very good," he said. "What triggered all this?"

"Me," she said. "I asked for what I wanted."

He did feel proud of her then. Because this was a different side of her. This was the side he always knew was there.

She was bright-eyed and eager. He had seen flashes of this. It was part of that sulky behavior, but this was it channeled. Directed.

"I want for us to work together. I would like for your resorts to consider carrying my line of home goods. We are expanding. Now that I have the contract with Anderson, I can afford to move into larger furnishings. I have several options that I think will suit the aesthetic of your chain. And we are willing to make certain things exclusive to the Rivelli brand."

"I assume that they are made from recycled materials?"

"You'll find the information on the carbon footprint in the paperwork. I think that you will be happy with it."

She shoved one folder at him.

He took it, and began to leaf through it. "I will need some time to…"

"That's fine. But while you consider that, there is one more thing that I need to speak to you about."

"And that is?"

"A custody agreement. You see, I'm pregnant, and I know that it's your baby. So we need to figure out the logistics of that deal as well."

CHAPTER EIGHT

SHE WAS SO proud of herself for not breaking into pieces the moment the words left her mouth. It was a challenge. More than a challenge.

But she had fantastic high heels and a plan.

What could go wrong?

She had rehearsed this in the mirror. She had spent hours putting her outfit together. She had been relatively unstable for the last several days. After her time with Dario had ended, she had gone home and decided to figure out what she was going to do with her business. She had thought a lot about what he said. About her bravery. And about her needing to use her connections. All good. And she had been feeling really confident about it. She had talked to her dad. It had been easier than she'd imagined it might be.

He was hesitant about a few things, but they weren't unreasonable. She could see he actually did respect her ideas. She'd been afraid he didn't. Like, very profoundly afraid. And when she'd actually spoken to him and he'd been open to it, it had been like a huge sigh of relief.

And then her period hadn't come. And that had been a worry.

Because the thing was, she'd never had sex before. So when your normally regular period took a vacation in the weeks following your first intercourse, it was a real concern.

It hadn't come. And it hadn't come. So then she took a pregnancy test. And she was pregnant.

She had called her doctor and had some words with her about that birth control pill.

The issue with low-dose pills, her doctor had told her, was that for some women they were less effective.

She had thrown her phone across the room. And thrown her pills in the trash. One by one for special effect.

She had considered all her options.

And then she had…

She had sat down in her room and looked at the framed photo she kept of her mother.

She could barely remember the way that her mother's voice had sounded now. She remembered her hands. She remembered how soft they were. How it had felt when she touched her.

She remembered that she had felt so loved. So cherished always.

And then she was gone.

That was when Lyssia had known that she was going to have the baby. Because that ghost of a memory was the most real thing she had ever experienced, and she wanted that. She wanted a child to love. She wanted to be a mother. And yes, there were going to be… Some issues. She was going to have to tell Dario. She was going to have to tell her father. She had decided that she could handle it. She had just made a very real business plan, and she had decided to attack custody the same way.

And so now here she was. It seemed a lot more reasonable in its inception. Now it seemed a little bit over the top.

"Lyssia…" He was speechless. She had rendered *Dario* speechless.

It had been a pretty shocking time for her, so it seemed fair.

"I didn't quite know the best way to tell you, but I thought that it would be best to speak when I had everything planned. So this is my proposal for custody..."

"Custody?" he asked, his voice dripping with disdain.

"Yes. Custody."

Above all else, as she had sat in that dark room and thought about her child. She had realized that she wanted her child to be proud of her. If she was going to share custody with Dario that meant that when the child was with their father, they would only be with him. When they were with her, they would only be with her. And she didn't want a child going from their wonderful, accomplished, type A father to a mother who wasn't as successful.

And that was when she had decided that she was going to get a contract with Dario's company too. Because she wanted her child to be able to be proud of her. It felt important. And that was holding her steady now. She wanted to be admirable. And this, she felt, was admirable. She was facing everything head-on, she was being mature and adult. She was owning her responsibilities.

"Yes," she said again. "*Custody.* Because of course we need to make sure that we have an amicable arrangement in place..."

"As if we will be... Co-parenting?"

"Yes," she said. "What else would we do? Unless... If you don't want to be part of the child's life, that is okay. I'm fully prepared to—"

"Absolutely not," he said. "Under no circumstances will any child of mine be abandoned by the father. And under no circumstances will any child of mine not live in my household. You will marry me, Lyssia."

She stood there, staring at him. And then, he was standing, and she had to look up, quite a bit up, to make eye contact with him. She was thankful the desk was between them because the impact of him was overwhelming. The memory of that night over a month ago was burned into her.

She would've thought that being with him like that might have demystified him. That she would feel... If not ambivalent, then at least like it was all settled. But instead, she felt like she was dangerously close to an electrical wire when she looked at him.

Like she was in danger of being shocked. And worse, like she might want to be.

She was trying to keep her guard up. Trying to keep herself from crumbling.

"We don't need to marry," she said.

"I do not want my child growing up in a broken home."

"My home was broken," she said. "It wasn't my mother's fault that she died. Our child will have both parents. That isn't a bad thing. And we've known each other for years. Surely we can be civil."

"We can be, but I won't be. I want to have our child living with married parents under one roof."

"Why?" she asked, feeling all of her control slipping.

She just couldn't handle this.

She had come to a place where she thought that she could do this. If anything, she had been worried that he wouldn't want the child. It had never occurred to her that he would demand that she marry him.

How could she...

How could she marry him? They weren't in a relationship. And she was just starting out with her business, and she was getting used to the idea of using her connections. But to be her father's daughter, and Dario's wife...

He's the father of your child either way. It isn't like you're going to get rid of your connection to him.

She gritted her teeth. Maybe. But he didn't love her. And she was definitely not in a position where she wanted to be tied to a man who could not fall in love with her. She'd never seen Dario have a relationship that lasted longer than a photo op.

She just had sex for the first time. There had to be more out there. She didn't know what sort of man she wanted. She didn't...

"That's ridiculous," she said.

"Why? What better reason to marry than a child?"

"Love?"

"Love is a fantasy. And some people do a very admirable job of getting lost in it. But those of us who live as I did don't have the luxury. And when you do not have that luxury you cannot buy into anything beyond what you can see and feel and touch."

"Dario..."

"I told you I lived on the streets. Everyone knows this."

"Yes, you did."

"But do you know how I got there?"

She shook her head. "No. How would I know unless you told me?"

"Then now I'll tell you. After my mother died he could no longer afford me. And he sold me. He sold me to a family who used me as manual labor, and believe me, I know that I did better than I might have. There are much worse uses people find for children. Instead, I was only expected to do hard labor. But that was how much my father loved me. I will not have any child of mine experience any potential instability."

It was like the room had been stripped of the ceiling, like the sky above was howling like a wolf.

Sold?

That boy she'd seen in her mind, sleeping on the streets, was suddenly right there again. Suddenly with her. And it was like everything was…pain. It was difficult for her to fully wrap her mind around what he had just said. She had conflicts with her father, and she had certainly let herself wallow in this idea that he might not love her quite as much as perhaps her mother had, or as much as he did Dario. But her father had never left her unsafe. And he would never have done anything like that. She knew in that moment, that if her father had been faced with abject poverty when her mother had died he would've taken care of her. Without question. He would have sacrificed it all for her.

And Dario…

He'd told her it was the usual sad story and it wasn't. There was nothing usual about this. It was barbaric and horrible and beyond imagination.

"I don't know what to say," she said. "It's horrible, it's awful, it's…"

"You can see why I insist on marriage."

"No. I don't. I don't understand why you think we need to be married in order to have these kinds of supports and stability in place. We can have a custody arrangement. We… We are in each other's lives, Dario, it isn't like we can't figure out a way to share a child. Nothing bad has happened between us."

"It isn't acceptable," he said. "I would give a child of mine everything."

"I didn't think you wanted children. Ever. As you are Dario Rivelli and if you wanted something you'd have had it by now."

"I didn't. But you are having one. And it is mine. There will be no other man raising my child. Did you harbor fantasies about that? Did you think perhaps you could convince golden retriever Carter to take on that role?"

"No," she said. "No. I didn't. I wouldn't. Ever. I came to you as soon as I figured out what I wanted to do. I came to you as soon as I had a plan. I'm doing what you said. I'm taking control. I'm not afraid. I think that this is the best—"

"You're wrong. The best thing for our child, the best thing for all of us would be if we were a family unit."

"What does that look like to you?"

"We will be married. Our child will not be subjected to censure. Think about it. Think about the sorts of articles that will be written about you and I if it does not look like we are in a real relationship."

"So that's what you're worried about. You know no one cares anymore if people are married."

"It is the principle. We do not wish to invite speculation. We will marry. It certainly doesn't matter if it's clear you were pregnant prior to the marriage, but there is no need for people to wonder or guess at the nature of our relationship."

"You would rather sell a lie."

"You're damn right I would. Instead of having… Online lists written about deadbeat billionaire father's or whatever else."

"I wasn't under the impression that you cared about that kind of thing," she said.

"I care about it in regard to my child. I will never give my child reason to doubt my care. My…my willingness to be there for them. I will never."

"I think that you're being—"

"Perhaps," he said. "But if we do this wrong we cannot go back and make it right. If we do this wrong, then we cannot go back and redo it. What is out there will be out there for all the world."

"I think the solution to that is to communicate with our child," she said.

"You want something from me, Lyssia. You want a business deal. Fine. Marry me, and it's yours."

"Are you kidding me? That is the most sexist, archaic thing that I have ever heard. I have to marry you in order to get a business deal. And it isn't going to be based on merit in any fashion."

"Did you think that it would be? You came in here with a business plan, yes, but you also came in bound and determined to tell me exactly how it was going to be with our child. Did you think that you were going to announce you are having my baby and then my decision as to whether or not I was going to go into business with you would be neutral?"

Well, she'd thought he was reasonable, and a businessman first. Every time she'd tried to bring up the subject of her issues with her father he'd been very black-and-white about all of it. If she was cared for, why was she mad? Like the finer emotional points didn't matter.

Given what she now knew about his childhood, she could understand that.

But still, she had expected him to take a cool approach to the idea of fatherhood. To be…appropriate, yes, but to want the bare minimum.

"I don't know," she said. "I don't know how to reach you. It never occurred to me that you would want to marry me. It never occurred to me that emotion would come into a business deal at all for you."

"You have never known me. I am not a cold man. I…"

He seemed at a loss for words, and that was an unusual thing. But did he really think he wasn't cold? He hadn't been during their time together, but then he'd cut her off like nothing had happened.

So yes, he could burn blazing hot, but he could definitely be cold. And his being filled with umbrage about it was a bit much for her.

"You acted as if nothing happened between us. When my father came to the house, it was like you were a stranger again." It made her vulnerable to admit that, but he had to know. They'd always had honesty between them. Even if it was easier to play with verbal knives before they'd become lovers. And now she felt wretched and upset but she wasn't going to lie.

"What exactly did you wish me to do? Did you wish me to lay you down across the rug as our rescuers descended upon us and give them an example of how we had spent the last days?"

"I don't know. I wanted something. You never reach out to me."

"And neither did you."

"Why would I?" she asked. "It did not feel to me like there was any reason to. You were the one that said you couldn't offer me anything. And now you're insisting on marriage."

"I can't offer you what you want."

"What did you think I wanted?"

"Most women want love," he said, his tone flat.

She made a show of looking around the office, a hand pressed to her forehead as if she was blocking out the sun to look far and wide.

"What are you doing?" he asked.

"Looking for all the women you've no doubt slept with, to see if they're loitering around wishing for love."

"Of course they are not here."

"So clearly they didn't need love. What makes you think I do? I might not want a marriage destined to be loveless, but I never said I was sitting around waiting for you to love me."

"In an ideal world I would not demand marriage of you, because I would hate to make you miserable."

"But you'll make me miserable for what you consider to be the sake of our child?"

"Yes. I will. There will be time enough to discuss logistics later. I am not suggesting that we live a traditional marriage for the entire life of our child. But I am suggesting that I want it as a foundation. I am not suggesting, I am demanding. And I will not be denied."

"And if I say no?"

"I cannot force you. But I would hope that you'd see reason. And I would hope that this business deal would be enough enticement."

"If it isn't, am I to expect threats?"

"No. There is no reason to issue threats. I'm correct. I think with time you'll realize that, but I do feel that it would be better if you would come to that conclusion quickly. You expect that we are to go to your father and tell him that you are having my baby and that you aren't going to marry me?"

"Is that your real concern? That my father will be angry at you?"

"It is a concern."

And he was Dario's family. She did understand that. But also, they were supposed to be something to each other and what he was proposing just seemed…outlandish.

"What does family mean to you?"

"Why do you need to know this?"

"I feel like I can't possibly marry you or even enter into a discussion until I know what it means. What is love to you, and what will you give to our child?"

He looked at her, his dark eyes intense. And she could see that he didn't want to be questioned. It was too bad. Because she was going to question him. She was going to question this.

It was fair. Because…

She wanted to know what she was potentially signing herself up for. It was only fair.

"Family is what your father has done for you," he said finally. "It is taking care of one another. It is the only place I have ever seen it. My own family did not treat love as if it was unconditional. What I know more than anything is what I don't want. And what I will not allow."

"And what about giving more than material wealth to your child?"

"I want to make a family, does that not demonstrate my desire to do so?"

"My father and I lived together in a family. He loves me but he has never known what to do with me. If you think marriage and living in a home can solve these things like a magic trick, then you're wrong."

"So if I am not perfect I cannot try?" he asked, his voice fierce. And she went cold at that. Regretful.

"I didn't say that."

"You are asking me to tell you all that I can ever be before we have ever even heard the child's heartbeat. How does that strike you as fair?"

It wasn't. She knew that. She sighed.

"Love," she said. "What does it mean to you?"

They weren't in love. She knew that. She knew there was a difference between sex and feelings. She wasn't that naive. Yes, what had happened between them was amazing. But it hadn't been worth it. Not really.

She felt guilty for thinking that. She wanted to put her

hand protectively over her stomach. Wanted to apologize to the little life blooming inside of her.

It hadn't asked to be created. She had to be sure that even though this wasn't planned she never passed on any resentment. It wasn't really a child that she resented. It was knowing that she had to solve this. That she had to take control of this and make it right. And standing in front of him right now with his demand of marriage hanging in the air she just wasn't sure what was right. More than that, she wasn't sure what her feelings were. But it felt disastrous.

She felt disastrous.

Wasn't this just the same? The same as it always was. He hadn't wanted her for her.

He wanted their child.

It was a hideous thing to be jealous of her own unborn baby, but there it was. It was never about her. He was even considering her father's feelings over hers.

It was just never about her.

"Does *marriage* mean something to you, then," she pressed. "If you can't tell me about love."

"It will mean, quite simply that you are my family. And if you are my family, then you will always be mine. I will take care of you. Always."

Taking care. It was what he saw from her father. That was how he interpreted the way her father provided for her.

That was hardly a declaration of love. But then, did she want one? She had imagined that she would get married someday, it just hadn't been anywhere near her radar. She had imagined that she might try and settle down in her thirties. And of course she had thought that it would be a union about love. Because otherwise what was the point?

Otherwise, why? Of course, there was a bigger answer to that question now. It was about the baby.

She wondered what her mother would do. Put in this situation. Her parents had loved each other very much. What would her mother have done if she had been faced with the prospect of marrying a man who didn't want to love, but wanted to create a family unit for the sake of their child. The truth was, life was fragile. And she had seen that firsthand. She had seen it at a young age. It had taken away some of the mystery and magic of life. The sense that things were charmed for her.

She had always thought that tragedy was something that befell others. And then it had befallen them. Their family, their kingdom had been shattered. And she'd had a little piece of life that was idyllic.

Sure, she was a nepo baby. But money didn't insulate you from tragedy.

If she married Dario, would she find that kingdom again? Or would it be impossible because it wasn't about love?

It is. It's about the love that you feel for your child. And how much you want that child to admire you.

Okay. That was true. But she just wanted to matter. If she had that business deal, then she would be an accomplished entrepreneur. She would be able to show her child what being a strong woman looked like. Maybe she wouldn't pale in comparison to Dario quite so much.

And that was the real issue. The rub. She didn't want to pale in comparison to Dario. She'd taken a step to finding a space to be different but effective with business, when it came to her father, but…she wanted to prove herself. She wanted to be special. Did she want everything? She kind of did.

"In terms of fidelity? Sex?"

"We have chemistry," he said. "I see no reason why we would have a marriage in name only."

The thought lit her on fire. She had been so convinced that those wild days in the snow were the only times they would ever have together.

But now he was talking about marriage. And sex. Sharing a life. Sharing a bed.

"And if you decide that you're tired of me?" she asked.

"I've never been with a woman long enough to tire of her."

"And so to that point you actually don't know how long it takes for you to get tired of a woman. If you do…"

"I'll let you know," he said.

If she ever became boring. If she ever had to be second to some random woman. The very idea made her feel sick.

"I won't be blindsided," she said. "Above all else, I won't be blindsided. I know what that's like. I was having a completely normal night. It was normal, and then my father came in to tell me that there was an accident and my mother was dead. And I have never gotten over that feeling. That you can be sitting there and everything will be just fine and the next moment your entire life is turned upside down. I will never sit there waiting for the other shoe to drop. Throw it to me first."

He nodded gravely and she was grateful she knew Dario was honest. Above all things, he was honest.

"You have my word. And the same applies to you. We can renegotiate the terms of the marriage at any time. But when it starts, we will be faithful. We will have a small child anyway."

She frowned. "Do you intend to be a hands-on father?"

"Yes. I do. Your father has been an incredible mentor to me. He is perhaps the only thing even near a father that I've ever experienced. I wish to give the same to our child."

"Yes, but you know small children don't want to hear about acquisitions and spreadsheets."

"I know that," he said.

"What if I tell you no?"

"You don't want to tell me no," he said. "Come now. Be reasonable. How would it benefit you to stay separate from me? Especially when I'm offering you a certain measure of freedom. You would rather walk into your father's office and tell him that you have decided not to marry me?"

"No," she said, suddenly and hideously appalled by that image. "I don't want to do that."

"I didn't think you did. And so here we are. At an impasse. Would you refuse for the sake of it? For the sake of your pride?" That galled her, because he was right. Half her issue was her pride. Half her issue was the fact that she didn't simply want to give him what he was asking for. It was a habit. Dario had vexed her for so many years it was difficult now to realize that she had to join forces with him. Even after those days they'd spent snowed in.

He had felt different then.

He had been such a wonderful lover. Courteous and generous and...

She needed to not think about that right now.

Was she going to do this? Agree to marry him and engage in all the spectacle that it would create? Agree to marry him and find herself back in his bed?

You want that.

She did. But she didn't want to want it. It was pointless. And worse, it was dangerous. What would happen if she ended up having feelings for him that he didn't return?

Isn't that already the case?

She shoved that thought to the side. She wasn't in love with him. But she did think about him quite a bit.

"Marry me," he said. "Join me. We will combine our companies and sit on top in business…"

Business. On top. Good God.

"You sound like Darth Vader, do you know that?" she asked, sounding a bit acidic.

He smiled. Looking grimly at her. "It is perhaps not a coincidence."

"Yes. Of course. You're so dark and bad."

Of course, saying that, even teasing made a little zip of arousal shiver through her. That was embarrassing. Really.

"Marry me," he said. "We will tell your father together. That he is going to be a grandfather, and that we are getting married."

"I…"

And she couldn't think of a reason not to. She absolutely couldn't.

Worst of all perhaps she wanted to say yes just for herself. But what would it get her? Well, this hot man would be her husband and they would spar ever after. But they would have a home and a child and perhaps that was all worth it?

Or maybe she was weak.

But if so, then she was weak.

She sighed.

"Well. How do you want to do this, then?"

"I'm canceling all of my plans, and we're going to dinner. I will then propose to you."

"Aren't you going to ask my father's permission?"

He frowned. "Neither of you would respect me if I did such a thing."

"It's traditional," she said.

"And you are not traditional. He may bluster about it, but he would rather I consult you than him. You know that, surely."

"I don't. But I'm glad that you do. Since he is clearly such a good friend to you."

"Don't be snappish," he said. "Go home and change. I will procure a ring for you, and then we will meet for dinner."

And that was how Lyssia found herself unofficially engaged, and stunned into complete silence.

CHAPTER NINE

DARIO'S MIND WAS working overtime to try and solve the intricacies of the situation. Of course, Nathan Anderson wouldn't be thrilled that Dario had gotten Lyssia pregnant out of wedlock, but he was a practical man, and he wouldn't be shocked by it. It wasn't as if he expected either of them to be chaste.

Pregnant.

She was pregnant with his child.

It had been all he could do not to threaten her. Threaten to take custody of the child, threaten to kidnap her. Beat his chest and climb the Empire State building like King Kong.

The problem was, this had hooked into something he hadn't known was in him.

He needed to make sure that there was every legal protection available to his child. He needed to make sure that no one could write scathing things about his child.

He needed to protect that child in all the ways that he wasn't protected, and marriage seemed the first step to doing that. Making sure that the circumstances surrounding his child's birth seemed clear. And he also didn't want to compromise his relationship with Lyssia's father. That was true too.

What does love mean to you?

There was no such thing as love. There was either care

or no care. And he cared. He cared about that child. About its future. And he knew what it was like when a parent forfeited that care. It was unconscionable.

It was cold and lonely and memories he refused to have.

How long were you on the street?

Maybe a year.

He knew every night but he refused to name them.

He called a private jeweler immediately and had them bring a tray of engagement rings into his office.

Likely, he should have asked Lyssia what she wanted. But this was not about her.

It wasn't.

His body had reacted strongly when Lyssia had first come into the room, but after that, everything had been red.

Because the only thing that really mattered was doing the right thing for their child.

And yes, he would have her. Why wouldn't he? He was certainly not going to leave her celibate so that she could go off and make planned love to Carter.

No.

The child was his. She was his.

It all made perfect sense to him.

He chose the largest and most ostentatious ring. He thought she would probably like it. There was nothing subtle about Lyssia. He thought about that white lingerie she'd worn the first time they were together. And the other outfits she'd worn in the times after.

He'd taken her in hot pink next to the shower. He'd stripped her of flimsy emerald green by the bathtub.

He bent her over the counter in the kitchen when she was in black, with matching heels.

He couldn't understand how she was pregnant. She'd said she was on the pill. He also knew that it was his child. Lyssia would never claim to be pregnant with his baby if it was someone else's. No. In fact, being pregnant with anyone else's baby would probably be an ideal situation for her. Then he called and arranged for a highly visible table at his favorite restaurant.

They would perform this. And when it was done, they would go and visit her father and tell him the news. As he sat at his desk, looking at the diamond ring, he called Lyssia. "I'll be at your house by six. We'll be having Italian."

"Well, that means it's probably going to be amazing," she said. "I doubt you would pick a bad Italian restaurant."

"You're correct. I am given to believe it is like old home cooking. I would hardly remember that. I barely remember what it's like to have a home in Italy much less anything cooked for me. But I like to think that my blood recalls."

"I assume I am to dress up?"

"Yes."

He got off the phone with her quickly, and cleared his schedule for the next three days. There would be nothing but working toward assembling this wedding, and finalizing that business deal with her. He would not sign anything for it until they were married. Using it as a carrot was perhaps low, but it was necessary.

He wasn't sure which thing had gotten to her. The offer to join in business, or the comment about her father.

Because he did know that Lyssia cared very much what her father thought.

At a quarter to six he made his way to Lyssia's penthouse in Midtown, where he left his driver idling at the front and entered the code for the building. Of course he had it. Her father had given it to him in case there was ever an emergency.

This was the right thing to do. Not just for the child. Her

father wanted him to take care of her. And this would not just protect their child, but her as well.

It was the right thing to do.

He went up the elevator to her floor, and walked down the hall. She opened it suddenly, her eyes wide. "What are you doing here this early?"

"I'm not early. Five minutes, maybe."

"Well, you didn't ask to be let up."

"I have a code. You didn't check to see who it was."

"I assumed it was somebody who works in the building. Or a neighbor."

She was half-dressed, wearing a silk nightgown.

"Are you all right?"

"Yes. I'm just… Trying to find something to wear."

"I can help."

"No thank you," she said.

"You don't think I have good taste?"

"I don't see the point of trying to look nice for a date with you if I then also show you all the things I try on. It doesn't actually make sense."

"It's not a date," he said. "We are putting on a performance."

"Right. Noted." He had clearly said the wrong thing. Or not. With Lyssia he could never really tell. Sometimes she acted put out just to fight with him.

"Don't be upset about it," he said. "You asked me what I think about love. I don't believe in it. Not as a philosophical concept. What I believe in is action. Taking care of the people that we have a responsibility to."

"Wow. Very romantic."

"I never said that it was romantic. But it is the truth."

"Why haven't you fallen in love with somebody yet? I mean, why didn't you have relationships in the past?"

She turned and walked toward her room. "You might as well come in," she said.

He walked in, and frowned. Her room was an explosion. Like her suitcase had been that first day. All of her things were strewn everywhere. And everything in the room was very pink.

"I never wanted a family," he said. "Or children. I have been single-minded and singularly focused since I was thirteen years old and decided to run away from the house I was being kept in." He was trying to decide if he should tell her the rest. Why not?

"There were children in that house. A married couple. The father was horrendously abusive. He beat me. He beat his own children. He beat his wife. It was another place that I saw men abusing the position they were in. A position that should be sacred. What is less honorable than taking people into your care and causing them harm."

He had never told anyone this. There had never seemed a point. He wasn't sure if he wanted her to understand him or if he wanted to prove to her that everything she was so concerned about was silly.

He would be a good father.

A damned sight better than his own. It would be impossible not to be. But all of this going on and on about love.

"There's nothing honorable about that," she said softly.

"No. I was only ever given bad examples of what it means to be the head of the family. Of what it means to take care of a wife and child. I never wanted it. And I felt that my drive made me unsuitable to it. But now you are pregnant. And it is no longer a discussion. It is reality."

"Everything can be a discussion now, Dario. We live in a very flexible era."

She looked so sincere. He almost felt sorry for her. "Yes, *cara*, but I am not a flexible man."

She wrinkled her nose. "I mean, I know that. I've met you."

"Yes. I understand that. You know me. I feel that it has made you rather bold in your dealings with me. You do not understand, do you, Lyssia? The manner of man that I am. But you will. When you are mine, you will."

She would be his. His wife. He would have his wife and his child in his home, that he was certain of, and he would not yield.

He was not a man capable of such a thing.

"Yes. I know. You are a big, scary billionaire."

She reached down and grabbed a dress off the floor, and he lifted a brow as she shook it out. "Maybe this."

"How about not."

He stood and went over to her closet. A vast, walk-in room that was larger than some places he had stayed in his youth. His eye was caught by a long, red dress at the back. "That one."

"Which one?" She appeared in the doorway.

"Red. Tonight, you will wear red for me."

"I like pink," she said, because she always had to challenge him.

"I like red," he said, taking hold of her chin and holding her gaze steady on his. "You will do what I say. You will give me what I want."

He could see that she wanted to argue, but he could also see arousal flare in her eyes. The very things that irritated her about him were also the things that drew her to him. He could relate.

It was Lyssia's very nature that made her undeniable. Her buoyancy. Her quick wit and temper. It was also what made her an irredeemable brat. Sadly for him, he quite liked a brat.

At least, this particular brat.

"Leave," she said, shooing him out of the closet. A few moments later, she came out, the silken fabric of the dress molding to her body as a second skin. She wasn't wearing a bra and he could see the natural outline of her breasts, her nipples.

It was decent enough, but his eye was drawn there, and he couldn't look away.

He also didn't wish for her to change the way the dress was styled. Because it was far too intoxicating.

"Yes," he said. "That one."

"I'll just be a moment."

She emerged from the bathroom perhaps two minutes later, her blond hair put up in a carefree clip, a swipe of shimmer on her eyes, a bit of red on her lips. She was just so beautiful naturally that it took almost nothing to transform her into a glamorous goddess.

Truthfully, he could not have planned this better. He had not intended to take a wife, but what better wife then Lyssia Anderson? She was from this world. He had business dealings with her father, her father was the dearest mentor he had ever known.

She would be the hostess that he needed her to be when it came to having events. She would be the perfect accessory at any business affair.

Yes, this was actually much better than he had originally thought. He had been uncertain about it. But it would be…

It would be a boon. He would make sure of it. If there was one thing Dario was good at, it was making a boon out of a difficult situation.

And as for Lyssia… He was handling her as he always did.

"Let's go, *cara*. Our table awaits."

The car was waiting out front when they got downstairs, and he opened the door for her, pressing his hand to the small of her back as he guided her into the vehicle.

There was a barrier between them and the driver, so they were able to speak privately.

"This is going to create a little firestorm, isn't it?" she asked.

"Yes," he agreed. "It is. I have chosen a table in a location designed to help fuel that fire. You understand."

"It's very important to you that this looks a certain way."

"I will not have anybody speculating on my child being a bastard."

"I think we're a bit past that as a society, don't you?"

"Perhaps. But I am not from this world. And there will be people who say that your father should never have taken me in as he did considering I impregnated his daughter and did not make it right. They will say that I took advantage of you. They will talk about our age gap. The fact that I've known you for so long. The narrative will ever be that I am a predator from the streets who never should have been trusted."

"That isn't fair," she said, a small crease appearing between her eyebrows. "I was involved in making this baby just as much is you were."

"To be certain. And there will be plenty of things said about you. Sexism is alive and well. But so is classism. I am ever to be a hardscrabble success story. But with that success story comes the inevitable truth of my roots. And what people will say about them."

"Do you actually care?"

The question sent a fire through his blood. "Yes. I did not spend all these years remaking myself into something new only to be cast in the mold that I came out of. I destroyed that. Broke it. Very deliberately. I have made myself new. I made myself safe, and I will make my child equally so."

He had not meant to say quite so much, and he could see that she was rocked by what he had said.

"I didn't think of it that way."

"All I have ever wanted is to put as much distance between that danger and myself as I could. I will not pass it on to my heir. I will not send it down my bloodline."

She nodded slowly. "I understand that. I do. I'm sorry if it seems like I'm insensitive. It's…it's exhausting all of this, isn't it? We bat awful things back and forth with our verbal rackets and try to respond and get in our own truths and… there isn't time, it doesn't feel like. For me to take all this in because I'm listening to you but I'm also just trying to breathe. To survive this. It's all unknown. Being a mother. I want to have this baby but I'm terrified."

"Do you think you have the monopoly on fear?"

She shook her head. "No. Though you handle it differently than I do. But I understand why you're afraid."

"You have experienced challenges in your life. I'm not denying that. But you don't know what it's like. To continually feel that you have to earn a place."

She looked out the window, and then back at him. "Not in the same way you do. But I do feel like I always have to earn a place. My mother loved having a child. It was, I think, the only thing she really wanted. My father would see me at dinnertime, and he enjoyed me, but it wasn't the same. I loved him. I love him. Please don't misunderstand. When my mother died, my father was bereft, and I could never shake the feeling that he had loved being her husband far more than he ever loved being my father. He never said that. But I always felt like I had to earn the right to still be there. To consume so much of his attention when what he wanted to do was sink into the sadness of having lost his wife, and I cannot blame him. I can't. He loved her so much. And I wanted to be able to fill that void, I wanted to be there for him. And then there was you. He met you, Dario, and it was like watching the light return to him. I think he always wanted a son. But he could never face the idea of marrying again. Because he would never love anyone other than my mother. And you were everything he ever wanted. And not a child. I think he never did know what to do with children. But an adult protégé who was good, better than he was, everything he valued? You were what healed him, not me. All I have ever wanted is to be the one bringing the light in, and I could never quite manage it."

She took a shuddering breath. "I'm not saying that I haven't had a certain amount of ease in my life. I have. And I'm not fool enough to think that I understand the struggle that you went through. I never had to do hard labor. I was never hungry. I was never afraid. I didn't move to a new country when I was a teenager and start over. I know that you did. But sometimes I felt invisible in my own house. I have always felt caught between all the things that I wanted. The love of my father, the desire for the right kind of success that would make him impressed with me, and the urge to be myself. Somewhere in all of that I think I never even quite figured out who I was."

It would be easy to brush these things aside. It would be easy to dismiss her as a poor little rich girl. But her pain was very real, and he did not relish it. It was the kind of pain he thought he might've had if his life had continued on in the normal fashion. If it hadn't been shattered so spectacularly. The kind of pain he might've experienced if his father had been human, rather than a monster who had abandoned his son. He and Lyssia were living in the fallout of things they could not control. They had both lost their mothers. They had both been left with fathers who had not been up to the task.

But her father had weathered it. He had stayed. His own had not.

Her pain was real. It didn't have to be about safety and survival to be real.

"You are every inch yourself," he said. "Whether you feel that or not. And I'm not certain that at twenty-three you're meant to fully understand who you are. Life has a way of changing our expectations, does it not?"

He was a decade older than she was, and yet he too was on the cusp of a profound change. She was going to be a mother and he was going to be a father.

A father.

There was no relationship on earth he had a more complicated feeling about.

Lyssia's father had been so good to him. His own so damaging.

He had vowed he would never be a father. Or a husband. Now he was to be both.

"I have gotten this far with great certainty of how everything would go. I never counted on you. On this. In that sense, perhaps neither of us know ourselves. Or at the very least we do not have great enough respect for how the world might intervene."

"Is it fate, do you think?"

"I think it was lust," he said. "Which has been undoing the greater plans of humanity for thousands of years."

She laughed softly. "Well. That's a good point. Though, not quite as romantic as fate." There was something hopeful in her eyes, and it made him ache. Because if she was hoping for real romance, there was no chance of him giving it. He thought of his own home. Back in Italy. Small and simple and filled with warmth.

His father had never been a bad man.

His father had always loved him. That was the frightening thing.

It was the truly frightening thing.

"Life is not overly romantic," he said. "And anyway, romance can be dangerous. I prefer to rest on careful planning."

"Isn't the topic of discussion about how plans fall apart?"

He smiled. "Then you make new plans."

"What is the saying, Dario? Man plans, God laughs?"

"Good thing I'm relatively adjacent to the divine, isn't it?"

"You have always been so arrogant. And I have always wanted to be more horrified by it than I am."

"What a tragedy for you, then, that you find me irresistible."

She looked at him and spread her hands. "Here I am, resisting."

"And after dinner?"

"Are we talking to my father after dinner?"

"Indeed."

"I'm going to guess that I won't be in the mood after that."

"We'll see." Because there was something about the bright burning between them that made him feel like this was something a little more familiar. Like it was something a bit more manageable.

The car pulled up to the restaurant then, the large picture windows lit up brilliantly, making the diners inside look as if they were part of a theatrical production.

Exactly perfect. Their table was right in the center.

"Let's go, then," he said, opening the door and getting

out, and helping her out of the car. He put his arm around her waist, and she let out a small sound. He looked at her. "Yes?"

"I don't know. This is strange. We… We might've been together quite a bit when we were snowed in, but that wasn't real life. This… This feels more real. And it's scary. Different. Because you're Dario. And I…"

Her eyes glittered, and he had to look away. "It was always going to be this way between us. I understand why you didn't see that." It wasn't like he had seen it either. He had great faith in his ability to resist her. Why wouldn't he? He had never been given any reason to suspect he wouldn't be able to resist their attraction. Because attraction when it came to feeling something for a specific woman had never meant much of anything to him. And yet, there she was. At his side, because he simply hadn't been able to turn away from the fire that built to his stomach every time he saw her.

He was undone by this woman that he had known all these years. And yet, had they truly known each other? There had been honesty between them. But it had been rooted in the present. In the moment. They'd volley back and forth and in those moments he felt he saw her, the her she really was. But this was different. They were peeling back layers, excavating each other's pasts, their feelings. Not a single person on earth knew these things about him. None but her.

He was as blindsided by all of it as she was, but he refused to let her know that.

Instead, he swept her into the restaurant where they were greeted by a spate of staff. "Bring us your specials," he said, as they took their seats.

"We're not even going to order off the menu?" she asked.

"No. You will trust me."

He wanted her trust, he realized.

Perhaps she wasn't the only one who still felt like she was earning her place.

He knew that she wasn't. If he wasn't still earning his way, then he wouldn't feel so strongly about marriage. He wouldn't feel so strongly about making sure they did this in such a way that he was above reproach.

He didn't want their child reading stories about him being some sort of predator, of course. But he also just didn't want… He had worked hard to get where he was. And he didn't want baseless assumptions made about him. Not for any reason.

He had earned more than that.

It was impossible, he realized that, to completely avoid judgment in the court of public opinion. It was how the internet worked. Everyone had a method by which to share their opinions, and every opinion was treated as discourse, often printed in the news.

He would mitigate as much as possible.

Dinner was served, and Lyssia went straight for the bread, and the pasta, and he could tell by the look on her face that she agreed with his choices.

He watched her enjoyment and felt a strange sort of satisfaction regarding it. He had done this. He had satisfied her in this way. Yes, he had satisfied her sexually the whole time they were together at the chalet. But tonight, he had satisfied her in a different way. He was caring for her. Whether she knew it or not. And yes, some of this was to guard himself and his own reputation. But a substantial amount of it was about her.

He had, on a whim, earlier today, looked her name up online. He didn't care much for those things, though of course he had an awareness of his own reputation. It was part of managing his image. Which was part of good business.

He'd never looked her up. The internet was harsh and cruel about her. They saw her as a socialite playing at having a business, and he could see where much of her insecurity had come from. If her father didn't rush in to fill the void left by her mother, then those voices were going to do it.

He didn't want that for her. Perhaps, what he needed to do was begin to fill that void. With words of his own. Today, she had been a different version of herself than he had seen before. Confident and fiery. She had a plan. She'd been self-assured. The ability for her to do that had always been there. But she was afraid. Afraid to try because it might lead to rejection.

It was difficult to see that, because she spoke freely. At least, she did with him.

"I have seen now," he said. "Those online articles you were referencing before."

"Oh, the ones talking about how I'm bad at things?"

"Yes. They don't know you. They are strangers."

"Are you really going to talk to me about how public opinion doesn't matter when we're sitting here engaged in a big PR gambit?"

"I'm not going to talk to you about that. Public opinion does matter, to the extent that it affects your business. And for a child, I worry it would affect how they felt about themselves, about us. But it doesn't affect how I feel about myself. And I feel that you have been made to feel bad about yourself because nobody was working to say good things to you. Positive things. You proved today that you were capable of putting together an amazing business plan. You are smart. Talented. Capable. You're artistic. You design the furniture and the home goods yourself, do you not?"

She was the mother of his child. And further to that she'd asked what he would do to support their child. So that their child didn't feel like she did. So that he didn't repeat the mistakes her father had made, and God knew, he didn't truly think he was a better man than Nathan Anderson. But he wanted to try.

"Yes," she said. "Everything in my apartment is something from my collection. You should… You should come see my studio sometime."

"You're right. I should."

He was not creative. He was good at building things. And not hiring the right people to design them. To execute them. People were his talent.

Lyssia seemed to have many talents, and she was not given credit for that.

"What made you decide to design these things?" He would never have thought of it. It was interesting. He felt big, he was good at that. But the truth was, it had been a natural extension for him to go into the business he had because he had come up working in hospitality.

"I…" She looked down, her cheeks turning the same color crimson of her lips.

"Tell me," he said. "Whatever it is inspired you to start a company. Whatever it is you have taken that inspiration and created many beautiful things with it. I want to know."

She smiled, lovely. Warm. It made something bloom within him.

"My mom loved to decorate. I associated all of these little touches around the house with her. They stayed the same for long time afterward. And then after I left the house, my dad sort of redid everything and made it very Spartan. He didn't add decorations. He didn't put knickknacks on shelves. He didn't have decorative lamps. I associated touches of home, of warmth with her. It can make you feel certain things. It can change your whole mood. I thought if I could help people change their surroundings, I can help them change the way that they felt. There is something about an attention to detail that can really create a whole new environment. I know my bedroom was really messy. But my house is stylized, but lived in. I don't like things to be to Spartan. It reminds me of… Of loss."

"I can think of few other better reasons to do anything."

He sat there watching, holding the stem on his wineglass between his thumb and forefinger, turning it absently. "I think one reason I was drawn to hospitality, other than the fact that a cruise ship allowed me to gain entry into the United States, was that it was about comfort. I had a shortage of it. For many years. And there was something about being able to give it to somebody else, and by doing that work, earning money so that I can have some myself, that gave me a sense of purpose. And of pride. I do not create things like you do. But it was still a lack of something that drew me to this life. I can do anything now. I could stop working. I could buy a different company. Get into a new sort of industry. I like what I do now."

"Do you… I know that you care a lot about the environment."

He sniffed. "It's expedient to be seen as doing so."

"Yes, your street cred is safe with me. I think you care about it. What other charities do you give to?"

"It isn't important," he said.

"Ah, so there are charities." She looked far too pleased with herself for divining that information. He found her irritating.

"I don't see what business it is of yours."

"We're sharing information. Having a conversation. Like humans. Humans that are about to be engaged."

"I have a foundation. I don't advertise it. For homeless

youth. And another for general housing and security. We've had old hotels and apartment buildings renovated into affordable housing. And we give classes, to help people re-enter society. One of the things people don't realize about growing up in that way, or living that way for a certain number of years, is that it isn't quite so simple as just deciding to step back into society. You have to learn. I was good at that. I was good at watching people and figuring it out on my own. But not everybody is. I was able to come up with a very convincing facade. One that helps me convince people that I belonged wherever I was. I don't take that for granted. Nor do I expect for everyone to be able to do it."

"You're a very compassionate person," she said.

He wanted to push against that. He had never thought of himself as compassionate. He had only ever thought of himself as practical. It wasn't right that people suffer on the streets if they wanted a different life. It wasn't right that children should suffer because of the choices that their parents had made. He didn't believe that people should be thrown away like garbage, he didn't consider that compassion, he considered it reasonable.

"Don't spin fantasies about me. I am the man that you have always known. The man you disliked this entire time. And now that I have given you pleasure, you seem to like me more."

"That isn't all you did. I'm having your baby."

"Yes, well. Don't go trying to spin that into a better situation by creating stories about me. I am still the man that you've known all this time. The one that you found cold and cruel at times."

"But you're also the man that I got to know in the chalet. You are also a man who hasn't forgotten where he came from. Maybe I shouldn't romanticize you, but isn't it fair to say that you're more than you've shown me?"

"You make it sound as if I have done something deliberate with you, and I have not." He chose his words carefully. Because they were sharp enough that they would slice beneath her skin, and she might not feel it just now. But she would later.

"None of this has been a game. And none of it has been a plan. I was not hiding something and then showing you. I did not think of you at all. I thought of myself. My own comfort, and my own enjoyment."

"Liar," she said.

Later. It would hurt later. It would make her think later.

The dessert came, and as soon as she finished the last bite, he moved from his chair and got down on one knee. "Lyssia, *cara*, will you marry me?"

CHAPTER TEN

UNTIL HE'D GOTTEN down on one knee, she'd forgotten it was a farce. Well, it wasn't a farce. She was really going to marry him because she was really having a baby.

But for a moment, they had just felt like two people who were connecting. Talking. Like two people who had chosen to share each other's company, rather than what they were. Two people performing a very specific farce for the world. One that had nothing to do with how he listened to her or made her feel validated or interesting. One that had nothing to do with her at all. It was all about him. Him and his reputation. And as he lifted the lid on the velvet box that contained the engagement ring, she forgot to breathe. Because she was struck dumb by how hurt she was. By how unfair this felt.

Because it was beautiful, this moment. Because she realized she felt some things for him that she would rather not. At this inopportune time.

Where he was there, being gorgeous and all the things he ever was, but fundamentally not... Hers.

She'd said yes to him. To this. But the enormity of the emotional mountain that separated them was so vast she didn't see how they could ever overcome it. And worse, he wouldn't want to.

And she had no choice. No choice but to smile. No choice

but to extend her hand while everyone in the restaurant looked on. And he took the most enormous ring she had ever seen out of the box and slid it onto her finger. She had never imagined this moment. Not really. Right then she realized it could only have ever been with him.

Because something about Dario had gotten under her skin and stayed there from the moment she'd first seen him.

Yes, when they'd first met she'd been a child, and it hadn't been at all like that. But she had lost someone then. And then... He had been there.

He had felt like arrival in many ways, and sometimes he still did.

He was significant, though. In a way she wouldn't be able to easily describe to anyone.

Right then, it felt confusing. Right then it felt horribly, and terribly poignant.

If she were going to write an article about it, then it would be a fairy tale.

They had known each other all of their lives. They were so different. They had both lost their mothers.

They had always been sparring partners. But then they'd become lovers.

They had fought their way through personality clashes and misunderstandings through an attraction that was undeniable. He had listened when she needed someone to talk to. He had encouraged her to be the best version of herself.

She only needed him to be him.

She made him tell her the nicer things about himself. Made him admit that he was a human and not a robot.

But that wasn't the truth.

It was just all the beautiful clues that he had strung together to lead to this moment. The assumptions that would be employed in order to make all of this seem magic. Rather than cold and calculated.

And part of her still felt caught up in it. Part of her still wanted to weep. Part of her still wanted to pretend that it was a fairy tale.

He stood, then lifted her up out of the chair and pulled her into his arms.

He hadn't touched her like this in six weeks.

The restaurant was their captive audience, and she had no time to respond before he brought his mouth down to hers, kissing her deep and long. Kissing her with intensity.

She clung to his arms, to keep herself from falling, from melting into a puddle at his feet. God knew she possibly might.

His mouth was firm and knowing. Not just of sex in general, but of her. As if he could reach in and read the deepest, most personal fantasies that she had.

His tongue swept hers, and she was transported. Back to that moment in the chalet when it had just been them.

This pure sort of reckoning of all that existed between them.

And when it was over, she felt dizzy, and displaced. Resentful that they were here in New York, and not back in their own cocoon.

But this was now. It was reality. They were having a baby. They were getting married. Her life was completely different now from how it had been. Her future was going to be something entirely separate to what she had imagined it would be.

Everything. Everything was different.

She had no idea how to reconcile that.

She wasn't even sure she wanted to. There was something almost comforting in the feeling of being outside of her body. Almost comforting in not feeling like herself. Not feeling like it was real.

"We should get to your father's as soon as possible. We don't want him to see it on the news."

"It'll probably just be on social media," she said. "And he won't see that."

He chuckled. "True."

She didn't know how he could laugh. She didn't know how he could be relaxed in any way. She felt like she was at the end of herself.

And she found herself being whisked out of the restaurant and back to his town car.

Being chauffeured out of the city and headed toward her father's house upstate.

It was an hour's drive, and she didn't quite know what to say as they burned through the miles on the highway.

"We will marry as soon as possible."

"We need to be able to actually put a wedding together," she said.

"The wedding doesn't matter," he said.

"How can you say that? After going to such great lengths to organize that spectacle of an engagement, how can you think that the wedding won't matter?"

"A small intimate ceremony with family and friends," he said as though he was reading the headline.

"Maybe that isn't what I want. Maybe I want to have an actual wedding. Did you ever think about that?"

"No," he said. "Have you?"

"No. I actually haven't thought that much about my wedding."

She leaned back against the seat.

Her father would give her away. Her mother was dead.

It actually made her want to cry.

"I want a dress, and I need it to be exactly right, and I want decorations and…"

"If you want a gorgeous dress then you are going to have to marry me sooner rather than later, because fit is going to become an issue."

She made an exasperated sound.

"I liked you better when you were pretending to be my date," she said.

She could see the intensity in his dark eyes as he looked at her in the dim light of the vehicle. "I wasn't pretending. I am actually interested in you. I do want to see your studio."

"Speaking of my studio, and my apartment, I assume that you expect me to move in with you."

"Yes. Though my penthouse in Manhattan is not far from yours, if you wish to maintain a studio in your space, and have an option for a place to sleep, that is fine with me."

He was being so reasonable. That was maybe the most annoying thing. That she wanted to rage at him, because he was making her feel raw and he was making her feel sensitive, but he was being perfectly… Correct. About so many things. The fact that he had held the business deal over her head was almost a courtesy. Because the truth was, she never would've been able to face her father telling him that she was pregnant with Dario's baby, and wasn't marrying him.

She hadn't really been able to think about that. She'd had to scale Mount Dario first.

But Dario knew.

Dario knew that she would never have been able to stand that. He knew that it would make her feel far too much like a disappointment. Like she was letting everyone down. Him and her father. He knew that, and he had known it was actually the only ammunition that he needed. So yes. Yet again, he was being far more reasonable than she would like. She would like some goads to kick against. It made her feel alive. She liked it when Dario was that way, because she felt like a piece of iron sharpening another piece of iron. Or at the very least, she didn't feel vulnerable. And right now, she felt a bit vulnerable. And he got to be charitable. Giving her the kind of arrangement that would make her feel safe and protected. Giving her something for her business so that she could look more accomplished than she was.

A sliver of uncertainty worked its way beneath her skin.

The thing was, he had said it, and she hadn't fully understood it. He hadn't really tailored himself to her either way. He wasn't really thinking of her. She had taken that to mean that he wasn't being manipulative, at least in the moment. Now it felt like maybe she was incidental, and it left her wounded. Breathless.

Finally, they pulled up to her father's palatial estate. The lights were on, and she knew that he was still awake. He had always been the sort of man who ran on very little sleep. He liked to work. And he liked to research things.

No wonder he and Dario got along so well. There was an intensity to both of them that just seemed a natural part of who they were. Her own father had never been hungry. Not in the way that Dario was, and yet it had been a natural thing for him to build and build and build his empire.

As natural as breathing.

And Dario… He had that spark that her father had, and yet he had been keen. Not just to survive, but to thrive. He had made a difference, not only in his own life, but in the lives of so many other people.

It really was no wonder that her father esteemed Dario so highly. Above anyone else on earth. She was just such a disaster. She'd been so confident there for a bit. And now life was…unrecognizable.

"Did you warn him that we were coming?"

"I did. I told him that we would see him tonight."

"Did you give him any indicator…"

"That I got you pregnant? No."

"How is it we are going to do this? Are we going to do both in the same breath? I'll be going to lead with the marriage…"

"The engagement, obviously. The news about the grandchild will come after that."

"For someone who doesn't have a lot of family, you have some decent insight into how to manage them."

That, she realized, landed a little bit more roughly than she had intended to.

"I didn't mean…"

"It's fine," he said. "I am aware that I am a functional orphan. I'm at peace with it."

They got out of the car and went to the front door.

Her father unlocked it without waiting for them to knock.

And there he was, waiting in the entry. She felt the need to hide her hands behind her back, because the ring suddenly felt so conspicuous it seemed like he would know before they ever even announced it.

Not that it was a bad thing, it was just… She was so near nervous. It was entirely unfathomable to her that only two months ago she would've said Dario was the most annoying man on earth, and now she was marrying him.

She still felt like he was the most annoying man on earth, but the marriage part was a real shift.

Her father would no doubt be shocked. He would probably figure out that they were getting married because of the baby. Would he be disappointed in her? Disappointed that she had lost her head and let her hormones prevail?

They had been responsible. Well. They hadn't really been irresponsible. She was on birth control, and it should've worked. It was just that it hadn't. And... And.

She felt a little bit faint.

"To what do I owe the visit?" her father asked.

In his early sixties, Nathan Anderson was still handsome and filled with energy.

"We have something to tell you," said Dario, plying her left hand out from behind her back. "Lyssia and I are engaged."

Her father looked stunned. The whole ten seconds, he didn't move.

"Well," he said. And then he took a step forward and gripped her by the shoulders. "That is the most wonderful news." He pulled her in and hugged her, and suddenly, Lyssia felt the urge to see if it was possible to break the moment. She didn't want to settle into this. Into her father's joy if it was only going to be compromised.

"I'm pregnant." She announced this, as if she was announcing that she was taking a nice trip down to Saks Fifth Avenue.

"Pregnant," her father said. He pulled away from her and looked to Dario, and then back at Lyssia. Here it was. Now he would rail. Now he would be angry.

"I'm going to be a grandfather," he said. He moved to Dario then, and clapped him on the shoulders. "You have made me a grandfather," he said. "My son."

She looked at Dario's face, and saw a myriad of emotions there. Unreadable. Unknowable. She felt a similar kaleidoscope in herself, because her dad was more invested right then in Dario than her and it galled, but she also knew Dario needed it, and that mattered. "I cannot tell you how happy this makes me. I never could have dreamed of such wonderful news. Was it being snowed in together?"

"That certainly was a factor," said Lyssia, her face getting hot.

Dario lifted a brow and gave her a scolding look.

"But there was always something about him," she said.

Because it was true anyway.

Dario moved, putting his hand on her lower back. "I have always been very fond of Lyssia. And I wanted to be very careful, because she's younger than me. Because I esteem you so much. Both of you. I never would have wanted to play lightly with her feelings. But I have been quite taken with her for a while. It was only spending uninterrupted time together that allowed us to understand what our connection really is."

"I don't need to know the details," her dad said. But he was smiling. "When is the wedding?"

"The sooner the better. We've known each other many years. There's no reason to delay," said Dario.

"Well, but we will want to have it in the Hamptons."

"I was thinking Rome," said Dario.

Rome? The place where he'd been homeless? Why? But now wasn't the time to ask.

"Rome," her father said. "That is a good idea."

"I know just where. It will overlook the sea. Don't worry about a thing. I will handle it all. And there will be no reason that the preparations should take more than two weeks. Whatever dress you want can be made, Lyssia," he said, cutting off her protests.

She blinked, but didn't say anything.

"Lyssia," her father said. "I have truly never been prouder."

Lyssia felt like she had been stabbed. Right through the

chest. Because somehow, it was something to do with Dario that made her father the proudest. It wasn't her job. It wasn't simply being her. It was incubating Dario's child.

It is your child too.

Yes. But it didn't feel like it. Everything felt… She just felt so raw.

She didn't know what to do about it. Didn't know how to combat these feelings inside of her.

"Let's have a drink."

They did. They ended up staying and having a drink with her father, and then after an hour, Dario said that they had to go. "It will take us an hour to get back to the city," said Dario. "We should head back."

"Of course, of course. Keep me posted on the wedding plans."

"We will."

"Lyssia," her father said. "Send me over the proposal for your redesign for the hotels."

That at least cheered her slightly. "I will."

"Of course I know you'll be very busy now. With your baby. You will be a wonderful mother."

It was perhaps the most definitively encouraging and kind thing he'd ever said.

They got back into the car, and she leaned her head back against the seat. "Don't worry," he said. "We're not going back to the city."

"Why did you tell my father we were?" she asked.

"Because he does not need to know that I intend to take you to a luxury bed-and-breakfast where I plan on sealing this arrangement in a very particular way."

The way that he looked at her. That dark need in his eyes.

It was the first thing that made her feel like she might

have some control here. And yet at the same time it made her feel undone.

They wanted each other. At the end of the day, it was her real power, and his.

They could claim all sorts of things. That by her agreeing she was making things easier with her father, that by him giving her the business deal he was improving her situation.

But mostly, she had the feeling they wanted each other. And if she didn't have him, some other woman might. If he didn't have her, perhaps other men would have her.

Maybe this was the truth of it. And that was both deeply comforting and confronting all at the same time.

"I am sorry, Lyssia," he said, softly.

"For what?" she asked.

The only sound was her heart beating and the tires on the road.

"I…feel as if I got more attention in that moment. And I am not… I am not his son."

He finally saw it. She felt bad, though, because while she'd had her own conflicting feelings about it…she hated everything she knew about Dario's childhood. She didn't begrudge him a relationship with her dad.

"I was happy," she said. "Happy that he's happy."

"But he should have been all there for you."

"He cares for you. It doesn't have to be a competition."

"But it has felt like one to you and that matters to me," he said. "We…you and I, we are a family now. This baby will be ours. There is nothing more important. Know that."

She held that close and turned it over. This small change in him. This insight. It mattered. But she had to resist the urge to make it more than it was.

They only drove five minutes away from her father's

house, and up to a glorious, rambling manor. "I rented the northern wing for us."

They walked inside, and she was struck by how quaint it was. How lovely. The walls were hunter green, with brown leather details all about the room. Hunting and fishing memorabilia from a bygone era added a warmth and a sense of another time to the place.

He went up to the polished mahogany desk and the woman behind the desk presented them with physical keys. They were given directions to the far side of the house. Where a library, a sitting room and a large bedroom with an en suite bathroom was theirs.

Two suitcases seemed to be produced from thin air, though she realized they had to come from the car.

"Did you… Take clothes from my house?"

"No," he said. "I purchased some things for you."

"Well, that…" She tried to muster up a fence, and instead she was intrigued. What sorts of things did Dario think that she should wear? Lyssia had a very strong sense of style. What did Dario see? That was the question. Of course, that was just a distraction from the actual, prevailing thought pounding through her. She was going to make love with Dario again.

And when he led her through the public area, back to the quarters that they would share. She didn't wait. Didn't hesitate. As soon as the door closed behind them, she stretched up on her toes, and she kissed him.

CHAPTER ELEVEN

DARIO HAD KNOWN that this was self-indulgent. But it was, in many ways, a fool's decision. But he could not go back. And wouldn't even if he could. Because the moment that he tasted Lyssia's mouth again, he wanted nothing else.

It had been torment tonight, standing with her in front of her father and keeping his hands to himself. Playing at being respectable. Not exposing the fact that the reason they were in the situation, the reason that they were getting married was because of the undeniable passion between them. Not feelings.

And then…and then her father had overlooked her, in his opinion, and everything in him had been twisted, turned sideways. It was all complicated and he didn't want that now. He wanted it simple.

He wanted her.

He wanted her to know she was his.

Maybe there was never going to be a way to untangle the emotional threads from all of this. But he wanted to stamp her, claim her, make her certain that she was his so that she would never look…hollow and alone as she had for a moment standing there in her father's entry.

He growled, moving his hand to her hair and pulling hard, drawing her head back, kissing her throat, down her collarbone.

She let out a sharp gasp.

"You are mine," he said. Something primitive was rioting through him. Something that made him feel like a stranger even to himself.

He wanted her. He was no stranger to sexual desire, but this was something else entirely. This was like a foreign entity had taken him over. This was something he was at the mercy of. And that was an entirely unfamiliar concept.

He couldn't wait. He was starving for her. He stripped her naked, bared her gorgeous body to his gaze.

The dress she had on was beautiful, but it had nothing on her bare skin.

Her breasts were full, pink tipped and lush.

He was held captive by the sight of the pale thatch of curls between her thighs.

His sex grew heavy with need, his heart pounding so hard he thought it would make its way out of his chest entirely.

She was everything.

"Take your hair down," he commanded.

He moved to a wingback chair in the corner and sat, watching her.

She was still wearing her high heels, her legs looking endless in those.

She reached behind her and undid the clip, let her blond hair fell down past her shoulders.

"Very good," he said. "I think that you should bring me a drink, Lyssia."

She looked at him, challenges parking in her blue eyes. "Why?"

"To see if you're any sweeter now that the promise of pleasure is before you. Sweeter than you were back when you were my assistant."

He felt compelled to marry those moments. This glorious need that he felt for her, combined with those past interactions. With that moment that he had first noticed her beauty when she'd walked into his office. When she had brought him the coffee and spilled it, gotten down on her knees before him.

"What would you like, Mr. Rivelli?" she asked, her voice sultry.

A satisfied, masculine sound sounded short and sharp in his throat. "Whiskey. Neat."

"Anything for you."

Still wearing heels, she walked to the sideboard and grabbed a bottle of amber liquid, pouring a measure of it into a tumbler. Then, with one hand at the bottom of the cup, and the other at the top, holding it as though she was grandly presenting, she made her way to him, her eyes never leaving his.

He took the whiskey from her hand.

"Do you remember, the day you came into my office, and spilled coffee all over the floor?"

"Yes," she said. "I was mortified."

"I wasn't. I was consumed by fantasies of you. You got on your knees before me, and all I could think of was how glorious your lips would look if they were wrapped around me."

She looked at him, her eyes dewy, full of questions.

"Get on your knees, Lyssia. Kneel before me."

At first he thought she would argue. And that would be its own kind of pleasure.

But she didn't. Instead, she went down in front of him. He moved his hands to his belt, undid his slacks. It freed his arousal. She leaned in, her lips brushing against the sensitive head of him.

"Take me in your mouth," he said.

She didn't argue. Finally, Lyssia obeyed him. Beautifully.

Sweetly. She wrapped her hand around the thick base of his shaft and took him into her mouth. Sucking him slowly.

Then she began to lick him like he was her favorite sweet.

Over and over again she took him like that. And he gripped her hair, steadying himself. Steadying them both.

He thrust his hips upward as she moved over him.

A swilling supplicant, naked before him.

She seemed bound and determined to take his pleasure that way.

"No," he said.

He lifted her, and brought her down onto his lap, bringing the heart of her to the blunt head of his arousal. He lowered her slowly onto him, until she was fully seated with him deep inside.

She let her head fall back, the sound of need emanating from her throat. She was wet. Unbearably so. Gloriously turned on by what had just happened between them.

She braced herself on his shoulders and she began to move. Rocking back and forth, and up and down over his length.

He had given the order, but she held him in thrall now.

"Lyssia," he growled.

And he lost himself. In the feel of her. The tight clasp of her body. That warm, wet heat.

All that glory.

Like he had never known.

They would marry for their child. For the public. For her father. But this, this was for them. When she had asked him what he would do if he tired of her he had lied. Because he would never tire of her. She was his. Utterly and completely. He had never had anything that belonged to him quite like this.

He had everything that he wanted that money could buy. That much was true.

But there was not a single person he could lay claim to.

He made connections, and he made them with ease. He had not connected with Lyssia using charm. He had not used his powers of assimilation. He had not given her only what she wanted to see. Their connection, from the beginning had been more real. The antagonism of it all more honest.

And that made this more.

He had charmed her into bed.

They had not played a game to get to this moment. What happened between them had been real. It had been undeniable.

It still was.

She brought herself down on him again and again. He didn't want it to end. He wanted to delay the moment of inevitable release for as long as possible. He wanted her. Only her. Always and ever her.

He moved his hand between their bodies, stroked the source of her pleasure there. Then captured it between his fingers and squeezed. She unraveled. Her pleasure a victory that he needed badly to win. Because finally, then and only then, did he surrender to his own need. Did he give himself over to the untamed thing inside of him.

Only then did he let himself go. Utterly and completely, his orgasm his undoing. In a way that nothing ever had been. She was singular. She was dangerous. He had never wanted in this way before. Even right after having her, he wanted.

He had dropped the whiskey. He had forgotten about it. It was on the floor, spilled, and there was something about that which felt symbolic in some regard. She had dropped the coffee the day he had first seen her.

And he was no longer aware of anything but her on this day. This day that she was bound to him. To marry him.

She would be his.

Unquestionably.

He looked at her, stroking her hair. "You're beautiful," he said. Because there was nothing deeper that he knew how to say.

"So are you," she said, her eyes looking sleepy.

"How do you find this?" he asked, stroking her cheek. "This association between the two of us. I am not Carter."

She blinked. "Who?" Then she laughed. "Seriously. I barely thought of him. It's probably unkind of me. But he and I never actually had a real commitment to each other. In fact, I think I might have overexaggerated the connection a little bit. I didn't want him. I wanted my life to feel different. I wanted to feel different. But in a way that I could control."

There was something about her words that resonated in him. He could understand them. He was a man who had re-made himself so many times. Who had created a smoother, more polished veneer with each and every iteration. He understood that.

The knowledge that he could no longer be what he'd once been. The knowledge that he needed to be something more.

More than himself. More than the people around him.

It fascinated him that a woman like Lyssia, who'd had things he had only ever dreamed of, could feel that same way. He had, these many years, imagined that he was unscathed by his life. After all, he was a billionaire. He was successful. He was well known. Highly regarded, in general.

He was fine, in other words. Except he could see the little ways in which Lyssia was cracked by the losses in her own life. By the wounds even a loving father had left behind.

"Is this what you had in mind? Because things are different now."

"I'm not in control of this," she said.

She moved her hands to his shirt, and began to undo the white buttons. She pressed her palm beneath the fabric, smoothing it over his skin. "But neither of us are, are we?"

Her words held a dangerous and reckless edge, and he felt them. They went deep.

"I want you," he said. It was the closest he could give her to confirmation.

"I know," she said. "I want you. It's a hideous thing, isn't it? We used to have lives. And they weren't about this."

"I only thought of you most of the time," he said.

She laughed. "Only *most* of the time? You did better than I did. I wanted... I wanted to call you so many times while we were apart. But it just seemed like a bad idea. I thought you were done with me."

"I intended to be," he said. He shrugged. "When I was a child... I never knew what might happen next. As a man I have sought to make my world one I can control. It's been a long time since life has surprised me in any fashion. I suppose I should thank you. For this. It is at least something entirely different."

And he had control now. He knew himself. He knew better than to let himself believe wholly in the fiction of everything around him.

When he was a child he hadn't known better. He had believed that his father loved him, and he had believed that love was a certain thing. Because his mother had told him that it was. His father had told him that it was. But when everything had gone wrong, his father hadn't protected him, he had sold him. Love had become something bitter. A betrayal. He would never believe in it again. Thus, in the decisions that he was making in regard to their child, he was using his head. Not his heart.

When it came to Lyssia, it was his body.

He could rationalize those things. And he found that to be very important.

Essential, even.

It was different from what he had imagined. But it wasn't beyond the boundaries that he had set forward for himself.

"Is that why you wish to marry in Rome?" she asked.

"Is what why?"

"More surprises?"

Something shifted within him. "Perhaps I just wish to return with everything in hand. Wealth, my wife, my child."

She shifted against him, but didn't speak.

"You should move in with me when we get back to Manhattan."

"I should?"

"Yes. It will be more convenient."

"For sex."

"Yes," he said. "What else would I mean?"

"Living with another person isn't only about sex. We will be sharing things. Our lives." But the whole time she was talking she was moving her hand beneath his shirt. Lower and lower still.

"You want to live with me. You want to be with me," he said. "In my bed."

"You're very arrogant," she said.

"Yes," he said. "I am."

"You want me to live with you because you can't bear to be apart from me. Because you want me naked, all the time. How long has it been, Dario? Has it really been since I spilled the coffee in your office?"

"Yes," he said, his voice hard. "I wanted things from

you that I knew then you could not even fathom. You were an adult, yes, but only technically. I was stunned by your beauty. And that is a rare thing. Because beauty is subjective. And it is everywhere. But there was something more with you. From the beginning. I wanted you."

"You should've had me then."

"A bad idea. I don't think you would've wanted to be my eighteen-year-old wife and mother to my child."

She laughed. "No. I am less of an idiot now than I was then."

"You will move in with me," he said.

"Yes. Of course. And I'll vacuum naked and in heels."

"Really?"

"Only if you cook me dinner naked."

"Sounds dangerous," he said. He gripped her chin. "Also, I have staff for that."

She laughed. "I do hope that your staff isn't naked."

"Of course not." But he did make a mental note to have there be clear times when no one else was in the house so that they did not always have to wear clothes.

He had never lived with a woman before.

Had never even thought about it.

It was a strange prospect. But one he quite liked. When the woman in question was Lyssia. She was interesting. She would perhaps be even more interesting in proximity.

"We didn't even make it to the bedroom."

"Feel free to lead the way. And explore what I brought in the suitcase."

Interest flared in her eyes.

There had been very few times in his life that Dario had ever considered himself happy. But right then, he felt like he might be.

CHAPTER TWELVE

THE NEXT MORNING, they spent some time wandering around the grounds of the bed-and-breakfast.

They had a leisurely meal in their quarters, and then began the drive back to Manhattan.

Lyssia felt like she was floating. And she had never especially felt like that before. She had never considered herself a romantic. Not really. But she was beginning to recognize that as being part of her very specific defense system.

It was not, she realized, in her nature to want everything.

Well. That wasn't true.

She did secretly want everything. It was just that she was afraid of putting too much of herself into it.

It was why Carter had seemed like a good idea.

He had seemed like a good idea because he had seemed safe. And ultimately, being safe was something that she valued perhaps more than having everything.

She'd realized that in some small part the first moment her lips had touched Dario's. But it was all becoming clearer as time went on.

She was happy. She didn't know what it meant. But she was hopeful, even, about the potential future.

About what they might have.

He was difficult to read sometimes. But so was she.

It wasn't like she was completely and totally emotionally available.

The truth was, she was somewhat stunted. It was because of her dedication to keeping things easy. Shallow.

She had tried having a business, and it wasn't like she hadn't put genuine heart into it. She had. Everything she had done had been genuine. Had been filled with actual effort. It was just that on some level, she had been holding back.

And she cared so much about what she did. The conversation she had with him at the restaurant had been clarifying in that regard. She wanted people to have a home the way that she did. She wanted everyone to be able to feel the kind of comfort that she'd once had. Including herself.

And when they arrived back at her apartment, she decided that she was going to show him everything.

"My studio… My office is in here."

She had a feeling that to the deeply organized Dario her method would seem haphazard. She looked around the room as someone who was unfamiliar with the place would. Taking in the bright pink walls, the patterned wallpaper that went up the wall her desk was flat against. Replete with palm fronds and birds of paradise. She knew that it was eclectic. To say the least. There were fabric swatches everywhere. Wood stain samples, glaze swatches, and any and many other things.

"This is it," she said. "I do most of the basic designs in here."

He was speechless, looking around the space, and she could imagine that part of the issue was he couldn't picture himself getting any work done here. She knew him. His workspace was always neat as a pin. Hers was… A bit haphazard.

"It's quite amazing," he said. "What do you sketch your designs on?"

"Anything," she said, surprised that he hadn't made a comment about her organization. "Everything. I have notebooks. And I like to put different fabrics next to the sketches. Sometimes I do it all in a virtual notebook, and then I can take fabric that I have imported into the tablet and get a good idea for how it will look virtually."

"Do you design some of the textiles?"

"Yes," she said. "This is my range. No one else has these fabrics."

He moved over to the fabric swatches and touched them.

"I can make exclusive textiles for your hotel chain," she said.

"You don't have to."

"I want to," she said keenly. "I want this to be important. Special."

"This is quite impressive, Lyssia. You should consider hiring more people."

"I have a good team. They all work remotely. I have people that liaise with manufacturers. I share some of the design work with a group of people."

"You haven't communicated much with them since I've been around you."

"Well, when I went to the chalet I was honestly thinking the whole business was winding down. I was ready to let it go. I felt like a failure."

"What changed your mind?"

"It really was talking to you. Well, and discovering I was pregnant. I was on the pill for my… For my periods, though, and it was a low dose. I have never tested it before, obviously. It turns out for me that wasn't sufficient. But you can bet I had a fight with my doctor about it. I spent three weeks going over and over what I was going to do. I was afraid to see you. I also missed you. I'm not used to going that long without seeing you. And we don't even usually talk or anything, but after the chalet I just…"

"I missed you," he said. "Even though you are a pain in the ass."

She felt flushed with pleasure over him saying that. It was perhaps the nicest thing Dario had ever said. "I really didn't expect that you would want to get married. Which is foolish, isn't it? You are very traditional down in your soul."

He seemed to withdraw from her then, even though he didn't move one bit. She could feel it. "I don't act out of a place of tradition. But security. What I am doing is for the good of our child. Here's what must be done. I will never let a child of mine suffer as I did, and that is not for the sake of tradition. And it could never be for feelings. Love is a foolish pursuit, Lyssia. It fails when we need it most. I believe in legally binding agreements. I do not believe in feelings. That is what has driven me here. Will continue to drive me. It is not tradition. It is practicality."

She felt wounded by that. And she was reminded again of what he had said to her. But he did not do any of this for her.

And that was the most important thing for her to hold on to. Except it made her sad. Because she was trying to embrace feeling more. Actually wanting more. Wanting everything. It was difficult to do that when he was reminding her at every turn just what reason she had to protect herself.

And she had already been hurt. That was a problem. She had been devastated by life. And it was so complicated with her father, because she didn't want to be whiny about that relationship, not when he meant well.

And he did.

He loved her, that was the thing. He wasn't a cold, unfeeling man. If he knew the ways in which he had made her insecure he would feel terrible about it. She knew that.

But she'd been hurt all the same.

And so she always tried to protect herself. To manage her expectations. To remind herself that everything would be fine today and could still go wrong tomorrow. What person who had experienced the more random side of life's cruelties at such a young age wouldn't do the same thing? But she really cared about him. And he made her feel things. Want things.

"I thought that I had love, but it didn't protect me. It didn't keep me safe. What was the purpose of it? It *lied* to me. My father lied to me. He failed me."

"But you won't fail our child," she said. "I know you won't. It isn't in you, Dario. It just isn't."

He shook his head. Once. Just once.

"I can't trust myself."

She wanted to deny it, instantly. "I have a very hard time believing that. You are a good man. And you're full of passion."

"I…"

And she realized that this was as far as he could go right now. And she needed to let it go. It wasn't like she could fall down to her knees and tell him that she loved him.

The idea made her feel disquieted. Because she was afraid that she was closer to that than she would like to be. "Your father bought this place for you, didn't he?"

"Yes," she said. Feeling very sharply aware that it was yet another thing that didn't really belong to her.

"Don't do that," he said. "Do not doubt yourself."

"I don't understand you," she said. "Because you made it very clear that nothing that you have done in the past couple of months was really all about me or for me. You tell me that you can't give me love. And then you don't want me to doubt myself."

"Because it's me," he said, deeply certain. "It isn't you. What you consider success to be. I trust nothing. I can't. Do you know…" He looked away from her, out the window. She was struck by his profile. He was such a beautiful man. Beautiful, troubled. Wounded. "My father told me that we were going to meet some friends. But he lied. He did not know them. I think he did not know what they intended for me. I was to help. And nothing more. A servant. But I didn't know that at first. I believed my father. I trusted him. I never saw him again. He left me there. I should be grateful that all they made me do was scrub the floors. Do the farm chores. Because the alternative was selling my body. And they knew many people who did that. I saw so clearly that day what love means. Nothing. He said he loved me. As easily as if he was stepping out to have a cigarette. He never came back. He didn't know what they intended for me. And he left me. He didn't know. He didn't care. That would have been a profound betrayal. For any adult to grab a child by the hand in the street and subject them to such a thing would be a profound betrayal. But mine came at the hands of my own father. I will never understand."

She moved to him. Rested her head on his chest, then her hands. She could feel his heart thundering. Could feel the weight of all this inside him. She felt it in herself.

She wanted to fix it. She knew she couldn't. Not because in this she doubted herself or felt inadequate, but because she didn't know if there was a cure for the kind of horrendous pain he'd been put through by the person who was supposed to care for him.

"Neither will I," she whispered. "I promise you, I am going to love your child. And take care of him. I promise."

He wrapped his arms around her. And held her.

"I know. I will take care of you both. You have my word."

But not his love. She could understand it now. Just a little bit more. A little bit better. Why that word specifically felt loaded. Like a lie. One it didn't seem anyone said it to him since? She didn't have to ask that.

They hadn't.

She knew they hadn't. Her father barely said it to her, and often only did when she said it first, not because he didn't feel it, but because he wasn't an overly emotive man. He would never say it to Dario. He would say he was like a son to him, clap him on the shoulder. Hug him, as he had the other night. But he wouldn't freely say that he loved him. And so Dario had gone and challenged all this time, and he had to work through his own issues.

And he had come out the other side with them only partly worked through.

"I'm going to pack up my essentials," she said, moving away from him.

"I have staff to do that."

"We don't need staff, Dario. I'm happy to spend the day with you if you're happy to spend it with me."

And that was how she found herself packing with Dario looming around. Asking if she really needed to bring all these things.

It was amusing. A stark contrast to the heavy moment early. It was strange and wonderful they could share these things. The dark, the light and the in-between.

"When did you decide to leave that family?"

"I was there for four years," he said. "Mostly because I didn't know what else to do. I ran away. I lived on the streets for nearly a year after that. We were very near a large cruise ship harbor. And I started hanging around. I pretended I was older. Someone at the port helped me manufacture some papers."

Her mouth dropped open. "Is your name really Dario Rivelli?"

He smiled. "That is what the paperwork says."

"But is it your name?"

"It is now."

"You're kidding me. You live under an assumed identity?"

"More or less."

"I was called *boy* by the family that I lived with. I was called nothing by the people on the streets. And I was given a new identity at thirteen and I have clung to it ever since"

He knew his own name. He just didn't want her to know it.

"So you sailed to America on a cruise ship."

"Yes. I did a few contracts. Three months doing passenger cruises. Mostly I did food service. I found I was quite good at it."

"I bet."

"I looked maybe seventeen. It was beneficial. Then the cruise company was moving the ship to sail from New York down to the Caribbean. I decided to sail over on the understanding that I would be continuing on. But instead I got off the ship. And I stayed in New York."

"Were you homeless in New York?"

"For a while. I moved between shelters, bus stations and the park. I managed to get myself a place in a very questionable part of the city. One room. No room for anything but a mattress. Shared bathroom down the hall. But it was mine. And you have no idea what that meant after everything."

"You're right," she said. "I don't. I can't. I've always had everything."

"But you're hurt by that comment," he said. "By pieces of your life anyway."

"I am."

"Amazing."

"Do you think I shouldn't be?"

He shook his head slowly. "No. That's not what I mean at all. Of course you can be hurt. I am only… I am turning over what that means for me."

"Did you think that you were healed?"

"I'm fine."

"Dario," she said. "You can't even speak your name to me. I don't think you're fine."

After that, they didn't speak much. They only packed up and made their way to his glorious Manhattan penthouse. It made her apartment look like a hovel. It was the entire top floor of the apartment building and overlooked the most brilliant views in New York. She imagined him coming here as a boy, and the way he must've looked up at these buildings. And the way he looked down now.

Looking at him, she knew that he had those exact thoughts. It wasn't an accident.

She had always seen Dario as difficult. And then as someone inflexible who looked down on her. She had never seen him as wounded. Now she was forced to. He was still so very much that boy that had come here with nothing. And she wondered how many of the things he did were based on that. She had her own issues, that much was certain. But not like him. She'd always had safety. That was the biggest difference. They had both experienced loss. They both understood that pain. But he had experienced scarcity, fear, uncertainty. Abuse. She had never had to contend with any of that. And still she was affected. How much more so must he be?

It made her want to give to him. Because hadn't he given so much to her already?

He had seen something in her that she hadn't fully seen herself. Something she'd been hopeful about, but hadn't been certain of. He had told her without reservation that she was smart. That she was talented.

He hadn't denigrated her workspace. Hadn't called her disorganized. He seemed interested.

She wanted to figure out how to heal him. But she didn't know how.

Not really.

She came from a much easier background, and she couldn't sort through exactly how somebody like her could help somebody like him.

She wanted to, though. More than anything.

And if those feelings were maybe a little bit more, a little bit beyond what she wanted, what she wished, well, she was just going to have to deal with it. Because it was, absolutely, but it was.

Dario had been a fixture in her life for a long time. And now they were going to be married.

It was impossible to not have feelings.

She was going to ask him if she was going to have her own room.

But before she could get the words out, he leaned in and kissed her.

And then she found herself being carried off to his bedroom.

And the logistics just suddenly didn't matter anymore.

Because she was here with Dario.

And they were going to make a life together, whatever that looked like.

And she was going to find a way to give him whatever he needed.

CHAPTER THIRTEEN

HIS HOUSE HAD changed since Lyssia had moved in. He supposed that was somewhat inevitable. She wasn't a neat or contained person. She was an eclectic explosion of color. There were clothes on the floor of his house.

He had always kept things neat. He didn't like chaos. He experienced enough of it in his life. But Lyssia was a soft, pink sort of chaos, and he found that part of him could actually enjoy it. Relish it, even.

He found himself thinking often of their honeymoon. He had decided that after their wedding in Rome he would spirit her off to Tahiti. Take her to a private island and enjoy looking at her in various bathing suits. He would work on acquiring a collection of bikinis between now and then. Today they were having a bridal gown fitting, in his home.

And he had been ushered out of the room. As if it mattered. As if he shouldn't be allowed to see her. He had said something about the fact that tradition meant little when the bride was already pregnant. Lyssia had slapped him on the shoulder and shooed him away.

And so he was standing as an exile in his own kitchen, drinking an espresso and wondering exactly how he had gotten here. He could recall that day when he had seen Lyssia in the chalet, and she had lost the entire contents of her suitcase.

He could recall, even then, the gnawing hunger he felt for her.

The way he was drawn to her.

And now she lived with him. Was marrying him.

She was on the verge of becoming... His family.

The word sat uncomfortably inside of him.

In some capacity, he had long thought of Nathan Anderson as a father figure. But there was a barrier. They were not family. Not really. Not truly. And now... Well. He and Lyssia would be family. Their child would be...

His heart felt like it had been grabbed and twisted.

He was having a child. A human that shared his DNA. Born of his blood.

He had lost his mother. His father had lost him.

He had not had a connection like that with another person in a long time.

Family.

Suddenly, and in so many ways. That traditional connection of marriage. That inevitable connection of blood.

And he knew that it was not simply blood that made a family. For if it did, the bond between him and his father could not have been broken, but it was. But still, it was a foundational connection, and one that forged a bond. It was up to him to not squander it. Up to him to do right by it.

He could figure out how to protect a child. But as much as he loved his mother, there had been no way for him to protect her from cancer. She had gotten ill, and that wasn't his fault.

That was, perhaps, the deepest and most unresolved issue of his life. That his father had failed him so grandly, and he would love to put every failure on his father's shoulders. But he couldn't.

Because it had been something far beyond the control of men that had taken his mother away.

She had gotten treatment. In that sense, his father had done right by his wife.

He wanted to vow to protect his family, but how could he, when he knew that there were some things that were beyond control? How could he protect Lyssia when the world was full of accidents and illness?

She knew that as well.

The thought of all this made his chest ache, and perhaps what he resented most of all was how often this new turn of events in his life made him think of these things.

Lyssia had brought up the subject of his old name.

He didn't even think it. He would never say it out loud.

A moment later, he heard voices, and the door to Lyssia's bedroom opened. She and the dress designer exited.

"Are you pleased?" he asked.

"Yes," she said, her eyes shining bright. With the promise of what, he wondered. Was it a future with him that made her so happy? Or was it simply this momentary satisfaction of finding a bridal gown that she liked?

He found he wasn't sure, and in fact, wanted to know.

He wanted to be the source of that happiness.

And yet, at the same time, he couldn't bear the idea.

Because… Because of everything.

He thanked the designer, and so did Lyssia, and when the door had closed and the woman had left, Lyssia came into the kitchen and wrapped her arms around his neck, pressing her body to him and kissing him. He held her lightly. It was strange, these casual moments of affection. He was accustomed to the wild and untamed need between them. Sort of.

But this… The way she touched him. The way she would kiss him, just to kiss him.

It was all beyond him.

"I'm looking forward to the wedding," she said. "Everything is coming together."

"Have your invitations gone out?"

"Yes. My father has graciously chartered a plane to bring my friends over."

"Friends from university?"

"Yes. Obviously I'm bragging because I'm marrying a very sexy billionaire. Who can blame me?"

He did not have a plane full of friends to bring. He had business associates. People he had made connections with.

"Well, I'm very glad for you."

"Am I not your trophy wife, Dario? Much younger… Etcetera. Etcetera."

"You are not that much younger than me."

"Yes, I am," she said, grinning. "In fact, that's one reason he felt as if you had to rush to marry me. The scandal of it all. But surely on some level it must appeal to your male ego."

"My ego is just fine."

That much was true. He was not a man given to insecurity. That had been a luxury he could never quite afford.

She laughed and moved away from him. He wanted to have sex with her. Because she had kissed him like that. Because turning it into sex made it feel more manageable. Because turning it into sex made it feel like something more than just casual affection. And for some reason casual affection felt… Impossible.

But she was moving about like a whirlwind, collecting her things.

"I have to go down to one of my showrooms. There is an issue with some supply that we got, and I have to look into it. Thank God it's a limited collection and not something we're manufacturing for you or my father. I don't need new disasters on that large of a scale."

"You cannot stay?"

He heard the need in his own voice and he despised himself for it.

"No," she said. "I can't stay. I have work to do. I'm sure you do too."

He growled, and moved closer to her, taking her hand and pressing it to the front of his slacks. Her eyebrows lifted. "Oh, my. Well. I'm sure that will keep for me."

"I want you," he said.

"And I want you," she said. "Always. But I have a work emergency."

And for the first time in his life, Dario found himself abandoned, aroused, by a woman.

He was proud of her too. For her resolve. For the new strides she was making in her career, even while managing all of this.

But she'd left him with nothing more than the impression of her soft lips against his, and an aching need for more.

Along with the swirling, cavernous feeling of need that he was assaulted by.

A need to protect her when he knew the world would not always allow it. A need to have her so that he could exist in the space that was not consumed with his desire for her.

Dio, but it was unbearable.

And he had to sit with the unbearableness of it until she returned hours later. And then, only then did he have her. And have her he did. On the couch, in the shower. In his bed.

Until he erased the memory of affection and replaced it with lust. Until he blotted out those open-ended emotional concerns from earlier and spun them into sex. Because that at least he knew he was good at. That at least he knew he could give her. It was a connection that was real and strong.

And it was what he would lean on.

Because in that at least, he knew his power.

As for the vagaries of the rest of the world and fatherhood?

It was best not to ponder it too deeply.

CHAPTER FOURTEEN

ROME WAS SPECTACULAR. Lyssia couldn't recall the last time she had been there. She had been a child, she was pretty sure, and dragged on a business trip of her father's after her mother had died.

Most of her time in Italy had been spent in the northern part of the country, and while she had done a fair amount of traveling, there had never been much occasion to go to Rome.

She watched Dario's face as they descended on their private jet, and then even closer still as they drove through the city, so overcrowded and teeming with people.

"I can't believe you lived on the streets here," she said.

He flicked a glance at her. "I survived."

"Does this feel like home to you?"

"No. This was home to a boy long since dead."

And yet, she knew that wasn't true. He was Italian. This was part of who he was. He sought to deny it. Because it was painful. She knew what it was like, to wonder what could've been. She wondered if those thoughts consumed him now.

She didn't say anything, however.

Instead, she kept her peace until they arrived at the hotel they would be staying at. Gloriously appointed, and of course with the room on the top floor because Dario simply had to look down on the world.

He had been so trapped before. She really could understand.

Their connection had always been powerfully sexual. But he had been even more intense this past week. Every interaction between them ended with sex. She wasn't complaining, it was just that she could feel him trying to avoid something via their passion.

It made her feel terribly sad for him.

And for herself. Because she was still trying to figure out exactly what she could give him.

What he could get from her that he couldn't get from anywhere else.

Her father arrived in Rome later that day, and the three of them went and had dinner near the Colosseum. It was crowded and dizzying, but she enjoyed it. She liked even more listening to Dario speak Italian, translating easily for them, and becoming more relaxed as the evening wore on.

He was relaxed, and she hadn't thought he would be. Whenever tension crept up in him, when they crossed a certain street, or the wind changed, she touched his hand. He would relax again. And she liked the feeling he was able to be happy here partly because of her.

I will have wealth, my wife and my child.

He'd said that about Rome. Perhaps this was what he'd needed to face it again. To feel different enough.

He was a fascinating man.

Brilliant. Exceptional.

Handsome.

It grieved her that his father had betrayed him. That he had thrown him away like so much garbage when...

Imagining him as a small boy, confused and left behind, filled her with aching sorrow. If they had a little boy, and he had dark eyes just like his father, she would hurt every time she looked at him for that small boy Dario had been. Left behind and left without love.

And she would give their son love doubly in response.

She couldn't explain it. But she knew it was going to be a boy. She just knew she was carrying Dario's son.

She blinked back impending tears that threatened to fall.

She kept on smiling. Because the moment was happy. Even if it was weighted with other things.

The night before the wedding she took up residence in a different hotel room, much to Dario's chagrin.

In the next morning, she felt completely undone, her heart fluttering continually, her hand shaking as her team of stylists got her ready.

She had chosen the dress because it reminded her of her mother. Her mother had always told her stories about the Fae Folk. And the soft gown with its plunging neckline and sleeves that trailed down along with the train reminded her of fairies. Elves. Something otherworldly.

She left her hair loose, with long ringlets. And she hoped that he would think she was beautiful. Her makeup was done expertly. Soft and natural to make her glow, but little more.

Her bouquet was made of cascading lilies, and she knew that the old church they were marrying in would be filled with candelabras and draped in flowers.

She had deliberately kept all of this from Dario, because she felt it fitting for the groom to be surprised.

Also, she hadn't wanted his opinion. He wasn't the one with design aesthetic. She was.

She got into the car that was waiting to take her to the church, and pressed her bouquet to her breast.

She was trying to calm the beating of her heart, or perhaps she just wanted to feel it.

She looked out at the city, and slowly, with each turn of the tires on the road, she realized something.

She wasn't marrying Dario for the sake of their child. In truth, she never had been.

She could've fought him on this. It would've been easy.

She had power, and her relationship with her father mattered to Dario, because his relationship with her father mattered.

She was not marrying him because he had forced her into it. Because he had coerced or blackmailed her in any way. She was marrying him because she wanted to.

The car pulled up to the church and her father was standing outside waiting for her, wearing a suit. The door opened and he reached his hand out, lifting her from the back of the car. His eyes were shining. "Lyssia," he said softly. "You are a beautiful bride."

That tenuous grasp on her emotional stability eroded, and she found herself crying and being thankful for waterproof makeup.

"Dad," she said. "I…"

She expected him to say something about how proud he was, because she was marrying Dario. Instead, he looked down at her, blue eyes sparkling. "I am amazed at the woman you've become. You're not a child anymore, and I know that. You haven't been one for quite some time. But I have always been reluctant to let go of you as my little girl. You're the only child that I have. I think sometimes I have not given you all the credit you deserve simply because I couldn't bear the idea that you were grown. I wanted you to need me. To need my advice. Perhaps even to need to work for my company because I wanted to keep you close. But you don't need that. You are an incredible person. Smart and ambitious. But far warmer than I've ever been. You are more like your mother that way. Your softness. Your creativity. She would be overjoyed today."

"It's been hard, Dad," she whispered. "There have been a lot of times I haven't felt like…like I mattered."

He closed his eyes. He looked pained. For the first time she realized he knew. And much the same way she'd been afraid to ask him for what she wanted, he'd been afraid to examine his failures. To hear them spoken out loud. Because they would no longer be doubts, they'd be confirmed.

"I am sorry," he said. "For all the things I didn't do when you were young. For all the things I couldn't give you, even when you deserved them. I am sorry."

"You don't have to be sorry," she said. "You're a good father."

"But you have not always felt loved, I don't think."

Bittersweetness lanced her chest. "No," she said. "I have always felt loved. Sometimes I didn't feel like you were proud of me. Sometimes I didn't feel like you understood me. But I always knew that you loved me, Dad. I never doubted that. I did think maybe you loved Dario a little bit more."

"I do love Dario," he said. "He is the son I never had. The son I never could've had. I never wanted anyone other than your mother. Not to live with. Not to have children with. He felt like a blessing because without him, there never would've been another child. You see? And now you're giving me a grandchild, with him. It is a gift. But it's not what I needed to be proud of you. And I don't need you to be like him."

"Thank you," she said.

"It was never that I didn't love you as much," he said. "I loved you so much it felt like breaking apart, and the only thing that ever felt like that was loving and losing your mother. I...never avoided you because you weren't enough."

"Oh, Dad." She wrapped her arms around him. It didn't erase his mistakes. But she loved him. He loved her. It was enough.

Part of her felt healed in that moment. She was enough. She always had been.

It was just that sometimes her father didn't show his feelings. And she didn't show hers. It was all part of being afraid of the ways the world would hurt you, she supposed.

Her father led her into the church, and toward the sanctuary.

They waited. Waited for their cue. And then the wedding coordinator signaled them, and the doors opened. And when she saw Dario standing there at the head of the aisle, suddenly she knew. She knew exactly what she needed to give him.

Love.

And right then she had the confidence in that. And the fact that her love mattered. And that it would mean something.

And it was also the moment when she knew, deep in her soul, that today she was marrying Dario because she loved him.

And that was the only reason.

Love.

When he saw Lyssia, the breath exited his body.

She was ethereal. An angel, on the arm of her father. Her dress was made of floating, diaphanous white fabric that rode around her like a cloud with each step she took. Her breasts were round and lush, highlighted by the low neckline.

Her face glowed, the joy there a sight so beautiful he nearly had to look away. Because he hardly deserved it.

Hardly deserved that bright, beautiful brilliance that she shone his way.

And when her father released his hold on her and passed her to Dario, he felt a brilliant weight of responsibility come down upon his shoulders.

She looked up at him with absolute trust in her eyes, took his hands, and they began their exchange of vows.

He spoke each one with heavy truth. Because whatever he had said in the beginning, he now intended to honor these vows. Forever. Forsaking all others, for as long as they lived.

He could not explain the intensity of this, he only knew it consumed him. Changed him. Became the essence of who he was.

In that moment, he became Lyssia's husband, as she became Dario's wife.

It seemed absurd that only a few months ago, it had taken a blizzard, and the lack of some boy in his twenties for the two of them to become what they were.

For they seemed to stretch beyond the fabric of time. Had there ever been a moment when Lyssia was not his? He could not recall it. Not truly.

The faces of the people in the crowd blurred before him. And he could see nothing but her.

They were married. He had spoken vows. There was, he came to realize, a reception planned for after the wedding, but the entire thing tried his patience. He didn't want a party. He wanted to be alone with her.

She danced with her friends, and with her father. He danced with her, but everything in him was demanding that he make her his in the most elemental way.

At first there was a cake. And he was thankful for the years he had spent learning charm, because he had to call upon all of those years now so that he could get through it with his humor intact.

She tossed her beautiful bouquet, and right after that he swept her away to the airport. To his private jet. They should've stayed an extra night in Rome, but he had been desirous to get her away from everyone and everything. To have her all to himself. So now they had a long flight overnight to the private island.

She was exhausted. And so he helped her out of her gown and did not ravish her as he wanted, but left her sleeping in the bedroom alone while he drank to try and drown the intensity of everything.

Sex helped him make sense of the intensity. When he was inside of her, when he was chasing the peak of need, then they could make all of that about sex.

But now, the ache in his chest felt like it was something else, and he did not care for it at all.

After this, they would return home. A home that they shared. They would have a baby.

A child together.

Their lives were being knit together as yarn becoming something new.

And he had never imagined that would be so.

Not for him.

It was like having a version of his past resurrected. A set of new choices given to him.

And this wild need that he felt for Lyssia terrified him,

because it compromised everything that he had ever told himself about connection.

About the decision he had made to marry her. And why it had been important. It had been about his child. Of course it had been. About the need to make sure they were both protected, but it didn't feel like it now.

It didn't feel like a decision made coolly with his mind and nothing more.

His feelings for Lyssia felt nothing like logic.

Nothing like himself.

He brooded on that all night, and when they touched down on the island, Lyssia emerged looking fresh, while he felt as if he had run a gauntlet.

"This is beautiful," she said as they walked up the trail that led to the home they would be staying in. Gorgeous and open to the jungle around them, because there were no other people to disturb them. The house was fully stocked, overlooking the water. There was a private dock with a small boat that they could take out at their leisure.

But he wanted none of that. Not now. He wanted nothing other than to have her. Nothing other than to make her his.

And when they arrived at the house, he did not wait to get inside. He grabbed hold of her on the sundeck and kissed her, deep and hard. Then he laid her down across one of the luxurious outdoor beds and began to strip her of all her clothes.

She was beautiful. Beyond.

Everything he had ever desired.

He had known. From that first moment in his office, he had known.

That whatever she had been to him before, she had become the woman of his dreams.

Dreams he hadn't even known he possessed.

He stripped her body and as he did, stripped layers of himself away. Of his protections. And he found he did not have the desire to resist. Either her or the need between them.

He sipped desire from between her legs and kissed his way back up her body. Sucking one nipple into his mouth and reveling in the intensity of what bloomed between them.

He had been alone. For so many years, he had been alone. And now he was with her. In a way he had never been. Never been with anyone.

She had gotten underneath his skin. She had gotten down to the very heart of who he was.

Something he wasn't entirely sure he had known before.

But she made him want to be better.

She made him want everything. And when he slid into her tight body, he felt himself coming home.

It was not wrong. It never could be. It was not an apartment at the top of the world.

Home, very quickly, had become this year, and that felt like a very dangerous thing.

But he couldn't turn away from it, not now. He was a slave to it. To her. He could do nothing but ride them both to the end. To completion.

But carry them both away on a cloud of desire. Because this was where it made sense. And this was where he could show her. It was where he would be able to manage this, because outside of this moment, outside of her body, it felt like a terrible thing. Great and awful, and like four walls and a home in Rome that he never wanted to revisit. Like a name he couldn't say, like a heart he could never allow to beat again. No. It had to be this. It could only ever be this. Always and forever.

"Dario," she said, shuddering out her pleasure as he found his own. As he shouted out his completion.

They clung to each other. And in the aftermath, he could hear only the sound of their hearts, and the waves.

"Dario," she said softly, looking up at him, those familiar blue eyes an integral part of the story of his life.

"I love you."

And the world shattered.

CHAPTER FIFTEEN

LYSSIA KNEW THAT it would be the harder road. She did. But she hadn't been able to hold back. Not anymore. Because the truth was, she loved him. And the truth was, she was certain that the only way forward was to allow herself to love him. Fully and openly. Because the only way she was ever going to reach him. The only way she was ever going to change him, was through that love.

She knew it as much as she knew that the ocean was out there, fathomless and blue. She knew it as much as she knew anything.

She had needed it to be said. Because she needed to let herself feel it. Without reservation. There was fear. But she had spent all of her life holding herself back. Out of fear. Out of the fear that she would find herself alone again, unloved.

She wasn't going to hold back, not anymore.

Never again.

There was no scope for fear.

Not when she loved him like she did. Not when she felt a burning desire to not simply be changed by him, but to change him in return.

He was, and had been, the most incredible influence on her life these past months. And even before that. He had made her feel a spirit of competition, and while she had resented that at times, she couldn't deny that it had driven her.

He had, without even meaning to, created a better version of Lyssia.

She wanted to make a better version of Dario.

What he had lost in his life, it was love. That was the thing that had felt tenuous to him. It was the thing that had felt conditional. The thing that had felt like a betrayal, and she had to make it steady. She had to make it real. She had to take the love and make it enduring. And it was terrifying, of course it was. Because she understood how random the world could be, she understood loss. She knew what it was like to feel like everything was fine one moment then have it be wrenched away the next, but she couldn't live in that space. Because they were going to have a child. And she had to love that child completely and wholly. With all of herself.

She had to find it within her to give that child love unreservedly, and it began here. Her father had loved her mother, so much. And even though he had been grief stricken in the years since he had lost her, she also knew that he wouldn't change a thing. She didn't even have to ask that. He was, now and ever, abundantly clear on what that love had meant to him. On how impacting it had been.

Love was not the enemy. It was fear.

Plain and simple. It was what had destroyed Dario's childhood. And it was what would continue to destroy him if she wasn't the brave one.

And she would be. At the expense of everything.

He said nothing. Because of course that was quintessentially Dario. To just ignore her, to pretend it hadn't happened. Rather than rounding on her or being cruel.

"I said that I love you," she said, drawing her knees up to her chest.

"I heard you," he said, his voice hard.

"Yes, well, you didn't acknowledge it, and many people might find that grounds for assuming they had been unheard." It was warm outside. As hot now as it had been cold at the chalet. When they had sat by the fireplace and shared sausages. When things had felt simpler.

Except… They felt more real now. More consequential. They felt terrifying.

The stakes had never been higher. And none of the wedding guests even knew about the pregnancy.

"I don't know what response you're looking for," he said.

"There is the usual response to that question, Dario."

"I told you what love was to me. Or rather, what it wasn't. I am not the person that you're looking for. Not in this."

"What if I told you I'm not actually looking for anything? What if I told you I was offering you love? And that is not an action item. You can take it, or you can simply let it sit there, but it doesn't change the fact that I love you."

He looked… Lost then. Sad and desperate. "Why? Why do you love me?"

It killed her. Because he didn't know. She could see that. She could feel it, that emptiness in him echoing in her.

She put her hand on his chest.

"Because you have made me see parts of myself that I didn't before. Because you are a good man, and I've seen it."

She thought of all that good while she said it. The way he encouraged her. The way he believed in her.

"Because you are strong in the face of great adversity, and because you know when to be soft, too. You have been with me. Whether you realize it or not. Because no matter how hard I try, I seem to not be able to stay away from you. Because you have introduced me to new aspects of my body, but of my soul too. You have made me a deeper person."

She didn't even recognize the girl who had come to the

chalet that had thought she had it all figured out. "You have made me a better person. I'm going to be a mother because of you. Because of us. It is really not overstating it to say that you're the single most important person in my life. That you have been for a very long time. I was running from you. That day that I showed up to the chalet with a suitcase full of lingerie, waiting for another man. I was running from you. I knew that you were the one that I needed. But I also knew that you were never going to be easy. Because a man who fought as hard as you did to get above all of that was never going to be easy. So I'm not asking you for anything. I'm just giving."

"I don't understand," he said, his voice rough. "Who loves someone without getting love in return?"

"That's what love is. It's not a transaction. It's not conditional. It's not yours to give when it's easy. It's not about convenience. And I know that you weren't taught that. Not in your life. I know that your father betrayed you. That he betrayed your trust. And I am so, so very sorry. But I will not love you that way. I will not love you when it's easy and convenient, and when I am getting enough out of it to call it sufficient. I love you because of everything that you are. You have already given enough to me. You are already enough."

"How can that be?" he asked.

"You said it yourself," she said, her heart breaking, just a bit. "I told you I wanted a summer rain kiss. You told me I needed a hurricane. This is the whole hurricane, Dario. I'm already in it. And I don't want anything else."

"I also told you, you wanted the villain. I'm the villain of the story, *cara*, not your hero."

"No," she said. "That was where you got it wrong. I never wanted the villain. But I wanted real. I wanted complicated. I didn't want a man who existed to make me feel better about myself. I wanted a man who made me better. And that's you."

"You are very young," he said.

It was so dismissive, and she knew he was doing it on purpose. Pushing her away. She wasn't going to let him.

"So what? Maybe that's what you need. Somebody young enough that they haven't done this before and they aren't afraid." She put her hands on his face and stared at him. "Because I know that it's going to take a lot of energy, but I have it. More than that, I need it. I can't keep part of myself back from you while giving everything to our child. I know that I can't. I have to open it all up. Slice into the vein and let it all just bleed out."

"You don't know what you're asking for…"

"Maybe I do. So here we are. This is what I have to give, and I know that it's good enough. And the reason I know it is good enough is because you have made me feel like I'm enough. So if you want to blame someone for this, blame yourself. A few months ago I would never have thought that this was a gift. My love. I would've laughed about that. Because what about my love could possibly be a gift? I just saw myself as a silly little rich girl. I know I see myself as a lot more. Because of you. I know that I deserve more. I know that we deserve more. We deserve everything. We don't deserve to be defined by our hardships. By the things that we've lost. We simply don't. We deserve everything. We deserve love."

He was reeling, and she could see that.

"We are on our honeymoon. I promise you this isn't conditional. I want to be on our honeymoon. I don't want to push you away. All I've ever wanted is to bring you closer."

"I don't need love," he said.

"You're wrong. It's the one thing that you need, more

than anything. You have billions, and you're still broken. You have billions and you still can't face the boy that you were. It's the one piece of yourself you haven't yet repaired. Your heart, Dario. Let me."

"Thank you, Lyssia," he said. "You are offering something I simply don't require. It isn't you. It isn't that you were wrong or insufficient. It is me. I simply don't need it. And I won't ask to hear it again. I can't."

And with that, he walked away from her, naked, each beautiful line of his body a rejection of what she had offered.

She sat there, the warm breeze blowing through her hair.

They were married. She knew him. He wasn't going to leave her. But he was going to wall himself off. Make himself a stranger. Pull away.

She thought perhaps she wouldn't see him for the whole rest of the honeymoon. Instead, he became voracious.

He made love to her multiple times a day, but he didn't speak to her after. And she allowed it. She let him soothe himself with her body, and each and every time she gave everything.

This was a real test of her strength. Of her endurance.

Because this was love rejected.

And if he had left her, then perhaps she could begin the cycle of healing. But they would never have separation. She would love him, alone. Isolated. And that was what she had offered. She had done it feeling like eventually he would come around. But he didn't. He was somehow distant and more near at the same time. And when they finished their two weeks on the island, they traded in all that sundrenched beauty for the gloom of Manhattan, for a shared space but not a shared life in a house in Midtown.

They didn't talk. Not often.

She felt like she had lost an integral part of him. Because

what she had lost was their connection. The one that they had before sex. The one that they'd always had. He had always been there.

She didn't invite him to her doctor appointments, because why?

The months melted together. Everything melted together.

And finally it was time for her to go and get her ultrasound where they could find out the gender of the baby. She knew that she wasn't going to actually speak to Dario until she texted him, to tell him that he could come to the appointment if he wanted to.

She didn't expect a response. But when she arrived at the doctor's office, he appeared. Looking every inch the thunder.

"Oh," she said. "I didn't expect you to actually show up."

"You invited me," he said.

They were ushered into the room right away, which was plush and glorious, and a perk, she knew, of her marriage.

They weren't kept waiting for long before an ultrasound technician came into the room.

"If you can undress and lie down I'll be back in a moment," the woman said.

Lyssia obeyed, and lay back on the table. She said nothing to Dario.

"I'm surprised you asked me," he said.

"Why? I'm not the one who made it weird. I just said that I loved you. You're the one that got distant. You're the one that quit talking to me."

"And you're the one that got upset when I refused to give you what I had said that I couldn't, and then you said it was offered freely. But you're angry. Why did you invite me if you find me so confounding?"

"Because I wanted you here."

The woman came back a moment later, and they stopped their discussion. She put gel on Lyssia's stomach, and that familiar watery sound filled the room. She'd had more than one scan and several Doppler appointments, so she had become somewhat familiarized with the state of her womb.

Still, she held her breath a little bit each time. Waiting for the heartbeat. Waiting for the definitive proof that her baby was still there. Still with her. She could feel it move now, a little bit. And she was the one who had chosen not to share that with Dario. So in that sense, he was right. She had offered to continue to love him, as if it was all the same, and she had become wounded about the whole thing.

But then, the heartbeat echoed in the room, and she could see their baby's profile. "Oh," she said. "There he is."

Dario looked confused. "He?"

"I just have a feeling. But we don't know yet."

"We will soon," said the ultrasound tech. "Provided the baby is not shy."

"He won't be," said Dario.

They were both so certain that when the ultrasound tech found the anatomy she was looking for and said, "It's a boy," Lyssia only smiled. "I knew it. I knew it was your son."

But Dario stood up, and suddenly looked pale. Ashen. And then he walked out of the room, leaving Lyssia sitting there staring at the ultrasound tech.

"Is he okay?" the woman asked.

"No. I think he has a load of childhood trauma that he isn't quite sure how to work through. But I'm going to need him to start doing it."

Dario was out on the streets. The high-rise looming over him, and people wandering all around him. It was like when he'd come here for the first time. It was like when he'd been a boy. Lost in the shuffle, lost in the madness. It was everything he was afraid of. Everything he had escaped.

A son.

He had known that there was a possibility of that, and had even felt certain along with Lyssia when she had said that. A son.

A little dark-eyed boy who would be like him.

It wrenched him. Tore him open.

He was going to have to relive this. Have to revisit it, and there was no getting away from it. He had made a decision to care for his son. But right then, he knew it wasn't enough. He knew he wasn't enough.

Lyssia had stood there, with truth shining out from her eyes when she had said that she now understood she was enough. Always, and forever. That her love was sufficient. How did he get there? How?

He knew the answer. But he hated the answer. He had to demolish the walls inside of himself, he didn't have another choice. He had to tear it all down. He had to find a way.

But the only way to do it was to make himself vulnerable, and the thought of that made him…

They lived in a home together. Happy home. And God, he had one of those before, and it had been wrenched away from him. It was hideous. To love someone as he had, and to lose her. And worse still, to love his father as he had and lose him.

To have him choose to walk away. Could he love Lyssia? Could he love his son?

Would it be enough?

How can you not?

Of course he had to. Of course he did. He couldn't breathe. He couldn't think.

Why was he wandering the streets like a homeless child? Why did he feel like a homeless child?

He was the same boy he'd always been.

Raphael.

He pushed that away. That name. That part of himself.

Raphael.

He was him again.

He had not escaped.

He was out there, alone. Abandoned.

And then he turned, and he saw her. Walking down the sidewalk, and it was as the crowd parted. Lyssia. Still coming for him. Even when he didn't deserve it.

"Dario," she said. "What… What's wrong?"

"A son," he said. "I will have a wife and a son, and I will fail him. I will fail you. I don't know… My father loved my mother too much, and then he couldn't bear it when she died. How can I be a good father, and a good husband?"

"Because you can withstand it. Because you can withstand it all. Because that is who you are. But I don't believe life will ask that from us."

"What if it does?"

"You will be the man you've become. In the face of everything. And so will I. It was not love that was weak when your father let you go. And deep down I think you know that."

"He did not love me. Not really."

"Or perhaps he didn't love himself. Perhaps he didn't see a way out. But it was his fear that won. Not his love. And it was not his love for your mother that caused him to do that, because if he truly loved her, if in that moment he could truly feel what he had felt for her when she was alive, he never would have left her son. I would kill you. I would come back and haunt your ass so hard, Dario. If you abandoned our child? No. Your tribute, your love for me would inspire you to be the best father you could be. My father did that. Even if imperfectly. And I am well, in spite of his imperfections. Love does not have to be perfect. It simply must endure."

"I do love you," he said, everything within him trembling now. "I do. But I am… I am afraid. Because I feel closer to the boy that I was now than I ever have been. I feel perilously close to losing everything."

"You've always been that boy. That boy is the one that got you here. Don't hate him. He was strong enough to bring you where you needed to go. He was strong enough to help turn you into the man that I love."

"I love you," he said.

"It means more here, doesn't it? Down in the street."

He nodded. "It reminds me of then. I… I." He took a breath and looked at her. "I spent three hundred and sixty-seven days on the street. Every night when I went to sleep I was afraid."

"Oh, Dario…"

"I dreamed of having a bed, but there wasn't one. I dreamed of rescue, but I couldn't find it. I was cold, scared, alone. And I was eaten up with hatred for my father. I knew he would not rescue me so I found the strength to rescue myself."

"Dario, our son will never need rescuing. We'll already be there."

They would be. Always. He knew it, with all of his heart. This was love. And it had been, from the moment she'd spilled coffee in his office and he'd seen the woman she'd become, and it had changed him. It had been, slowly, in all the years since.

Every fight, every battle, had begun to tear at the layers of defense he'd put up. She was the only one he'd never tried to charm. She was the only one who knew him.

And he knew it was time.

"I was born Raphael Vicente. I made vows to you as Dario. And now I make them as Raphael. I will stay with you, honor you, and love you. With all of me."

A sob racked her frame and she threw herself into his arms. "Raphael," she whispered. "I feel like I always knew you. Like I knew him."

He held her tightly, emotion cascading over him in a wave. "Because you were the only one who looked at me and saw the truth. Saw it all."

She smiled through her tears. "It's mutual. You saw me when I didn't."

"You are kisses in a summer rain, Lyssia. And a whole hurricane besides. You are everything. You are mine, and I am yours. With you, I lose control and feel more grounded all at once. With you, I'm not afraid anymore. Not of love, not of the future, not of those three hundred and sixty-seven nights. With you, there is only love. Always."

She nodded gravely, and then she took his hands, as if they were making vows then and there. Again. "And I will stay with you. I will. Always. I promise." She leaned in, pressing her mouth to his. "You told me once you were what the world needed, spontaneously created to fill a void. But I don't think so. You weren't for the world. You were for me. You were never the villain, Dario. You were always my hero. From the very beginning."

Dario Rivelli had very expensive custom-made shoes, and for the first time in his life he did not have a plan. Instead, he was filled entirely with nothing beyond love. For the woman in front of him. And he knew that he needed to know nothing. Except for them. Except for this. And so he would. Always.

EPILOGUE

WHEN THEIR SON was born, the joy that Lyssia felt was so far beyond any pain she had ever suffered it was like a beacon of light that changed everything around her. The entire world.

But then, that seemed to happen, daily, since falling in love with Dario.

They were in a private hospital suite, looking down at their baby. Her father had been brought to tears by the enormity of seeing his grandson.

A little boy with black hair and dark eyes, just like his father.

"Have you thought of the name yet?" She looked up at her husband, who hadn't taken his eyes off his son from the moment he had entered the world.

"I want... I want to name him Raphael," he said.

Tears stung her eyes. "You do? That will not be too painful for you?"

"All of this is pain in the most beautiful way. Because it is real. Because this is all that was meant to be. Because this is love. At its deepest and most powerful. Because it is everything. And I aim to change the story. The story of Raphael. He will be a boy that is loved. Always. From beginning to end. From here to all of eternity. He will be smart and ingenious like his mother. And like his father. But he will not have to strive. And when there is hardship, we will be there for him. We will make mistakes, because love is never perfect. But there will be love."

"Yes," she whispered. "There will be. Always."

And that much she knew was true. Because if there was one thing she had seen in her own life, through loss, and through mistakes and imperfections, it was that love, when given without fear, did in fact endure. It was in the memories of her mother, and the joy of her father. It was in the glow that existed between herself and Dario. It was in the deepest part of her soul.

And it shone so much brighter than fear ever could.

"Raphael Rivelli. I like it. And for his middle name?"

"Nathan," Dario said.

She smiled. "Raphael Nathan Rivelli. A tribute. To the life you should have had, and the man who loves us both."

"I am grateful for your father. I wonder if I could've found my way to this without him. Without his example."

"I think you could have. Although I'm grateful that you had him."

"Why is that?"

"Because true love always wins. And that's what we have. True love."

* * * * *

COMING SOON!

We really hope you enjoyed reading this book.
If you're looking for more romance
be sure to head to the shops when
new books are available on

Thursday 1st February

To see which titles are coming soon, please visit

millsandboon.co.uk/nextmonth

MILLS & BOON®

Coming next month

CINDERELLA'S ONE-NIGHT BABY
Michelle Smart

Skimming her fingers up his arm, Gabrielle placed her palm on his chest.

He sucked in a breath. His grip on her hip tightened. The thuds of his heartbeat perfectly matched the thuds of her own.

Andrés was a strictly short-term relationship man. He wouldn't want more than she could give, and all she could give him was one night. It was all she could give to herself.

This was meant to be, she realised, staring even deeper into his eyes. It had been from the start. If she'd known he was single, she would have refused point blank to attend the party with him, would have spent the night alone in her tiny apartment unaware that he held the key to unlocking all the desires she'd kept buried so deep she'd hardly been aware they existed.

For this one night she could put those desires first, and do so with the sexiest man to roam the earth, the man who had the power to turn her to liquid without even touching her.

A man who wouldn't want anything more from her.

She moved her face closer. Their lips brushed like feathers. The heat of his breath filled her senses.

Continue reading
CINDERELLA'S ONE-NIGHT BABY
Michelle Smart

Available next month
millsandboon.co.uk

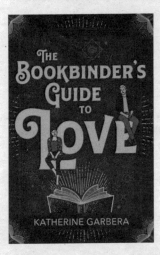

OUT NOW!

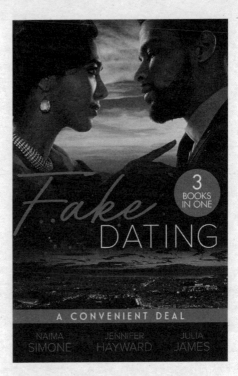

3
BOOKS
IN ONE

Fake
DATING

A CONVENIENT DEAL

NAIMA
SIMONE

JENNIFER
HAYWARD

JULIA
JAMES

Available at
millsandboon.co.uk

MILLS & BOON

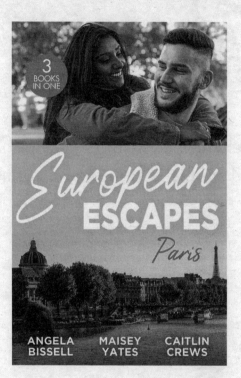

LET'S TALK

Romance

For exclusive extracts, competitions and special offers, find us online:

 MillsandBoon

@MillsandBoon

@MillsandBoonUK

@MillsandBoonUK

Get in touch on 01413 063 232

MILLS & BOON

THE HEART OF ROMANCE

A ROMANCE FOR EVERY READER

MODERN

Prepare to be swept off your feet by sophisticated, sexy and seductive heroes, in some of the world's most glamourous and romantic locations, where power and passion collide.

HISTORICAL

Escape with historical heroes from time gone by. Whether your passion is for wicked Regency Rakes, muscled Vikings or rugged Highlanders, awaken the romance of the past.

MEDICAL

Set your pulse racing with dedicated, delectable doctors in the high-pressure world of medicine, where emotions run high and passion, comfort and love are the best medicine.

True Love

Celebrate true love with tender stories of heartfelt romance, from the rush of falling in love to the joy a new baby can bring, and a focus on the emotional heart of a relationship.

HEROES

The excitement of a gripping thriller, with intense romance at its heart. Resourceful, true-to-life women and strong, fearless men face danger and desire - a killer combination!

From showing up to glowing up, these characters are on the path to leading their best lives and finding romance along the way – with plenty of sizzling spice!

To see which titles are coming soon, please visit

millsandboon.co.uk/nextmonth